Enoch Arnold Bennett, the son of a :   y,
Staffordshire. At twenty-one, he mov   a
solicitor's clerk, but he soon turned ι |
editing a women's magazine. After the
From the North in 1898, he became a pι   ...∪ved to Paris
and became a man of cosmopolitan and ι ..ι..ιng tastes.

Bennett's great reputation is built upon the success of his novels and short
stories set in the Potteries, an area of north Staffordshire that he recreated as
the 'Five Towns'. *Anna of the Five Towns* and *The Old Wives' Tale* show the
influence of Flaubert, Maupassant and Balzac as Bennett describes provincial
life in great detail. Arnold Bennett is an important link between the English
novel and European realism.

He wrote several plays and lighter works such as *The Grand Babylon
Hotel* and *The Card*.

Arnold Bennett died in 1931.

BY THE SAME AUTHOR
ALL PUBLISHED BY HOUSE OF STRATUS

THE CLAYHANGER SERIES:
CLAYHANGER
HILDA LESSWAYS
THESE TWAIN

FIVE TOWNS SERIES:
A MAN FROM THE NORTH
ANNA OF THE FIVE TOWNS
THE CARD
THE OLD WIVES' TALE
THE REGENT
TALES OF THE FIVE TOWNS

FANTASIAS:
THE CITY OF PLEASURE
THE GHOST

NOVELS:
ACCIDENT
BURIED ALIVE
THE GLIMPSE
THE GRAND BABYLON HOTEL
LORD RAINGO
PRETTY LADY
RICEYMAN STEPS
TERESA OF WATLING STREET

NON-FICTION:
HOW TO LIVE ON 24 HOURS A DAY

ARNOLD BENNETT

THE ROLL CALL

HOUSE OF
STRATUS

This edition published by House of Stratus, an imprint of Stratus Books Ltd, 21 Beeching Park, Kelly Bray, Cornwall, PL17 8QS, UK.

www.houseofstratus.com

Typeset, printed and bound by House of Stratus.

A catalogue record for this book is available from the British Library and the Library of Congress.

ISBN 07551-165-5-0
EAN 97807551-165-5-3

CONTENTS

PART I

I

THE NEW LODGING

In the pupils' room of the offices of Lucas & Enwright, architects, Russell Square, Bloomsbury, George Edwin Cannon, an articled pupil, leaned over a large drawing-board and looked up at Mr. Enwright, the head of the firm, who with cigarette and stick was on his way out after what he called a good day's work. It was past six o'clock on an evening in early July 1901.

To George's right was an open door leading to the principals' room, and to his left another open door leading to more rooms and to the staircase. The lofty chambers were full of lassitude; but round about George, who was working late, there floated the tonic vapour of conscious virtue. Haim, the factotum, could be seen and heard moving in his cubicle which guarded the offices from the stairs. In the rooms shortly to be deserted and locked up, and in the decline of the day, the three men were drawn together like survivors.

"I gather you're going to change your abode," said Mr. Enwright, having stopped.

"Did Mr. Orgreave tell you, then?" George asked.

"Well, he didn't exactly tell me...."

John Orgreave was Mr. Enwright's junior partner; and for nearly two years, since his advent in London from the Five Towns, George had lived with Mr. and Mrs. Orgreave at Bedford Park. The Orgreaves, too, sprang from the Five Towns. John's people and George's people were closely entwined in the local annals.

Pupil and principal glanced discreetly at one another, exchanging in silence vague, malicious, unutterable critical verdicts upon both John Orgreave and his wife.

"Well, I am!" said George at length.

"Where are you going to?"

"Haven't settled a bit," said George. "I wish I could live in Paris."

"Paris wouldn't be much good to you yet," Mr. Enwright laughed benevolently.

"I suppose it wouldn't. Besides, of course-"

George spoke in a tone of candid deferential acceptance, which flattered Mr. Enwright very much, for it was the final proof of the prestige which the grizzled and wrinkled and peculiar Fellow and Member of the Council of the Royal Institute of British Architects had acquired in the estimation of that extremely independent, tossing sprig, George Edwin Cannon. Mr. Enwright had recently been paying a visit to Paris, and George had been sitting for the Intermediate Examination. "You can join me here for a few days after the exam., if you care to," Mr. Enwright had sent over. It was George's introduction to the Continent, and the circumstances of it were almost ideal. For a week the deeply experienced connoisseur of all the arts had had the fine, eager, responsive virgin mind hi his power. Day after day he had watched and guided it amid entirely new sensations. Never had Mr. Enwright enjoyed himself more purely, and at the close he knew with satisfaction that he had put Paris in a proper perspective for George, and perhaps saved the youth from years of groping misapprehension. As for George, all his preconceived notions about Paris had been destroyed or shaken. In the quadrangles of the Louvre, for example, Mr. Enwright, pointing to the under part of the stone bench that foots so much of the walls, had said: "Look at that curve." Nothing else. No ecstasies about the sculptures of Jean Goujon and Carpeaux, or about the marvellous harmony of the East facade! But a flick of the cane towards the half-hidden moulding! And George had felt with a thrill what an exquisite curve and what an original curve and what a modest curve that curve was. Suddenly and magically his eyes had been opened. Or it might have been that a deceitful mist had rolled away and the real Louvre been revealed in its esoteric and sole authentic beauty....

"Why don't you try Chelsea?" said Mr. Enwright over his shoulder, proceeding towards the stairs.

"I was thinking of Chelsea."

"You were!" Mr. Enwright halted again for an instant. "It's the only place in London where the structure of society is anything like Paris. Why, dash it, in the King's Road the grocers know each other's business!" Mr. Enwright made the last strange remark to the outer door, and vanished.

"Funny cove!" George commented tolerantly to Mr. Haim, who passed through the room immediately afterwards to his nightly task of collecting and inspecting the scattered instruments on the principal's august drawing-board.

But Mr. Haim, though possibly he smiled ever so little, would not

4

compromise himself by an endorsement of the criticism of his employer. George was a mere incident in the eternal career of Mr. Haim at Lucas & Enwright's.

When the factotum came back into the pupils' room, George stood up straight and smoothed his trousers and gazed admiringly at his elegant bright socks.

"Let me see," said George in a very friendly manner. "You live somewhere in Chelsea, don't you?"

"Yes," answered Mr. Haim.

"Whereabouts, if it isn't a rude question?"

"Well," said Mr. Haim, confidentially and benignantly, captivated by George's youthful charm, "it's near the Redcliffe Arms." He mentioned the Redcliffe Arms as he might have mentioned the Bank, Piccadilly Circus, or Gibraltar. "Alexandra Grove. No. 8. To tell you the truth, I own the house."

"The deuce you do!"

"Yes. The leasehold, that is, of course. No freeholds knocking about loose in that district!"

George saw a new and unsuspected Mr. Haim. He was impressed. And he was glad that he had never broken the office tradition of treating Mr. Haim with a respect not usually accorded to factotums. He saw a, property-owner, a tax-payer, and a human being behind the spectacles of the shuffling, rather shabby, ceremonious familiar that pervaded those rooms daily from before ten till after six. He grew curious about a living phenomenon that hitherto had never awakened his curiosity.

"Were you really looking for accommodation?" demanded Mr. Haim suavely.

George hesitated. "Yes."

"Perhaps I have something that might suit you."

Events, disguised as mere words, seemed to George to be pushing him forward.

"I should like to have a look at it," he said. He had to say it; there was no alternative.

Mr. Haim raised a hand. "Any evening that happens to be convenient."

"What about tonight, then?"

"Certainly," Mr. Haim agreed. For a moment George apprehended that Mr. Haim was going to invite him to dinner. But Mr. Haim was not going to invite him to dinner. "About nine, shall we say?" he suggested, with a courtliness softer even than usual.

Later, George said that he would lock up the office himself and leave the key with the housekeeper.

"You can't miss the place," said Mr. Haim on leaving. "It's between the Workhouse and the Redcliffe."

2

At the corner dominated by the Queen's Elm, which on the great route from Piccadilly Circus to Putney was a public-house and halt second only in importance to the Redcliffe Arms, night fell earlier than it ought to have done, owing to a vast rain-cloud over Chelsea. A few drops descended, but so warm and so gently that they were not like real rain, and sentimentalists could not believe that they would wet. People, arriving mysteriously out of darkness, gathered sparsely on the pavements, lingered a few moments, and were swallowed by omnibuses that bore them obscurely away. At intervals an individual got out of an omnibus and adventured hurriedly forth and was lost in the gloom. The omnibuses, all white, trotted on an inward curve to the pavement, stopped while the conductor, with hand raised to the bell-string, murmured apathetically the names of streets and of public-houses, and then they jerked off again on an outward curve to the impatient double ting of the bell. To the east was a high defile of hospitals, and to the west the Workhouse tower faintly imprinted itself on the sombre sky.

The drops of rain grew very large and heavy, and the travellers, instead of waiting on the kerb, withdrew to the shelter of the wall of the Queen's Elm. George was now among the group, precipitated like the rest, as it were, out of the solution of London. George was of the age which does not admit rain or which believes that it is immune from the usual consequences of exposure to rain. When advised, especially by women, to defend himself against the treacheries of the weather, he always protested confidently that he would 'be all right.' Thus with a stick and a straw hat he would affront terrible dangers. It was a species of valour which the event often justified. Indeed he generally was all right. But tonight, afoot on the way from South Kensington Station in a region quite unfamiliar to him, he was intimidated by the slapping menace of the big drops. Reality faced him. His scared thought ran: "Unless I do something at once I shall get wet through." Impossible to appear drenched at old Haim's! So he had abandoned all his pretensions to a magical invulnerability, and rushed under the eave of the Queen's Elm to join the omnibus group.

He did not harmonize with the omnibus group, being both too elegant and too high-spirited. His proper role in the circumstances would have been to 'jump into a hansom'; but there were no empty hansoms, and moreover, for certain reasons of finance, he had sworn off hansoms until a given date. He regarded the situation as 'rather a lark,' and he somehow knew that the group understood and appreciated and perhaps resented his superior and tolerant attitude. An omnibus rolled palely into the radiance of the Queen's Elm lamp, the horses' flanks and the lofty driver's apron gleaming with rain. He sprang towards the vehicle; the whole group sprang. "Full inside!" snapped the conductor inexorably. Ting, ting! It was gone, glimmering with its enigmatic

6

load into the distance. George turned again to the wall, humiliated. It seemed wrong that the conductor should have included him with the knot of common omnibus-travellers and late workers. The conductor ought to have differentiated.... He put out a hand. The rain had capriciously ceased! He departed gaily and triumphantly. He was re-endowed with the magical invulnerability.

The background of his mind was variegated. The incidents of the tremendous motor-car race from Paris to Berlin, which had finished nearly a week earlier, still glowed on it. And the fact that King Edward VII had driven in a car from Pall Mall to Windsor Castle in sixty minutes was beautifully present. Then, he was slightly worried concerning the Mediterranean Fleet. He knew nothing about it, but as a good citizen he suspected in idle moments, like a number of other good citizens, that all was not quite well with the Mediterranean Fleet. As for the war, he had only begun to be interested in the war within the last six months, and already he was sick of it. He knew that the Boers had just wrecked a British military train, and his attitude towards such methods of fighting was rather severe and scornful; he did not regard them as 'war.' However, the apparent permanence of the war was splendidly compensated by the victory of the brothers Doherty over the American lawn-tennis champions in the Gentlemen's Doubles at Wimbledon. Who could have expected the brothers to win after the defeat of R.H. by Mr. Gore in the Singles? George had most painfully feared that the Americans would conquer, and their overthrowing by the twin brothers indicated to George, who took himself for a serious student of affairs, that Britain was continuing to exist, and that the new national self-depreciative, yearning for efficiency might possibly be rather absurd after all.

In the midst of these and similar thoughts, and of innumerable minor thoughts about himself, in the very centre of his mind and occupying nearly the whole of it, was the vast thought, the obsession, of his own potential power and its fulfilment. George's egotism was terrific, and as right as any other natural phenomenon. He had to get on. Much money was included in his scheme, but simply as a by-product. He had to be a great architect, and - equally important - he had to be publicly recognized as a great architect, and recognition could not come without money. For him, the entire created universe was the means to his end. He would not use it unlawfully, but he would use it.

He was using it, as well as he yet knew how, and with an independence that was as complete as it was unconscious. In regard to matters upon which his instinct had not suggested a course of action, George was always ready enough to be taught; indeed his respect for an expert was truly deferential. But when his instinct had begun to operate he would consult nobody and consider nobody, being deeply sure that infallible wisdom had been granted to him.

7

(Nor did experience seem to teach him.) Thus, in the affair of a London lodging, though he was still two years from his majority and had no resources save the purse of his stepfather, Edwin Clayhanger, he had decided to leave the Orgreaves without asking or even informing his parents. In his next letter home he would no doubt inform them, casually, of what he meant to do or actually had done, and if objections followed he would honestly resent them.

A characteristic example of his independence had happened when at the unripe age of seventeen he left the Five Towns for London. Upon his mother's marriage to Edwin Clayhanger his own name had been informally changed for him to Clayhanger. But a few days before the day of departure he had announced that, as Clayhanger was not his own name and that he preferred his own name, he should henceforth be known as 'Cannon,' his father's name. He did not invite discussion.

Mr. Clayhanger had thereupon said to him privately and as one man of the world to another: "But you aren't really entitled to the name Cannon, sonny."

"Why?"

"Because your father was what's commonly known as a bigamist, and his marriage with your mother was not legal. I thought I'd take this opportunity of telling you. You needn't say anything to your mother - unless of course you feel you must."

To which George had replied: "No, I won't. But if Cannon was my father's name I think I'll have it all the same." And he did have it. The bigamy of his father did not apparently affect him. Upon further inquiry he learnt that his father might be alive or might be dead, but that if alive he was in America.

The few words from Mr. Enwright about Chelsea had sufficed to turn Chelsea into Elysium, Paradise, almost into Paris. No other quarter of London was inhabitable by a rising architect. As soon as Haim had gone George had begun to look up Chelsea in the office library, and as Mr. Enwright happened to be an active member of the Society for the Survey of the Memorials of Greater London, the library served him well. In an hour and a half he had absorbed something of the historical topography of Chelsea. He knew that the Fulham Road upon which he was now walking was a boundary of Chelsea. He knew that the Queen's Elm public-house had its name from the tradition that Elizabeth had once sheltered from a shower beneath an elm tree which stood at that very corner. He knew that Chelsea had been a 'village of palaces,' and what was the function of the Thames in the magnificent life of that village. The secret residence of Turner in Chelsea, under the strange alias of Admiral Booth, excited George's admiration; he liked the idea of hidden retreats and splendid, fanciful pseudonyms. But the master-figure of Chelsea for George was Sir Thomas More. He could see Sir Thomas More walking in his majestic garden by the river with the King's arm round his neck, and Holbein close by, and respectful august prelates and a nagging wife in the background. And he could see Sir Thomas More taking his barge for the last journey to the Tower, and Sir Thomas More's daughter coming back in the same barge with her father's head on board. Curious! He envied Sir Thomas More.

"Darned bad tower for a village of palaces!" he thought, not of the Tower of London, but of the tower of the Workhouse which he was now approaching. He thought he could design an incomparably better tower than that. And he saw himself in the future, the architect of vast monuments, strolling in a grand garden of his own at evening with other distinguished and witty persons.

But there were high-sounding names in the history of Chelsea besides those of More and Turner. Not names of people! Cremorne and Ranelagh! Cremorne to the west and Ranelagh to the east. The legend of these vanished resorts of pleasure and vice stirred his longings and his sense of romantic beauty - especially Ranelagh with its Rotunda. (He wanted, when the time came, to be finely vicious, as he wanted to be everything. An architect could not be great without being everything.) He projected himself into the Rotunda, with its sixty windows, its countless refreshment-boxes, its huge paintings, and the orchestra in the middle, and the expensive and naughty crowd walking round and round and round on the matting, and the muffled footsteps and the swish of trains on the matting, and the specious smiles and whispers, and the blare of the band and the smell of the lamps and candles.... Earl's Court was a poor, tawdry, unsightly thing after that.

When he had passed under the Workhouse tower he came to a side street which, according to Haim's description of the neighbourhood, ought to have been Alexandra Grove. The large lamp on the corner, however, gave no indication, nor in the darkness could any sign be seen on the blind wall of either of the corner houses in Fulham Road. Doubtless in daytime the street had a visible label, but the borough authorities evidently believed that night endowed the stranger with powers of divination. George turned hesitant down the mysterious gorge, which had two dim lamps of its own, and which ended in a high wall, whereat could be descried unattainable trees - possibly the grove of Alexandra. Silence and a charmed stillness held the gorge, while in Fulham Road not a hundred yards away omnibuses and an occasional hansom rattled along in an ordinary world. George soon decided that he was not in Alexandra Grove, on account of the size of the houses. He could not conceive Mr. Haim owning one of them. They stood lofty in the gloom, in pairs, secluded from the pavement by a stucco garden-wall and low bushes. They were double-fronted, and their doors were at the summits of flights of blanched steps that showed through the bars of iron gates. They had three stories above a basement. Still, he looked for No. 8. But just as the street had no name, so the houses had no numbers. No. 16 alone could be distinguished; it had figures on its faintly illuminated fanlight. He walked back, idly counting.

Then, amid the curtained and shuttered facades, he saw, across the road, a bright beam from a basement. He crossed and peeped through a gate, and an interior was suddenly revealed to him. Near the window of a room sat a young woman bending over a table. A gas-jet on a bracket in the wall, a few inches higher than her head and a foot distant from it, threw a strong radiance on her face and hair. The luminous living picture, framed by the window in blackness, instantly entranced him. All the splendid images of the past faded and were confuted and invalidated and destroyed by this intense reality so present and so near to him. (Nevertheless, for a moment he thought of her as the daughter of Sir Thomas More.) She was drawing. She was drawing with her whole mind and heart. At intervals, scarcely moving her head, she would glance aside at a paper to her left on the table.... She seemed to search it, to drag some secret out of it, and then she would resume her drawing. She was neither dark nor fair; she was comely, perhaps beautiful; she had beautiful lips, and her nose, behind the nostrils, joined the cheek in a lovely contour, like a tiny bulb. Yes, she was superb. But what mastered him was less her fresh physical charm than the rapt and extreme vitality of her existing.... He knew from her gestures and the tools on the table that she could be no amateur. She was a professional. He thought: Chelsea!... Marvellous place, Chelsea! He ought to have found that out long ago. He imagined Chelsea full of such pictures - the only true home of beauty and romance.

Then the impact of a single idea startled his blood. He went hot. He flushed. He had tingling sensations all down his back, and in his legs and in his arms. It was as though he had been caught in a dubious situation. Though he was utterly innocent, he felt as though he had something to be ashamed of. The idea was: she resembled old Haim, facially! Ridiculous idea! But she did resemble old Haim, particularly in the lobal termination of the nose. And in the lips too. And there was a vague, general resemblance. Absurd! It was a fancy.... He would not have cared for anybody to be watching him then, to surprise him watching her. He heard unmistakable footsteps on the pavement. A policeman darkly approached. Policemen at times can be very apposite. George moved his gaze and looked with admirable casualness around.

"Officer, is this Alexandra Grove?" (His stepfather had taught him to address all policemen as 'officer.')

"It is, sir."

"Oh! Well, which is No. 8? There're no numbers."

"You couldn't be much nearer to it, sir," said the policeman dryly, and pointed to a large number, fairly visible, on the wide gate-post. George had not inspected the gate-post.

"Oh! Thanks!"

He mounted the steps, and in the thick gloom of the portico fumbled for the bell and rang it. He was tremendously excited and expectant and apprehensive and puzzled. He heard rain flatly spitting in big drops on the steps. He had not noticed till then that it had begun again. The bell jangled below. The light in the basement went out. He flushed anew. He thought, trembling: "She's coming to the door herself!"

3

"It had occurred to me some time ago," said Mr. Haim, "that if ever you should be wanting rooms I might be able to suit you."

"Really!" George murmured. After having been shown into the room by the young woman, who had at once disappeared, he was now recovering from the nervousness of that agitating entry and resuming his normal demeanour of an experienced and well-balanced man of the world. He felt relieved that she had gone, and yet he regretted her departure extremely, and hoped against fear that she would soon return.

"Yes!" said Mr. Haim, as it were triumphantly, like one who had whispered to himself during long years: "The hour will come." The hour had come.

Mr. Haim was surprising to George. The man seemed much older in his own parlour than at the office - his hair thinner and greyer, and his face more wrinkled. But the surprising part of him was that he had a home and was master in it, and possessed interests other than those of the firm of Lucas & Enwright. George had never until that day conceived the man apart from Russell Square. And here he was smoking a cigarette in an easy-chair and wearing red morocco slippers, and being called 'father' by a really stunning creature in a thin white blouse and a blue skirt.

The young girl, opening the front door, had said: "Do you want to see father?" And instantly the words were out George had realized that she might have said: "Did you want to see father?" ... in the idiom of the shop-girl or clerk, and that if she had said 'did' he would have been gravely disappointed and hurt. But she had not. Of course she had not! Of course she was incapable of such a locution, and it was silly of him to have thought otherwise, even momentarily. She was an artist. Entirely different from the blonde and fluffy Mrs. John Orgreave - (and a good thing too, for Mrs. John with her eternal womanishness had got on his nerves) - Miss Haim was without doubt just as much a lady, and probably a jolly sight more cultured, in the true sense. Yet Miss Haim had not in the least revealed herself to him in the hall as she indicated the depository for his hat and stick and opened the door of the sitting-room. She had barely smiled. Indeed she had not smiled. She had not mentioned the weather. On the other hand, she had not been prim or repellent. She had revealed nothing of herself. Her one feat had been to stimulate mightily his curiosity and his imagination concerning her - rampant enough even before he entered the house!

The house - what he saw of it - suited her and set her off, and, as she was

11

different from Mrs. John, so was the house different from the polished, conventional abode of Mrs. John at Bedford Park. To George's taste it knocked Bedford Park to smithereens. In the parlour, for instance, an oak chest, an oak settee, an oak gate-table, one tapestried easy chair, several rush-bottomed chairs, a very small brass fender, a self-coloured wall-paper of warm green, two or three old engravings in maple-wood or tarnished gilt frames, several small portraits in maple-wood frames, brass candlesticks on the mantelpiece and no clock, self-coloured brown curtains across the windows (two windows opposite each other at either end of the long room), sundry rugs on the dark-stained floor, and so on! Not too much furniture, and not too much symmetry either. An agreeable and original higgledy-piggledyness! The room was lighted by a fairly large oil-lamp, with a paper shade hand-painted in a design of cupids - delightful personal design, rough, sketchy, adorable! She had certainly done it.

George sat on the oak settle, fronting the old man in the easy chair. It was a hard, smooth oak settle; it had no upholstering nor cushion; but George liked it.

"May I smoke?" asked George.

"Please do. Please do," said Mr. Haim, who was smoking a cigarette himself, with courteous hospitality. However, it was a match and not a cigarette that he offered to George, who opened his own dandiacal case.

"I stayed rather late at the office tonight," said George, as he blew out those great clouds with which young men demonstrate to the world that the cigarette is actually lighted. And as Mr. Haim, who was accustomed to the boastings of articled pupils, made no comment, George proceeded, lolling on the settle and showing his socks: "You know, I like Chelsea. I've always had a fancy for it." He was just about to continue cosmopolitanly: "It's the only part of London that's like Paris. The people in the King's Road," etc., when fortunately he remembered that Mr. Haim must have overheard these remarks of Mr. Enwright, and ceased, rather awkwardly. Whereupon Mr. Haim suggested that he should see the house, and George said eagerly that he should like to see the house.

"We've got one bedroom more than we want," Mr. Haim remarked as he led George to the hall.

"Oh yes!" said George politely.

The hall had a small bracket-lamp, which Mr. Haim unhooked, and then he opened a door opposite to the door of the room which they had quitted.

"Now this is a bedroom," said he, holding the lamp high.

George was startled. A ground-floor bedroom would have been unthinkable at Bedford Park. Still, in a flat.... Moreover, the idea had piquancy. The bedroom was sparsely furnished. Instead of a wardrobe it had a corner curtained off with cretonne.

"A good-sized room," said Mr. Haim.

"Very," said George. "Two windows, too, like the drawing-room." Then they went upstairs to the first floor, and saw two more bedrooms, each with two windows. One of them was Miss Haim's; there was a hat hung on the looking-glass, and a table with a few books on it. They did not go to the second floor. The staircase to the second floor was boarded up at the point where it turned.

"That's all there is," said Mr. Haim on the landing. "The studio people have the second floor, but they don't use my front door." He spoke the last words rather defiantly.

"I see," said George untruthfully, for he was mystified. But the mystery did not trouble him.

There was no bathroom, and this did not trouble him either, though at Bedford Park he could never have seriously considered a house without a bathroom.

"You could have your choice of ground floor or first floor," said Mr. Haim confidentially, still on the landing. He moved the lamp about, and the shadows moved accordingly on the stairs.

"Oh, I don't mind in the least," George answered. "Whichever would suit you best."

"We could give you breakfast, and use of sitting-room," Mr. Haim proceeded in a low tone. "But no other meals."

"That would be all right," said George cheerfully. "I often dine in town. Like that I can get in a bit of extra work at the office, you see."

"Except on Sundays," Mr. Haim corrected himself. "You'd want your meals on Sundays, of course. But I expect you're out a good deal, what with one thing or another."

"Oh, I am!" George concurred.

The place was perfect, and he was determined to establish himself in it. Nothing could baulk him. A hitch would have desolated him completely.

"I may as well show you the basement while I'm about it," said Mr. Haim.

"Do!" said George ardently.

They descended. The host was very dignified, as invariably at the office, and his accent never lapsed from the absolute correctness of an educated Londoner. His deportment gave distinction and safety even to the precipitous and mean basement stairs, which were of stone worn as by the knees of pilgrims in a crypt. All kinds of irregular pipes ran about along the ceiling of the basement; some were covered by ancient layers of wall-paper and some were not; some were painted yellow, and some were painted grey, and some were not painted. Mr. Haim exhibited first the kitchen. George saw a morsel of red amber behind black bars, a white deal table and a black cat crouched on a corner of the table, a chair, and a tea-cloth drying over the back thereof. He liked the scene; it reminded him of the Five Towns, and showed reassuringly - if he needed reassurance, which he did not - that all houses are the same at heart. Then Mr. Haim, flashing a lamp-ray on the coal-hole and the area door as he turned, crossed the stone passage into the other basement room.

"This is our second sitting-room," said Mr. Haim, entering.

There she was at work, rapt, exactly as George had seen her from the outside. But now he saw the right side of her face instead of the left. It was wonderful to him that within the space of a few minutes he should have developed from an absolute stranger to her into an acquaintance of the house, walking about in it, peering into its recesses, disturbing its secrets, which were hers. But she remained as mysterious, as withdrawn and intangible, as ever. And then she shifted round suddenly on the chair, and her absorbed, intent face softened into a most beautiful, simple smile - a smile of welcome. An astonishing and celestial change!... She was not one of those queer girls, as perhaps she might have been. She was a girl of natural impulses. He smiled back, uplifted.

"My daughter designs bookbindings," said Mr. Haim. "Happens to be very busy tonight on something urgent."

He advanced towards her, George following.

"Awfully good!" George murmured enthusiastically, and quite sincerely, though he was not at all in a condition to judge the design. Strange, that he should come to the basement of an ordinary stock-size house in Alexandra Grove to see bookbindings in the making! This was a design for a boy's book. He had possessed many such books. But it had never occurred to him that the gay bindings of them were each the result of individual human thought and labour. He pulled at his cigarette.

There was a sound of pushing and rattling outside.

"What's that?" exclaimed Mr. Haim.

"It's the area door. I bolted it. I dare say it's Mrs. Lobley," said the girl indifferently.

Mr. Haim moved sharply.

"Why did you bolt it, Marguerite? No, I'll go myself."

He picked up the lamp, which he had put down, and shuffled quickly out in his red morocco slippers, closing the door.

Marguerite? Yes, it suited her; and it was among the most romantic of names. It completed the picture. She now seemed to be listening and waiting, her attention on the unseen area door. He felt shy and yet very happy alone with her. Voices were distinctly heard. Who was Mrs. Lobley? Was Mr. Haim a little annoyed with his daughter, and was Marguerite exquisitely defiant? Time hung. The situation was slightly awkward, he thought. And it was obscure, alluring.... He stood there, below the level of the street, shut in with those beings unknown, provocative, and full of half-divined implications. And all

14

Chelsea was around him and all London around Chelsea.

"Father won't be a moment," said the girl. "It's only the charwoman."

"Oh! That's quite all right," he answered effusively, and turning to the design: "The outlining of that lettering fairly beats me, you know."

"Not really!... I get that from father, of course."

Mr. Haim was famous in the office as a letterer.

She sat idly glancing at her own design, her plump, small hands lying in the blue lap. George compared her, unspeakably to her advantage, with the kind, coarse young woman at the chop-house, whom he had asked to telephone to the Orgreaves for him, and for whom he had been conscious of a faint penchant.

"I can't colour it by gaslight," said Marguerite Haim. "I shall have to do that in the morning."

He imagined her at work again early in the morning. Within a week or so he might be living in this house with this girl. He would be, - watching her life! Seducing prospect, scarcely credible! He remembered having heard when he first went to Lucas & Enwright's that old Haim was a widower.

"Do excuse me," said Mr. Haim, urgently apologetic, reappearing.

A quarter of an hour later, George had left the house, having accepted Mr. Haim's terms without the least argument. In five days he was to be an inmate of No. 8 Alexandra Grove. The episode presented itself to him as a vast, romantic adventure, staggering and enchanting. His luck continued, for the rain-cloud was spent. He got into an Earl's Court bus. The dimly perceived travellers in it seemed all of them in a new sense to be romantic and mysterious.... "Yes," he thought, "I did say good-night to her, but I didn't shake hands."

2

MARGUERITE

More than two months later George came into the office in Russell Square an hour or so after his usual time. He had been to South Kensington Museum to look up, for professional purposes, some scale drawings of architectural detail which were required for a restaurant then rising in Piccadilly under the direction of Lucas & Enwright. In his room Mr. Everard Lucas was already seated. Mr. Lucas was another articled pupil of the firm; being a remote cousin of the late senior partner, he had entered on special terms. Although a year older than George he was less advanced, for whereas George had passed the Intermediate, Mr. Lucas had not. But in manly beauty, in stylishness, in mature tact, and especially in persuasive charm, he could beat George.

"Hallo!" Lucas greeted. "How do you feel? Fit?"

"Fit?" said George enthusiastically "I feel so fit I could push in the side of a house."

"What did I tell you?" said Lucas.

George rubbed his hand all over Lucas's hair, and Lucas thereupon seized George's other hand and twisted his arm, and a struggle followed. In this way they would often lovingly salute each other of a morning. Lucas had infected George with the craze for physical exercises as a remedy for all ills and indiscretions, including even late nights and excessive smoking. The competition between them to excel in the quality of fitness was acute, and sometimes led to strange challenges. After a little discussion about springing from the toes, Lucas now accused George's toes of a lack of muscularity, and upon George denying the charge, he asserted that George could not hang from the mantelpiece by his toes. They were both men of the world, capable of great heights of dignity, figures in an important business, aspirants to a supreme art and profession. They were at that moment in a beautiful late-eighteenth-century house of a stately and renowned square, and in a room whose proportions and ornament admittedly might serve as an exemplar to the student; and not the least lovely feature of the room was the high carved mantelpiece. The morning itself was historic, for it was the very morning upon which, President McKinley having expired, Theodore Roosevelt ascended the throne and inaugurated a new era. Nevertheless, such was their peculiar time of life that George, a minute later, was as a fact hanging by his toes from the mantelpiece, while Lucas urged him to keep the blood out of his head. George had stood on his hands on a box and lodged his toes on the mantelpiece, and then raised his hands - and Lucas had softly pushed the box away. George's watch was dangling against his flushed cheek.

"Put that box back, you cuckoo!" George exploded chokingly.

Then the door opened and Mr. Enwright appeared. Simultaneously some shillings slipped out of George's pocket and rolled about the floor. The hour was Mr. Enwright's customary hour of arrival, but he had no fair excuse for passing through that room instead of proceeding along the corridor direct to the principals' room. His aspect, as he gazed at George's hair and at the revealed sateen back of George's waistcoat, was unusual. Mr. Enwright commonly entered the office full of an intense and aggrieved consciousness of his own existence - of his insomnia, of the reaction upon himself of some client's stupidity, of the necessity of going out again in order to have his chin lacerated by his favourite and hated Albanian barber. But now he had actually forgotten himself.

"What is this?" he demanded.

Lucas having quickly restored the box, George subsided dangerously thereon, and arose in a condition much disarrayed and confused, and beheld Mr. Enwright with shame.

"I - I was just looking to see if the trap of the chimney was shut," said George. It was foolish in the extreme, but it was the best he could do, and after all it was a rather marvellous invention. Lucas sat down and made no remark.

"You might respect the mantelpiece," said Mr. Enwright bitterly, and went into the principals' room, where John Orgreave could be heard dictating letters. George straightened his clothes and picked up his money, and the two men of the world giggled nervously at each other.

Mr. Haim next disturbed them. The shabby, respectable old man smiled vaguely, with averted glance.

"I think he's heard the result," said he.

Both men knew that 'he' was Mr. Enwright, and that the 'result' was the result of the open competition for the L150,000 Law Courts which a proud provincial city proposed to erect for itself. The whole office had worked very hard on the drawings for that competition throughout the summer, while cursing the corporation which had chosen so unusual a date for sending-in day. Even Lucas had worked. George's ideas for certain details, upon which he had been engaged on the evening of his introduction to Mr. Haim's household, had been accepted by Mr. Enwright. As for Mr. Enwright, though the exigencies of his beard, and his regular morning habit of inveighing against the profession at great length, and his inability to decide where he should lunch, generally prevented him from beginning the day until three o'clock in the afternoon, Mr. Enwright had given many highly concentrated hours of creative energy to the design. And Mr. Haim had adorned the sheets with the finest lettering. The design was held to be very good. The principals knew the identity of all the other chief competitors and their powers, and they knew also the idiosyncrasies of the Assessor; and their expert and impartial opinion was that the Lucas & Enwright design ought to win and would win. This view, indeed, was widespread in the arcana of the architectural world. George had gradually grown certain of victory. And yet, at Mr. Haim's words, his hopes sank horribly away.

"Have we won?" he asked sharply.

"That I can't say, Mr. Cannon," answered Haim.

"Well, then, how do you know he's heard? Has he told you?"

"No," said the factotum mysteriously. "But I think he's heard." And upon this Mr. Haim slouched off quite calmly. Often he had assisted at the advent of such vital news in the office - news obtained in advance by the principals through secret channels - and often the news had been bad. But the firm's calamities seemed never to affect the smoothness of Mr. Haim's earthly passage.

The door into the principals' room opened, and Mr. Enwright's head showed. The gloomy, resenting eyes fixed George for an instant.

"Well, you've lost that competition," said Mr. Enwright, and he stepped into full view. His unseen partner had ceased to dictate, and the shorthand-clerk could be heard going out by the other door.

"No!" said George, in a long, outraged murmur. The news seemed incredible and quite disastrous; and yet at the same time had he not, in one unvisited corner of his mind, always foreknown it? Suddenly he was distressed, discouraged, disillusioned about the whole of life. He thought that Everard Lucas, screwing up a compass, was strangely unmoved. But Mr. Enwright ignored Lucas.

"Who's got it?" George asked.

"Whinburn."

"That chap!... Where are we?"

"Nowhere."

"Not placed?"

"Not in it. Skelting's second. And Grant third. I shouldn't have minded so much if Grant had got it. There was something to be said for his scheme. I knew we shouldn't get it. I knew that perfectly well - not with Corver assessing."

George wondered that his admired principal should thus state the exact opposite of what he had so often affirmed during the last few weeks. People were certainly very queer, even the best of them. The perception of this fact added to his puzzled woe.

"But Whinburn's design is grotesque!" he protested borrowing one of Mr. Enwright's adjectives.

"Of course it is."

"Then why does Sir Hugh Corver go and give him the award? Surely he must know - -"

"Know!" Mr. Enwright growled, destroying Sir Hugh and his reputation and his pretensions with one single monosyllable.

"Then why did they make him Assessor - that's what I can't understand."

"It's quite simple," rasped Mr. Enwright. "They made him assessor because he's got so much work to do it takes him all his time to trot about from one job to another on his blooming pony. They made him assessor because his pony's a piebald pony. Couldn't you think of that for yourself? Or have you been stone deaf in this office for two years? It stands to reason that a man who's responsible for all the largest new eyesores in London would impress any corporation. Clever chap, Corver! Instead of wasting his time in travel and study, he made a speciality of learning how to talk to committees. And he was always full of ideas like the piebald pony, ever since I knew him."

"It's that facade that did for us," broke in another voice. John Orgreave stood behind Mr. Enwright. He spoke easily; he was not ruffled by the immense disappointment, though the mournful greatness of the topic had drawn him irresistibly into the discussion. John Orgreave had grown rather fat and coarse. At one period, in the Five Towns, he had been George's hero. He was so no longer. George was still fond of him, but he had torn him down from the pedestal and established Mr. Enwright in his place. George in his heart now somewhat patronized the placid Orgreave, regarding him as an excellent person who comprehended naught that was worth comprehending, and as a husband who was the dupe of his wife.

"You couldn't have any other facade," Mr. Enwright turned on him, "unless you're absolutely going to ignore the market on the other side of the Square. Whinburn's facade is an outrage - an outrage. Give me a cigarette. I must run out and get shaved."

While Mr. Enwright was lighting the cigarette, George reflected in desolation upon the slow evolving of the firm's design for the Law Courts. Again and again in the course of the work had he been struck into a worshipping enthusiasm by the brilliance of Mr. Enwright's invention and the happy beauty of his ideas. For George there was only one architect in the world; he was convinced that nobody could possibly rival Mr. Enwright, and that no Law Courts ever had been conceived equal to those Law Courts. And he himself had contributed something to the creation. He had dreamed of the building erected and of being able to stand in front of some detail of it and say to himself: "That was my notion, that was." And now the building was destroyed before its birth. It would never come into existence. It was wasted. And the prospect for the firm of several years' remunerative and satisfying labour had vanished. But the ridiculous, canny Whinburn would be profitably occupied, and his grotesque building would actually arise, and people would praise it, and it would survive for centuries - at any rate for a century.

Mr. Enwright did not move.

"It's no use regretting the facade, Orgreave," he said suddenly. "There's such a thing as self-respect."

"I don't see that self-respect's got much to do with it," Orgreave replied lightly.

("Of course you don't," George thought. "You're a decent sort, but you don't see, and you never will see. Even Lucas doesn't see. I alone see." And he felt savage and defiant.)

"Better shove my self-respect away into this cupboard, I suppose!" said Mr. Enwright, with the most acrid cynicism, and he pulled open one door of a long, low cupboard whose top formed a table for portfolios, dusty illustrated books, and other accumulations.

The gesture was dramatic, and none knew it better than Mr. Enwright. The cupboard was the cupboard which contained the skeleton. It was full of designs rejected in public competitions. There they lay, piles and piles of them, the earliest dating from the late seventies. The cupboard was crammed with the futility of Enwright's genius. It held monuments enough to make illustrious a score of cities. Lucas & Enwright was a successful firm. But, confining itself chiefly to large public works, it could not escape from the competition system; and it had lost in far more competitions than it had won. It was always, and always would be, at the mercy of an Assessor. The chances had always been, and always would be, against the acceptance of its designs, because they had the fatal quality of originality combined with modest adherence to the classical tradition. When they conquered, it was by sheer force. George glanced at the skeleton, and he was afraid. Something was very wrong with architecture. He agreed with Mr. Enwright's tiresomely reiterated axiom that it was the Cinderella of professions and the chosen field of ghastly injustice. He had embraced architecture; he had determined to follow exactly in the footsteps of Mr. Enwright; he had sworn to succeed. But could he succeed? Suppose he failed! Yes, his faith faltered. He was intensely, miserably afraid. He was the most serious man in Russell Square. Astounding that only a few minutes ago he had hung triumphantly by his feet from the mantelpiece!

Mr. Enwright kicked-to the door of the cupboard.

"Look here," he said to his partner, "I shan't be back just yet. I have to go and see Bentley. I'd forgotten it."

Nobody was surprised at this remark. Whenever Mr. Enwright was inconveniently set back he always went off to visit Bentley, the architect of the new Roman Catholic Cathedral at Westminster, on the plea of an urgent appointment.

"You had a look at the cathedral lately?" he demanded of George as he left.

"No, I haven't," said George, who, by reason of a series of unaccountable omissions, and of the fullness of his life as an architect and a man of the world, had never seen the celebrated cathedral at all.

"Well," said Mr. Enwright sarcastically, "better take just a glance at it - some time before they've spoilt the thing with decorations. There's a whole lot of 'em only waiting till Bentley's out of the way to begin and ruin it."

2

Before the regular closing hour of the office the two articled pupils had left and were walking side by side through Bloomsbury. They skirted the oval garden of Bedford Square, which, lying off the main track to the northern termini, and with nothing baser in it than a consulate or so, took precedence in austerity and selectness over Russell Square, which had consented to receive a grand hotel or 'modern caravanserai' and a shorthand school. Indeed the aspect of Bedford Square, where the great institution of the basement and area still flourished in perfection, and wealthy menials with traditional manners lived sensually in caves beneath the spacious, calm salons of their employers and dupes, - the aspect of Bedford Square gave the illusion that evolution was not, and that Bloomsbury and the whole impressive structure of British society could never change. Still, from a more dubious Bloomsbury, demure creatures with inviting, indiscreet eyes were already traversing the prim flags of Bedford Square on their way to the evening's hard diplomacy. Mr. Lucas made quiet remarks about their qualities, but George did not respond.

"Look here, old man," said Lucas, "there's no use in all this gloom. You might think Lucas & Enwright had never put up a building in their lives. Just as well to dwell now and then on what they have done instead of on what they haven't done. We're fairly busy, you know. Besides - "

He spoke seriously, tactfully, with charm, and he had a beautiful voice.

"Quite right! Quite right!" George willingly agreed, swinging his stick and gazing straight ahead. And he thought: "This chap has got his head screwed on.

He's miles wiser than I am, and he's really nice. I could never be nice like that."

In a moment they were at the turbulent junction of Tottenham Court Road and Oxford Street, where crowds of Londoners, deeply unconscious of their own vulgarity, and of the marvellous distinction of Bedford Square, and of the moral obligation to harmonize socks with neckties, were preoccupying themselves with omnibuses and routes, and constituting the spectacle of London. The high-heeled, demure creatures were lost in this crowd, and Lucas and George were lost in it.

"Well," said Lucas, halting on the pavement. "You're going down to the cathedral."

"It'll please the old cock," answered George, anxious to disavow any higher motive. "You aren't coming?"

Lucas shook his head. "I shall just go and snatch a hasty".... 'Cup of tea' was the unuttered end of the sentence.

"Puffin's?"

Lucas nodded. Puffin's was a cosy house of sustenance in a half-new street on the site of the razed slums of St. Giles's. He would not frequent the orthodox tea-houses, which were all alike and which had other serious disadvantages. He adventured into the unusual, and could always demonstrate that what he found was subtly superior to anything else.

"That affair still on?" George questioned.

"It's not off."

"She's a nice little thing - that I will say."

"It all depends," Lucas replied sternly. "I don't mind telling you she wasn't so jolly nice on Tuesday."

"Wasn't she?" George raised his eyebrows.

Lucas silently scowled, and his handsomeness vanished for an instant.

"However - " he said.

As George walked alone down Charing Cross Road, he thought: "That girl will have to look out," - meaning that in his opinion Lucas was not a man to be trifled with. Lucas was a wise and an experienced man, and knew the world. And what he did could not be other than right. This notion comforted George, who had a small affair of his own, which he had not yet even mentioned to Lucas. Delicacy as well as diffidence had prevented him from doing so. It was a very different affair from any of Lucas's, and he did not want Lucas to misesteem it; neither did he want Lucas to be under the temptation to regard him as a ninny.

Not the cathedral alone had induced George to leave the office early. The dissembler had reflected that if he called in a certain conventional tea-shop near Cambridge Circus at a certain hour he would probably meet Marguerite Haim. He knew that she had an appointment with one of her customers, a firm of bookbinders, that afternoon, and that on similar occasions she had been to the tea-shop. In fact he had already once deliciously taken tea with her therein. To-day he was disappointed, to the extent of the tea, for he met her as she was coming out of the shop. Their greetings were rather punctilious, but beneath superficial formalities shone the proofs of intimacy. They had had large opportunities to become intimate, and they had become intimate. The immediate origin of and excuse for the intimacy was a lampshade. George had needed a lampshade for his room, and she had offered to paint one. She submitted sketches. But George also could paint a bit. Hence discussions, conferences, rival designs, and, lastly, an agreement upon a composite design. Before long, the lampshade craze increasing in virulence, they had between them re-lampshaded the entire house. Then the charming mania expired; but it had done its work. During the summer holiday George had written twice to Marguerite, and he had thought pleasurably about her the whole time. He had hoped that she would open the door for him upon his return, and that when he saw her again he would at length penetrate the baffling secret of her individuality. She had opened the door for him, exquisitely, but the secret had not yielded itself. It was astonishing to George, how that girl could combine the candours of honest intimacy with a profound reserve.

"Were you going in there for tea?" she asked, looking up at him gravely.

"No," he said. "I don't want any tea. I have to wend my way to the Roman Catholic Cathedral - you know, the new one, near Victoria. I suppose you wouldn't care to see it?"

"I should love to," she answered, with ingenuous eagerness. "I think it might do me good."

A strange phrase, he thought! What did she mean?

"Would you mind walking?" she suggested.

"Let me take that portfolio, then."

So they walked. She had her usual serious expression, as it were full of the consciousness of duty. It made him think how reliable she would always be. She held herself straight and independently, and her appearance was very simple and very trim. He considered it wrong that a girl with such beautiful lips should have to consult callous bookbinders and accept whatever they chose to say. To him she was like a lovely and valiant martyr. The spectacle of her was touching. However, he could not have dared to hint at these sentiments. He had to pretend that her exposure to the stresses of the labour-market was quite natural and right. Always he was careful in his speech with her. When he got to know people he was apt to be impatient and ruthless; for example, to John Orgreave and his wife, and to his mother and stepfather, and sometimes even to Everard Lucas. He would bear them down. But he was restrained from such freedoms with Enwright, and equally with Marguerite Haim. She did not intimidate him, but she put him under a spell.

Crossing Piccadilly Circus he had a glimpse of the rising walls and the scaffolding of the new restaurant. He pointed to the building without a word. She nodded and smiled.

In the Mall, where the red campanile of the cathedral was first descried, George began to get excited. And he perceived that Marguerite sympathetically responded to his excitement. She had never even noticed the campanile before, and the reason was that the cathedral happened not to be on the route between Alexandra Grove and her principal customers. Suddenly, out of Victoria Street, they came up against the vast form of the Byzantine cathedral. It was hemmed in by puny six-story blocks of flats, as ancient cathedrals also are hemmed in by the dwellings of townsfolk. But here, instead of the houses having gathered about the cathedral, the cathedral had excavated a place for itself amid the houses. Tier above tier the expensively curtained windows of dark drawing-rooms and bedrooms inhabited by thousands of the well-to-do blinked up at the colossal symbol that dwarfed them all. George knew that he was late. If the watchman's gate was shut for the night he would look a fool. But his confidence in his magic power successfully to run risks sustained him in a gallant and assured demeanour. The gate in the hoarding that screened the west front was open. With a large gesture he tipped the watchman a shilling, and they passed in like princes. The transition to the calm and dusty interior was instantaneous and almost overwhelming. Immense without, the cathedral seemed still more immense within. On one side of the nave was a steam-engine; on the other some sort of a mill; and everywhere lay in heaps the wild litter of construction, among which moved here and there little parties of aproned pygmies engaged silently and industriously on sub-contracts; the main army of labourers had gone. The walls rose massively clear out of the white-powdered confusion into arches and high domes; and the floor of the choir, and a loftier floor beyond that, also rose clear. Perspectives ended in shadow and were illimitable, while the afternoon light through the stone grille of the western windows made luminous spaces in the gloom.

The sensation of having the mysterious girl at his elbow in that wonder-striking interior was magnificent.

He murmured, with pride:

"Do you know this place has the widest nave of any cathedral in the world? It's a much bigger cathedral than St. Paul's. In fact I'm not sure if it isn't the biggest in England."

"You know," he said again, "in the whole of the nineteenth century only one cathedral was built in England."

"Which was that?"

"Truro.... And you could put Truro inside this and leave a margin all round. Mr. Enwright says this is the last cathedral that ever will be built, outside America."

They gazed, more and more aware of a solemn miracle.

"It's marvellous - marvellous!" he breathed.

After a few moments, glancing at her, a strong impulse to be confidential mastered him. He was obliged to tell that girl.

"I say, we've lost that competition - for the Law Courts."

He smiled, but the smile had no effect.

"Oh!" She positively started.

He saw that her eyes had moistened, and he looked quickly away, as though he had seen something that he ought not to have seen. She cared! She cared a great deal! She was shocked by the misfortune to the firm, by the injustice to transcendent merit! She knew nothing whatever about any design in the competition. But it was her religion that the Lucas & Enwright design was the best, and by far the best. He had implanted the dogma, and he felt that she was ready to die for it. Mystery dropped away from her. Her soul stood bare to him. He was so happy and so proud that the intensity of his feeling dismayed him. But he was enheartened too, and courage to surmount a thousand failures welled up in him as from an unimagined spring.

"I wonder who that is?" she said quietly and ordinarily, as if a terrific event had not happened.

On the highest floor, at the other extremity of the cathedral, in front of the apse, a figure had appeared in a frock-coat and a silk hat. The figure stood solitary, gazing around in the dying light.

"By Jove! It's Bentley! It's the architect!"

George literally trembled. He literally gave a sob. The vision of Bentley within his masterpiece, of Bentley whom Enwright himself worshipped, was too much for him. Renewed ambition rushed through him in electric currents. All was not wrong with the world of architecture. Bentley had succeeded. Bentley, beginning life as an artisan, had succeeded supremely. And here he stood on the throne of his triumph. Genius would not be denied. Beauty would conquer despite everything. What completed the unbearable grandeur of the scene was that Bentley had cancer of the tongue, and was sentenced to death. Bentley's friends knew it; the world of architecture knew it; Bentley knew it.... "Shall I tell her?" George thought. He looked at her; he looked at the vessel which he had filled with emotion. He could not speak. A highly sensitive decency, an abhorrence of crudity, restrained him. "No," he decided, "I can't tell her now. I'll tell her some other time."

3

With no clear plan as to his dinner he took her back to Alexandra Grove. The dusk was far advanced. Mounting the steps quickly Marguerite rang the bell. There was no answer. She pushed up the flap of the letter-aperture and looked within.

"Have you got your latchkey?" she asked, turning round on George. "Father's not come home - his hat's not hanging up. He promised me certain that he would be here at six-thirty at the latest. Otherwise I should have taken the big key."

She did not show resentment against her father; nor was there impatience in her voice. But she seemed to be firmly and impassively judging her father, as his equal, possibly even as somewhat his superior. And George admired the force of her individuality. It flattered him that a being so independent and so strong should have been so meltingly responsive to him in the cathedral.

An adventurous idea occurred to him in a flash and he impulsively adopted it. His latchkey was in his pocket, but if the house door was once opened he would lose her - he would have to go forth and seek his dinner and she would remain in the house; whereas, barred out of the house, she would be bound to him - they would be thrust together into exquisite contingencies, into all the deep potentialities of dark London.

"Dash it!" he said, first fumbling in one waistcoat pocket, and then ledging the portfolio against a step and fumbling in both waistcoat pockets simultaneously. "I must have left it in my other clothes."

It is doubtful whether his conscience troubled him. But he had a very exciting sense of risk and of romance and of rapture, as though he had done something wonderful and irremediable.

"Ah! Well!" she murmured, instantly acquiescent, and without the least hesitation descended the steps.

How many girls (he demanded) would or could have made up their minds and faced the situation like that? Her faculty of decision was simply masculine! He looked at her in the twilight and she was inimitable, unparalleled. And yet by virtue of the wet glistening of her eyes in the cathedral she had somehow become mystically his! He. permitted himself the suspicion: "Perhaps she guesses that I'm only pretending about the latchkey." The suspicion which made her an accessory to his crime did not lower her in his eyes. On the contrary, the enchanting naughtiness with which it invested her only made her variety more intoxicant and perfection more perfect. His regret was that the suspicion was not a certainty.

Before a word could be said as to the next move, a figure in a grey suit and silk hat, and both arms filled with packages, passed in front of the gate and then halted.

"Oh! It's Mr. Buckingham Smith!" exclaimed Marguerite. "Mr. Buckingham Smith, we're locked out till father comes." She completed the tale of the mishap, to George's equal surprise and mortification.

Mr. Buckingham Smith, with Mr. Alfred Prince, was tenant of the studio at the back of No. 8. He raised his hat as well as an occupied arm would allow.

"Come and wait in the studio, then," he suggested bluntly.

"You know Mr. Cannon, don't you?" said Marguerite, embarrassed.

George and Mr. Buckingham Smith had in fact been introduced to one another weeks earlier in the Grove by Mr. Haim. Thereafter Mr. Buckingham Smith had, as George imagined, saluted George with a kind of jealous defiance and mistrust, and the acquaintance had not progressed. Nor, by the way, had George's dreams been realized of entering deeply into the artistic life of Chelsea. Chelsea had been no more welcoming than Mr. Buckingham Smith. But now Mr. Buckingham Smith grew affable and neighbourly. Behind the man's inevitable insistence that George should accompany Miss Haim into the studio was a genuine, eager hospitality.

The studio was lofty and large, occupying most of the garden space of No. 8. Crimson rep curtains, hung on a thick, blackened brass rod, divided it into two unequal parts. By the wall nearest the house a staircase ran up to a door high in the gable, which door communicated by a covered bridge with the second floor of No. 8, where the artists had bedrooms. The arrangement was a characteristic example of the manner in which building was added to building in London contrary to the intention of the original laying-out, and George in his expert capacity wondered how the plans had been kept within the by-laws of the borough, and by what chicane the consent of the ground-landlord had been obtained.

Mr. Alfred Prince, whom also George knew slightly, was trimming a huge oil-lamp which depended by a wire from the scarcely visible apex of the roof. When at length the natural perversity of the lamp had been mastered and the metal shade replaced, George got a general view of the immense and complex disorder of the studio. It was obviously very dirty - even in the lamplight the dust could be seen in drifts on the moveless folds of the curtains - it was a pigsty; but it was romantic with shadowed spaces, and gleams of copper and of the pale arms of the etching-press, and glimpses of pictures; and the fellow desired a studio of his own! He was glad, now, that Mr. Buckingham Smith had invited them in. He had wanted to keep Marguerite Haim to himself; but it was worth while to visit the studio, and it was especially worth while to watch her under the illumination of the lamp.

"Lucky we have a clean tablecloth," said Mr. Buckingham Smith, opening his packages and setting a table. "Brawn, Miss Haim! And beer, Miss Haim! That is to say, Pilsener. From the only place in Chelsea where you can get it."

And his packages really did contain brawn and beer (four bottles of the Pilsener); also bread and a slice of butter. The visitors learnt that they had happened on a feast, a feast which Mr. Buckingham Smith had conceived and ordained, a feast to celebrate the triumph of Mr. Alfred Prince. An etching by Mr. Prince had been bought by Vienna. Mr. Buckingham Smith did not say that the etching had been bought by any particular gallery in Vienna. He said 'by

Vienna,' giving the idea that all Vienna, every man, woman, and child in that distant and enlightened city where etchings were truly understood, had combined for the possession of a work by Mr. Prince. Mr. Buckingham Smith opined that soon every gallery in Europe would be purchasing examples of Alfred Prince. He snatched from a side-table and showed the identical authentic letter from Vienna to Mr. Alfred Prince, with its official heading, foreign calligraphy, and stilted English. The letter was very complimentary.

In George's estimation Mr. Prince did not look the part of an etcher of continental renown. He was a small, pale man, with a small brown beard, very shabby, and he was full of small nervous gestures. He had the innocently-red nose which pertains to indigestion. His trousers bagged horribly at the knees, and he wore indescribable slippers. He said little, in an extremely quiet, weak voice. His eyes, however, were lively and attractive. He was old, probably at least thirty-five. Mr. Buckingham Smith made a marked contrast to him. Tall, with newish clothes, a powerful voice and decisive gestures, Mr. Buckingham Smith dominated, though he was younger than his friend. He tried to please, and he mingled the grand seigneurial style with the abrupt. It was he who played both the parlourmaid and the host. He forced Marguerite to have some brawn, serving her with a vast portion; but he could not force her to take Pilsener.

"Now, Mr. Cannon," he said, pouring beer into a glass with an up-and-down motion of the bottle so as to put a sparkling head on the beer.

"No, thank you," said George decidedly. "I won't have beer."

Mr. Buckingham Smith gazed at him challengingly out of his black eyes. "Oh! But you've got to," he said. It was as if he had said: "I am generous. I love to be hospitable, but I am not going to have my hospitality thwarted, and you needn't think it."

George accepted the beer and joined in the toasting of Mr. Alfred Prince's health.

"Old chap!" Mr. Buckingham Smith greeted his chum, and then to George and Marguerite, informingly and seriously: "One of the best."

It was during the snack that Mr. Buckingham Smith began to display the etchings of Mr. Alfred Prince, massed in a portfolio. He extolled them with his mouth half-full of brawn, or between two gulps of Pilsener. They impressed George deeply - they were so rich and dark and austere.

"Old Princey boy's one of the finest etchers in Europe to-day, if you ask me," said Mr. Buckingham Smith off-handedly, and with the air of stating the obvious. And George thought that Mr. Prince was. The etchings were not signed 'Alfred Prince,' but just 'Prince,' which was quietly imposing. Everybody agreed that Vienna had chosen the best one.

"It's a dry-point, isn't it?" Marguerite asked, peering into it. George started. This single remark convinced him that she knew all about etching, whereas he himself knew nothing. He did not even know exactly what a dry-point was.

"Mostly," said Mr. Prince. "You can only get that peculiar quality of line in dry-point."

George perceived that etching was an entrancing subject, and he determined to learn something about it - everything about it.

Then came the turn of Mr. Buckingham Smith's paintings. These were not signed 'Smith' as the etchings were signed 'Prince.' By no means! They were signed 'Buckingham Smith.' George much admired them, though less than he admired the etchings. They were very striking and ingenious, in particular the portraits and the still-life subjects. He had to admit that these fellows to whom he had scarcely given a thought, these fellows who existed darkly behind the house, were prodigiously accomplished.

"Of course," said Mr. Buckingham Smith negligently, "you can't get any idea of them by this light - though," he added warningly, "it's the finest artificial light going. Better than all your electricity."

There was a pause, and Mr. Prince sighed and said:

"I was thinking of going up to the Promenades tonight, but Buck won't go."

George took fire at once. "The Glazounov ballet music?"

"Glazounov?" repeated Mr. Prince uncertainly. "No. I rather wanted to hear the new Elgar."

George was disappointed, for he had derived from Mr. Enwright positive opinions about the relative importance of Elgar and Glazounov.

"Go often?" he asked.

"No," said Mr. Prince. "I haven't been this season yet, but I'm always meaning to." He smiled apologetically. "And I thought tonight - " Despite appearances, he was not indifferent after all to his great Viennese triumph; he had had some mild notion of his own of celebrating the affair.

"I suppose this is what etchings are printed with," said George to Mr. Buckingham Smith, for the sake of conversation, and he moved towards the press. The reception given to the wonderful name of Glazounov in that studio was more than a disappointment for George; he felt obscurely that it amounted to a snub.

Mr. Buckingham Smith instantly became the urbane and alert showman. He explained how the pressure was regulated. He pulled the capstan-like arms of the motive wheel and the blanketed steel bed slid smoothly under the glittering cylinder. Although George had often been in his stepfather's printing works he now felt for the first time the fascination of manual work, of artisanship, in art, and he regretted that the architect had no such labour. He could indistinctly hear Mr. Prince talking to Marguerite.

"This is a monotype," said Mr. Buckingham Smith, picking up a dusty print off the window-sill. "I do one occasionally."

"Did you do this?" asked George, who had no idea what a monotype was and dared not inquire.

"Yes. They're rather amusing to do. You just use a match or your finger or anything."

"It's jolly good," said George. "D'you know, it reminds me a bit of Cezanne."

Of course it was in Paris that he had heard of the great original, the martyr and saviour of modern painting. Equally of course it was Mr. Enwright who had inducted him into the esoteric cult of Cezanne, and magically made him see marvels in what at the first view had struck him as a wilful and clumsy absurdity.

"Oh!" murmured Buck, stiffening.

"What do you think of Cezanne?"

"Rule it out!" said Buck, with a warning cantankerous inflection, firmly and almost brutally reproving this conversational delinquency of George's. "Rule it out, young man! We don't want any of that sort of mountebanking in England. We know what it's worth."

George was cowed. More, his faith in Cezanne was shaken. He smiled sheepishly and was angry with himself. Then he heard Mr. Prince saying calmly and easily to Miss Haim - the little old man could not in fact be so nervous as he seemed:

"I suppose you wouldn't come with me to the Prom?"

George was staggered and indignant. It was inconceivable, monstrous, that those two should be on such terms as would warrant Mr. Prince's astounding proposal. He felt that he simply could not endure them marching off together for the evening. Her acceptance of the proposal would be an outrage. He trembled. However, she declined, and he was lifted from the rack.

"I must really go," she said. "Father's sure to be home by now."

"May I?" demanded Mr. Buckingham Smith, stooping over Marguerite's portfolio of designs, and glancing round at her for permission to open it. Already his hand was on the tape.

"On no account!" she cried. "No! No!... Mr. Cannon, please take it from him!" She was serious.

"Oh! All right! All right!" Mr. Buckingham Smith rose to the erect good-humouredly.

After a decent interval George took the portfolio under his arm. Marguerite was giving thanks for hospitality. They left. George was singularly uplifted by the fact that she never concealed from him those designs upon which Mr. Buckingham Smith had not been allowed to gaze. And, certain contretemps and disappointments notwithstanding, he was impressed by the entity of the studio. It had made a desirable picture in his mind: the romantic paraphernalia, the etchings, the canvases, the lights and shadows, the informality, the warm odours of the lamp and of the Pilsener, the dazzling white of the tablecloth, the quick, positive tones of Buckingham Smith, who had always to be convincing not only others but himself that he was a strong man whose views were unassailable, the eyes of Buckingham Smith like black holes in his handsome face, the stylish gestures and coarse petulance of Buckingham Smith, the shy assurance of little old Prince. He envied the pair. Their existence had a cloistral quality which appealed to something in him. They were continually in the studio, morning, afternoon, evening. They were independent. They had not to go forth to catch omnibuses and trains, to sit in offices, to utilize the services of clerks, to take orders, to 'Consider the idiosyncrasies of superiors. They were self-contained, they were consecrated, and they were free. No open competitions for them! No struggles with committees and with contractors! And no waiting for the realization of an idea! They sat down and worked, and the idea came at once to life, complete, without the necessity of other human co-operation! They did not sit in front of a painting or etching and say, as architects had too often to say in front of their designs: "That is wasted! That will never come into being." Architecture might be the art of arts, and indeed it was, but there were terrible drawbacks to it....

And next he was outside in the dark with Marguerite Haim, and new, intensified sensations thrilled him. She was very marvellous in the dark.

Mr. Haim had not returned.

"Well!" she muttered; and then dreamily: "What a funny little man Mr. Prince is, isn't he?" She spoke condescendingly.

"Anyhow," said George, who had been respecting Mr. Alfred Prince, "anyhow, I'm glad you didn't go to the concert with him."

"Why?" she asked, with apparent simplicity. "I adore the Proms. Don't you?"

"Let's go, then," he suggested. "We shan't be very late, and what else is there for you to do?"

His audacity frightened him. There she stood with him in the porch, silent, reflective. She would never go. For sundry practical and other reasons she would refuse. She must refuse.

"I'll go," she said, as if announcing a well-meditated decision. He could scarcely believe it. This could not be London that he was in.

They deposited the portfolio under the mat in the porch.

4

When they got into the hall the band was sending forth a tremendous volume of brilliant exhilarating sound. A vast melody seemed to ride on waves of brass. The conductor was very excited, and his dark locks shook with the violence of his gestures as he urged onward the fingers and arms of the executants flying madly through the maze of the music to a climax. There were flags; there was a bank of flowers; there was a fountain; there were the huge crimson-domed lamps that poured down their radiance; and there was the packed crowd of straw-hatted and floral-hatted erect figures gazing with upturned, intent faces at the immense orchestral machine. Then came a final crash, and for an instant the thin, silvery tinkle of the fountain supervened in an enchanted hush; and then terrific applause, with yells and thuds above and below the hand-clapping, filled and inflamed the whole interior. The conductor, recovering from a collapse, turned round and bowed low with his hand on his shirt-front; his hair fell over his forehead; he straightened himself and threw the hair back again, and so he kept on, time after time casting those plumes to and fro. At last, sated with homage, he thought of justice, and pointed to the band and smiled with an unconvincing air of humility, as if saying: "I am naught. Here are the true heroes." And on the end of his stick he lifted to their feet eighty men, whose rising drew invigorated shouts. Enthusiasm reigned; triumph was accomplished. Even when the applause had expired, enthusiasm still reigned; and every person present had the illusion of a share in the triumph. It was a great night at the Promenades.

George and Marguerite looked at each other happily. They both were inspired by the feeling that life was a grand thing, and that they had reached suddenly one of the summits of existence. George, observing the excitement in her eyes, thought how wonderful it was that she too should be excited.

"What was that piece?" she asked.

"I don't quite know," he said. "There don't appear to be any programmes about." He wished he had been able to identify the piece, but he was too content to be ashamed of his ignorance. Moreover, his ignorance was hers also, and he liked that.

The music resumed. He listened, ready to put himself into the mood of admiration if it was the Glazounov item. Was it Glazounov? He could not be certain. It sounded fine. Surely it sounded Russian. Then he had a glimpse of a programme held by a man standing near, and he peered at it. "No. 4. Elgar - Sea-Pictures." No. 5 was the Glazounov.

"It's only the Elgar," he said, with careless condescension, perceiving at once, by the mere virtue of a label, that the music was not fine and not Russian. He really loved music, but he happened to be at that age, from which some people never emerge, at which the judgment depends almost completely on extraneous suggestion.

"Oh!" murmured Marguerite indifferently, responding to his tone.

"Glazounov's next," he said.

"I suppose we couldn't sit down," she suggested.

Yet it was she who had preferred the Promenade to the Grand Circle or the Balcony.

"We'll find something," he said, with his usual assurance. And in the corridor that surrounded the hemicycle they climbed up on to a narrow ledge in the wall and sat side by side in perfect luxury, not dreaming that they were doing anything unusual or undignified. As a fact, they were not. Other couples were perched on other ledges, and still others on the cold steam-pipes. A girl with a big face and heavy red lips sat alone, lounging, her head aslant. She had an open copy of Home Notes in one hand. Elgar had sent the simple creature into an ecstasy, and she never stirred; probably she did not know anyone named Enwright. Promenaders promenaded in and out of the corridor, and up and down the corridor, and nobody troubled to glance twice either at the heavy-lipped, solitary girl or at the ledged couples.

Through an arched doorway could be seen the orchestra and half the auditorium.

"This is the best seat in the hall," George observed proudly. Marguerite smiled at him.

When the "Sea-Pictures" were finished she gave a sigh of appreciation, having forgotten, it seemed, that persons who had come to admire Glazounov ought not to relish Elgar. And George, too, reflecting upon the sensations produced within him by Elgar, was ready to admit that, though Elgar could of course not be classed with the foreigner, there might be something to be said for him after all.

"This is just what I needed," she murmured.

"Oh?"

"I was very depressed this afternoon," she said.

"Were you?" He had not noticed it.

"Yes. They've cut down my price from a pound to seventeen and six." 'They' were the employing bookbinders, and the price was the fixed price for a design - side and back.

He was shocked, and he felt guilty. How was it that he had noticed nothing in her demeanour? He had been full of the misfortune of the firm, and she had made the misfortune her own, keeping silence about the grinding harshness of bookbinders. He was an insensible egotist, and girls were wondrous. At any rate this girl was wondrous. He had an intense desire to atone for his insensibility and his egotism by protecting her, spoiling her, soothing her into forgetfulness of her trouble.... Ah! He understood now what she meant when she had replied to his suggestion as to visiting the cathedral: "It might do me good."

"How rotten!" he exclaimed, expressing his sympathy by means of disgust. "Couldn't you tell them to go to the dickens?"

"You have to take what they'll give," she answered. "Especially when they begin to talk about bad trade and that sort of thing."

"Well, it's absolutely rotten!"

It was not the arbitrary reduction of her earnings that he resented, but the fact of her victimhood. Scandalous, infamous, that this rare and delicate creature should be defenceless against commercial brutes!

The Glazounov ballet music, "The Seasons," started. Knowing himself justified, he surrendered himself to it, to its exoticism, to its Russianism, to its wilful and disconcerting beauty. And there was no composer like Glazounov. Beneath the sensory spell of the music, his memory wandered about through the whole of his life. He recalled days in his mother's boarding-house at Brighton; musical evenings, at which John Orgreave was present, at his stepfather's house in the Five Towns; and in all kinds of scenes at the later home at Ladderedge Hall - scenes in which his mother again predominated, becoming young again and learning sports and horsewomanship as a girl might have learnt them.... And they were all beautiful beneath the music. The music softened; the fountain was heard; the striking of matches was heard.... Still, all was beautiful. Then he touched Marguerite's hand as it rested a little behind her on the ledge. The effect of contact was surprising. With all his other thoughts he had not ceased to think of the idea of shielding and enveloping her. But now this idea utterly possessed him. The music grew louder, and as it were under cover of the music he put his hand round her hand. It was a venturesome act with such a girl; he was afraid.... The hand lay acquiescent within his! He tightened the pressure. The hand lay acquiescent; it accepted. The flashing realization of her compliance overwhelmed him. He was holding the very symbol of wild purity, and there was no effort to be free. None guessed. None could see. They two had the astonishing, the incredible secret between them. He looked at her profile, taking precautions. No sign of alarm or disturbance. Her rapt glance was fixed steadily on the orchestra framed in the arched doorway.... Incredible, the soft, warm delicacy of the cotton glove!

The applause at the end of the number awoke them. He released her hand. She slipped neatly down from the ledge.

"I think I ought to be going back home.... Father ..." she murmured. She met his eyes; but his embarrassed eyes would not meet hers.

"Certainly!" he agreed quickly, though they had been in the hall little more than half an hour. He would have agreed to any suggestion from her. It seemed to him that the least he could do at that moment was to fulfil unquestioningly her slightest wish. Then she looked away, and he saw that a deep blush gradually spread over her lovely face. This was the supreme impressive phenomenon. Before the blush he was devotional.

5

They walked down Regent Street almost in silence, enjoying simultaneously the silence and solitude of the curving thoroughfare and the memory of the bright, crowded, triumphant scene which they had left. At Piccadilly Circus

George inquired for the new open motor-buses which had just begun to run between the Circus and Putney, passing the Redcliffe Arms. Already, within a year, the time was historically distant when a policeman had refused to allow the automobile of a Member of Parliament to enter Palace Yard, on the ground that there was no precedent for such a desecration. The new motor-buses, however, did not run at night. Human daring had limits, and it was reported that at least one motor-driver, succumbing to the awful nervous strain of guiding these fast expresses through the traffic of the West End, had been taken to the lunatic asylum. George called a hansom, of which there were dozens idling about. Marguerite seemed tacitly to object to this act as the germ of extravagance; but it was the only classic thing to do, and he did it.

The hansom rolled rapidly and smoothly along upon that well-established novelty, india-rubber tyres. Bits of the jingling harness oscillated regularly from side to side. At intervals the whip-thong dragged gently across the horse's back, and the horse lifted and shook its head. The shallow and narrow interior of the hansom was constructed with exactitude to hold two. Neither occupant could move in any direction, and neither desired to move. The splendidly lighted avenues, of which every detail could be discerned as by day, flowed evenly past the vehicle.

"I've never been in a hansom before," said Marguerite timidly - because the situation was so dismaying in its enchantment.

He, from the height of two years of hansom-using, was touched, delighted, even impressed. The staggering fact increased her virginal charm and its protectiveness. He thought upon the simplicity of her existence. Of course she had never been in a hansom! Hansoms were obviously outside her scheme. He said nothing, but he sought for and found her hand beneath the apron. She did not resist. He reflected "Can she resist? She cannot." Her hand was in a living swoon. Her hand was his; it was admittedly his. She could never deny it, now. He touched the button of the glove, and undid it. Then, moving her passive hand, he brought both his to it, and with infinitely delicate and considerate gestures he slowly drew off the glove, and he held her hand ungloved. She did not stir nor speak. Nothing so marvellous as her exquisite and confiding stillness had ever happened.... The hansom turned into Alexandra Grove, and when it stopped he pushed the glove into her hand, which closed on it. As they descended the cabman, accustomed to peer down on loves pure and impure, gave them a beneficent look.

"He's not come in," said Marguerite, glancing through the flap of the front door. She was exceedingly self-conscious, but beneath her self-consciousness could be noticed an indignant accusation against old Haim. She had rung the bell and knocked.

"Are you sure? Can you see the hat-stand?"

"I can see it enough for that."

"Look here," George suggested, with false lightness, "I expect I could get in through my window." His room was on the ground floor, and not much agility was needed to clamber up to its ledge from the level of the area. He might have searched his pockets again and discovered his latchkey, but he would not. Sooner than admit a deception he would have remained at the door with her all night.

"Think you could?"

"Yes. I could slide the window-catch."

He jumped down the steps and showed her how he could climb. In two minutes he was opening the front door to her from the inside. She moved towards him in the gloom.

"Oh! My portfolio!" She stopped, and bent down to the mat.

Then she busily lighted the little hall-lamp with his matches, and hurried down, taking the matches, to the kitchen. After a few moments George followed her; he was obliged to follow her. She had removed her coat; it lay on the sole chair. The hat and blouse which she wore seemed very vivid in the kitchen - vestiges of past glorious episodes in concert-halls and hansoms. She had lighted the kitchen-lamp and was standing apparently idle. The alarum-clock on the black mantelpiece ticked noisily. The cat sat indifferently on the corner of the clean, bare table. George hesitated in the doorway. He was extremely excited, because the tremendous fact of what he had done and what she had permitted, with all the implications, had to be explicitly acknowledged between them. Of course it had to be acknowledged! They were both fully aware of the thing, she as well as he, but spoken words must authenticate its existence as only spoken words could.

She said, beginning sternly and finishing with a peculiar smile:

"I do think this business of father and Mrs. Lobley is going rather far."

And George had a sudden new sense of the purely feminine adroitness of women. In those words she had clearly conceded that their relations were utterly changed. Never before had she made even the slightest, most distant reference to the monstrous household actuality, unadmitted and yet patent, of the wooing of Mrs. Lobley the charwoman by her father, the widower of her mother. If Mr. Haim stayed away from home of an evening, Mrs. Lobley was the siren who deflected him from the straight domestic path. She knew it; George surmised it; the whole street had its suspicions. But hitherto Marguerite had given no sign. She now created George the confidant of her resentment. And her smile was not an earnest of some indulgence for her father - her smile was for George alone.

He went boldly up to her, put his arms round her, and kissed her. She did not kiss. But she allowed herself to be kissed, and she let her body loose in his embrace. She looked at him with her eyes nearly upon his, and her eyes glittered with a mysterious burning; he knew that she was content. That she should be content, that it should please her to let him have the unimaginable experience of holding that thrilled and thrilling body close to his, seemed to him to be a marvellous piece of sheer luck and overwhelming good fortune. She was so sensuous and yet so serious. Her gaze stimulated not only love but conscience. In him ambition was superlatively vigorous. Nevertheless he felt then as though he had never really known ambition till that moment. He thought of the new century and of a new life. He perceived the childishness and folly of his favourite idea that an artist ought to pass through a phase of Don Juanism. He knew that the task of satisfying the lofty and exacting and unique girl would be immense, and that he could fulfil it, but on the one condition that it monopolized his powers. Thus he was both modest and proud, anxious and divinely elated. His mind was the scene of innumerable impulses and sensations over which floated the banner of the male who has won an impassioned allegiance.

"Don't let's tell anyone yet," she murmured.

"No."

"I mean for a long time," she insisted.

"No, we won't," he agreed, and added scornfully: "They'd only say we're too young."

The notion of secrecy was an enchanting notion.

She cut magic cake and poured out magic milk. And they ate and drank together, for they were hungry. And at this point the cat began to show an interest in their doings.

And after they were both in their beds, but not after they were asleep, Mr. Haim, by the clicking of a latchkey in a lock, reminded them of something which they had practically forgotten - his disordered existence.

3

THE CHARWOMAN

George entered Alexandra Grove very early the next evening, having dined inadequately and swiftly so that he might reach the neighbourhood of Marguerite at the first moment justifiable. He would have omitted dinner and trusted to Marguerite's kitchen, only that, in view of the secrecy resolved upon, appearances had to be preserved. The secrecy in itself was delicious, but even the short experiences of the morning had shown both of them how extremely difficult it would be for two people who were everything to each other to behave as though they were nothing to each other. George hoped, however, that Mr. Haim would again be absent, and he was anticipating exquisite hours.

At the precise instant when he put his latchkey in the door the door was pulled away from him by a hand within, and he saw a woman of about thirty-five, plump but not stout, in a blue sateen dress, bonneted but not gloved. She had pleasant, commonplace features and brown hair. Several seconds elapsed before George recognized in her Mrs. Lobley, the charwoman of No. 8, and when he did so he was a little surprised at her presentableness. He had met her very seldom in the house. He was always late for breakfast, and his breakfast was always waiting for him. On Sundays he was generally out. If he did catch sight of her, she was invariably in a rough apron and as a rule on her knees. Their acquaintance had scarcely progressed far enough for him to call her 'Mrs. Lob' with any confidence. He had never seen her at night, though upon occasion he had heard her below in the basement, and for him she was associated with mysterious nocturnal goings and comings by the basement door. That she should be using the front door was as startling as that she should be so nobly attired in blue sateen.

"Good evening - Mr. Cannon," she said, in her timid voice, too thin for her body. He noticed that she was perturbed. Hitherto she had always addressed him as 'sir.'

"Excuse me," she said, and with an apologetic air she slipped past him and departed out of the house.

Mr. Haim was visible just within the doorway of the sitting-room, and behind him the table with the tea-things still on it. George had felt considerably self-conscious in Mr. Haim's presence at the office; and he was so preoccupied by his own secret mighty affair that his first suspicion connected the strange apparition of a new Mrs. Lobley and the peculiar look on Mr. Haim's face with some disagreeable premature and dramatic explosion of the secret mighty affair. His thoughts, though absurd, ran thus because they could not run in any other way.

"Ah, Mr. Cannon!" said Mr. Haim queerly. "You're in early tonight."

"A bit earlier," George admitted, with caution. "Have to read, you know." He was using the word 'read' in the examination sense.

"If you could spare me a minute," smiled Mr. Haim

"Certainly."

"Have a cigarette," said Mr. Haim, as soon as George had deposited his hat and come into the room. This quite unprecedented offer reassured George, who in spite of reason had continued to fear that the landlord had something on his mind about his daughter and his lodger. Mr. Haim presented his well-known worn cigarette-case, and then with precise and calm gestures carefully shut the door.

"The fact is," said he, "I wanted to tell you something. I told Mr. Enwright this afternoon, as I thought was proper, and it seems to me that you are the next person who ought to be informed."

"Oh yes?"

"I am going to be married."

"The deuce you are!"

The light words had scarcely escaped from young George before he perceived that his tone was a mistake, and that Mr. Haim was in a state of considerable emotion, which would have to be treated very carefully. And George too now suddenly partook of the emotion. He felt himself to be astonished and even shaken by Mr. Haim's news. The atmosphere of the interview changed in an instant. Mr. Haim moved silently on slippered feet to the mantelpiece, out of the circle of lamplight, and dropped some ash into the empty fire-place.

"I congratulate you," said George.

"Thank you!" said Mr. Haim brightly, seizing gratefully on the fustian phrase, eager to hall-mark it as genuine and put it among his treasures. Without doubt he was flattered. "Yes," he proceeded, as it were reflectively, "I have asked Mrs. Lobley to be my wife, and she has done me the honour to consent." He had the air of having invented the words specially to indicate that Mrs. Lobley was descending from a throne in order to espouse him. It could not have occurred to him that they had ever been used before and that the formula was classic. He smiled again, and went on: "Of course I've known and admired Mrs. Lobley for a long time. What we should have done without her valuable help in this house I don't like to think. I really don't."

"'Her help in this house,'" thought the ruthless George, behind cigarette smoke. "Why doesn't he say right out she's the charwoman? If I was marrying a charwoman, I should say I was marrying a charwoman." And then he had a misgiving: "Should I? I wonder whether I should." And he remembered that ultimately the charwoman was going to be his own mother-in-law. He was aware of a serious qualm.

"Mrs. Lobley has had an uphill fight since her first husband's death," said Mr. Haim. "He was an insurance agent - the Prudential. She's come out of it splendidly. She's always kept up her little home, though it was only two rooms, and she'll only leave it because I can offer her a better one. I have always admired her, and I'm sure the more you know her the more you'll like her. She's a woman in a thousand, Mr. Cannon."

"I expect she is," George agreed feebly. He could not think of anything to say.

"And I'm thankful I can offer her a better home. I don't mind telling you now that at one time I began to fear I shouldn't have a home. I've had my ambitions, Mr. Cannon. I was meant for a quantity surveyor. I was one - you may say. But it was not to be. I came down in the world, but I kept my head above water. And then in the end, with a little money I had I bought this house. L575. It needed some negotiation. Ground-rent L10 per annum, and seventy years to run. You see, all along I had had the idea of building a studio in the garden. I was one of the first to see the commercial possibilities of studios in Chelsea. But of course I know Chelsea. I made the drawings for the studio myself. Mr. Enwright kindly suggested a few improvements. With all my experience I was in a position to get it put up as cheaply as possible. You'd be surprised at the number of people in the building line anxious to oblige me. It cost under L300. I had to borrow most of it. But I've paid it off. What's the consequence? The consequence is that the rent of the studio and the top rooms brings me in over eight per cent on all I spent on the house and the studio together. And I'm living rent free myself."

"Jolly good!"

"Yes.... If I'd had capital, Mr. Cannon, I could have made thousands out of studios. Thousands. I fancy I've the gift. But I've never had the capital. And that's all there is to it." He smacked his lips, and leaned back against the mantelpiece. "You may tell me I've realized my ambitions. Not all of them, Mr. Cannon. Not all of them. If I'd had money I should have had leisure, and I should have improved myself. Reading, I mean. Study. Literature. Music. Painting. History of architecture. All that sort of thing. I've got the taste for it. I know I've got the taste for it. But what could I do? I gave it up. You'll never know how lucky you are, Mr. Cannon. I gave it up. However, I've nothing to be ashamed of. At any rate I hope not."

George nodded appreciatively. He was touched. He was even impressed. He admitted the naivete of the ageing man, his vanity, his sentimentality. But he saw himself to be in the presence of an achievement. And though the crown of Mr. Haim's achievement was to marry a charwoman, still the achievement impressed. And the shabby man with the lined, common face was looking back at the whole of his life - there was something positively formidable in that alone. He was at the end; George was at the beginning, and George felt callow and deferential. The sensation of callowness at once heightened his resolve to succeed. All George's sensations seemed mysteriously to transform themselves into food for this great resolve.

"And what does Miss Haim say to all this?" he asked, rather timidly and wildly. It was a venturesome remark; it might well have been called an impertinence; but the mage of Marguerite was involved in all the workings of his mind, and it would not be denied expression.

Mr. Haim lifted his back from the mantelpiece sharply. Then he hesitated, moving forward a little.

"Mr. Cannon," he said, "it's curious you should ask that." His voice trembled, and at the vibration George was suddenly apprehensive. Mr. Haim had soon recovered from his original emotion, but now he seemed to be in danger of losing control of himself.

George nervously cleared his throat and apologized.

"I didn't mean - "

"I'd better tell you," Mr. Haim interrupted him, rather loudly. "We've just had a terrible scene with my daughter, a terrible scene!" He seldom referred to Marguerite by her Christian name, "Mr. Cannon, I had hoped to get through my life without a scandal, and especially an open scandal. But it seems as if I shouldn't - if I know my daughter! It was not my intention to say anything. Far from it. Outsiders ought not to be troubled.... I - I like you, Mr. Cannon. She left us a few minutes ago And as she didn't put her hat on she must be either at the studio or at Agg's...."

"She went out of the house?" George questioned awkwardly.

Mr. Haim nodded, and then without warning he dropped like an inert lump on to a chair and let his head fall on to his hand.

George was frightened as well as mystified. The spectacle of the old man - at one moment boasting ingenuously of his career, and at the next almost hysterical with woe - roused his pity in a very disconcerting manner, and from his sight the Lucas & Enwright factotum vanished utterly, and was supplanted by a tragic human being. But he had no idea how to handle the unexampled situation with dignity; he realized painfully his own lack of experience, and his over-mastering impulse was to get away while it was still possible to get away. Moreover, he desired intensely to see and hear Marguerite.

"Perhaps I had better find out where she is," he absurdly suggested, and departed from the room feeling like a criminal reprieved.

The old man did not stir.

2

"Can I come in?" said George, hatless, pushing open the door of the studio, which was ajar.

There were people in the bright and rather chilly studio, and none of them moved until the figure arriving out of the darkness was identified. Mr. Prince, who in the far corner was apparently cleaning or adjusting his press, then came forward with a quiet, shy, urbane welcome. Marguerite herself stood nearly under the central lamp, talking to Agg, who was seated. The somewhat celebrated Agg immediately rose and said in her somewhat deep voice to Marguerite:

"I must go."

Agg was the eldest daughter of the Agg family, a broad-minded and turbulent tribe who acknowledged the nominal headship of a hard-working and successful barrister. She was a painter, and lived and slept in semi-independence in a studio of her own in Manresa Road, but maintained close and constant relations with the rest of the tribe. In shape and proportions fairly tall and fairly thin, she counted in shops among the stock-sizes; but otherwise she was entitled to call herself unusual. She kept her hair about as short as the hair of a boy who has postponed going to the barber's for a month after the proper time, and she incompletely covered the hair with the smallest possible hat. Her coat was long and straight and her skirt short. Her boots were high, reaching well up the calf, but they had high heels and were laced in some hundreds of holes. She carried a cane in a neatly gloved hand. She was twenty-seven. In style Marguerite and Agg made a great contrast with one another. Each was fully aware of the contrast, and liked it.

"Good evening, Mr. Cannon," said Agg firmly, not shaking hands.

George had met her once in the way of small-talk at her father's house. Having yet to learn the important truth that it takes all sorts to make a world, he did not like her and wondered why she existed. He could understand Agg being fond of Marguerite, but he could not understand Marguerite being fond of Agg; and the friendship between these two, now that he actually for the first time saw it in being, irked him.

"Is anything the matter?... Have you seen father?" asked Marguerite in a serious, calm tone, turning to him. Like George, she had run into the studio without putting on any street attire.

George perceived that there was no secret in the studio as to the crisis in the Haim family. Clearly the topic had been under discussion. Prince as well as Agg was privy to it. He did not quite like that. He was vaguely jealous of both Prince and Agg. Indeed he was startled to find that Marguerite could confide such a matter to Prince - at any rate without consulting himself. While not definitely formulating the claim in his own mind, he had somehow expected of Marguerite that until she met him she would have existed absolutely sole, without any sentimental connexions of any sort, in abeyance, waiting for his miraculous advent. He was glad that Mr. Buckingham Smith was not of the conclave; he felt that he could not have tolerated Mr. Buckingham Smith.

"Yes, I've seen him," George answered.

"Did he tell you?"

"Yes."

Mr. Prince, after a little hovering, retired to his press, and a wheel could be heard creaking.

"What did he tell you?"

"He told me about - the marriage.... And I gathered there'd been a bit of a scene."

"Nothing else?"

"No."

Agg then interjected, fixing her blue eyes on George:

"Marguerite is coming to live with me in my studio."

And her challenging gaze met George's.

"Oh!" George could not suppress his pained inquietude at this decision having been made without his knowledge. Both girls misapprehended his feeling. "That's it, is it?"

"Well," said Agg, "what can Mr. Haim expect? Here Marguerite's been paying this woman two shillings a day and her food, and letting her take a parcel home at nights. And then all of a sudden she comes dressed up for tea, and sits down, and Mr. Haim says she's his future wife. What does he expect? Does he expect Marguerite to kiss her and call her mamma? The situation's impossible."

"But you can't stop people from falling in love, Agg, you know. It's not a crime," said Mr. Prince in his weak voice surprisingly from the press.

"I know it's not a crime," said Agg sharply. "And nobody wants to stop people from falling in love. If Mr. Haim chooses to go mad about a charwoman, when his wife, and such a wife, 's been dead barely three years, that's his concern. It's true the lady isn't much more than half his age, and that the whole business would be screamingly funny if it wasn't disgusting; but still he's a free agent. And Marguerite's a free agent too, I hope. Of course he's thunder-struck to discover that Marguerite is a free agent. He would be!"

"He certainly is in a state," said George, with an uneasy short laugh.

Agg continued:

"And why is he in a state? Because Marguerite says she shall leave the house? Not a bit. Only because of what he thinks is the scandal of her leaving. Mr. Haim is a respectable man. He's simply all respectability. Respectability's his god - Father, Son, and Holy Ghost. Always has been. He'd sacrifice everything to respectability - except the lovely Lobley. It's not respectable in a respectable family for a girl to leave home on account of her stepmother. And so he's in a state, if you please!... If he wanted to carry on with Mrs. Lobley, let him carry on with her. But no! That's not respectable. He's just got to marry her!" Agg sneered.

George was startled, perhaps excusably, at the monstrous doctrine implied in Agg's remarks. He had thought himself a man of the world, experienced, unshockable. But he blenched, and all his presence of mind was needed to preserve a casual, cool demeanour. The worst of the trial was Marguerite's tranquil acceptance of the attitude of her friend. She glanced at Agg in silent, admiring approval. He surmised that until that moment he had been perfectly ignorant of what girls really were.

"I see," said George courageously. And then, strangely, he began to admire too. And he pulled himself together.

"I think I shall leave tomorrow," Marguerite announced. "Morning. It will be much better. She can look after him. I don't see that I owe any duty ..."

"Yes, you do, dear," Agg corrected her impressively. "You owe a duty to your mother - to her memory. That's the duty you owe. I'll come round for you tomorrow myself in a four-wheeler - let me see, about eleven."

George hated the sound of the word 'duty.'

"Thank you, dear," Marguerite murmured, and the girls shook hands; they did not kiss.

"Bye-bye, Princey."

"Bye-bye, Agg."

"Good night, Mr. Cannon."

Agg departed, slightly banging the door.

"I think I'll go back home now," said Marguerite, in a sweet, firm tone. "Had they gone out?"

"Who? Your father and What's-her-name? She's gone, but he hasn't. If you don't want to meet him tonight again, hadn't you better - "

"Oh! If she's gone, he'll be gone too by this time. Trust him!"

Mr. Prince approached them, urging Marguerite soothingly to stay as long as she liked. She shook her head, and pressed his hand affectionately.

3

When George and Marguerite re-entered No. 8 by the front door, Mr. Haim was still sitting overcome at the tea-table. They both had sight of him through the open door of the parlour. Marguerite was obviously disturbed to see him there, but she went straight into the room. George moved into the darkness of his own room. He heard the voices of the other two.

"Then you mean to go?" Haim asked accusingly.

Marguerite answered in a calm, good-humoured, sweet tone:

"Of course, if you mean to marry Mrs. Lobley."

"Marry Mrs. Lobley! Of course I shall marry her!" Haim's voice rose. "What right have you to settle where I shall marry and where I shan't?"

"I've fixed everything up with Celia Agg," said Marguerite very quietly.

"You've soon arranged it!"

No reply from Marguerite. The old man spoke again:

"You've no right - It'll be an open scandal."

Then a silence. George now thought impatiently that a great fuss was being made about a trifle, and that a matter much more important deserved attention. His ear caught a violent movement. The old man came out of the parlour, and, instead of taking his hat and rushing off to find the enchantress, he walked slowly and heavily upstairs, preceded by his immense shadow thrown from the hall-lamp. He disappeared round the corner of the stairs. George, under the influence of the apparition, was forced to modify his view that all the fuss was over a trifle. He tiptoed into the parlour. Marguerite was standing at the table. As soon as George came in she began to gather the tea-things together on the tray.

"I say!" whispered George.

Marguerite's bent, tranquil face had a pleasant look as she handled the crockery.

"I shall get him a nice breakfast tomorrow," she said, also in a whisper. "And as soon as he's gone to the office I shall pack. It won't take me long, really."

"But won't Mrs. Lobley be here?"

"What if she is? I've nothing against Mrs. Lobley. Nor, as far as that goes, against poor father either - you see what I mean."

"He told me you'd had a terrible scene. That's what he said' - a terrible scene."

"It depends what you call a scene," she said smoothly. "I was rather upset just at first - who wouldn't be? - but ..." She stopped, listening, with a glance at the ceiling. There was not the slightest sound overhead. "I wonder what he's doing?"

She picked up the tray.

"I'll carry that," said George.

"No! It's all right. I'm used to it. You might bring me the tablecloth. But you won't drop the crumbs out of it, will you?"

He followed her with the bunched-up tablecloth down the dangerous basement steps into the kitchen. She passed straight into the little scullery, where the tray with its contents was habitually left for the attention of Mrs. Lobley the next morning. When she turned again, he halted her, as it were, at the entrance from the scullery with a question.

"Shall you be all right?"

"With Agg?"

"Yes."

"How do you mean - 'all right'?"

"Well, for money, and so on."

"Oh yes!" She spoke lightly and surely, with a faint confident smile.

"I was thinking as they'd cut down your prices - "

"I shall have heaps. Agg and I - why, we can live splendidly for next to nothing. You'll see."

He was rebuffed. He felt jealous of both Agg and Prince, but especially of Prince. It still seemed outrageous to him that Prince should have been taken into her confidence. Prince had known of the affair before himself. He was more than jealous; he had a greater grievance. Marguerite appeared to have forgotten all about love, all about the mighty event of their betrothal. She appeared to have put it away, as casually as she had put away the tray. Yet ought not the event to count supreme over everything else - over no matter what? He was desolate and unhappy.

"Did you tell Agg?" he asked.

"What about?"

"Our being engaged - and so on."

She started towards him.

"Dearest!" she protested, not in the least irritated or querulous, but kindly, affectionately. "Without asking you first? Didn't we agree we wouldn't say anything to anybody? But we shall have to think about telling Agg."

He met her and suddenly seized her. They kissed, and she shut her eyes. He was ecstatically happy.

"Oh!" she murmured in his embrace. "I'm so glad I've got you."

And she opened her eyes and tears fell from them. She cried quietly, without excitement and without shame. She cried with absolute naturalness. Her tears filled him with profound delight. And in the exquisite subterranean intimacy of the kitchen, he saw with his eyes and felt with his arms how beautiful she was. Her face, seen close, was incredibly soft and touching. Her nose was the most wonderful nose ever witnessed. He gloated upon her perfection. For, literally, to him she was perfect. With what dignity and with what a sense of justice she had behaved, in the studio, in the parlour, and here. He was gloriously reassured as he realized how in their joint future he would be able to rely upon her fairness, her conscientiousness, her mere pleasantness which nothing could disturb. Throughout the ordeal of the evening she had not once been ruffled. She had not said an unkind word, nor given an unkind gesture, nor exhibited the least trace of resentment. Then, she had taste, and she was talented. But perhaps the greatest quality of all was her adorable beauty and charm. And yet no! The final attraction was that she trusted him, depended on him, cried in his embrace.... He loosed her with reluctance, and she deliciously wiped her eyes on his handkerchief, and he took her again.

"I suppose I must leave here too, now," he said.

"Oh, George!" she exclaimed. "You mustn't! Why should you? I don't want you to."

"Don't you? Why?"

"Oh! I don't! Truly. You'll be just as well looked after as if I was here. I do hope you'll stay."

That settled it. And Manresa Road was not far off.

She sat on the table and leaned against him a long time. Then she said she must go upstairs to her room - she had so much to do. He could not forbid, because she was irresistible. She extinguished the kitchen-lamp, and, side by side, they groped up the stairs to the first floor. The cat nonchalantly passed them in the hall.

"Put the lights out here, will you, when you go to bed?" she whispered. He felt flattered.

She offered her face.... The lovely thing slipped away upstairs with unimaginable, ravishing grace. She vanished. There was silence. After a moment George could hear the clock ticking in the kitchen below. He stood motionless, amid the dizzying memories of her glance, her gestures, the softness of her body. What had happened to him was past belief. He completely forgot the existence of the old man in love.

4

THE LUNCHEON

George, having had breakfast in bed, opened his door for the second time that morning, and duly found on the mat the can of hot water (covered with a bit of old blanket) and the can of cold water which comprised the material for his bath. There was no sound in the house. The new spouse might be upstairs or she might be downstairs - he could not tell; but the cans proved that she was immanent and regardful; indeed, she never forgot anything. And George's second state at No. 8 was physically even better than his first. In the transition through autumn from summer to winter - a transition which, according to the experience of tens of thousands of London lodgers, is capable of turning comparative comfort into absolute discomfort - Mrs. Haim had behaved with benevolence and ingenuity. For example, the bedroom fire, laid overnight, was now burning up well from the mere touch of the lodger's own match. Such things are apt to count, and they counted with George.

As for Mr. Haim, George knew that he was still in bed, because, since his marriage, Mr. Haim had made a practice of staying in bed on Sunday mornings. The scheme was his wife's; she regarded it as his duty to himself to exercise this grand male privilege of staying in bed; to do so gave him majesty, magnificence, and was a sign of authority. A copy of The Referee, fresh as fruit new-dropped from the bough, lay in the hall at the front door. Mr. Haim had read The Referee since The Referee was. He began his perusal with the feature known as "Mustard and Cress," which not only amused him greatly, but convinced him that his own ideas on affairs were really very sagacious. His chief and most serious admiration, however was kept for "Our Hand-Book." "It's my Bible," he had once remarked, "and I'm not ashamed to say it. And there are scores and scores of men who'd say the same." Church bells could not be heard at No. 8. The Referee lying in the hall was the gracious sign of Sabbath morning. Presently Mrs. Haim would carry it upstairs, respectfully. For her it was simply and unanalysably The Referee. She did not dream of looking into it. Mr. Haim did not expect her to look into it. Her mission was to solace and to charm, his alone to supply the intellectual basis upon which their existence reposed. George's nose caught the ascending beautiful odour of bacon; he picked up his cans and disappeared.

When he was dressed, he brought forward the grindstone to the fire, and conscientiously put his nose to it, without even lighting a cigarette. It had been agreed between himself and Marguerite that there should be no more cigarettes until after lunch. It had also been agreed that he should put his nose to the grindstone that Sunday morning, and that she should do the same away in Manresa Road. George's grindstone happened to be Miers and Crosskey's *The Soil in Relation to Health*. He was preparing for his Final Examination. In addition to the vast imperial subject of Design, the Final comprised four other subjects - Construction, Hygiene, Properties and Uses of Building Materials, and Ordinary Practice of Architecture. George was now busy with one branch of the second of these subjects. Perhaps he was not following precisely the order of tactics prescribed by the most wily tacticians, for as usual he had his own ideas and they were arbitrary; but he was veritably and visibly engaged in the slow but exciting process of becoming a great architect. And he knew and felt that he was. And the disordered bed, and the untransparent bath-water, and the soap-tin by the side of the bath, and the breakfast-tray on a chair, were as much a part of the inspiring spectacle as himself tense and especially dandiacal in the midst.

Nevertheless appearances deceived. On a table were the thirteen folio and quarto glorious illustrated volumes of Ongania's *Basilica di San Marco*, which Mr. Enwright had obtained for him on loan, and which had come down to No. 8 in a big box by Carter Paterson van. And while George sat quite still with his eyes and his volition centred fiercely on Miers and Crosskey, his brain would keep making excursions across the room to the Church of St. Mark at Venice. He brought it back again and again with a jerk but he could not retain it in place. The minutes passed; the quarters passed, until an hour and a half had gone. Then he closed Miers and Crosskey. He had sworn to study Miers and Crosskey for an hour and a half. He had fought hard to do so, and nobody could say that he had not done so. He was aware, however, that the fight had not been wholly successful; he had not won it; on the other hand neither had he lost it. Honour was saved, and he could still sincerely assert that in regard to the Final Examination he had got time fiercely by the forelock. He rose and strolled over to the Basilica di San Marco, and opened one or two of those formidable and enchanting volumes. Then he produced a cigarette, and struck a match, and he was about to light the cigarette, when squinting down at it he suddenly wondered: "Now how the deuce did that cigarette come into my mouth?" He replaced the cigarette in his case, and in a moment he had left the house.

He was invited to Mrs. John Orgreave's new abode at Bedford Park for lunch. In the early part of the year, Mrs. John had inherited money - again, and the result had been an increase in the spaciousness of her existence. George had not expected to see the new house, for he had determined to have nothing more to do with Mrs. John. He was, it is to be feared, rather touchy. He and Mrs. John had not openly quarrelled, but in their hearts they had quarrelled. George had for some time objected to her attitude towards him as a boarder. She would hint that, as she assuredly had no need of boarders, she was conferring a favour on him by boarding him. It was of course true, but George considered that her references to the fact were offensive. He did not understand and make allowances for Adela. Moreover, he thought that a woman who had been through the Divorce Court ought to be modest in demeanour towards people who had not been through the Divorce Court. Further, Adela resented his frequent lateness for meals. And she had said, with an uncompromising glance: "I hope you'll turn over a new leaf when we get into the new house." And he had replied, with an uncompromising glance: "Perhaps I shan't get into the new house." Nothing else. But that ended it. After that both felt that mutual detestation had set in. John Orgreave was not implicated in the discreet rupture. Possibly he knew of it; possibly he didn't; he was not one to look for trouble, and he accepted the theory that it was part of George's vital scheme to inhabit Chelsea. And then Adela, all fluffiness and winsomeness, had called, in the previous week, at Russell Square and behaved like a woman whose sole aim in life is to please and cosset men of genius. "I shall be dreadfully hurt if you don't come to one of my Sunday lunches, George!" she had said. And also: "We miss you, you know," and had put her head on one side.

Marguerite had thoroughly approved his acceptance of the invitation. She thought that he 'ought' to accept. He had promised, as she had an urgent design to do, not to arrive at the studio before 8 p.m., and he had received a note from her that morning to insist on the hour.

2

The roads were covered with a very even, very thin coating of mud; it was as though a corps of highly skilled house-painters had laid on the mud, and just vanished. The pavements had a kind of yellowish-brown varnish. Each of the few trees that could be seen - and there were a few - carried about six surviving leaves. The sky was of a blue-black with golden rents and gleams that travelled steadily eastwards. Except the man with newspapers at the corner of

Alexandra Grove, scarcely a sign of life showed along the vistas of Fulham Road; but the clock over the jeweller's was alive and bearing the usual false witness. From the upper open galleries of the Workhouse one or two old men and old women in uniform looked down indifferently upon the free world which they had left for ever. Then an omnibus appeared faintly advancing from the beautiful grey distance of the straight and endless street. George crossed the road on his way towards Redcliffe Gardens and Earl's Court. He was very smart, indeed smarter than ever, having produced in himself quite naturally and easily a fair imitation of the elegant figures which, upon his visits to the restaurant-building in Piccadilly, he had observed airing themselves round about Bond Street. His hair was smooth like polished marble; his hat and stick were at the right angle; his overcoat was new, and it indicated the locality of his waist; the spots of colour in his attire complied with the operative decrees. His young face had in it nothing that obviously separated him from the average youth of his clothes. Nobody would have said of him, at a glance, that he might be a particularly serious individual. And most people would have at once classed him as a callow pleasure-seeking person in the act of seeking pleasure.

Nevertheless he was at that moment particularly serious, and his seriousness was growing. His secret engagement had affected him, in part directly, and in part by the intensification of ambitious endeavour which had resulted from contact with that fount of seriousness, Marguerite. Although still entirely dependent - even to cigarette money - upon the benevolence of a couple of old individuals a hundred and fifty miles off, he reckoned that he was advancing in the world. The Intermediate Examination was past, and already he felt that he had come to grips with the Final and would emerge victorious. He felt too that his general knowledge and the force and variety of his ideas were increasing. At times, when he and Marguerite talked, he was convinced that both of them had achieved absolute knowledge, and that their criticisms of the world were and would always be unanswerable. After the Final, he hoped, his uncle would buy him a share in the Lucas & Enwright practice. In due season, his engagement would be revealed, and all would be immensely impressed by his self-restraint and his good taste, and the marriage would occur, and he would be a London architect, an established man - at the mature age of, say, twenty-two.

No cloud would have obscured the inward radiance caused by the lovely image of Marguerite and by his confidence in himself, had it not been for those criticisms of the world. He had moods of being rather gravely concerned as to the world, and as to London. He was recovering from the first great attack of London. He saw faults in London. He was capable of being disturbed by, for example, the ugliness and the inefficiency of London. He even thought that something ought to be done about it. Upon this Sunday morning, fresh from visions of Venice, and rendered a little complacent by the grim execution of the morning's programme of work, he was positively pained by the aspect of Redcliffe Gardens. The Redcliffe Arms public-house, locked and dead, which was the daily paradise of hundreds of human beings, and had given balm and illusion to whole generations, seemed simply horrible to him in its Sunday morning coma. The large and stuffy unsightliness of it could not be borne. (However, the glimpse of a barmaid at an upper window interested him pleasantly for a moment.) And the Redcliffe Arms was the true gate to the stucco and areas of Redcliffe Gardens. He looked down into the areas and saw therein the furtive existence of squalor behind barred windows. All the obscene apparatus of London life was there. And as he raised his eyes to the drawing-room and bedroom stories he found no relief. His eyes could discover nothing that was not mean, ugly, frowzy, and unimaginative. He pictured the heavy, gloomy, lethargic life within. The slatternly servants pottering about the bases of the sooty buildings sickened and saddened him. A solitary Earl's Court omnibus that lumbered past with its sinister, sparse cargo seemed to be a spectacle absolutely tragic - he did not know why. The few wayfarers were obviously prim and smug. No joy, no elegance, anywhere! Only, at intervals, a feeling that mysterious and repulsive wealth was hiding itself like an ogre in the eternal twilight of fastnesses beyond the stuccoed walls and the grimy curtains.... The city worked six days in order to be precisely this on the seventh. Truly it was very similar to the Five Towns, and in essentials not a bit better. - A sociological discovery which startled him! He wanted to destroy Redcliffe Gardens, and to design it afresh and rebuild it under the inspiration of St. Mark's and of the principles of hygiene as taught for the Final Examination. He had grandiose ideas for a new design. As for Redcliffe Square, he could do marvels with its spaces.

He arrived too soon at Earl's Court Station, having forgotten that the Underground Railway had a treaty with the Church of England and all the Nonconformist churches not to run trains while the city, represented by possibly two per cent of its numbers, was at divine worship. He walked to and fro along the platforms in the vast echoing cavern peopled with wandering lost souls, and at last a train came in from the void, and it had the air of a miracle, because nobody had believed that any train ever would come in. And at last the Turnham Green train came in, and George got into a smoking compartment, and Mr. Enwright was in the compartment.

Mr. Enwright also was going to the Orgreave luncheon. He was in what the office called 'one of his moods.' The other occupants of the compartment had a stiff and self-conscious air: some apparently were proud of being abroad on Sunday morning; some apparently were ashamed. Mr. Enwright's demeanour was as free and natural as that of a child. His lined and drawn face showed worry and self-absorption in the frankest manner. He began at once to explain how badly he had slept; indeed he asserted that he had not slept at all; and he complained with extreme acerbity of the renewal of his catarrh. 'Constant secretion. Constant secretion,' was the phrase he used to describe the chief symptom. Then by a forced transition he turned to the profession of architecture, and restated his celebrated theory that it was the Cinderella of professions. The firm had quite recently obtained a very important job in a manufacturing quarter of London, without having to compete for it; but Mr. Enwright's great leading ideas never fluctuated with the fluctuation of facts. If the multiplicity of his lucrative jobs had been such as to compel him to run round from one to another on a piebald pony in the style of Sir Hugh Corver, his view of the profession would not have altered. He spoke with terrible sarcasm apropos of a rumour current in architectural circles that a provincial city intended soon to invite competitive designs for a building of realty enormous proportions, and took oath that in no case should his firm, enter for the competition. In short, his condition was markedly pessimistic.

George loved him, and was bound to humour him; and in order to respond sympathetically to Enwright's pessimism he attempted to describe his sensations concerning the London Sunday, and in particular the Sunday morning aspect of Earl's Court streets. He animadverted with virulence, and brought forward his new startling discovery that London was in truth as provincial as the provinces.

"Well, I don't think it is," said Enwright, instantly becoming a judicial truth-seeker.

"Why don't you?"

"Simply because it's bigger - so much bigger. That's the principal difference, and you'll never get over it. You must appreciate size. An elephant is a noble animal, but it wouldn't be if it was only as big as a fly. London's an elephant, and forget it not."

"It's frightfully ugly, most of it, anyhow, and especially on Sunday morning," George persisted.

"Is it? I wonder whether it is, now. The architecture's ugly. But what's architecture? Architecture isn't everything. If you can go up and down London and see nothing but architecture, you'll never be an A1 architect." He spoke in a low, kindly, and reasonable tone. "I like London on Sunday mornings. In fact it's marvellous. You say it's untidy and all that ... slatternly, and so on. Well, so it ought to be when it gets up late. Jolly bad sign if it wasn't. And that's part of it! Why, dash it, look at a bedroom when you trail about, getting up! Look how you leave it! The existence of a big city while it's waking up - lethargy business - a sort of shamelessness - it's like a great animal! I think it's marvellous, and I always have thought so."

George would not openly agree, but his mind was illuminated with a new light, and in his mind he agreed, very admiringly.

The train stopped; people got out; and the two were alone in the compartment.

"I thought all was over between you and Adela," said Mr. Enwright, confidentially and quizzically.

George blushed a little. "Oh no!"

"I don't know what I'm going to her lunch for, I'm sure. I suppose I have to go."

"I have, too," said George.

"Well, she won't do you any good, you know. I was glad when you left there."

George looked worldly. "Rum sort, isn't she?"

I'll tell you what she is, now. You remember Aida at the Paris Opera. The procession in the second act where you lost your head and said it was the finest music ever written. And those girls in white, waving palms in front of the hero - What's-his-name. There are some women who are born to do that and nothing else. Thin lips. Fixed idiotic smile. They don't think a bit about what they're doing. They're thinking about themselves all the time. They simply don't care a damn about the hero, or about the audience, or anything, and they scarcely pretend to. Arrogance isn't the word. It's something more terrific - it's stupendous! Mrs. John's like that. I thought of it as I was coming along here."

"Is she?" said George negligently. "Perhaps she is. I never thought of her like that."

Turnham Green Station was announced.

3

Despite the fresh pinky horrors of its external architecture, and despite his own desire and firm intention to the contrary, George was very deeply impressed by the new Orgreave home. It was far larger than the previous house. The entrance was spacious, and the drawing-room, with a great fire at either end, immense. He had never been in an interior so splendid. He tried to be off-hand in his attitude towards it, but did not fully succeed. The taste shown in the decoration and furniture was almost unexceptionable. White walls - Heppel-white; chintz - black, crackling chintz strewn with tens of thousands of giant roses. On the walls were a few lithographs - John's contribution to the general effect. John having of late years begun to take himself seriously as a collector of lithographs.

One-third of the room was divided from the rest by an arched and fretted screen of red lacquer, and within this open cage stood Mrs. John, surveying winsomely the expanse of little tables, little chairs, big chairs, huge chairs, sofas, rugs, flower-vases, and knick-knacks. She had an advantage over most blondes nearing the forties in that she had not stoutened. She was in fact thin as well as short; but her face was too thin. Still, it dimpled, and she held her head knowingly on one side, and her bright hair was wonderfully done up. Dressed richly as she was, and assisted by the rejuvenating magic of jewels, she produced, in the shadow of the screen, a notable effect of youthful vivacity, which only the insult of close inspection could destroy. With sinuous gestures she waved Mr. Enwright's metaphorical palm before the approaching George. Her smile flattered him; her frail, dinging hand flattered him. He had known her in her harsh morning moods; he had seen that persuasive, manufactured mask vanish for whole minutes, to reveal a petty egotism, giving way, regardless of appearances, to rage; he clearly observed now the hard, preoccupied eyes. Nevertheless, the charm which she exercised was undeniable. Her husband was permanently under its spell. There he stood, near her, big, coarsening, good-natured, content, proud of her. He mixed a cocktail and he threw a match into the fire, in exactly the old Five Towns manner, which he would never lose. But as for her, she had thrown off all trace of the Five Towns; she had learnt London, deliberately, thoroughly. And even George, with the unmerciful, ruthless judgment of his years, was obliged to admit that she possessed a genuine pertinacity and had marvellously accomplished an ambition. She had held John Orgreave for considerably over a decade; she had had the tremendous courage to Leave the heavy provincial manufacturer, her first husband; she had passed through the Divorce Court as a respondent without blenching; she had slowly darned her reputation with such skill that you could scarcely put your finger on the place where the hole had been; and lo! she was reigning in Bedford Park and had all she wanted - except youth. Nor did she in the least show the resigned, disillusioned air of women who have but recently lost their youth. She bore herself just as though she still had no fear of strong lights, and as though she was still the dazzling, dashing blonde of whom John in his earliest twenties used to say, with ingenuous enthusiasm, that she was 'ripping' - the ripping Mrs. Chris Hamson. An epical creature!

This domestic organism created by Mrs. John inspired George, and instantly he was rapt away in dreams of his own future. He said to himself again, and more forcibly, that he had a natural taste for luxury and expensiveness, and that he would have the one and practise the other. He invented gorgeous interiors which would be his and in which he would be paramount and at ease. He positively yearned for them. He was impatient to get back home and resume the long labours that would lead him to them. Every grand adjunct of life must be his, and he could not wait. Absurd to apprehend that Marguerite would not rise to his dreams! Of course she would! She would fit herself perfectly into them, completing them. She would understand all the artistic aspects of them, because she was an artist; and in addition she would be mistress, wife, hostess, commanding impeccable servants, receiving friends with beauty and unsurpassable sweet dignity, wearing costly frocks and jewels as though she had never worn anything else. She had the calm power, she had the individuality, to fulfil all his desires for her. She would be the authentic queen of which Mrs. John was merely the imitation. He wanted intensely to talk to her about the future.... And then he had the seductive idea of making presentable his bed-sitting-room at Mr. Haim's. He saw the room instantaneously transformed; he at once invented each necessary dodge for absolutely hiding during the day the inconvenient fact that it had to serve as a bedroom at night; he refurnished it; he found the money to refurnish it. And just as he was impatient to get back home in order to work, so he was impatient to get back home in order to transform his chamber into the ideal. Delay irked him painfully. And yet he was extremely happy in the excitement of the dreams that ached to be fulfilled.

"Now, Mr. Enwright," said Mrs. John in an accent to draw honey out of a boulder. "You haven't told me what you think of it."

Enwright was wandering about by himself.

"He's coming on with his lithographs," he replied, as if after a decision. "One or two of these are rather interesting."

"Oh! I don't mean the lithographs. You know those are all Jack's affairs. I mean - well, the room. Now do pay me a compliment."

The other guests listened.

Enwright gave a little self-conscious smile, characteristic of him in these dilemmas, half kind and half malicious.

"You must have taken a great deal of trouble over it," he said, with bright amiability; and then relapsing from the effort: "it's all very nice and harmless."

"Oh! Mr. Enwright! Is that all?" She pouted, though still waving the palm. "And you so fond of the eighteenth century, too!"

"But I heard a rumour at the beginning of this year that we're living in the twentieth," said Enwright.

"And I thought I should please you!" sighed Adela. "What ought I to have done?"

"Well, you might have asked me to design you some furniture. Nobody ever has asked me yet." He rubbed his eyeglasses and blinked.

"Oh! You geniuses.... Janet darling!"

Mrs. John moved forward to meet Miss Orgreave, John's appreciably elder sister, spinster, who lived with another brother, Charles, a doctor at Ealing. Janet was a prim emaciated creature, very straight and dignified, whose glance always seemed to hesitate between benevolence and fastidiousness. Janet and Charles had consented to forget the episode of the Divorce Court. Marion, however, the eldest Orgreave sister, mother of a family of daughters, had never received the divorcee. On the other hand the divorcee, obeying her own code, had obstinately ignored the wife of Jim Orgreave, a younger brother, who, according to the universal opinion, had married disgracefully.

When the sisters-in-law had embraced, with that unconvincing fulsomeness which is apt to result from a charitable act of oblivion, Janet turned lovingly to George and asked after his mother. She was his mother's most intimate friend. In the past he had called her Auntie, and was accustomed to kiss her and be kissed. Indeed he feared that she might want to kiss him now, but he was spared. As with negligence of tone he answered her fond inquiries, he was busy reconstructing quite anew his scheme for the bed-sittingroom - for it had actually been an eighteenth-century scheme, and inspired by the notions of Mrs. John!

At the lunch-table George found that the party consisted of ten persons, of whom one, seated next to himself, was a youngish, somewhat plump woman who had arrived at the last moment. He had not been introduced to her, nor to the four other strangers, for it had lately reached Bedford Park that introductions were no longer the correct prelude to a meal. A hostess who wished to be modern should throw her guests in ignorance together and leave them to acquire knowledge by their own initiative. This device added to the piquancy of a gathering. Moreover, there was always a theory that each individual was well known, and that therefore to introduce was subtly to insult. On Mrs. John's right was a beautifully braided gentleman of forty or so, in brown, with brown necktie and hair to match, and the hair was so perfect and ended so abruptly that George at first took it for a wig; but soon afterwards he decided that he had been unkind. Mr. Enwright was opposite to this brown gentleman.

Mrs. John began by hoping that the brown gentleman had been to church.

"I'm afraid I haven't," he replied, with gentle regret in his voice.

And in the course of the conversation he was frequently afraid. Nevertheless his attitude was by no means a fearful attitude; on the contrary it was very confident. He would grasp the edge of the table with his hands, and narrate at length, smiling amiably, and looking from side to side regularly like a public speaker. He narrated in detail the difficulties which he had in obtaining the right sort of cutlets rightly cooked at his club, and added: "But of course there's only one club in London that would be satisfactory in all this - shall I say? - finesse, and I'm afraid I don't belong to it."

"What club's that?" John Orgreave sent the inquiry down the table.

"The Orleans."

"Oh yes, the Orleans! I suppose that is the best."

And everybody seemed glad and proud that everybody had known of the culinary supremacy of the Orleans.

"I'm afraid you'll all think I'm horribly greedy," said the brown gentleman apologetically. And then at once, having noticed that Mr. Enwright was gazing up at the great sham oak rafters that were glued on to the white ceiling, he started upon this new architectural picturesqueness which was to London and the beginning of the twentieth century what the enamelled milking-stool had been to the provinces and the end of the nineteenth century - namely, a reminder that even in an industrial age romance should still survive in the hearts of men. The brown gentleman remarked that with due deference to 'you professional gentlemen,' he was afraid he liked the sham rafters, because they reminded him of the good old times and all that sort of thing.

He was not only a conscientious conversationalist, but he originated talk in others, and listened to them with his best attention. And he invariably stepped into gaps with praise-worthy tact and skill. Thus the chat meandered easily from subject to subject - the Automobile Club's tour from London to Southsea, the latest hotel, Richter, the war (which the brown gentleman treated with tired respect, as some venerable survival that had forgotten to die), the abnormally early fogs, and the abnormally violent and destructive gales. An argument arose as to whether these startling weather phenomena were or were not a hint to mankind from some undefined Higher Power that a new century had in truth begun and that mankind had better mind what it was about. Mrs. John favoured the notion, and so did Miss Orgreave, whereas John Orgreave coarsely laughed at it. The brown gentleman held the scales admirably; he was chivalrously sympathetic to the two ladies, and yet he respected John's materialism. He did, however, venture to point out the contradictions in the character of 'our host,' who was really very responsive to music and art, but who seemed curiously to ignore certain other influences - etc. etc.

"How true that is!" murmured Mrs. John.

The brown gentleman modestly enjoyed his triumph. With only three people had he failed - Mr. Enwright, George, and the youngish woman next to George.

"And how's Paris, Miss Ingram?" he pointedly asked the last.

George was surprised. He had certainly taken her for a married woman, and one of his generalizations about life was that he did not like young married women; hence he had not liked her. He now regarded her with fresh interest. She blushed a little, and looked very young indeed.

"Oh! Paris is all right!" she answered shortly.

The brown gentleman after a long, musing smile, discreetly abandoned the opening; but George, inquiring in a low voice if she lived in Paris, began a private talk with Miss Ingram, who did live in Paris. He had his doubts about her entire agreeableness, but at any rate they got on to a natural, brusque footing, which contrasted with the somewhat ceremonious manner of the general conversation. She exceeded George in brusqueness, and tended to patronize him as a youngster. He noticed that she had yellow eyes.

"What do you think of his wig?" she demanded in an astonishing whisper, when the meal was over and chairs were being vacated.

"Is it a wig?" George exclaimed ingenuously.

"Oh, you boys!" she protested, with superiority. "Of course it's a wig."

"But how do you know it's a wig?" George insisted stoutly.

"'Is it a wig!'" she scorned him.

"Well, I'm not up in wigs," said George. "Who is he, anyhow?"

"I forget his name. I've only met him once, here at tea. I think he's a tea-merchant. He seemed to remember me all right."

"A tea-merchant! I wonder why Mrs. John put him on her right, then, and Mr. Enwright on her left." George resented the precedence.

"Is Mr. Enwright really very great, then?"

"Great! You bet he is.... I was in Paris with him in the summer. Whereabouts do you live in Paris?"

She improved, especially at the point where she said that Mr. Enwright's face was one of the most wonderful faces that she had ever seen. Evidently she knew Paris as well as George knew London. Apparently she had always lived there. But their interchanges concerning Paris, on a sofa in the drawing-room, were stopped by a general departure. Mr. Enwright began it. The tea-merchant instantly supported the movement. Miss Ingram herself rose. The affair was at an end. Nothing interesting had been said in the general talk, and little that was sincere. No topic had been explored, no argument taken to a finish. No wit worth mentioning had glinted. But everybody had behaved very well, and had demonstrated that he or she was familiar with the usages of society and with aspects of existence with which it was proper to be familiar. And everybody - even Mr. Enwright - thanked Mrs. John most heartily for her quite delightful luncheon; Mrs. John insisted warmly on her own pleasure and her appreciation of her guests' extreme good nature in troubling to come, and she was beyond question joyously triumphant. And George, relieved, thought, as he tried to rival the rest in gratitude to Mrs. John:

"What was it all about? What did they all come for? I came because she made me. But why did the others come?"

The lunch had passed like a mild nightmare, and he felt as though, with the inconsequence of dream-people, these people had gone away without having accomplished some essential act which had been the object of their gathering.

4

When George came out of the front door, he beheld Miss Ingram on the kerb, in the act of getting into a very rich fur coat. A chauffeur, in a very rich livery, was deferentially helping her. Behind them stretched a long, open motor-car. This car, existing as it did at a time when the public acutely felt that automobiles splashed respectable foot-farers with arrogant mud and rendered unbearable the lives of the humble in village streets, was of the immodest kind described, abusively, as 'powerful and luxurious.' The car of course drew attention, because it had yet occurred to but few of anybody's friends that they might themselves possess even a modest car, much less an immodest one. George had not hitherto personally known a single motor-car owner.

But what struck him even more than the car was the fur coat, and the haughty and fastidious manner in which Miss Ingram accepted it from the chauffeur, and the disdainful, accustomed way in which she wore it - as though it were a cheap rag - when once it was on her back. In her gestures he glimpsed a new world. He had been secretly scorning the affairs of the luncheon and all that it implied, and he had been secretly scorning himself for his pitiful lack of brilliancy at the luncheon. These two somewhat contradictory sentiments were suddenly shrivelled in the fire of his ambition which had flared up anew at contact with a spark. And the spark was the sight of the girl's costly fur coat. He must have a costly fur coat, and a girl in it, and the girl must treat the fur coat like a cheap rag. Otherwise he would die a disappointed man.

"Hallo!" called Miss Ingram.

"Hallo!" She had climbed into the car, and turned her head to look at him. He saw that she was younger even than he had thought. She seemed quite mature when she was still, but when she moved she had the lithe motions of immaturity. As a boy, he now infallibly recognized a girl.

"Which way are you going?"

"Well - Chelsea more or less."

"I'll give you a lift."

He ought to have said: "Are you sure I shan't be taking you out of your way?" But he said merely: "Oh! Thanks awfully!"

The chauffeur held the door for him, and then arranged a fur rug over the knees of the boy and the girl. To be in the car gave George intense pleasure, especially when the contrivance thrilled into life and began to travel. He was thankful that his clothes were as smart as they ought to be. She could not think ill of his clothes - no matter who her friends were.

"This is a great car," he said. "Had it long?"

"Oh! It's not mine," answered Miss Ingram. "It's Miss Wheeler's."

"Who's Miss Wheeler, if I may ask?"

"Miss Wheeler! She's a friend of mine. She lives in Paris. But she has a flat in London too. I came over with her. We brought the car with us. She was to have come to the Orgreaves's to-day, but she had a headache. So I took the car - and her furs as well. They fit me, you see.... I say, what's your Christian name? I hate surnames, don't you?"

"George. What's yours?"

"Mine's Lois."

"What? How do you spell it?"

She spelt it, adding 'Of course.' He thought it was somehow a very romantic name. He decidedly liked the name. He was by no means sure, however, that he liked the girl. He liked her appearance, though she was freckled; she was unquestionably stylish; she had ascendancy; she imposed herself; she sat as though the world was the instrument of her individuality. Nevertheless he doubted if she was kind, and he knew that she was patronizing. Further, she was not a conversationalist. At the luncheon she had not been at ease; but here in the car she was at ease absolutely, yet she remained taciturn.

"D'you drive?" he inquired.

"Yes," she said. "Look here, would you like to sit in front? And I'll drive."

"Good!" he agreed vigorously. But he had a qualm about the safety of being driven by a girl.

She abruptly stopped the car, and the chauffeur swerved to the pavement.

"I'm going to drive, Cuthbert," she said.

"Yes, miss," said the chauffeur willingly. "It's a bit side-slippy, miss."

She gave no answer to this remark, but got out of the car with a preoccupied, frowning air, as if she was being obliged to take a responsible post, which she could fill better than anybody else, rather against her inclination. A few persons paused to watch. She carefully ignored them; so did George.

As soon as she had seized the wheel, released the brake and started the car, she began to talk, looking negligently about her. George thought: "She's only showing off." Still, the car travelled beautifully, and there was a curious illusion that she must have the credit for that. She explained the function of handles, pedals, and switches, and George deemed it proper to indicate that he was not without some elementary knowledge of the subject. He leaned far back, as Lois leaned, and as the chauffeur had leaned, enjoying the brass fittings, the indicators, and all the signs of high mechanical elaboration.

He noticed that Lois sounded her horn constantly, and often upon no visible provocation. But once as she approached cross-roads at unslackened speed, she seemed to forget to sound it and then sounded it too late. Nothing untoward happened; Sunday traffic was thin, and she sailed through the danger-zone with grand intrepidity.

"I say, George," she remarked, looking now straight in front of her. ("She's a bit of a caution," he reflected happily.) "Have you got anything special on this afternoon?"

"Nothing what you may call deadly special," he answered. He wanted to call her 'Lois,' but his volition failed at the critical moment.

"Well, then, won't you come and have tea with Miss Wheeler and me? There'll only be just a few people, and you must be introduced to Miss Wheeler."

"Oh! I don't think I'd better." He was timid.

"Why not?" She pouted.

"All right, then. Thanks. I should like to."

"By the way, what's your surname?"

("She is a caution," he reflected.)

"I wasn't quite sure," she said, when he had told her.

He was rather taken aback, but he reassured himself. No doubt girls of her environment did behave as she behaved. After all, why not?

They entered Hammersmith. It was a grand and inspiring sensation to swing through Hammersmith thus aristocratically repudiating the dowdy Sunday crowd that stared in ingenuous curiosity. And there was a wonderful quality in the spectacle of the great, formidable car being actuated and controlled by the little gloved hands and delicately shod feet of this frail, pampered, wilful girl.

In overtaking a cab that kept nearly to the middle of the road, Lois hesitated in direction, appeared to defy the rule, and then corrected her impulse.

"It's rather confusing," she observed, with a laugh. "You see, in France you keep to the right and overtake things on their left."

"Yes. But this is London," said George dryly.

Half a minute later, just beyond the node of Hammersmith, where bright hats and frocks were set off against the dark-shuttered fronts of shops, Lois at quite a good speed inserted the car between a tramcar and an omnibus, meeting the tram and overtaking the omnibus. The tram went by like thunder, all its glass and iron rattling and shaking; the noise deafened, and the wind blew hard like a squall. There appeared to be scarcely an inch of space on either side of the car. George's heart stopped. For one horrible second he expected a tremendous smash. The car emerged safe. He saw the omnibus-driver gazing down at them with reproof. After the roar of the tram died he heard the trotting of the omnibus horses and Lois's nervous giggle. She tried, and did not fail, to be jaunty; but she had had a shock, and the proof was that by mere inadvertence she nearly charged the posts of the next street-refuge.... George switched off the current. She herself had shown him how to do it. She now saw him do it. The engine stopped, and Lois, remembering in a flash that her dignity was at stake, raised her hand and drew up fairly neatly at the pavement.

"What's the matter?" she demanded imperiously.

"Are you going to drive this thing all the way into London, Lois?" he demanded in turn.

They looked at each other. The chauffeur got down. "Of course."

"Not with me in it, anyhow!"

She sneered. "Oh! You boys! You've got no pluck."

"Perhaps not," he returned viciously. "Neither have you got any sense of danger. Girls like you never have. I've noticed that before." Even his mother with horses had no sense of danger.

"You're very rude," she replied. "And it was very rude of you to stop the car."

"I dare say. But you shouldn't have told me you could drive."

He was now angry. And she not less so. He descended, and slammed the door.

"Thanks so much," he said, raised his hat, and walked away. She spoke, but he did not catch what she said. He was saying to himself: "Pluck indeed!" (He did not like her accusation.) "Pluck indeed! Of all the damned cheek!... We might all have been killed - or worse. The least she could have done was to apologize. But no! Pluck indeed! Women oughtn't to be allowed to drive. It's too infernally silly for words."

He glanced backward. The chauffeur had started the car again, and was getting in by Lois's side. Doubtless he was a fatalist by profession. She drove off.

"Yes!" thought George. "And you'd drive home yourself now even if you knew for certain you'd have an accident. You're just that stupid kind."

The car looked superb as it drew away, and she reclined in the driver's seat with a superb effrontery. George was envious; he was pierced by envy. He hated that other people, and especially girls, should command luxuries which he could not possess. He hated that violently. "You wait!" he said to himself. "You wait! I'll have as good a car as that, and a finer girl than you in it. And she won't want to drive either. You wait." He was more excited than he knew by the episode.

5

THE TEA

"Tea is ready, Mr. Cannon," said Mr. Haim in his most courteous style, coming softly into George's room. And George looked up at the old man's wrinkled face, and down at his crimson slippers, with the benevolent air of a bookworm permitting himself to be drawn away from an ideal world into the actual. Glasses on the end of George's nose would have set off the tableau, but George had outgrown the spectacles which had disfigured his boyhood. As a fact, since his return that afternoon from Mrs. John's, he had, to the detriment of modesty and the fostering of conceit, accomplished some further study for the Final, although most of the time had been spent in dreaming of women and luxury.

"All right," said he. "I'll come."

"I don't think that lamp's been very well trimmed to-day," said Mr. Haim apologetically, sniffing.

"Does it smell?"

"Well, I do notice a slight odour."

"I'll open the window," said George heartily. He rose, pulled the curtains, and opened the front French window with a large gesture. The wild, raw, damp air of Sunday night rushed in from the nocturnal Grove, and instantly extinguished the lamp.

"Oh!" exclaimed Mr. Haim, rather nervously.

"Saved me the trouble," said George.

As he emerged after Mr. Haim from the dark room, he was thinking that it was ridiculous not to have electricity, and that he must try to come to some arrangement with Mr. Haim for the installation of electricity. Fancy oil-lamps in the middle of London in the twentieth century! Shocks were waiting in George's mind for Mr. Haim. He intended, if he could, to get the room on the first floor, empty since the departure of Marguerite, and to use it for a bedroom, while keeping the ground-floor room exclusively for work and society. His project would involve shocks also for Mr. Edwin Clayhanger in the Five Towns, who would be called upon to pay; but George had an airy confidence in the ability of his stepfather to meet such shocks in a satisfactory manner.

To George's surprise, Mr. Alfred Prince was in the sitting-room. Shabby and creased as usual, he looked far more like a clerk in some establishment where clerks were not morally compelled to imitate dandies than like an etcher of European renown. But, also as usual, he was quietly at ease and conversational; and George at once divined that he had been invited with the object of relieving the social situation created by the presence of the brilliant young lodger at tea. This tea was the first meal to be taken by George with Mr. and Mrs. Haim, for he was almost never at home on Sunday afternoons, and he was not expected to be at home. The table showed, as Mr. Haim's nervousness had shown, that the importance of the occasion had been realized. It was an obviously elaborate table. The repast was ready in every detail; the teapot was under the cosy; the cover was over the hot crumpets; Mrs. Haim alone lacked.

"Where's missus?" asked George lightly. Mr. Haim had not come into the room.

"I don't know," said Mr. Prince. "She brought the tea in a minute ago. You been working this afternoon?"

At that moment Mr. Haim entered. He said:

"Mrs. Haim isn't feeling very well. She's upstairs. She says she's sure she'll be all right in a little while. In the meantime she prefers us to go on with our tea."

Mr. Prince and Mr. Haim looked at each other, and George looked at Mr. Haim. The older men showed apprehension. The strange idea of unconquerable destiny crossed George's mind - destiny clashing ruthlessly with ambition and desire. The three males sat down in obedience to the wish of the woman who had hidden herself in the room above. All of them were dominated by the thought of her. They did not want to sit down and eat and drink, and they were obliged to do so by the invisible volitional force of which Mr. Haim was the unwilling channel. Mr. Haim, highly self-conscious, began to pour out the tea. Mr. Prince, highly self-conscious, suggested that he should make himself useful by distributing the crumpets while they were hot. George, highly selfconscious, accepted a crumpet. Mr. Prince chatted; George responded in a brave worldly fashion; Mr. Haim said 'Yes,' 'Ye-es,' very absently.

And then Mrs. Haim appeared smiling in the doorway. "Ah!" breathed everybody, assuaged. "Ah!" Mr. Haim moved from in front of the tea-tray to the next seat. Mrs. Haim was perhaps somewhat pale, but she gave a sincere, positive assurance that she was perfectly well again. Reassurance spread throughout the company. Forebodings vanished; hearts lightened; gladness reigned; the excellence of crumpets became apparent. And all this swift, wonderful change was brought about by the simple entry of the woman. But beneath the genuine relief and satisfaction of the men there stirred vaguely the thought of the mysteriousness of women, of the entire female sex. Mrs. Haim, charwoman, was just as mysterious as any other woman. As for George, despite the exhilaration which he could feel rising in him effortless and unsought, he was preoccupied by more than women's mysteriousness; the conception of destiny lingered and faintly troubled him. It was as though he had been walking on a clear path through a vast and empty and safe forest, and the eyes of a tiger had gleamed for an instant in the bush and gone. Not a real tiger! And if a real tiger, then a tiger that would never recur, and the only tiger in the forest!... Yet the entire forest was transformed.

Mrs. Haim was wearing the blue sateen. It was a dress unsuited to her because it emphasized her large bulk; but it was her best dress; it shone and glittered; it imposed. Her duty was to wear it on that Sunday afternoon. She was shy, without being self-conscious. To preside over a society consisting of young bloods, etchers of European renown, and pillars of the architectural profession was an ordeal for her. She did not pretend that it was not an ordeal. She did not pretend that the occasion was not extraordinary. She was quite natural in her calm confusion. She was not even proud, being perhaps utterly incapable of social pride. Her husband was proud for her. He looked at her earnestly, wistfully. He could not disguise his anxiety for her success. Was she equal to the role? She was. Of course she was. He had never doubted that she would be (he said to himself). His pride increased, scarcely escaped being fatuous.

"I must congratulate you on the new front doormat, Mrs. Haim," said Mr. Prince, with notable conversational tact. "I felt it at once in the dark."

Mrs. Haim smiled.

"I do like a good doormat," she said. "It saves so much work, I always think. I told Mr. Haim I thought we needed a new one, and bless me if he didn't take me straight out to buy one."

The new doormat expressed Mrs. Haim's sole and characteristic criticism of the organism into which she had so unassumingly entered. Secure in the adoration of Mr. Haim, she might safely have turned the place upside-down and proved to the Grove that she could act the mistress with the best of them; but she changed nothing except the doormat. The kitchen and scullery had already been hers before the eye of Mr. Haim had fallen upon her; she was accustomed to them and had largely fashioned their arrangements. Her own furniture, such of it as was retained, had been put into the spare bedroom and the kitchen, and was hardly noticeable there. The dramatic thing for her to do would have been to engage another charwoman. But Mrs. Haim was not dramatic; she was accommodating. She fitted herself in. The answer to people who asked what Mr. Haim could see in her, was that what Mr. Haim first saw was her mere way of existing, and that in the same way she loved. At her tea-table, as elsewhere, she exhibited no special quality; she said little; she certainly did not shine. Nevertheless the three men were quite happy and at ease, because her way of existing soothed and reinspired them. George especially got gay; and he narrated the automobile adventure of the afternoon with amusing gusto. He was thereby a sort of hero, and he liked that. He was bound by his position in the world and by his clothes and his style to pretend to some extent that the adventure was much less extraordinary to him than it seemed to them. The others made no pretence. They were open-mouthed. Their attitude admitted frankly that above them was a world to which they could not climb, that they were not familiar with it and knew nothing about it. They admired George; they put it to his credit that he was acquainted with these lofty matters and moved carelessly and freely among them; and George too somehow thought that credit was due to him and that his superiority was genuine.

"And do you mean to say she'd never met you before?" exclaimed Mr. Haim.

"Never in this world!"

Mr. Prince remarked calmly: "You must have had a very considerable effect on her then." His eyes twinkled.

George flushed slightly. The idea had already presented itself to him with great force. "Oh no!" He negligently pooh-poohed it.

"Well, does she go about asking every man she meets what his Christian name is?"

"I expect she just does."

There was silence for a moment. Mrs. Haim refilled a cup.

"Something will have to be done soon about these motor-cars," observed Mr. Haim at length, sententiously, in the vein of 'Mustard and Cress.' "That's very evident."

"They cost so much," said Mr. Prince. "Why! They cost as much as a house, some of them."

"More!" said George.

"Nay, nay!" Mr. Haim protested. The point had come at which his imagination halted.

"Anyhow, you had a lucky escape," said Mr. Prince. "You might have been lamed for life - or anything."

George laughed.

"I am always lucky," said he. He thought: "I wonder whether I am!" He was afraid.

Mrs. Haim was half-way towards the door before any of the men noticed what she was about. She had risen silently and quickly; she could manoeuvre that stout frame of hers with surprising facility. There was a strange, silly look on her face as she disappeared, and the face was extremely pale. Mr. Haim showed alarm, and Mr. Prince concern. Mr. Haim's hands clasped the arms of his chair; he bent forward hesitatingly.

"What - ?"

Then was heard the noise of a heavy subsidence, apparently on the stairs. George was out of the room first. But the other two were instantly upon him. Mrs. Haim had fallen at the turn of the stairs; her body was distributed along the little half-landing there.

"My God! She's fainted!" muttered Mr. Haim.

"We'd better get her into the bedroom," said Mr. Prince, with awe.

The trouble had come back, but in a far more acute form. The prostrate and unconscious body, all crooked and heaped in the shadow, intimidated the three men, convicting them of helplessness and lack of ready wit. George stood aside and let the elder pair pass him. Mr. Haim hurried up the stairs, bent over his wife, and seized her under the arms. Mr. Prince took her by the legs. They could not lift her. They were both thin little men, quite unaccustomed to physical exertion. Mrs. Haim lay like a giantess, immovably recumbent between their puny, straining figures.

"Here, let me try," said George eagerly, springing towards the group.

With natural reluctance Mr. Haim gave way to him. George stooped and braced himself to the effort. His face was close to the blanched, blind face of Mrs. Haim. He thought she looked very young, astonishingly young in comparison with either Haim or Prince. Her complexion was damaged but not destroyed. Little fluffy portions of her hair seemed absolutely girlish. Her body was full of nice curves, which struck George as most enigmatically pathetic. But indeed the whole of her was pathetic, very touching, very precious and fragile. Even her large, shiny, shapeless boots and the coarse sateen stuff of her dress affected him. A lump embarrassed his throat. He suddenly understood the feelings of Mr. Haim towards her. She was inexpressibly romantic.... He lifted her torso easily; and pride filled him because he could do easily what others could not do at all. Her arms trailed limp. Mr. Haim and Mr. Prince jointly raised her lower limbs. George staggered backwards up the remainder of the stairs. As they steered the burden into the bedroom, where a candle was burning, Mrs. Haim opened her eyes and, gazing vacantly at the ceiling, murmured in a weak, tired voice:

"I'm all right. It's nothing. Please put me down."

"Yes, yes, my love!" said Mr. Haim, agitated.

They deposited her on the bed. She sighed; then smiled. A slight flush showed on her cheek under the light of the candle which Mr. Prince was holding aloft. Mysterious creature, with the mysterious forces of life flowing and ebbing incomprehensibly within her! To George she was marvellous, she was beautiful, as she lay defenceless and silently appealing.

"Thank you, Mr. Cannon. Thank you very much," said Mr. Haim, turning to the strong man.

It was a dismissal. George modestly departed from the bedroom, which was no place for him. After a few minutes Mr. Prince also descended. They stood together at the foot of the stairs in the draught from the open window of George's room.

"Hadn't I better go for a doctor?" George suggested.

"That's what I said," replied Mr. Prince. "But she won't have one."

"But - "

"Well, she won't."

The accommodating, acquiescent dame, with scarcely strength to speak, was defeating all three of them on that one point.

"What is it?" asked George confidentially.

"Oh! I don't suppose it's anything, really."

2

That George should collect the tea-things together on the tray, and brush and fold the cloth, and carry the loaded tray downstairs into the scullery, was sufficiently strange. But it was very much more strange that he should have actually had the idea of washing-up the tea-things himself. In his time, in the domestic crises of Bursley, he had boyishly helped ladies to wash-up, and he reckoned that he knew all about the operation. There he stood, between the kitchen and the scullery, elegantly attired, with an inquiring eye upon the kettle of warm water on the stove, debating whether he should make the decisive gesture of emptying the kettle into the large tin receptacle that lay on the slop-stone. Such was the miraculous effect on him of Mrs. Haim's simplicity, her weakness, and her predicament. Mrs. Haim was a different woman for him now that he had carried her upstairs and laid her all limp and girlish on the solemn conjugal bed! He felt quite sure that old Haim was incapable of washing-up. He assuredly did not want to be caught in the act of washing-up, but he did want to be able to say in his elaborately nonchalant manner, answering a question about the disappearance of the tea-things: "I thought I might as well wash-up while I was about it." And he did want Mrs. Haim to be put in a flutter by the news that Mr. George Cannon had washed-up for her. The affair would positively cause a sensation.

He was about to begin, taking the risks of premature discovery, when he heard a noise above. It was Mr. Haim at last descending the stairs to the ground floor. George started. He had been alone in the lower parts of the house for a period which seemed long. (Mr. Prince had gone to the studio, promising to return later.) The bedroom containing Mr. and Mrs. Haim had become for him the abode of mystery. The entity of the enchanted house had laid hold of his imagination. He had thought of Marguerite as she used to pervade the house, and of his approaching interview with her at the Manresa Road studio. He had thought very benevolently of Marguerite and also of, Mr. and Mrs. Haim. He had involved them all three, in his mind, in a net of peace and goodwill. He saw the family quarrel as something inevitable, touching, absurd - the work of a maleficent destiny which he might somehow undo and exorcise by the magic act of washing-up, to be followed by other acts of a more diplomatic and ingenious nature. And now the dull, distant symptoms of Mr. Haim on the stairs suddenly halted him at the very outset of his benignant machinations. He listened. If the peace of the world had depended upon his washing-up he could not have permitted himself to be actually seen in the role of kitchen-girl by Mr. Haim - so extreme was his lack of logic and right reason. There was a silence, a protracted silence, and then Mr. Haim unmistakably came down the basement stairs, and George thanked God that he had not allowed his impulse to wash-up run away with his discretion, to the ruin of his dignity.

Mr. Haim, hesitating in the kitchen doorway, peered in front of him as if at a loss. George had shifted the kitchen lamp from its accustomed place.

"I'm here," said George, moving slightly in the dim light. "I thought I might as well make myself useful and clear the table for you. How is she going on?" He spoke cheerfully, even gaily, and he expected Mr. Haim to be courteously appreciative - perhaps enthusiastic in gratitude.

"Mrs. Haim is quite recovered, thank you. It was only a passing indisposition," said Mr. Haim, using one of his ridiculously stilted phrases. His tone was strange; it was very strange.

"Good!" exclaimed George, with a gaiety that was now forced, a bravado of gaiety.

He thought:

"The old chump evidently doesn't like me interfering. Silly old pompous ass!" Nevertheless his attitude towards the huffy landlord, if scornful, was good-humoured and indulgent.

Then he noticed that Mr. Haim held in his hand a half-sheet of note-paper which disturbingly seemed familiar. "What is the meaning of this, Mr. Cannon?" Mr. Haim demanded, advancing towards the brightness of the lamp and extending the paper. He was excessively excited. Excitement always intensified his age.

The offered document was the letter which George had that morning received from Marguerite. The missive was short, a mere note, but its terms could leave no doubt as to the relations between the writer and the recipient.

Moreover, it ended with a hieroglyphic sign, several times repeated, whose significance is notorious throughout the civilized world.

"Where did you get that?" muttered George, with a defensive menace half formed in his voice. He faltered. His mood had not yet become definitive.

Mr. Haim answered:

"I have just picked it up in the hall, sir. The wind must have blown it off the table in your room, and the door was left open. I presume that I have the right to read papers I find lying about in my own house."

George was dashed. On returning home from Mrs. John's lunch he had changed his suit for another one almost equally smart, but of Angora and therefore more comfortable. He liked to change. He had taken the letter out of a side-pocket of the jacket and put it with his watch, money, and other kit on the table while he changed, and he had placed everything back into the proper pockets, everything except the letter. Carelessness! A moment of negligence had brought about the irremediable. The lovely secret was violated. The whole of his future life and of Marguerite's future life seemed to have been undermined and contaminated by that single act of omission. Marguerite wrote seldom to him because of the risks. But precautions had been arranged for the occasions when she had need to write, and she possessed a small stock of envelopes addressed by himself, so that Mr. Haim might never by chance, picking up an envelope from the hall floor, see George's name in his daughter's hand. And now Mr. Haim had picked up an actual letter from the hall floor. And the fault for the disaster was George's own.

"May I ask, sir, are you engaged to my daughter?" demanded Mr. Haim, getting every instant still more excited.

George had once before seen him agitated about Marguerite, but by no means to the same degree. He trembled. He shook. His dignity had a touch of the grotesque; yet it remained dignity, and it enforced respect. For George, destiny seemed to dominate the kitchen and the scullery like a presence. He and the old man were alone together in that presence, and he was abashed. He was conscious of awe. The old man's mien accused him of an odious crime, of something base and shameful. Useless to argue with himself that he was entirely guiltless, that he had the right to be the betrothed of either Mr. Haim's daughter or any other girl, and to publish or conceal the betrothal as he chose and as she chose. Yes, useless! He felt, inexplicably, a criminal. He felt that he had committed an enormity. It was not a matter of argument; it was a matter of instinct. The old man's frightful and irrational resentment was his condemnation. He could not face the old man.

He thought grievously: "I am up against this man. All politeness and conventions have vanished. It's the real, inmost me, and the real, inmost him." Nobody else could take a part in the encounter. And he was sad, because he could not blame the old man. Could he blame the old man for marrying a charwoman? Why, he could only admire him for marrying the charwoman. In marrying the charwoman the old man had done a most marvellous thing. Could he blame Marguerite? Impossible. Marguerite's behaviour was perfectly comprehensible. He understood Marguerite and he understood her father; he sympathized with both of them. But Marguerite could not understand her father, and her father could not understand either his daughter or George. Never could they understand! He alone understood. And his understanding gave him a melancholy, hopeless feeling of superiority, without at all lessening the strange conviction of guilt. He had got himself gripped by destiny. Destiny had captured all three of them. But not the fourth. The charwoman possessed the mysterious power to defy destiny. Perhaps the power lay in her simplicity.... Fool! An accursed negligence had eternally botched his high plans for peace and goodwill.

"Yes," he said. "I am."

"And how long have you been engaged, sir?"

"Oh! Since before Marguerite left here." He tried to talk naturally and calmly.

"Then you've been living here all this time like a spy - a dirty spy. My daughter behaves to us in an infamous manner. She makes an open scandal. And all the time you're - "

George suddenly became very angry. And his anger relieved and delighted him. With intense pleasure he felt his anger surging within him. He frowned savagely. His eyes blazed. But he did not move.

"Excuse me," he interrupted, with cold and dangerous fury. "She didn't do anything of the kind."

Mr. Haim went wildly on, intimidated possibly by George's defiance, but desperate:

"And all the time, I say, you stay on here, deceiving us, spying on us. Going every night to that wicked, cruel, shameful girl and tittle-tattling. Do you suppose that if we'd had the slightest idea - "

George walked up to him.

"I'm not going to stand here and listen to you talking about Marguerite like that."

Their faces were rather close together. George forced himself away by a terrific effort and left the kitchen.

"Jackanapes!"

George swung round, very pale. Then with a hard laugh he departed. He stood in the hall, and thought of Mrs. Haim upstairs. The next moment he had got his hat and overcoat and was in the street. A figure appeared in the gloom. It was Mr. Prince.

"Hallo! Going out? How are things?"

"Oh! Fine!" He could scarcely articulate. A ghastly sob impeded the words.

Tears gushed into his eyes. The dimly glowing oblongs in the dark facades of the Grove seemed unbearably tragic.

3

No. 6 Romney Studios, Manresa Road, Chelsea, was at the end of the narrow alley which, running at right angles to the road, had a blank wall on its left and Romney Studios on its right. The studios themselves were nondescript shanties which reminded George of nothing so much as the office of a clerk-of-the-works nailed together anyhow on ground upon which a large building is in course of erection. They were constructed of brick, wood, waterproof felting, and that adaptable material, corrugated iron. No two were alike. None had the least pretension to permanency, comeliness, or even architectural decency. They were all horribly hot in summer, and they all needed immense stoves to render them habitable in winter. In putting them up, however, cautiously and one by one, the landlord had esteemed them to be the sort of thing that was good enough for artists and that artists would willingly accept. He had not been mistaken. Though inexpensive they were dear, but artists accepted them with eagerness. None was ever empty. Thus it was demonstrated once more that artists were exactly what capitalists and other sagacious persons had always accused them of being.

When George knocked on the door of No. 6, the entire studio, and No. 5 also, vibrated. As a rule Agg, the female Cerberus of the shanty, answered any summons from outside; but George hoped that tonight she would be absent; he knew by experience that on Sunday nights she usually paid a visit to her obstreperous family in Alexandra Grove.

The door was opened by a young man in a rich but torn and soiled eighteenth-century costume, and he looked, in the half-light of the entrance, as though he was just recovering from a sustained debauch. The young man stared haughtily in silence. Only after an appreciable hesitation did George see through the disguise and recover himself sufficiently to remark with the proper nonchalance:

"Hallo, Agg! What's the meaning of this?"

"You're before your time," said she, shutting the door.

While he took off his overcoat Agg walked up the studio. She made an astonishingly life-like young man. George and Agg were now not unfriendly; but each constantly criticized the other in silence, and both were aware of the existence of this vast body of unspoken criticism. Agg criticized more than George, who had begun to take the attitude that Agg ought to be philosophically accepted as incomprehensible rather than criticized. He had not hitherto seen her in male costume, but he would not exhibit any surprise.

"Where's Marguerite?" he inquired, advancing to the Stove and rubbing his hands above it.

"Restrain your ardour," said Agg lightly. "She'll appear in due season. I've told you - you're before your time."

George offered no retort. Despite his sharp walk, he was still terribly agitated and preoccupied, and the phenomena of the lamplit studio had not yet fully impressed his mind. He saw them, including Agg, as hallucinations gradually turning to realities. He could not be worried with Agg. His sole desire was to be alone with Marguerite immediately, and he regarded the fancy costume chiefly as an obstacle to the fulfilment of that desire, because Agg could not depart until she had changed it for something else.

Then his gaze fell upon a life-size oil-sketch of Agg in the eighteenth-century male dress. The light was bad, but it disclosed the sketch sufficiently to enable some judgment on it to be formed. The sketch was exceedingly clever, painted in the broad, synthetic manner which Steer and Sickert had introduced into England as a natural reaction from the finicking, false exactitudes of the previous age. It showed Agg, glass in hand, as a leering, tottering young drunkard in frills and velvet. The face was odious, but it did strongly resemble Agg's face. The hair was replaced by a bag wig.

"Who did that?"

"I did, of course," said Agg. She pointed to the large mirror at the opposite side of the studio.

"The dickens you did!" George murmured, struck. But now that he knew the sketch to be the work of a woman he at once became more critical, perceiving in it imitative instead of original qualities. "What is it? I mean, what's the idea at the back of it, if it isn't a rude question, Agg?"

"Title: 'Bonnie Prince Charlie,'" said Agg, without a smile. She was walking about, in a convincingly masculine style. Unfortunately she could not put her hands in her pockets, as the costume was without pockets.

"Is that your notion of the gent?"

"Didn't you know I'm supposed to be very like him?" cried Agg, vain. The stern creature had frailties. Then she smiled grimly. "Look at my cold blue eyes, my sharp chin, my curly-curly lips, my broad forehead, my clear complexion. And I hope I'm thin enough. Look!" She picked up the bag wig, which was lying on a chair, and put it on, and posed. The pose was effective.

"You seem to know a lot about this Charlie."

"Well, our well-beloved brother Sam is writing a monograph on him, you see. Besides, every one - "

"But what's the idea? What's the scheme? Why is he drunk?"

"He always was drunk. He was a confirmed drunkard at thirty. Both his fair ladies had to leave him because he was just a violent brute. And so on and so on. I thought it was about time Charlie was shown up in his true colours. And I'm doing it!... After all the sugar-stick Academy pictures of him, my picture will administer a much-needed tonic to our dear public. I expect I can get it into next year's New English Art Club, and if I do it will be the sensation of the show.... I haven't done with it yet. In fact I only started yesterday. There's going to be a lot more realism in it. All those silly Jacobite societies will furiously rage together.... And it's a bit of pretty good painting, you know."

"It is," George agreed. "But it's a wild scheme."

"Not so wild as you think, my minstrel boy. It's very, much needed. It's symbolic, that picture is. It's a symbolic antidote. Shall I tell you what put me on to it? Look here."

She led him to Marguerite's special work-table, under the curtained window. There, on a sheet of paper stretched upon a drawing-board, was the finished design which Marguerite had been labouring at for two days. It was a design for a bookbinding, and the title of the book was, The Womanly Woman, and the author of the book was Sir Amurath Onway, M.D., D.Sc., F.R.S., a famous specialist in pathology. Marguerite, under instruction from the bookbinders, had drawn a sweet picture, in quiet colours, of a womanly woman in a tea-gown, sitting in a cosy corner of a boudoir. The volume was destined to open the spring season of a publishing firm of immense and historic respectability.

"Look at it! Look at it!" Agg insisted. "I've read the book myself. Poor Marguerite had to go through the proofs, so that she could be sure of getting the spirit of the binding right. Do you know why he wrote it? He hates his wife - that's why. His wife isn't a womanly woman, and he's put all his hatred of her into this immortal rubbish. Read this great work, and you will be made to see what fine, noble creatures we men are" - she strode to and fro - "and how a woman's first duty is to recognize her inferiority to us, and be womanly.... Damme!... As soon as I saw what poor Marguerite had to do I told her I should either have to go out and kill some one, or produce an antidote. And then it occurred to me to tell the truth about one of the leading popular heroes of history." She bowed in the direction of the canvas. "I began to feel better at once. I got the costume from a friend of the learned Sam's, and I've ruined it.... I'm feeling quite bright tonight."

She gazed at George with her cold blue eyes, arraigning in his person the whole sex which she thought she despised but which her deepest instinct it was to counterfeit. George, while admiring, was a little dismayed. She was sarcastic. She had brains and knowledge and ideas. There was an intellectual foundation to her picture. And she could paint - like a witch! Oh! She was ruthlessly clever! Well, he did not like her. What he wanted, though he would not admit it, was old Onway's womanly woman. And especially in that hour he wanted the womanly woman.

"What's Marguerite up to?" he asked quietly.

"After the heat and the toil of the day she's beautifying herself for your

75

august approval," said Agg icily. "I expect she's hurrying all she can. But naturally you expect her to be in a permanent state of waiting for you - fresh out of the cotton-wool."

The next instant Marguerite appeared from the cubicle or dressing-room which had been contrived in a corner of the studio to the left of the door. She was in her plain, everyday attire, but she had obviously just washed, and her smooth hair shone from the brush.

"Well, George."

"Well, Marguerite."

Both spoke casually. Celia Agg was the only person in the world privy to their engagement; but they permitted themselves no freedoms in front of her. As Marguerite came near to George, she delicately touched his arm - nothing more. She was smiling happily, but as soon as she looked close at his face under the lamp, her face changed completely. He thought: "She understands there's something up."

She said, not without embarrassment:

"George, I really must have some fresh air. I haven't had a breath all day. Is it raining?"

"No. Would you like to go for a walk?"

"Oh! I should!"

He was very grateful, and also impressed by the accuracy of her intuitions and her quick resourcefulness. She had comprehended at a glance that he had a profound and urgent need to be alone with her. She was marvellously comforting, precious beyond price. All his susceptibilities, wounded by the scene at Alexandra Grove, and further irritated by Agg, were instantaneously salved and soothed. Her tones, her scarcely perceptible gesture of succour, produced the assuaging miracle. She fulfilled her role to perfection. She was a talented and competent designer, but as the helpmeet of a man she had genius. His mind dwelt on her with rapture.

"You'll be going out as soon as you've changed, dear?" she said affectionately to Agg.

"Yes," answered Agg, who at the mirror was wiping from her face the painted signs of alcoholism. She had thrown off the bag wig. "You'd better take the key with you. You'll be back before I am." She sat down on one of the draped settees which were beds in disguise, and Marguerite got a hat, cloak, and gloves.

While George was resuming his overcoat, which Marguerite held for him, Agg suddenly sprang up and rushed towards them.

"Good night, Flora Macdonald," she murmured in her deep voice in Marguerite's ear, put masculine arms round her, and kissed her. It was a truly remarkable bit of male impersonating, as George had to admit, though he resented it.

Then she gave a short, harsh laugh.

"Good night, old Agg," said Marguerite, with sweet responsiveness, and smiled ingenuously at George.

George, impatient, opened the door, and the damp wind swept anew into the studio.

4

It was a fine night; the weather had cleared, and the pavements were drying. George, looking up in a pause of the eager conversational exchanges, drew tonic air mightily into his lungs.

"Where are we?" he asked.

"Tite Street," said Marguerite. "That's the Tower House." And she nodded towards the formidable sky-scraper which another grade of landlord had erected for another grade of artists who demanded studios from the capitalist. Marguerite, the Chelsea girl, knew Chelsea, if she knew nothing else; her feet turned corners in the dark with assurance, and she had no need to look at street-signs. George regarded the short thoroughfare made notorious by the dilettantism, the modishness, and the witticisms of art. It had an impressive aspect. From the portico of one highly illuminated house a crimson carpet stretched across the pavement to the gutter; some dashing blade of the brush had maliciously determined to affront the bourgeois Sabbath. George stamped on the carpet; he hated it because it was not his carpet; and he swore to himself to possess that very carpet or its indistinguishable brother.

"I was a most frightful ass to leave that letter lying about!" he exclaimed.

"Oh! George!" she protested lovingly. "It could so easily happen - a thing like that could. It was just bad luck."

A cushion! The divinest down cushion! That was what she was! She was more. She defended a man against himself. She restored him to perfection. Her affectionate faith was a magical inspiration to him; it was, really, the greatest force in the world. Most women would have agreed with him, however tactfully, that he had been careless about the letter. An Adela would certainly have berated him in her shrewish, thin tones. A Lois would have been sarcastic, scornfully patronizing him as a 'boy.' And what would Agg have done?... They might have forgiven and even forgotten, but they would have indulged themselves first. Marguerite was exteriorly simple. She would not perhaps successfully dominate a drawing-room. She would cut no figure playing with lives at the wheel of an automobile. After all, she would no doubt be ridiculous in the costume of Bonnie Prince Charlie. But she was finer than the other women whose images floated in his mind. And she was worth millions of them. He was overpowered by the sense of his good fortune in finding her. He went cold at the thought of what he would have missed if he had not found her. He would not try to conceive what his existence would be without her, for it would be unendurable. Of this he was convinced.

"Do you think he'll go talking about it?" George asked, meaning of course Mr. Haim.

"More likely she will," said Marguerite.

He positively could feel her lips tightening. Futile to put in a word for Mrs. Haim! When he had described the swoon, Marguerite had shown neither concern nor curiosity. Not the slightest! Antipathy to her stepmother had radiated from her almost visibly in the night like the nimbus round a street lamp. Well, she did not understand; she was capable of injustice; she was quite wrong about Mrs. Haim. What matter? Her whole being was centralized on himself. He was aware of his superiority.

He went on quietly:

"If the old man gets chattering at the office, the Orgreaves will know, and the next minute the news'll be in the Five Towns. I can't possibly let my people hear from anybody else of my engagement before they hear from me. However, if it comes to the point, we'll tell everybody. Why not?"

"Oh, but dearest! It was so nice it being a secret. It was the loveliest thing in the world."

"Yes, it was jolly."

"Perhaps father will feel differently in the morning, and then you can - "

"He won't," said George flatly. "You don't know what a state he's in. I didn't tell you - he called me a spy in the house, a dirty spy. Likewise a jackanapes. Doubtless a delicate illusion to my tender years."

"He didn't!"

"He did, honestly."

"So that was what upset you so!" Marguerite murmured. It was her first admission that she had noticed his agitation.

"Did I look so upset, then?"

"George, you looked terrible. I felt the only thing to do was for us to go out at once."

"Oh! But surely I wasn't so upset as all that?" said George, finding in Marguerite's statement a reflection upon his ability to play the part of an imperturbable man of the world. "Agg didn't seem to see anything."

"Agg doesn't know you like I do."

She insinuated her arm into his. He raised his hand and took hold of hers. In the left pocket of his overcoat he could feel the somewhat unwieldy key of the studio. He was happy. The domestic feel of the key completed his happiness.

"Of course I can't stay on there," said he.

"At father's? Oh! I do wish father hadn't talked like that." She spoke sadly, not critically.

"I suppose I must sleep there tonight. But I'm not going to have my breakfast there tomorrow morning. No fear! I'll have it up town. Lucas'll be able to put me up to some new digs. He always knows about that sort of thing. Then I'll drive down and remove all my worldly in a four-wheeler."

He spoke with jauntiness, in his role of male who is easily equal to any situation. But she said in a low, tenderly commiserating voice:

"It's a shame!"

"Not a bit!" he replied. Then he suddenly stood still and brought her to a halt. Under his erratic guidance they had turned along Dilke Street, and northwards again, past the Botanical Garden. "And this is Paradise Row!" he said, surveying the broad street which they had come into.

"Paradise Row?" she corrected him softly. "No, dear, it's Queen's Road. It runs into Pimlico Road."

"I mean it used to be Paradise Row," he explained. "It was the most fashionable street in Chelsea, you know. Everybody that was anybody lived here."

"Oh! Really!" She showed an amiable desire to be interested, but her interest did not survive more than a few seconds. "I didn't know. I know Paradise Walk. It's that horrid little passage down there on the right."

She had not the historic sense; and she did not understand his mood, did not in the slightest degree suspect that events had been whipping his ambition once more, and that at that moment he was enjoying the seventeenth and even the sixteenth centuries, and thinking of Sir Thomas More and Miss More, and all manner of grandiose personages and abodes, and rebelling obstinately against the fact, that he was as yet a nonentity in Chelsea, whereas he meant in the end to yield to nobody in distinction and renown. He knew that she did not understand, and he would not pretend to himself that she did. There was no reason why she should understand. He did not particularly want her to understand.

"Let's have a look at the river, shall we?" he suggested, and they moved towards Cheyne Walk.

"Dearest," she said, "you must come and have breakfast at the studio tomorrow morning. I shall get it myself."

"But Agg won't like me poking my nose in for breakfast."

"You great silly! Don't you know she simply adores you?"

He was certainly startled by this remark, and he began to like Agg.

"Old Agg! Not she!" he protested, pleased, but a little embarrassed. "Will she be up?"

"You'll see whether she'll be up or not. Nine o'clock's the time, isn't it?"

They reached the gardens of Cheyne Walk. Three bridges hung their double chaplets of lights over the dark river. On the southern shore the shapes of high trees waved mysteriously above the withdrawn woodland glades that in daytime were Battersea Park. Here and there a tiny red gleam gave warning that a pier jutted out into the stream; but nothing moved on the water. The wind that swept clean the pavements had unclouded ten million stars. It was a wind unlike any other wind that ever blew, at once caressing and roughly challenging. The two, putting it behind them, faced eastward, and began to pass one by one the innumerable ornate gas-lamps of Chelsea Embankment, which stretched absolutely rectilinear in front of them for a clear mile. No soul but themselves was afoot. But on the left rose gigantic and splendid houses, palaces designed by modern architects, vying with almost any houses in London, some dark, others richly illuminated and full of souls luxurious, successful, and dominant. As the girl talked creatively about the breakfast, her arm pressed his, and his fingers clasped her acquiescent fingers, and her chaste and confiding passion ran through him in powerful voltaic currents from some inexhaustible source of energy in her secret heart. It seemed to him that since their ride home in the hansom from the Promenade concert her faculty for love had miraculously developed. He divined great deeps in her, and deeps beyond those deeps. The tenderness which he felt for her was inexpressible. He said not a word, keeping to himself the terrific resolves to which she, and the wind, and the spectacular majesty of London inspired him. He and she would live regally in one of those very houses, and people should kowtow to her because she was the dazzling wife of the renowned young architect, George Cannon. And he would show her to Mrs. John Orgreave and to Lois, and those women should acknowledge in her a woman incomparably their superior. They should not be able to hide their impressed astonishment when they saw her.

Nothing of all this did he impart to her as she hung supported and inspiring on his arm. He held it all in reserve for her. And then, thinking again for a moment of what she had said about Agg's liking for him, he thought of Agg's picture and of Marguerite's design which had originated the picture. It was a special design, new for Marguerite, whose bindings were generally of conventional patterns; it was to be paid for at a special price because of its elaborateness; she had worked on it for nearly two days; in particular she had stayed indoors during the whole of Sunday to finish it; and it was efficient, skilful, as good as it could be. It had filled her life for nearly two days - and he had not even mentioned it to her! In the ruthless egotism of the ambitious man he had forgotten it, and forgotten to imagine sympathetically the contents of her mind. Sharp remorse overcame him; she grew noble and pathetic in his eyes.... Contrast her modest and talented industry with the exacting, supercilious, incapable idleness of a Lois!

"That design of yours is jolly good," he said shortly without any introductory phrases.

She perceptibly started.

"Oh! George! I'm so glad you think so. I was afraid. You know it was horribly difficult - they give you no chance."

"I know. I know. You've come out of it fine."

She was in heaven; he also, because it was so easy for him to put her there. He glanced backwards a few hours into the past, and he simply could not comprehend how it was that he had been so upset by the grotesque scene with Mr. Haim in the basement of No. 8. Everything was all right; everything was utterly for the best.

6

THE DINNER

Early on the morning of a Tuesday in the second half of June 1903, George
Cannon was moving fast on a motor-bicycle westwards down the slope of
Piccadilly. At any rate he had the sensation of earliness, and was indeed thereby
quite invigorated; it almost served instead of the breakfast which he had not
yet taken. But thousands of people travelling in the opposite direction in
horse-omnibuses and in a few motor-buses seemed to regard the fact of their
being abroad at that hour as dully normal. They had fought, men and girls, for
places in the crammed vehicles; they had travelled from far lands such as
Putney; they had been up for hours, and the morning, which was so new to
George, had lost its freshness for them; they were well used to the lustrous
summer glories of the Green Park; what they chiefly beheld in the Green Park
was the endless lines of wayfarers, radiating from Victoria along the various
avenues, on the way, like themselves, to offices, ware-houses, and shops. Of the
stablemen, bus-washers, drivers, mechanics, chauffeurs, and conductors, who
had left their beds much in advance even of the travellers, let us not speak -
even they had begun the day later than their wives, mothers, or daughters. All
this flying population, urged and preoccupied by pitiless time, gazed down
upon George and saw a gay young swell without a care in the world rushing
on 'one of those motor-bikes' to freedom.

George was well aware of the popular gaze, and he supported it with
negligent pride. He had the air of having been born to greatness; cigarette
smoke and the fumes of exploded petrol and the rattle of explosions made a
fine wake behind his greatness. In two years, since he had walked into Mr.
Haim's parlour, his body had broadened, his eyes had slightly hardened, and

his complexion and hair had darkened. And there was his moustache, very sprightly, and there was a glint of gold in his teeth. He had poor teeth, but luxuriant hair, ruthlessly cut and disciplined and subjugated. His trousers were clipped tightly at the ankles, and his jacket loosely buttoned by the correct button; his soft felt hat achieved the architect's ideal of combining the perfectly artistic with the perfectly modish. But the most remarkable and envy-raising portion of his attire was the loose, washable, yellow gloves, with large gauntlets, designed to protect the delicately tended hands when they had to explore among machinery.

He had obtained the motor-bicycle in a peculiar way. On arriving at Axe Station for the previous Christmas holidays, he had seen two low-hung lamps brilliantly flashing instead of the higher and less powerful lamps of the dogcart, and there had been no light-reflecting flanks of a horse in front of the lamps. The dark figure sitting behind the lamps proved to be his mother. His mother herself had driven him home. He noted calmly that as a chauffeur she had the same faults as the contemned Lois Ingram. Still, she did drive, and they reached Ladderedge Hall in safety. He admired, and he was a little frightened by, his mother's terrific volition to widen her existence. She would insist on doing everything that might be done, and nobody could stop her. Who would have dreamt that she, with her narrow, troubled past, and her passionate temperament rendered somewhat harsh by strange experiences, would at the age of forty-six or so be careering about the country at the wheel of a motor-car? Ah! But she would! She would be a girl. And by her individual force she successfully carried it off! Those two plotters, she and his stepfather, had conspired to buy a motor-car in secret from him. No letter from home had breathed a word of the motor-car. He was thunder-struck, and jealous. He had spent the whole of the Christmas holidays in that car, and in four days could drive better than his mother, and also - what was more difficult - could convince her obstinate self-assurance that he knew far more about the mechanism than she did. As a fact, her notions of the mechanism, though she was convinced of their rightness, were mainly fantastic. George of course had had to punish his parents. He had considered it his duty to do so. "The least you can do," he had said discontentedly and menacingly, "the least you can do is to give me a decent motor-bike!" The guilty pair had made amends in the manner thus indicated for them. George gathered from various signs that his stepfather was steadily and rapidly growing richer. George had acted accordingly - not only in the matter of the motor-bicycle, but in other matters.

Now, on this June morning he had just begun to breast the slope rising from the hollow to Hyde Park Corner when a boy shot out from behind a huge, stationary dust-cart on the left and dashed unregarding towards him. George shouted. The boy, faced with sudden death, was happily so paralysed that he fell down, thus checking his momentum by the severest form of friction. George swerved aside, missing the small, outstretched hands by an inch or two, but missing also by an inch or two the front wheel of a tremendous motor-bus on his right. He gave a nervous giggle as he flashed by the high red side of the motor-bus; and then he deliberately looked back at the murderous boy, who had jumped up. At the same moment George was brought to a sense of his own foolishness in looking back by a heavy jolt. He had gone over half a creosoted wood block which had somehow escaped from a lozenge-shaped oasis in the road where two workmen were indolently using picks under the magic protection of a tiny, dirty red flag. Secure in the guardianship of the bit of bunting, which for them was as powerful and sacred as the flag of an empire, the two workmen gazed with indifference at George and at the deafening traffic which swirled affronting but harmless around them. George slackened speed, afraid lest the jar might have snapped the plates of his accumulator. The motor-bicycle was a wondrous thing, but as capricious and delicate as a horse. For a trifle, for nothing at all, it would cease to function. The high-tension magneto and the float-feed carburetter, whose invention was to transform the motor-bicycle from an everlasting harassment into a means of loco-motion, were yet years away in the future. However, the jar had done no harm. The episode, having occupied less than ten seconds, was closed. George felt his heart thumping. He thought suddenly of the recent Paris-Madrid automobile race, in which the elite of the world had perished. He saw himself beneath the motor-bus, and a futile staring crowd round about. Simply by a miracle was he alive. But this miracle was only one of a score of miracles. He believed strongly in luck. He had always believed in it. The smoke of the cigarette displayed his confidence to all Piccadilly. Still, his heart was thumping.

And it had not ceased to thump when a few minutes later he turned into Manresa Road. Opposite the entrance to the alley of Romney Studios, there happened to be a small hiatus in the kerbstone. George curved the machine largely round and, mounting the pavement through this hiatus, rode gingerly up the alley, in defiance of the regulations of a great city, and stopped precisely at the door of No. 6. It was a matter of honour with him to arrive thus. Not for a million would he have walked the machine up the alley. He got off, sounded a peremptory call on the horn, and tattooed with the knocker. No answer came. An apprehension visited him. By the last post on the previous night he had received a special invitation to breakfast from Marguerite. Never had he been kept waiting at the door. He knocked again. Then he heard a voice from the side of the studio:

"Come round here, George."

In the side of the studio was a very small window from which the girls, when unpresentable, would parley with early tradesmen. Agg was at the window. He could see only her head and neck, framed by the window. Her short hair was tousled, and she held a dressing-gown tight about her neck. For the first time she seemed to him like a real feminine girl, and her tones were soft as they never were when Marguerite was present with her.

"I'm very sorry," she said. "You woke me. I was fast asleep. You can't come in."

"Anything up?" he questioned, rather anxiously. "Where's Marguerite?"

"Oh, George! A dreadful night!" she answered, almost plaintively, almost demanding sympathy from the male - she, Agg! "We were wakened up at two o'clock. Mr. Prince came round to fetch Marguerite to go to No. 8."

"To go to No. 8?" he repeated, frightened, and wondered why he should be frightened. "What on earth for?"

"Mrs. Haim very ill!" Agg paused. "Something about a baby."

"And did she go?"

"Yes; she put on her things and went off at once."

He was silent. He felt the rough grip of destiny, of some strange power irresistible and unescapable, just as he had momentarily felt it in the basement of No. 8 more than eighteen months before, when the outraged Mr. Haim had quarrelled with him. The mere idea of Marguerite being at No. 8 made him feel sick. He no longer believed in his luck. "How soon d'ye think she'll be back?"

"I - I don't know, George. I should have thought she'd have been back before this."

"I'll run round there," he said curtly.

Agg was disconcertingly, astoundingly sympathetic. Her attitude increased his disturbance.

2

When George rang the bell at No. 8 Alexandra Grove his mysterious qualms were intensified. He dreaded the moment when the door should open, even though it should be opened by Marguerite herself. And yet he had a tremendous desire to see Marguerite - merely to look at her face, to examine it, to read it. His summons was not answered. He glanced about. The steps were dirty. The brass knob and the letter-flap had not been polished. After a time he pushed up the flap and gazed within, and saw the interior which he knew so well and which he had not entered for so many months. Nothing was changed in it, but it also had a dusty and neglected air. Every detail roused his memory. The door of what had once been his room was shut; he wondered what the room was now. This house held the greatest part of his history. It lived in his mind as vitally as even the boarding-house kept by his mother in a side-street in Brighton, romantic and miserable scene of his sensitive childhood. It was a solemn house for him. Through the basement window on a dark night he had first glimpsed Marguerite. Unforgettable event! Unlike anything else that had ever happened to anybody!... He heard a creak, and caught sight through the letter-aperture of a pair of red slippers, and then the lower half of a pair of trousers, descending the stairs. And he dropped the flap hurriedly. Mr. Haim was coming to open the door. Mr. Haim did open the door, started at the apparition of George, and stood defensively and forbiddingly in the very centre of the doorway.

"Oh!" said George nervously. "How is Mrs. Haim?"

"Mrs. Haim is very ill indeed." The reply was emphatic and inimical.

"I'm sorry."

Mr. Haim said nothing further. George had not seen him since the previous Saturday, having been excused by Mr. Enwright from the office on Monday on account of examination work. He did not know that Mr. Haim had not been to the office on Monday either. In the interval the man had shockingly changed. He seemed much older, and weaker too; he seemed worn out by acute anxiety. Nevertheless he so evidently resented sympathy that George was not sympathetic, and regarded him coldly as a tiresome old man. The official relations between the two had been rigorously polite and formal. No reference had ever been made by either to the quarrel in the basement or to the cause of it. And for the world in general George's engagement had remained as secret as before. Marguerite had not seen her father in the long interval, and George had seen only the factotum of Lucas & Enwright. But he now saw Marguerite's father again - a quite different person from the factotum.... Strange, how the house seemed forlorn! 'Something about a baby,' Agg had said vaguely. And it was as though something that Mr. Haim and his wife had concealed had burst from its concealment and horrified and put a curse on the whole Grove. Something not at all nice! What in the name of decent propriety was that slippered old man doing with a baby? George would not picture to himself Mrs. Haim lying upstairs. He did not care to think of Marguerite secretly active somewhere in one of those rooms. But she was there; she was initiated. He did not criticize her.

"I should like to see Marguerite," he said at length. Despite himself he had a guilty feeling.

"My daughter!" Mr. Haim took up the heavy role.

"Only for a minute," said George boyishly, and irritated by his own boyishness.

"You can't see her, sir."

"But if she knows I'm here, she'll come to me," George insisted. He saw that the old man's hatred of him was undiminished. Indeed, time had probably strengthened it.

"You can't see her, sir. This is my house."

George considered himself infinitely more mature than in the November of

1901 when the old man had worsted him. And yet he was no more equal to this situation than he had been to the former one.

"But what am I to do, then?" he demanded, not fiercely, but crossly.

"What are you to do? Don't ask me, sir. My wife is very ill indeed, and you come down the Grove making noise enough to wake the dead" - he indicated the motor-bicycle, of which the silencer was admittedly defective - "and you want to see my daughter. My daughter has more important work to do than to see you. I never heard of such callousness. If you want to communicate with my daughter you had better write - so long as she stays in this house."

Mr. Haim shut the door, which rendered his advantage over George complete.

From the post office nearly opposite the end of the Grove George dispatched a reply-paid telegram to Marguerite:

"Where and when can I see you? - George. Russell Square."

It seemed a feeble retort to Mr. Haim, but he could think of nothing better.

On the way up town he suddenly felt, not hungry, but empty, and he called in at a tea-shop. He was the only customer, in a great expanse of marble-topped tables. He sat down at a marble-topped table. On the marble-topped table next to him were twenty-four sugar-basins, and on the next to that a large number of brass bells, and on another one an infinity of cruets. A very slatternly woman was washing the linoleum in a corner of the floor. Two thin, wrinkled girls in shabby black were whispering together behind the counter. The cash-den was empty. Through the open door he could keep an eye on his motor-bicycle, which was being surreptitiously regarded by a boy theoretically engaged in cleaning the window. A big van drove up, and a man entered with pastry on a wooden tray and bantered one of the girls in black. She made no reply, being preoccupied with the responsibility of counting cakes. The man departed and the van disappeared. Nobody took the least notice of George. He might have been a customer invisible and inaudible. After the fiasco of his interview with Mr. Haim, he had not the courage to protest. He framed withering sentences to the girls in black, such as: "Is this place supposed to be open for business, or isn't it?" but they were not uttered. Then a girl in black with a plain, ugly white apron and a dowdy white cap appeared on the stairs leading from the basement, and removed for her passage a bar of stained wood lettered in gilt: 'Closed,' and she halted at George's table. She spoke no word. She just stood over him, unsmiling, placid, flaccid, immensely indifferent. She was pale, a poor sort of a girl, without vigour. But she had a decent, honest face. She was not aware that she ought to be bright, welcoming, provocative, for a penny farthing an hour. She had never heard of Hebe. George thought of the long, desolating day that lay before her. He looked at her seriously. His eyes did not challenge hers as they were accustomed to challenge Hebe's. He said in a friendly, matter-of-fact tone:

"A meat-pie, please, and a large coffee."

And she repeated in a thin voice:

"Meat-pie. Large coffee."

A minute later she dropped the order on the table, as it might have been refuse, and with it a bit of white paper. The sadness of the city, and the inexplicable sadness of June mornings, overwhelmed George as he munched at the meat-pie and drank the coffee, and reached over for the sugar and reached over for the mustard. And he kept saying to himself:

"She doesn't see her father at all for nearly two years, and then she goes off to him like that in the middle of the night - at a word."

3

The office was not at its normal. The empty cubicle of the factotum looked strange enough. But there was more than that in the abnormality. There were currents of excitement in the office. The door of the principals' room was open, and George saw John Orgreave and Everard Lucas within, leaning over one of the great flat desks. The hour was early for Lucas, and self-satisfaction was on Lucas's face as he raised it to look at the entering of George.

"I say," he remarked quietly through the doorway, "that town hall scheme is on again."

"Oh!" said George, depositing his hat and gloves and strolling into the principals' room. "Good morning, Mr. Orgreave. Got the conditions there?" For a moment his attitude of interest was a pose, but very quickly it became sincere. Astonishing how at sight of a drawing-board and a problem he could forget all that lay beyond them! He was genuinely and extremely disturbed by the course of affairs at Chelsea; nevertheless he now approached Mr. Orgreave and Lucas with eagerness, and Chelsea slipped away into another dimension.

"No," said John Orgreave, "the conditions aren't out yet. But it's all right this time. I know for a fact."

The offices of all the regular architectural competitors in London were excited that morning. For the conception of the northern town hall was a vast one. Indeed, journalists had announced, from their mysterious founts of information, that the town hall would be the largest public building erected in England during half a century. The scheme had been the sport of municipal politics for many months, for years. Apparently it could not get itself definitely born. And now the Town Clerk's wife had brought about the august parturition. It is true that her agency was unintentional. The Town Clerk had belonged to a powerful provincial dynasty of town clerks. He had the illusion that without him a great town would cease to exist. There was nothing uncommon in this illusion, which indeed is rife among town clerks; but the Town Clerk in question had the precious faculty of being able to communicate it to mayors, aldermen, and councillors. He was a force in the municipal council. Voteless, he exercised a moral influence over votes. And he happened to be opposed to the scheme for the new town hall. He gave various admirable reasons for the postponement of the scheme, but he never gave the true reasons, even to himself. The true reasons were, first, that he hated and detested the idea of moving office, and, second, that he wanted acutely to be able to say in the fullness of years that he had completed half a century of municipal work in one and the same room. If the pro-scheme party had had the wit to invent a pretext for allowing the Town Clerk to remain in the old municipal buildings, the scheme would instantly have taken life. The Town Clerk, being widowed, had consoled himself with a young second wife. This girl adored dancing; the Town Clerk adored her; and therefore where she danced he deemed it prudent to attend. Driving home from a January ball at 4 a.m. the Town Clerk had caught pneumonia. In a week he was dead, and his dynasty with him. In a couple of months the pro-scheme party had carried the council off its feet. Such are the realities, never printed in newspapers, of municipal politics in the grim north.

Sketches of the site had appeared in the architectural press. John Orgreave and Lucas were pencilling in turn upon one of these, a page torn out of a weekly. George inserted himself between them, roughly towards Lucas and deferentially towards Mr. John.

"But you've got the main axis wrong!" he exclaimed.

"How, wrong?" John Orgreave demanded.

"See here - give me the pencil, Looc."

George felt with a little thrill of satisfaction the respect for him which underlay John Orgreave's curt tone of a principal - and a principal from the Midlands. He did not miss, either, Lucas's quick, obedient, expectant gesture in surrendering the pencil. Ideas for the plan of the building sprang up multitudinously in his mind. He called; they came. He snatched towards him a blank sheet of tracing-paper, and scrawled it over with significant lines.

"That's my notion. I thought of it long ago," he said. "Or if you prefer - "

The other two were impressed. He himself was impressed. His notion, which he was modifying and improving every moment, seemed to him perfect and ever more perfect. He was intensely and happily stimulated in the act of creation; and they were all three absorbed.

"Why hasn't my desk been arranged?" said a discontented voice behind them. Mr. Enwright had arrived by the farther door from the corridor.

Lucas glanced up.

"I expect Haim hasn't come again to-day," he answered urbanely, placatingly.

"Why hasn't he come?"

"I hear his wife's very ill," said George.

"Who told you?"

"I happened to be round that way this morning."

"Oh! I thought all was over between you two."

George flushed. Nothing had ever been said in the office as to his relations with Haim, though it was of course known that George no longer lodged with the factotum. Mr. Enwright, however, often had disconcerting intuitions concerning matters to which Mr. Orgreave and Lucas were utterly insensible.

"Oh no!" George haltingly murmured.

"Well, this is all very well, this is - !" Mr. Enwright ruthlessly proceeded, beginning to marshal the instruments on his desk.

He had been a somewhat spectacular martyr for some time past. A mysterious facial neuralgia had harried his nights and days. For the greater part of a week he had dozed in an arm-chair in the office under the spell of eight tabloids of aspirin per diem. Then a specialist had decided that seven of his side teeth, already studded with gold, must leave him. Those teeth were not like any other person's teeth, and in Mr. Enwright's mind the extracting of them had become a major operation, as, for example, the taking off of a limb. He had spent three days in a nursing home in Welbeck Street. His life was now saved, and he was a convalescent, and passed several hours daily in giving to friends tragi-farcical accounts of existence in a nursing home. Mr. Enwright's career was one unending romance.

"I was just looking at that town hall affair," said John Orgreave.

"What town hall?" his partner snapped.

"The town hall," answered the imperturbable John. "George here has got an idea."

"I suppose you know Sir Hugh Corver, Bart., is to be the assessor," said Mr. Enwright in a devastating tone.

Sir Hugh Corver, formerly a mere knight, had received a baronetcy, to Mr. Enwright's deep disgust. Mr. Enwright had remarked that any decent-minded man who had been a husband and childless for twenty-four years would have regarded the supplementary honour as an insult, but that Sir Hugh was not decent-minded and, moreover, was not capable of knowing an insult when he got one. This theory of Mr. Enwright's, however, did not a bit lessen his disgust.

"Oh yes," John Orgreave admitted lamely.

"I for one am not going in for any more competitions with Corver as assessor," said Mr. Enwright. "I won't do it."

Faces fell. Mr. Enwright had previously published this resolve, but it had not been taken quite seriously. It was entirely serious. Neuralgia and a baronetcy had given it the consistency of steel.

"It isn't as if we hadn't got plenty of work in the office," said Mr.

Enwright.

This was true. The firm was exceedingly prosperous.

Nobody else spoke.

"What can you expect from a fellow like Corver?" Mr. Enwright cried, with a special glance at George. "He's the upas-tree of decent architecture."

George's mood changed immediately. Profound discouragement succeeded to his creative stimulation. Mr. Enwright had reason on his side. What could you expect from a fellow like Corver? With all the ardour of a disciple George dismissed the town hall scheme, and simultaneously his private woes surged up and took full possession of him. He walked silently out of the room, and Lucas followed. As a fact, Mr. Enwright ought not to have talked in such a way before the pupils. A question of general policy should first have been discussed in private between the partners, and the result then formally announced to the staff. Mr. Enwright was not treating his partner with proper consideration. But Mr. Enwright, as every one said at intervals, was 'like that'; and his partner did not seem to care greatly.

Lucas shut the door between the principals' room and the pupils' room.

"I say," said Lucas importantly. "I've got a show on tonight. Women. Cafe Royal. I want a fourth. You must come."

"Yes," sneered George. "And what about my exam., I should like to know.... Besides, I can't."

The Final was due to begin on Thursday.

"That's all right," Lucas answered, with tact. "That's all right. I'd thought of the exam., of course. You'll have tomorrow to recover. It'll do you all the good in the world. And you know you're more than ready for the thing. You don't want to be overtrained, my son. Besides, you'll sail through it. As for 'can't,' 'can't' be damned. You've got to."

A telegraph boy, after hesitating at the empty cubicle, came straight into the room.

"Name of Cannon?"

George nodded, trembling.

The telegram read:

"Impossible to-day. - Marguerite."

It was an incredible telegram, as much by what it said as by what it didn't say. It overthrew George.

"Seven forty-five, and I'll drive you round," said Lucas.

"'Tis well," said George.

Immediately afterwards Mr. Enwright summoned Lucas.

4

The two young men of fashion were silent that evening as they drove to the

Cafe Royal in the car which Lucas loosely called 'my car,' but which was his mother's and only to be obtained by him upon his own conditions after delicate diplomacies. The chief of his conditions was that the chauffeur should not accompany the car. Lucas, having been engaged upon outdoor work for the firm, had not seen George throughout the day. Further, he was late in calling for George, and therefore rather exacerbated in secret; and if George had not been ready and waiting for him at the club trouble might have arisen. George understood his host's mood and respected it. Lucas drove rapidly and fiercely, with appropriate frowns and settings of cruel teeth; his mien indeed had the arrogance of the performer who, having given only a fraction of his time to the acquirement of skill, reckons that he can beat the professional who has given the whole of his time. Lucas's glances at chauffeurs who hindered his swiftness were masterpieces of high disdain, and he would accelerate, after circumventing them, with positive ferocity.

George himself, an implacable critic, could not find fault with the technique of Lucas's driving. But exacerbation tells, even in the young, and at Piccadilly Circus, Lucas, in obeying a too suddenly uplifted hand of a policeman, stopped his engine. The situation, horribly humiliating for Lucas and also for George, provided pleasure for half the chauffeurs and drivers in Piccadilly Circus, and was the origin of much jocularity of a kind then fairly new. Lucas cursed the innocent engine, and George leapt down to wield the crank. But the engine, apparently resenting curses, refused to start again. No, it would not start. Lucas leapt down too. "Get out of the way," he muttered savagely to George, and scowled at the bonnet as if saying to the engine: "I'm not going to stand any of your infernal nonsense!" But still the engine refused to start.

The situation, humiliating before, was now appalling. Two entirely correct young gentlemen, in evening dress, with light overcoats and opera hats, struggling with a refractory car that in its obstinacy was far more dignified than themselves - and the car obstructing traffic at the very centre of the world in the very hour when the elect of Britain were driving by on the way to Tristan at the Opera! Sebastians both, they were martyrized by the poisoned arrows of vulgar wit, shot at them from all sides and especially from the lofty thrones of hansom-cab drivers. The policeman ordered them to shove the car to the kerb, and with the aid of a boy and the policeman himself they did so, opposite the shuttered front of Swan & Edgar's.

The two experts then examined the engine in a professional manner; they did everything but take it down; they tried in vain all known devices to conquer the recalcitrancy of engines; and when they had reached despair and fury George, startlingly visited by an idea, demanded:

"Any petrol in the tank?..." In those days men of fashion were apt to forget, at moments of crisis, that the first necessity of the engine was petrol. George behaved magnanimously. He might have extinguished Lucas with a single inflection as Lucas, shamed to the uttermost, poured a spare half-tin of petrol into the tank. He refrained.

In one minute, in less than one minute, they were at the side entrance to the Cafe Royal, which less than a minute earlier had been inconceivably distant and unattainable. Lucas dashed first into the restaurant. To keep ladies waiting in a public place was for him the very worst crime, surpassing in turpitude arson, embezzlement, and the murder of innocents. The ladies must have been waiting for a quarter of an hour, half an hour! His reputation was destroyed!

However, the ladies had not arrived.

"That's all right," Lucas breathed, at ease at last. The terrible scowl had vanished from his face, which was perfectly recomposed into its urbane, bland charm.

"Now perhaps you'll inform me who they are, old man," George suggested, relinquishing his overcoat to a flunkey, and following Lucas into the cloister set apart for the cleansing of hands which have meddled with machinery.

"The Wheeler woman is one - didn't I tell you?" Lucas answered, unsuccessfully concealing his pride.

"Wheeler?"

"Irene Wheeler. You know."

George was really impressed. Lucas had hitherto said no word as to his acquaintance with this celebrated woman. It was true that recently Lucas had been spreading himself in various ways - he had even passed his Intermediate - but George had not anticipated such a height of achievement as the feat of entertaining at a restaurant a cynosure like Irene Wheeler. George had expected quite another sort of company at dinner, for he had publicly dined with Lucas before. All day he had been abstracted, listless, and utterly desolate. All day he had gone over again and again the details of the interview with Mr. Haim, his telegram to Marguerite and her unspeakable telegram to him, hugging close a terrific grievance. Only from pique against Marguerite had he accepted Lucas's invitation. The adventure in Piccadilly Circus had somewhat enlivened him, and now the fluttering prospect of acquaintance with the legendary Irene Wheeler pushed Marguerite into the background of his mind, and excitement became quite pleasant. "And a Miss Ingram," Lucas added.

"Not Lois Ingram?" exclaimed George, suddenly dragging the names of Ingram and Wheeler out of the same drawer of his memory.

"No. Laurencine. But she has a sister named Lois. What do you know about her?" Lucas spoke challengingly, as if George had trespassed on preserves sacred to himself alone. He had not yet admitted that it was merely Mrs. John Orgreave who had put him in the way of Irene Wheeler.

George was surprised and shocked that it had never occurred to him to identify Lois Ingram's wealthy friend Miss Wheeler with the Irene Wheeler of society columns of newspapers. And Lois Ingram rose in his esteem, not because of the distinction of her friend, but because she had laid no boastful stress on the distinction of her friend.

"Don't you remember?" he said. "I told you once about a girl who jolly nearly got me into a motor accident all through her fancying herself as a chauffeur. That was Lois Ingram. Paris girl. Same lot, isn't it?"

"Oh! Was that Lois?" Lucas murmured. "Well, I'm dashed!"

They returned in a hurry to the entrance-hall, fearful lest the ladies might have arrived. However, the ladies had not arrived. Lucas had the inexpressible satisfaction of finding in an illustrated weekly a full-page portrait of Miss Irene Wheeler.

"Here you are!" he ejaculated, with an air of use, as though he was habitually picking up from the tables of fashionable restaurants high-class illustrated papers containing portraits of renowned beauties to whom he said "Come!" and they came. It was a great moment for Lucas.

Ten minutes later the ladies very calmly arrived, seeming perfectly unaware that they were three-quarters of an hour behind time. Lucas felt that, much as he already knew about life, he had learned something fresh.

To George, Irene Wheeler was not immediately recognizable as the original of her portrait. He saw the resemblance when he looked for it, but if after seeing the photograph he had met the woman in the street he would have passed her by unknowing. At first he was disappointed in her. He had never before encountered celebrated people - except architects, who, Enwright always said, never could be really celebrated - and he had to learn that celebrated people seldom differ in appearance from uncelebrated people. Nevertheless it was not to be expected that George should escape where the most experienced and the most wary of two capitals had not escaped. He did not agree that she was beautiful, but her complexion enthralled him. He had never seen such a complexion; nobody had ever seen such a complexion. It combined extremely marvellous whites and extremely marvellous pinks, and the skin had the exquisite, incredible softness of a baby's. Next he was struck by her candid, ingenuous, inquiring gaze, and by her thin voice with the slight occasional lisp. The splendid magnificence of her frock and jewels came into play later. Lastly her demeanour imposed itself. That simple gaze showed not the slightest diffidence, scarcely even modesty; it was more brazen than effrontery. She preceded the other three into the restaurant, where electricity had finally conquered the expiring daylight, and her entry obviously excited the whole room; yet, guided by two waving and fawning waiters, and a hundred glances upon her, she walked to the appointed table without a trace of self-consciousness - as naturally as a policeman down a street. When she sat down, George on her right, Lucas on her left, and the tall, virginal Laurencine Ingram opposite, she was the principal person in the restaurant. George had already passed from disappointment to an impressed nervousness. The inquisitive diners might all have been quizzing him instead of Irene Wheeler. He envied Lucas, who was talking freely to both Miss Wheeler and Laurencine about what he had ordered for dinner. That morning over a drawing-board and an architectural problem, Lucas had been humble enough to George, and George by natural right had laid the law down to Lucas; but now Lucas, who - George was obliged to admit - never said anything brilliant or original, was outshining him.... It was unquestionable that in getting Irene Wheeler to dinner, Lucas, by some mysterious talent which he possessed, had performed a feat greater even than George had at first imagined - a prodigious feat.

George waited for Irene Wheeler to begin to talk. She did not begin to talk. She was content with the grand function of existing. Lucas showed her the portrait in the illustrated paper, which he had kept. She said that it was comparatively an old one, and had been taken at the Durbar in January. "Were you at the Durbar?" asked the simpleton George. Irene Wheeler looked at him. "Yes. I was in the Viceroy's house-party," she answered mildly. And then she said to Lucas that she had sat three times to photographers that week - "They won't leave me alone" - but that the proofs were none of them satisfactory.

At this Laurencine Ingram boldly and blushingly protested, maintaining that one of them was lovely. George was attracted to Laurencine, in whom he saw no likeness to her sister Lois. She could not long have left school. She was the product finished for the world; she had been taught everything that was considered desirable - even to the art of talking easily and yet virginally on all subjects at table; and she was a nice, honest, handsome girl, entirely unspoilt by the mysterious operations practised upon her. She related how she had been present when a famous photographer arrived at Miss Wheeler's flat with his apparatus, and what the famous photographer had said. The boys laughed. Miss Wheeler smiled faintly. "I'm glad we didn't have to go to that play tonight," she remarked. "However, I shall have to go tomorrow night. And I don't care for first nights in London, only they will have me go."

In this last phrase, and in the intonation of it, was the first sign she had given of her American origin; her speech was usually indistinguishable from English English, which language she had in fact carefully acquired years earlier. George gathered that Lucas's success in getting Miss Wheeler to dinner was due to the accident of a first night being postponed at the last moment and Miss Wheeler thus finding herself with an empty evening. He covertly examined her. Why was the feat of getting Miss Wheeler to dinner enormous? Why would photographers not leave her alone? Why would theatrical managers have her accept boxes gratis which they could sell for money? Why was she asked to join the Viceregal party for the Durbar? Why was the restaurant agog? Why was he himself proud and flattered - yes, proud and flattered - to be seen at the same table with her?... She was excessively rich, no doubt; she was reputed to be the niece of a railway man in Indianapolis who was one of the major rivals of Harriman. She dressed superbly, perhaps too superbly. But there were innumerable rich and well-dressed women on earth. After all, she put her gold bag and her gloves down on the table with just the same gesture as other women did; and little big Laurencine had a gold bag too. She was not witty. He questioned whether she was essentially kind. She was not young; her age was an enigma. She had not a remarkable figure, nor unforgettable hair, nor incendiary eyes. She seemed too placid and self-centred for love. If she had loved, it must have been as she sat to photographers or occupied boxes on first nights - because 'they' would have it so. George was baffled to discover the origin of her prestige. He had to seek it in her complexion. Her complexion was indubitably miraculous. He enjoyed looking at it, though he lacked the experience to know that he was looking at a complexion held by connoisseurs who do naught else but look at complexions to be a complexion unique in Europe. George, unsophisticated, thought that the unaffected simplicity - far exceeding self-confidence - with which she acquiesced in her prestige was perhaps more miraculous than her complexion. It staggered him.

The dinner was a social success. Irene Wheeler listened adroitly, if without brilliance, and after one glass of wine George found himself quite able to talk in the Enwright manner about architecture and the profession of architecture, and also to talk about automobiles. The casualness with which he mentioned his Final Examination was superb - the examiners might have been respectfully waiting for him to arrive and discomfit them. But of course the main subject was automobiles. Even Laurencine knew the names of all the leading makers, and when the names of all the leading makers had been enumerated and their products discussed, the party seemed to think that it had accomplished something that was both necessary and stylish. When the tablecloth had been renewed, and the solemn moment came for Everard Lucas to order liqueurs, George felt almost gay. He glanced round the gilded and mirrored apartment, now alluringly animated by the subdued yet vivacious intimacies of a score of white tables, and decided that the institution of restaurants was a laudable and agreeable institution. Marguerite had receded further than ever into the background of his mind; and as for the Final, it had diminished to a formality.

"And you?" Everard asked Laurencine, after Miss Wheeler.

George had thought that Laurencine was too young for liqueurs. She had had no wine. He expected her to say 'Nothing, thanks,' as conventionally as if her late head mistress had been present. But she hesitated, smiling, and then, obedient to the profound and universal instinct which seems to guide all young women to the same liqueur, she said:

"May I have a creme de menthe? I've never had creme de menthe."

George was certainly shocked for an instant. But no one else appeared to be shocked. Miss Wheeler, in charge of Laurencine, offered no protest. And then George reflected: "And why not? Why shouldn't she have a creme de menthe?" When Laurencine raised the tiny glass to her firm, large mouth, George thought that the sight of the young virginal thing tasting a liqueur was a fine and a beautiful sight.

"It's just heavenly!" murmured Laurencine ecstatically.

Miss Wheeler was gazing at George.

"What's the matter?" he demanded, smiling, and rested one elbow on the table and looked enigmatically through the smoke of his cigar.

"I was just wondering about you," said Miss Wheeler. Her voice, always faint, had dropped to a murmur which seemed to expire as it reached George's ear.

"Why?" He was flattered.

"I've been wanting to see you."

"Really!" he laughed, rather too loudly. "What a pity I didn't know earlier!" He was disturbed as well as flattered, for such a remark from such a person as Irene Wheeler to such a person as himself was bound to be disturbing. His eyes sought audaciously to commune with hers, but hers were not responsive; they were entirely non-committal.

"You are the man that wouldn't let my friend Lois drive him in my car, aren't you?"

"Yes," he said defiantly, but rather guiltily. "Did she tell you about that? It's an awful long time ago."

"She told me something about it."

"And you've remembered it all this long while!"

"Yes," she answered, and her thin, queer tone and her tepid, impartial glance had the effect of a challenge to him to justify himself.

"And don't you think I was quite right?" he ventured.

"She drives very well." It was not the sort of answer he was expecting. His desire was to argue.

"She didn't drive very well then," he said, with conviction.

"Was that a reason for your leaving her to drive home alone?"

Women were astounding!

"She ought to have let the chauffeur drive," he maintained.

"Ah! A man mustn't expect too much from a woman."

"But I was risking my life in that car! Do you mean to say I ought to have kept on risking it?"

"I don't express any opinion on that. That was for you to decide.... You must admit it was very humiliating for poor Lois."

He felt himself cornered, but whether justly or unjustly he was uncertain.

"Was she vexed?"

"No, she wasn't vexed. Lois isn't the woman to be vexed. But I have an idea she was a little hurt."

"Did she say so?"

"Say so? Lois? She'd never say anything against anybody. Lois is a perfect angel.... Isn't she, Laurencine?"

Laurencine was being monopolized by Everard.

"What did you say?" the girl asked, collecting herself.

"I was just saying what an angel Lois is."

"Oh, she is!" the younger sister agreed, with immense and sincere emphasis.

George, startled, said to himself suddenly:

"Was I mistaken in her? Some girls you are mistaken in! They're regular bricks, but they keep it from you at first."

Somehow, in spite of a slight superficial mortification, he was very pleased by the episode of the conversation, and his curiosity was titillated.

"Lois would have come tonight instead of Laurencine," Miss Wheeler went on, "only she wasn't feeling very well."

"Is she in London? I've only seen her once from that day to this, and then we didn't get near each other owing to the crush. So we didn't speak. It was at Mrs. Orgreave's."

"Yes, I know."

"Did she tell you?"

"Yes."

"Is she at your flat?"

"Yes; but she's not well."

"Not in bed, I hope, or anything like that?"

"Oh no! She's not in bed."

Laurencine threw laughingly across the table:

"She's as well as I am."

It was another aspect of the younger sister.

When they left the restaurant it was nearly empty. They left easily, slowly, magnificently. The largesse of Everard Lucas - his hat slightly raked - in the foyer and at the portico was magnificent in both quantity and manner. There was no need to hurry; the hour, though late for the end of dinner, was early for separation. They moved and talked without the slightest diffidence, familiar and confident; the whole world was reformed and improved for them by the stimulus of food and alcohol. The night was sultry and dark. The two women threw their cloaks back from their shoulders, revealing the whiteness of toilettes. At the door the head-lights of Miss Wheeler's automobile shot horizontally right across Regent Street. The chauffeur recognized George, and George recognized the car; he was rather surprised that Miss Wheeler had not had a new car in eighteen months. Lucas spoke of his own car, which lay beyond in the middle of the side-street like a ship at anchor. He spoke in such a strain that Miss Wheeler deigned to ask him to drive her home in it. The two young men went to light the head-lights. George noticed the angry scowl on Everard's face when three matches had been blown out in the capricious breeze. The success of the fourth match restored his face to perfect benignity. He made the engine roar triumphantly, imperiously sounded his horn, plunged forward, and drew the car up in front of Miss Wheeler's. His bliss, when Miss Wheeler had delicately inserted herself into the space by his side, was stern and yet radiant. The big car, with George and Laurencine on board, followed the little one like a cat following a mouse, and Laurencine girlishly interested herself in the chase. George, with his mind on Lois, kept saying to himself: "She's been thinking about that little affair ever since last November but one. They've all been thinking about it." He felt apprehensive, but his satisfaction amounted to excitement. His attitude was: "At any rate I gave them something to think about!" Also he breathed appreciatively the atmosphere of the three women - two seen and one unseen. How extraordinarily different all of them were from Agg! They reminded him acutely of his deep need of luxury. After all, the life lived by those two men about town, George and Everard, was rather humdrum and monotonous. In spite of Everard's dash, and in spite of George's secret engagement, neither of them met enough women or enough sorts of women. George said to himself: "I shall see her tonight. We shall go up to the flat. She isn't in bed. I shall see her tonight." He wanted to see her because he had hurt her, and because she had remembered and had talked about him and had raised curiosity about him in others. Was she really unwell? Or had she been excusing herself! Was she an angel? He wanted to see her again in order to judge for himself whether she was an angel. If Laurencine said she was an angel she must be an angel. Laurencine was a jolly, honest girl. To be in the car with her was agreeable. But she was insipid. So he assessed the splendidly budding Laurencine, patronizing her a little. Miss Wheeler gave him pause. Her simple phrases had mysterious intonations. He did not understand her glance. He could not settle the first question about her - her age. She might be very wicked; certainly she could be very ruthless. And he had no hold over her. He could give her nothing that she wanted. He doubted whether any man could.

"Have you been in London long?" he asked Laurencine.

"A week," she said. "I came over with Miss Wheeler. I didn't think mother would let me, but she did."

"And did your sister come with you?"

"No; Lois only came yesterday."

"By herself?"

"Yes."

"I suppose you go about a lot?"

"Oh, we do It's such a change from Paris."

99

"Well, I should prefer Paris."

"You wouldn't! London's much more romantic. Paris is so hard and matter-of-fact."

"So's London."

She squirmed about lissomly on the seat.

"You don't know what I mean," she said. "I never can make people see what I mean - about anything."

He smiled indulgently and dropped the point.

"Miss Wheeler taken you to Mrs. Orgreave's yet?"

"Yes; we were there on Saturday afternoon."

"Well, what do you think of Mrs. Orgreave?"

"Oh! She's very nice," Laurencine answered, with polite tepidity; and added eagerly: "Mr. Orgreave's a dear."

George was glad that she had not been enthusiastic about Mrs. Orgreave. Her reserve showed that she could discriminate. Ecstasy was not altogether a habit. If she said that Lois was an angel, Lois probably was an angel.

The cars stopped at the foot of a huge block of masonry in a vast leafy square. George suddenly became very nervous. He thought: "I shall be seeing her in a minute."

Then, as he got out of the car, he heard Miss Wheeler saying to Lucas:

"Well, good night. And thank you so much. It's been most delightful.... We expect you soon, of course."

She actually was not asking them to go up! George was excessively disappointed. He watched Miss Wheeler and Laurencine disappear into the rich and guarded interior with envy, as though they had entered a delectable paradise to which he could not aspire; and the fact that Miss Wheeler had vaguely invited him to call did not brighten him very much. He had assumed that he would see Lois the angel that night.

5

The young men finished the evening at Pickering's.

Pickering's was George's club. George considered, rightly, that in the matter of his club he had had great luck. Pickering's was a small club, and it had had vicissitudes. Most men whose worldly education had been completed in St. James's were familiar with its historical name, but few could say off-hand where it was. Its address was Candle Court, and Candle Court lay at the end of Candle Alley (a very short passage), between Duke Street and Bury Street. The Court was in fact a tiny square of several houses, chiefly used by traders and agents of respectability - as respectability is understood in St. James's; it had a lamp-post of its own. The report ran, and was believed by persons entitled to an opinion, that the Duke of Wellington had for some years hidden there the lovely desire of his heart from an inquisitive West End. Pickering's had, of course, originally been a coffee-house; later, like many other coffee-houses in the neighbourhood, it had developed into a proprietary club. Misfortunes due to the caprices of taste and to competition had brought about an arrangement by which the ownership was vested in a representative committee. The misfortunes had continued, and at the beginning of the century a crisis was reached, and Pickering's tried hard to popularize itself, thereby doing violence to its feelings. Rules were abated, and the entrance-fee fell. It was in this period that Everard Lucas, whose ears were always open for useful items, heard of it and suggested it to George. George wanted to join Lucas's club, which was in St. James's Street itself, but Lucas wisely pointed out that if they belonged to different clubs each would in practice have two clubs. Moreover, he said that George might conceivably get a permanent bedroom there. The first sight of the prim, picturesque square, the first hint of scandal about the Duke of Wellington, decided George. It was impossible for a man about town to refuse the chance of belonging to a club in a Court where the Duke of Wellington had committed follies.

George was proposed, seconded, and duly elected, together with other new blood. Some of the old blood naturally objected, but the feud was never acute. Solely owing to the impression which his young face made on the powerful and aged hall-porter, George obtained a bedroom. It was small, and at the top of the house; but it was cheap, it solved the even more tiresome and uncomfortable problem of lodging; and further it was a bedroom at Pickering's, and George could say that he lived at his club - an imposing social advantage. He soon learnt how to employ the resources of the club for his own utmost benefit. Nobody could surpass him in choosing a meal inexpensively. He could have his breakfast in his bedroom for tenpence, or even sixpence when his appetite was poor. He was well served by a valet who apparently passed his whole life on stairs and landings. This valet, courteous rather in the style of old Haim, had a brain just equal to the problems presented by his vocation. Every morning George would say: "Now, Downs, how soon can I have my bath?" or "Now, Downs, what can I have for breakfast?" And Downs would conscientiously cerebrate, and come forth after some seconds with sound solutions, such as: "I'll see if I can put you in before Mr. de Gales if you're in a hurry, sir," or "Scrambled eggs, sir - it'll make a bit of a change." And when George agreed, Downs would exhibit a restrained but real satisfaction. Yes, George had been very lucky. The club too was lucky. The oldest member, who being paralysed had not visited the club for eleven years, died and bequeathed ten thousand pounds to the institution where he had happily played cards for several decades. Pickering's was refurnished, and the stringency of its rules re-established. The right wing of the committee wished that the oldest member could have managed to die a year or two earlier and so obviated the crisis. It was recognized, however, by the more reasonable, that you cannot have everything in this world.

Pickering's was very dull; but it was still Pickering's. George was often bored at Pickering's. He soon reached the stage at which a club member asserts gloomily that the club cookery is simply damnable. Nevertheless he would have been desolated to leave Pickering's. The place was useful to him in another respect than the purely material. He learnt there the code which governs the familiar relations of men about town.

On the night of the Cafe Royal dinner, George and Lucas reclined in two easy chairs in the inner smoking-room of Pickering's. They were alone. Through the wide archway that marked the division between the inner and the outer smoking-rooms they could see one solitary old gentleman dozing in an attitude of abandonment, a magazine on his knees. Ash-trays were full of ash and cigarette ends and matches. Newspapers were scattered around, some folded inside out, some not folded, some whose component sheets had been divided for ever like the members of a ruined family. The windows were open, and one gave a view of the Court's watchful lamp-post, and the other of the house - now occupied by an art dealer and a commission agent - where the Duke had known both illusion and disillusion. The delicate sound of the collision of billiard-balls came from somewhere, and the rat-tatting of a tape-machine from somewhere else. The two friends had arrived at the condition of absolute wisdom and sagacity and tolerance which is apt to be achieved at a late hour in clubs by young and old men who have discussed at length the phenomena of society.

"Well, I must be toddling," said Lucas, yawning as he looked idly at the coloured horses on each wall who were for ever passing winning-posts or soaring over bullfinches or throwing riders into brooks.

"Here! Hold on!" George protested. "It's early."

"Is it?"

They began again to smoke and talk.

"Nice little thing, What's-her-name! What's her funny name?"

"Laurencine, do you mean? Yes." Lucas spoke coldly, with a careful indifference. George, to whom insight had not been denied, understood that Everard did not altogether care for Laurencine to be referred to as a little thing, that he had rendered Laurencine sacred by his secret approval.

"I say," said George, sitting up slightly, and increasing the intimacy of his tone, "devilish odd, wasn't it, that the Wheeler woman didn't ask us up?"

Hitherto they had avoided this question in their profound gossip. It had lain between them untouched, like a substance possibly dangerous and explosive. Yet they could not have parted without touching it, and George, with characteristic moral courage or rashness, had touched it first. Lucas was of a mind to reply succinctly that the Wheeler woman's conduct was not a bit devilish odd. But sincerity won. The dismissal at the entrance to the Mansions had affected him somewhat deeply. It had impaired the perfection of his most notable triumph. The temptation to release his feelings was too strong.

"Well, if you ask me," he answered, it was. After a little pause he went on:

"Especially seeing that she practically asked me to ask them to dinner." His nice features loosened to dissatisfaction. "The deuce she did!"

"Yes! Practically asked me! Anyhow, gave me the tip What can you do?" He implied that, far from deriving unique and unhoped-for glory from the condescension of Irene Wheeler in consenting to dine with him, he had conferred a favour on her by his invitation. He implied that brilliant women all over London competed for his invitations. His manner was entirely serious; it probably deceived even himself. George's manner corresponded, instinctively, chivalrously; but George was not deceived - at any rate in the subconscious depth of his mind.

"Exactly!" murmured George.

"Yes" said Lucas. "She said: 'I could bring Laurencine with me, if you can get another man. That would make a four.' She said she wanted to wake Laurencine up."

"Did you tell her you should ask me?" George questioned.

"Oh! She seemed to know all about you, my boy."

"Well, but she couldn't know all about me," said George insincerely. "Well, if you want to know then, she suggested I should ask you."

"But she'd never seen me!"

"She's heard of you. Mrs. Orgreave, I expect."

"Odd!... Odd!" George now pretended to be academically assessing an announcement that had no intrinsic interest for him. In reality he was greatly excited.

"Well you know what those sort of women are!" Lucas summed up wisely, as if referring to truths of knowledge common among men of their kidney.

"Oh, of course!"

The magazine slid from the knees of the sleeper. The sleeper snorted and woke up. The spell was broken. Lucas rose suddenly. "Bye-bye!" He was giving an ultimatum as to his departure.

George rose also, but slowly. "All that doesn't explain why she didn't ask us up," said he. But in his heart he thought he knew why Miss Wheeler hadn't asked them up. The reason was that she maliciously wanted to tantalize him, George. She had roused his curiosity about Lois, and then she had said to herself: "You think you're going to see her tonight, but you just aren't." Such, according to George, was Irene Wheeler the illustrious. He reflected on the exasperating affair until he had undressed and got into bed. But as soon as he had put out the light Marguerite appeared before him, and at the back of her were the examiners for the Final. He slept ill.

7

THE RUPTURE

During the whole of the next day George waited for a letter from Marguerite. There was nothing at the club by the first post; he went to the office, hoping that as he had addressed his telegram from Russell Square she might have written to Russell Square; there was nothing at Russell Square. At lunch-time no word had arrived at the club; when the office closed no word had arrived at the office; the last post brought nothing to the club. He might have sent another telegram to Alexandra Grove, but he was too proud to do so. He dined alone and most miserably at the club. Inspired by unhappiness and resentment, he resolved to go to bed; in bed he might read himself to sleep. But in the hall of the club his feet faltered. Perhaps it was the sight of hats and sticks that made him vacillate, or a glimpse of reluctantly dying silver in the firmament over Candle Court. He wavered; he stood still at the foot of the stairs. The next moment he was in the street. He had decided to call on Agg at the studio. Agg might have the clue to Marguerite's astounding conduct, though he had it not. He took a hansom, after saying he would walk; he was too impatient for walking. Possibly Marguerite would be at the studio; possibly a letter of hers had miscarried; letters did miscarry. He was in a state of peculiar excitement as he paid the cabman - an enigma to himself.

The studio was quite dark. Other studios showed lights, but not Agg's. From one studio came the sound of a mandolin - he thought it was a mandolin - and the sound seemed pathetic, tragic, to his ears. Agg was perhaps in bed; he might safely arouse her; she would not object. But no! He would not do that. Pride again! It would be too humiliating for him, the affianced, to have to ask Agg: "I say, do you know anything about Marguerite?" The affianced ought to be the leading authority as to the doings of Marguerite. He turned away, walked a little, and perceived the cabman swinging himself cautiously down from his perch in order to enter a public-house. He turned back. Marguerite too might be in bed at the studio. Or the girls might be sitting in the dark, talking - a habit of theirs.... Fanciful suppositions! At any rate he would not knock at the door of the studio, would not even enter the alley again. What carried him into the Fulham Road and westwards as far as the Workhouse tower and the corner of Alexandra Grove? Feet! But surely the feet of another person, over which he had no control! He went in the lamplit dimness of Alexandra Grove like a thief; he crept into it. The silver had not yet died out of the sky; he could see it across the spaces between the dark houses; it was sad in exactly the same way as the sound of the mandolin had been sad.

What did he mean to do in the Grove? Nothing! He was just walking in it by chance. He could indeed do nothing. For if he rang at No. 8 old Haim would again confront him in the portico. He passed by No. 8 on the opposite side of the road. No light showed, except a very dim glow through the blind of the basement window to the left of the front door. Those feet beneath him strolled across the road. The basement window was wide open. The blind being narrower than the window-frame, he could see, through the railings, into the room within. He saw Marguerite. She was sitting, in an uncomfortable posture, in the rather high-seated arm-chair in which formerly, when the room was her studio, she used to sit at her work. Her head had dropped, on one shoulder. She was asleep. On the table a candle burned. His heart behaved strangely. He flushed. All his flesh tingled. The gate creaked horribly as he tiptoed into the patch of garden. He leaned over the little chasm between the level of the garden and the window, and supported himself with a hand on the lower sash. He pushed the blind sideways with the other hand.

"Marguerite!" in a whisper. Then louder: "Marguerite!"

She did not stir. She was in a deep sleep. Her hands hung limp. Her face was very pale and very fatigued. She liberated the same sadness as the sound of the mandolin and the gleam of silver in the June sky, but it was far more poignant. At the spectacle of those weary and unconscious features and of the soft, bodily form, George's resentment was annihilated. He wondered at his resentment. He was aware of nothing in himself but warm, protective love. Tenderness surged out from the impenetrable secrecy of his heart, filled him, overflowed, and floated in waves towards the sleeper. In the intense sadness, and in the uncertainty of events, he was happy.

An older man might have paused, but without hesitancy George put his foot on the window-sill, pushed down the window farther, and clambered into the room in which he had first seen Marguerite. His hat, pressing backward the blind, fell off and bounced its hard felt on the floor, which at the edges was uncarpeted. The noise of the hat and the general stir of George's infraction disturbed Marguerite, who awoke and looked up. The melancholy which she was exhaling suddenly vanished. Her steady composure in the alarm delighted George.

"Couldn't wake you," he murmured lightly. It was part of his Five Towns upbringing to conceal excitement. "Saw you through the window."

"Oh! George! Was I asleep?"

Pleasure shone on her face. He deposited his stick and sprang to her. He sat on the arm of the chair. He bent her head back and examined her face. He sat on her knee and held her. She did not kiss; she was kissed; he liked that. Her fatigue was adorable.

"I came here for something, and I just sat down for a second because I was so tired, and I must have gone right off.... No! No!"

The admonishing negative was to stop him from getting up off her knee. She was exhausted, yet she had vast resources of strength to bear him on her knee. She was wearing her oldest frock. It was shabby. But it exquisitely suited her then. It was the frock of her capability, of her great labours, of her vigil, of her fatigue. It covered, but did not hide, her beautiful contours. He thought she was marvellously beautiful - and very young, far younger than himself. As for him, he was the dandy, in striking contrast to her. His dandyism as he sat on her knee pleased both of them. He looked older than his years, his shoulders had broadened, his dark moustache thickened. In his own view he was utterly adult, as she was in hers. But their young faces so close together, so confident, were touchingly immature. As he observed her grave satisfaction at his presence, the comfort which he gave her, he felt sure of her, and the memory of his just resentment came to him, and he was tenderly reproachful.

"I expected to hear from you," he said. The male in him relished the delicate accusation of his tone.

Marguerite answered with a little startled intake of breath:

"She's dead!"

"Dead?"

"She died this afternoon. The layer-out left about half an hour ago."

Death parted them. He rose from her knee, and Marguerite did not try to prevent him. He was profoundly shocked. With desolating vividness he recalled the Sunday afternoon when he had carried upstairs the plump, living woman now dead. He had always liked Mrs. Lob - it was as Mrs. Lob that he thought of her. He had seen not much of her. Only on that Sunday afternoon had he and she reached a sort of intimacy - unspoken but real. He had liked her. He had even admired her. She was no ordinary being. And he had sympathized with her for Marguerite's quite explicable defection. He had often wished that those two, the charwoman and his beloved, could somehow have been brought together. The menaces of death had brought them together. Mrs. Lob was laid out in the bedroom which he had once entered. Mrs. Lob had been dying while he dined richly with Miss Wheeler and Laurencine, and while he talked cynically with Everard Lucas. And while he had been resenting Marguerite's neglect Marguerite was watching by the dying bed. Oh! The despicable superficialities of restaurants and clubs! He was ashamed. The mere receding shadow of death shamed him.

"The baby's dead too, of course," Marguerite added. "She ought never to have had a baby. It seems she had had two miscarriages."

There were tears in Marguerite's eyes and in her voice. Nevertheless her tone was rather matter-of-fact as she related these recondite and sinister things. George thought that women were very strange. Imagine Marguerite quietly talking to him in this strain! Then the sense of the formidable secrets that lie hidden in the history of families, and the sense of the continuity of individual destinies, overwhelmed him. There was silence.

"And your exam. begins tomorrow," whispered the astonishing Marguerite.

"Where's the old gentleman?"

"He's sitting in the parlour in the dark."

It was a terrible house: they two intimidated and mournful in the basement; the widower solitary on the ground floor; the dead bodies, the wastage and futility of conception and long bearing, up in the bedroom. And in all the house the light of one candle! George suddenly noticed, then, that Marguerite was not wearing the thin, delicate ring which he had long ago given her. Had she removed it because of her manual duties? He wanted to ask the question, but, even unspoken, it seemed too trivial for the hour....

There was a shuffling sound beyond the door, and a groping on the outer face of the door. Marguerite jumped up. Mr. Haim stumbled into the room. He had incredibly aged; he looked incredibly feeble. But as he pointed a finger at George he was in a fury of anger, and his anger was senile, ridiculous, awful.

"I thought I heard voices," he said, half squeaking. "How did you get in? You didn't come in by the door. Out of my house! My wife lying dead upstairs, and you choose this night to break in!" He was implacable against George, absolutely; and George recoiled.

The opening of the door had created a draught in which the candle-flame trembled, and the shadow of the old man trembled on the door.

"You'd better go. I'll write. I'll write," Marguerite murmured to George very calmly, very gently, very persuasively. She stood between the two men. Her manner was perfect. It eternally impressed itself on George. "Father, come and sit down."

The old man obeyed her. So did George. He snatched his hat and stick. By the familiar stone steps of the basement, and along the familiar hall, he felt his way to the door, turned the familiar knob, and departed.

2

The examination began the next day. Despite his preoccupation about Marguerite, George's performances during the first days were quite satisfactory to himself. Indeed, after a few minutes in the examination-room, after the preliminary critical assessing of the difficulty of the problems in design, and the questions, and of his ability to deal with them, George successfully forgot everything except the great seven-day duel between the self-constituted autocratic authorities backed by prestige and force, and the aspirants who had naught but their wits to help them. He was neither a son, nor a friend, nor a lover; he ceased to have human ties; he had become an examinee. Marguerite wrote him two short letters which were perfect, save that he always regarded her handwriting as a little too clerical, too like her father's. She made no reference whatever to the scene in the basement room. She said that she could not easily arrange to see him immediately, and that for the sake of his exam. he ought not to be distracted. She would have seen him on the Saturday, but on Saturday George learnt that her father was a little unwell and required, even if he did not need, constant attention. The funeral, unduly late, occurred by Mr. Haim's special desire on the Sunday, most of which day George spent with Everard Lucas. On the Monday he had a rendezvous at eight o'clock with Marguerite at the studio.

She opened the door herself; and her welcome was divine. Her gestures spoke, delicate, and yet robust in their candour. But she was in deep mourning.

"Oh!" he said, holding her. "You're wearing black, then."

"Of course!" she answered sweetly. "You see, I had to be there all through the funeral. And father would have been frightfully shocked if I hadn't been in black - naturally."

"Of course!" he agreed. It was ridiculous that he should be surprised and somewhat aggrieved to find her in mourning; still, he was surprised and somewhat aggrieved.

"Besides - " she added vaguely.

And that 'besides' disquieted him, and confirmed his grievance. Why should she wear mourning for a woman to whom she was not related, whom she had known simply as a charwoman, and who had forced her to leave her father's house? There was no tie between Marguerite and her stepmother. George, for his part, had liked the dead woman, but Marguerite had not even liked her. No, she was not wearing black in honour of the dead, but to humour the living. And why should her father be humoured? George privately admitted the unreasonableness, the unsoundness, of these considerations - obviously mourning wear was imperative for Marguerite - nevertheless they were present in his mind.

"That frock's a bit tight, but it suits you," he said, advancing with her into the studio.

"It's an old one," she smiled.

"An old one?"

"It's one I had for mother."

He had forgotten that she had had a mother, that she had known what grief was, only a very few years earlier. He resented these bereavements and the atmosphere which they disengaged. He wanted a different atmosphere.

"Is the exam. really all right?" she appealed to him, taking both his hands and leaning against him and looking up into his face.

"What did I tell you in my letter?"

"Yes, I know."

"The exam. is as right as rain."

"I knew it would be."

"You didn't," he laughed. He imitated her: "'Is the exam. really all right?'" She just smiled. He went on confidently: "Of course you never know your luck, you know. There's the viva tomorrow.... Where's old Agg?"

"She's gone home."

"Thoughtful child! How soon will she be back?"

"About nine," said Marguerite, apparently unaware that George was being funny.

"Nine!"

"Oh, George!" Marguerite exclaimed, breaking away from him. "I'm awfully sorry, but I must get on with my packing."

"What packing?"

"I have to take my things home."

"What home?"

"Father's, I mean."

She was going to live with her father, who would not willingly allow him, George, to enter the house! How astounding girls were! She had written to him twice without giving the least hint of her resolve. He had to learn it as it were incidentally, through the urgency of packing. She did not tell him she was going - she said she must get on with her packing! And there, lying on the floor, was an open trunk; and two of her drawing-boards already had string round them.

George inquired:

"How is the old man - to-day?"

"He's very nervy," said Marguerite briefly and significantly. "I'd better light the lamp; I shall see better." She seemed to be speaking to herself. She stood on a chair and lifted the chimney off the central lamp. George absently passed her his box of matches.

As she, was replacing the chimney, he said suddenly in a very resolute

109

tone:

"This is all very well, Marguerite. But it's going to be jolly awkward for me."

She jumped lightly down from the chair, like a little girl.

"Oh! George! I know!" she cried. "It will be awkward for both of us. But we shall arrange something." She might have resented his tone. She might have impulsively defended herself. But she did not. She accepted his attitude with unreserved benevolence. Her gaze was marvellously sympathetic.

"I can't make out what your father's got against me," said George angrily, building his vexation on her benevolence. "What have I done, I should like to know."

"It's simply because you lived there all that time without him knowing we were engaged. He says if he'd known he would never have let you stay there a day." She smiled, mournfully, forgivingly, excusingly.

"But it's preposterous!"

"Oh! It is."

"And how does he behave to you? Is he treating you decently?"

"Oh! Fairly. You see, he's got a lot to get over. And he's most frightfully upset about - his wife. Well, you saw him yourself, didn't you?"

"That's no reason why he should treat you badly."

"But he doesn't, George!"

"Oh! I know! I know! Do you think I don't know? He's not even decent to you. I can hear it in your voice. Why should you go back and live with him if he isn't prepared to appreciate it?"

"But he expects it, George. And what am I to do? He's all alone. I can't leave him all alone, can I?"

George burst out:

"I tell you what it is. Marguerite. You're too good-natured. That's what it is. You're too good-natured. And it's a very bad thing."

Tears came into her eyes; she could not control them. She was grieved by his remark.

"I'm not, George, truly. You must remember father's been through a lot this last week. So have I."

"I know! I know! I admit all that. But you're too good-natured, and I'll stick to it."

She was smiling again.

"You only think that because you're fond of me. Nobody else would say it, and I'm not. Help me to lift this trunk on to the chest."

While the daylight withdrew, and the smell of the lamp strengthened and then faded, and the shadows cast by the lamp-rays grew blacker, she went on rapidly with her packing, he serving her at intervals. They said little. His lower lip fell lower and lower. The evening was immensely, horribly different from what he had expected and hoped for. He felt once more the inescapable grip of destiny fastening upon him.

"Why are you in such a hurry?" he asked, after a long time.

"I told father I should be back at a quarter-past nine."

This statement threw George into a condition of total dark disgust. He made no remark. But what remarks he could have made - sarcastic, bitter, unanswerable! Why indeed in the name of heaven should she promise her father to be back at a quarter-past nine, or at a quarter-past anything? Was she a servant? Had she no rights? Had he himself, George, no rights?

A little before nine Agg arrived. Marguerite was fastening the trunk.

"Now be sure, Agg," said Marguerite. "Don't forget to hang out the Carter Paterson card at the end of the alley tomorrow morning. I must have these things at home tomorrow night for certain. The labels are on. And here's twopence for the man."

"Do I forget?" retorted Agg cheerfully. "By the way, George, I want to talk to you." She turned to Marguerite and repeated in quite a different voice: "I want to talk to him, dear, tonight. Do, let him stay. Will you?"

Marguerite gave a puzzled assent.

"I'll call after I've taken Marguerite to Alexandra Grove, Agg - on my way back to the club."

"Oh no, you won't!" said Agg. "I shall be gone to bed then. Look at that portrait and see how I've worked. My family's concerned about me. It wants me to go away for a holiday."

George had not till then noticed the portrait at all.

"But I must take Marguerite along to the Grove," he insisted. "She can't go alone."

"And why can't she go alone? What sort of a conventional world do you think you live in? Don't girls go home alone? Don't they come in alone? Don't I? Anybody would think, to listen to some people, that the purdah flourished in Chelsea. But it's all pretence. I don't ask for the honour of a private interview with you every night. You've both of you got all your lives before you. And for once in a way Marguerite's going out alone. At least, you can take her to the street, I don't mind that. But don't be outside more than a minute."

Agg, who had sat down, rose and slowly removed her small hat. With pins in her mouth she said something about the luggage to Marguerite.

"All right! All right!" George surrendered gloomily. In truth he was not sorry to let Marguerite depart solitary. And Agg's demeanour was very peculiar; he would have been almost afraid to be too obstinate in denying her request. He had never seen her hysterical, but a suspicion took him that she might be capable of hysteria.... You never knew, with that kind of girl, he thought sagaciously.

In the darkness of the alley George said to Marguerite, feigning irritation: "What on earth does she want?"

"Agg? Oh! It's probably nothing. She does get excited sometimes, you know."

The two girls had parted with strange, hard demonstrations of affection from Agg.

"I suppose you'll write," said George coldly.

"Tomorrow, darling," she replied quite simply and gravely.

Her kiss was warm, complete, faithful, very loving, very sympathetic. Nothing in her demeanour as she left him showed that George had received it in a non-committal manner. Yet she must have noticed his wounded reserve. He did not like such duplicity. He would have preferred her to be less miraculously angelic.

When he re-entered the studio, Agg, who very seldom smoked, was puffing violently at a cigarette. She reclined on one elbow on the settee, her eyes fixed on the portrait of herself. George was really perturbed by the baffling queerness of the scenes through which he was passing.

"Look here, infant-in-arms," she began immediately. "I only wanted to say two words to you about Marguerite. Can you stand it?"

There was a pause. George walked in front of her, hiding the easel.

"Yes," he said gruffly.

"Well, Marguerite's a magnificent girl. She's extraordinarily capable. You'd think she could look after herself as well as anyone. But she can't. I know her far better than you do. She needs looking after. She'll make a fool of herself if she isn't handled."

"How do you mean?"

"You know how I mean."

"D'you mean about the old man?"

"I mean about the perfectly horrid old man.... Ah! If I was in your place, if I was a man," she said passionately, "do you know what I should do with Marguerite? I should carry her off. I should run away with her. I should drag her out of the house, and she should know what a real man was. I'm not going to discuss her with you. I'm not going to say any more at all. I'm off to bed. But before you go, I do think you might tell me my portrait's a pretty good thing."

And she did not say any more.

3

The written part of the examination lasted four days; and then there was an interval of one day in which the harassed and harried aspirants might restore themselves for the two days' ordeal of the viva voce. George had continued to be well satisfied with his work up to the interval. He considered that he had perfectly succeeded in separating the lover and the examinee, and that nothing foreign to the examination could vitiate his activity therein. It was on the day of repose, a Wednesday, that a doubt suddenly occurred to him as to the correctness of his answer, in the "Construction" paper, to a question which began with the following formidable words: "A girder, freely supported at each end and forty feet long, carries a load of six tons at a distance of six feet from one end and another load of ten tons - " Thus it went on for ten lines. He had always been impatient of detail, and he hated every kind of calculation. Nevertheless he held that calculations were relatively easy, and that he could do them as well as the driest duffer in the profession when he set his mind to them. But the doubt as to the correctness of his answer developed into a certainty. Facing the question in private again, he obtained four different solutions in an hour; it was John Orgreave who ultimately set him right, convicting him of a most elementary misconception. Forthwith his faith in his whole "Construction" paper vanished. He grumbled that it was monstrous to give candidates an unbroken stretch of four hours' work at the end of a four-day effort. Yet earlier he had been boasting that he had not felt the slightest fatigue. He had expected to see Marguerite on the day of repose. He did not see her. She had offered no appointment, and he said to himself that he had not the slightest intention of running after her. Such had become the attitude of the lover to the beloved.

On the Thursday morning, however, he felt fit enough to face a dozen oral examiners, and he performed his morning exercises in the club bedroom with a positive ferocity of vigour. And then he was gradually overtaken by a black moodiness which he could not explain. He had passed through similar though less acute moods as a boy; but this was the first of the inexplicable sombre humours which at moments darkened his manhood. He had not the least suspicion that prolonged nervous tension due to two distinct causes had nearly worn him out. He was melancholy, and his melancholy increased. But he was proud; he was defiant. His self-confidence, as he looked back at the years of genuine hard study behind him, was complete. He disdained examiners. He knew that with all their damnable ingenuity they could not floor him.

The crisis arrived in the afternoon of the first of the two days. His brain was quite clear. Thousands of details about drainage, ventilation, shoring, architectural practice, lighting, subsoils, specifications, iron and steel construction, under-pinning, the properties of building materials, strains, thrusts, water-supply; thousands of details about his designs - the designs in his 'testimonies of study,' the design for his Thesis, and the designs produced during the examination itself - all these peopled his brain; but they were in order; they were under control; they were his slaves. For four and a half hours, off and on, he had admirably displayed the reality of his knowledge, and then he was sent into a fresh room to meet a fresh examiner. There he stood in the room alone with his designs for a small provincial town hall - a key-plan, several one-eighth scale-plans, a piece of half-inch detail, and two rough perspective sketches which he knew were brilliant. The room was hot; through the open window came the distant sound of the traffic of Regent Street. The strange melancholy of a city in summer floated towards him from the outside and reinforced his own.

The examiner, who had been snatching tea, entered briskly and sternly. He was a small, dapper, fair man of about fifty, with wonderfully tended finger-nails. George despised him because Mr. Enwright despised him, but he had met him once in the way of the firm's business and found him urbane.

"Good afternoon," said George politely.

The examiner replied, trotting along the length of the desk with quick, short steps:

"Now about this work of yours. I've looked at it with some care - " His speech was like his demeanour and his finger-nails.

"Boor!" thought George. But he could not actively resent the slight. He glanced round at the walls; he was in a prison. He was at the mercy of a tyrant invested with omnipotence.

The little tyrant, however, was superficially affable. Only now and then in his prim, courteous voice was there a hint of hostility and cruelty. He put a number of questions, the answers to which had to be George's justification. He said "H'm!" and "Ah!" and "Really?" He came to the matter of spouting.

"Now, I object to hopper-heads," he said. "I regard them as unhygienic."

And he looked coldly at George with eyebrows lifted. George returned the gaze.

"I know you do, sir," George replied.

Indeed it was notorious that hopper-heads to vertical spouting were a special antipathy of the examiner's; he was a famous faddist. But the reply was a mistake. The examiner, secure in his attributes, ignored the sally. A little later, taking up the general plan of the town hall, he said:

"The fact is, I do - not - care for this kind of thing. The whole tendency - "

"Excuse me, sir," George interrupted, with conscious and elaborate respectfulness. "But surely the question isn't one of personal preferences. Is the design good or is it bad?"

"Well, I call it bad," said the examiner, showing testiness. The examiner too could be impulsive, was indeed apt to be short-tempered. The next instant he seized one of the brilliant perspective sketches, and by his mere manner of holding it between his thumb and finger he sneered at it and condemned it.

He snapped out, not angrily - rather pityingly:

"And what the devil's this?"

George, furious, retorted:

114

"What the hell do you think it is?"

He had not foreseen that he was going to say such a thing. The traffic in Regent Street, which had been inaudible to both of them, was loud in their ears.

The examiner had committed a peccadillo, George a terrible crime. The next morning the episode, in various forms, was somehow common knowledge and a source of immense diversion. George went through the second day, but lifelessly. He was sure he had failed. Apart from the significance of the fact that the viva voce counted for 550 marks out of a total of 1200, he felt that the Royal Institute of British Architects would know how to defend its dignity. On the Saturday morning John Orgreave had positive secret information that George would be plucked.

4

On that same Saturday afternoon George and Marguerite went out together. She had given him a rendezvous in Brompton Cemetery, choosing this spot partly because it was conveniently near and partly in unconscious obedience to the traditional instinct of lovers for the society of the undisturbing dead. Each of them had a roofed habitation, but neither could employ it for the ends of love. No. 8 was barred to George as much by his own dignity as by the invisible sword of the old man; and of course he could not break the immemorial savage taboo of a club by introducing a girl into it. The Duke of Wellington himself, though Candle Court was his purdah, could never have broken the taboo of even so modest a club as Pickering's. Owing to the absence of Agg, who had gone to Wales with part of her family, the studio in Manresa Road was equally closed to the pair.

Marguerite was first at the rendezvous. George saw her walking sedately near the entrance. Despite her sedateness she had unmistakably the air of waiting at a tryst. Anybody at a glance would have said that she was expecting a man. She had the classical demure innocency of her situation. George did not care for that. Why? She in fact was expecting a man, and in expecting him she had nothing to be ashamed of. Well, he did not care for it. He did not care for her being like other girls of her class. In his pocket he had an invitation from Miss Wheeler for the next evening. Would Miss Wheeler wait for a man in a public place, especially a cemetery? Would Lois Ingram? Would Laurencine? He could not picture them so waiting. Oh, simpleton, unlearned in the world! A snob too, no doubt! (He actually thought that Hyde Park would have been 'better' than the cemetery for their rendezvous.) And illogical! If No. 8 had been open to them, and the studio, and the club, he would have accepted with gusto the idea of an open-air rendezvous. But since there was no alternative to an open-air rendezvous the idea of it humiliated and repelled him.

Further, in addition to her culpable demure innocency, Marguerite was wearing black. Of course she was. She had no choice. Still, he hated her mourning. Moreover, she was too modest; she did not impose herself. Some girls wore mourning with splendid defiance. Marguerite seemed to apologize; seemed to turn the other cheek to death.... He arrived critical, and naturally he found matter to criticize.

Her greeting showed quite candidly the pleasure she had in the sight of him. Her heart was in the hand she gave him; he felt its mystic throbbings there.

"How are things?" he began. "I rather thought I should have been hearing from you." He softened his voice to match the tenderness of her smile, but he did it consciously.

She replied:

"I thought you'd have enough to worry about with the exam. without me."

It was not a wise speech, because it implied that he was capable of being worried, of being disturbed in the effort of absorption necessary for the examination. He laughed a little harshly.

"Well, you see the result!"

He had written to tell her of the disastrous incident and that failure was a certainty; a sort of shame had made him recoil from telling her to her face; it was easier to be casual in writing than in talking; the letter had at any rate tempered for both of them the shock of communication. Now, he was out of humour with her because he had played the ass with an ass of an examiner - not because she was directly or indirectly responsible for his doing so; simply because he had done so. She was the woman. It was true that she in part was indirectly responsible for the calamity, but he did not believe it, and anyhow would never have admitted it.

"Oh! George! What a shame it was!" As usual, not a trace of reproach from her: an absolute conviction that he was entirely blameless. "What shall you do? You'll have to sit again."

"Sit again? Me?" he exclaimed haughtily. "I never shall! I've done with exams." He meant it.

"But - shall you give up architecture, then?"

"Certainly not! My dear girl, what are you thinking of? Of course I shan't give up architecture. But you needn't pass any exams, to be an architect. Anybody can call himself an architect, and be an architect, without passing exams. Exams. are optional. That's what makes old Enwright so cross with our beautiful profession."

He laughed again harshly. All the time, beneath his quite genuine defiance, he was thinking what an idiot he had been to cheek the examiner, and how staggeringly simple it was to ruin years of industry by one impulsive moment's folly, and how iniquitous was a world in which such injustice could be.

Marguerite was puzzled. In her ignorance she had imagined that professions were inseparably connected with examinations. However, she had to find faith to accept his dictum, and she found it.

"Now about this afternoon," he said. "I vote we take a steamboat down the river. I've made up my mind I must have a look at Greenwich again from the water. And we both need a blow."

"But won't it take a long time?" she mildly objected.

He turned on her violently, and spoke as he had never spoken:

"What if it does?"

He knew that she was thinking of her infernal father, and he would not have it. He remembered all that Agg had said. Assuredly Agg had shown nerve, too much nerve, to tackle him in the way she did, and the more he reflected upon Agg's interference the more he resented it as impertinent. Still, Agg had happened to talk sense.

"Oh, nothing!" Marguerite agreed quickly, fearfully. "I should like to go. I've never been. Do we go to Chelsea Pier? Down Fernshaw Road will be the nearest."

"We'll go down Beaufort Street," he decided. He divined that she had suggested Fernshaw Road in order to avoid passing the end of the Grove, where her father might conceivably see them. Well, he was not going out of his way to avoid her father. Nay, he was going slightly out of his way in order to give her father every chance of beholding them together.

Although the day was Saturday there was no stir on Chelsea Pier. The pier-keeper, indeed, was alone on the pier, which rose high on the urgent flood-tide, so that the gangway to it sloped unusually upwards. No steamer was in sight, and it seemed impossible that any steamer should ever call at that forlorn and decrepit platform that trembled under the straining of the water. Nevertheless, a steamer did after a little while appear round the bend, in Battersea Reach; she dropped her funnel, aimed her sharp nose at an arch of Battersea Bridge, and finally, poising herself against the strong stream, bumped very gently and neatly into contact with the pier. The pier-keeper went through all the classic motions of mooring, unbarring, barring, and casting off, and in a few seconds the throbbing steamer, which was named with the name of a great Londoner, left the pier again with George and Marguerite on board. Nobody had disembarked. The shallow and handsome craft, flying its gay flags, crossed and recrossed the river, calling at three piers in the space of a few minutes; but all the piers were like Chelsea Pier; all the pier-keepers had the air of castaways upon shaking islets. The passengers on the steamer would not have filled a motor-bus, and they carried themselves like melancholy adventurers who have begun to doubt the authenticity of the inspiration which sent them on a mysterious quest. Such was travel on the Thames in the years immediately before Londoners came to a final decision that the Thames was meet to be ignored by the genteel town which it had begotten.

George and Marguerite sat close together near the prow, saying little, the one waiting to spring, the other to suffer onslaught. It was in Lambeth Reach that the broad, brimming river challenged and seized George's imagination. A gusty, warm, south-west wind met the rushing tide and blew it up into foamy waves. The wind was powerful, but the tide was irresistible. Far away, Land's End having divided the Atlantic surge, that same wind was furiously driving vast waters up the English Channel and round the Forelands, and also vast waters up the west coast of Britain. The twin surges had met again in the outer estuary of the Thames and joined their terrific impulses to defy the very wind which had given them strength, and the mighty flux swept with unregarding power through the mushroom city whose existence on its banks was a transient episode in the everlasting life of the river.

The river seemed to threaten the city that had confined it in stone. And George, in the background of his mind, which was obsessed by the tormenting enigma of the girl by his side, also threatened the city. With the uncompromising arrogance of the student who has newly acquired critical ideas, he estimated and judged it. He cursed the Tate Gallery and utterly damned Doulton's works. He sternly approved Lambeth Palace, the Houses of Parliament, Westminster Abbey, Somerset House, Waterloo Bridge, and St. Paul's. He cursed St. Thomas's Hospital and the hotels. He patronized New Scotland Yard. The "Isambard Brunel" penetrated more and more into the heart of the city, fighting for every yard of her progress. Flags stood out straight in the blue sky traversed by swift white clouds. Huge rudder-less barges, each with a dwarf in the stern struggling at a giant's oar, were borne westwards broadside on like straws upon the surface of a hurrying brook. A launch with an orchestra on board flew gaily past. Tugs with a serpentine tail of craft threaded perilously through the increasing traffic. Railway trains, cabs, coloured omnibuses, cyclists, and footfarers mingled in and complicated the scene. Then the first ocean-going steamer appeared, belittling all else. And then the calm, pale beauty of the custom-house at last humbled George, and for an instant made him think that he could never do anything worth doing. His pride leapt up, unconquerable. The ocean-going steamers, as they multiplied on the river, roused in him wild and painful longings to rush to the ends of the earth and gorge himself on the immense feast which the great romantic earth had to offer.

"By Jove!" he exclaimed passionately. "I'd give something to go to Japan."

"Would you?" Marguerite answered with mildness. She had not the least notion of what he was feeling. Her voice responded to him, but her imagination did not respond. True, as he had always known, she had no ambition! The critical quality of his mood developed. The imperious impulse came to take her to task.

"What's the latest about your father?" he asked, with a touch of impatient, aggrieved disdain. Both were aware that the words had opened a crucial interview between them. She moved nervously on the seat. The benches that ran along the deck-rails met in an acute angle at the stem of the steamer, so that the pair sat opposite each other with their knees almost touching. He went on: "I hear he hasn't gone back to the office yet."

"No," said Marguerite. "But he'll start again on Monday, I think."

"But is he fit to go back? I thought he looked awful."

She flushed slightly - at the indirect reference to the episode in the basement on the night of the death.

"It will do him good to go back," said Marguerite. "I'm sure he misses the office dreadfully."

George gazed at her person. Under the thin glove he suddenly detected the form of her ring. She was wearing it again, then. (He could not remember whether she had worn it at their last meeting, in Agg's studio. The very curious fact was that at their last meeting he had forgotten to look for the ring.) Not only was she wearing the ring, but she carried a stylish little handbag which he had given her. When he bought that bag, in the Burlington Arcade, it had been a bag like any other bag. But now it had become part of her, individualized by her personality, a mysterious and provocative bag. Everything she wore, down to her boots and even her bootlaces so neatly threaded and knotted, was mysterious and provocative. He examined her face. It was marvellously beautiful; it was ordinary; it was marvellously beautiful. He knew her to the depths; he did not know her at all; she was a chance acquaintance; she was a complete stranger.

"How are you getting on with him? You know you really ought to tell me."

"Oh, George!" she said, earnestly vivacious. "You're wrong in thinking he's not nice to me. He is He's quite forgiven me."

"Forgiven you!" George took her up. "I should like to know what he had to forgive."

"Well," she murmured timorously. "You understand what I mean."

He drummed his elegant feet on the striated deck. Out of the corner of his left eye he saw the mediaeval shape of the Tower rapidly disappearing. In front were the variegated funnels and masts of fleets gathered together in St. Katherine's Dock and London Dock. The steamer gained speed as she headed from Cherry Gardens Pier towards the middle of the river. She was a frail trifle compared with the big boats that lined the wharves; but in herself she had size and irresistible force, travelling quite smoothly over the short, riotous, sparkling waves which her cut-water divided and spurned away on either side. Only a tremor faintly vibrated throughout her being.

"Has he forgiven you for being engaged?" George demanded, with rough sarcasm.

She showed no resentment of his tone, but replied gently:

"I did try to mention it once, but it was no use - he wasn't in a condition. He made me quite afraid - not for me of course, but for him."

"Well, I give it up!" said George. "I simply give it up! It's past me. How soon's he going to be in condition? He can't keep us walking about the streets for ever."

"No, of course not!" She smiled to placate him.

There was a pause, and then George, his eyes fixed on her hand, remarked:

"I see you've got your ring on."

She too looked at her hand.

"My ring? Naturally. What do you mean?"

He proceeded cruelly:

"I suppose you don't wear it in the house, so that the sight of it shan't annoy him."

She flushed once more.

"Oh, George, dear!" Her glance asked for mercy, for magnanimity.

"Do you wear it when you're in the house, or don't you?"

Her eyes fell.

"I daren't excite him. Truly, I daren't. It wouldn't do. It wouldn't be right."

She was admitting George's haphazard charge against her. He was astounded. But he merely flung back his head and raised his eyebrows. He thought:

"And yet she sticks to it he's nice to her! My God!"

He said nothing aloud. The Royal Hospital, Greenwich, showed itself in the distance like a domed island rising fabulously out of the blue-green water. Even far off, before he could decipher the main contours of the gigantic quadruple pile, the vision excited him. His mind, darkened by the most dreadful apprehensions concerning Marguerite, dwelt on it darkly, sardonically, and yet with pleasure. And he proudly compared his own disillusions with those of his greatest forerunners. His studies, and the example of Mr. Enwright, had inspired him with an extremely enthusiastic worship of Inigo Jones, whom he classed, not without reason, among the great creative artists of Europe. He snorted when he heard the Royal Hospital referred to as the largest and finest charitable institution in the world. For him it was the supreme English architectural work. He snorted at the thought of that pompous and absurd monarch James I ordering Inigo Jones to design him a palace surpassing all palaces and choosing a sublime site therefor, and then doing nothing. He snorted at the thought of that deluded monarch Charles I ordering Inigo Jones to design him a palace surpassing all palaces, and receiving from Inigo Jones the plans of a structure which would have equalled in beauty and eclipsed in grandeur any European structure of the Christian era - even Chambord, even the Escurial, even Versailles - and then accomplishing nothing beyond a tiny fragment of the sublime dream. He snorted at the thought that Inigo Jones had died at the age of nearly eighty ere the foundations of the Greenwich palace had begun to be dug, and without having seen more than the fragment of his unique Whitehall - after a youth spent in arranging masques for a stupid court, and an old age spent in disappointment. But then no English monarch had ever begun and finished a palace. George wished, rather venturesomely, that he had lived under Francis I!...

The largest and finest charitable institution! The ineffable William and Mary had merely turned it into a charitable institution because they did not know what else to do with it. The mighty halls which ought to have resounded to the laughter of the mistresses of Charles II were diverted to the inevitable squalor of almsgiving. The mutilated victims of the egotism and the fatuity of kings were imprisoned there together under the rules and regulations of charity, the cruellest of all rules and regulations. And all was done meanly - that is, all that interested George. Christopher Wren, who was building St. Paul's and fighting libels and slanders at a salary of two hundred a year, came down to Greenwich and for years worked immortally for nothing amid material difficulties that never ceased to multiply; and he too was beaten by the huge monster. Then Vanbrugh arrived and blithely finished in corrupt brick and flaming manifestations of decadence that which the pure and monumental genius of Inigo Jones had first conceived. The north frontages were marvels of beauty; the final erections to the south amounted to an outrage upon Jones and Wren. Still, the affair was the largest and finest charitable institution on earth! What a country, thought George, hugging injustice! So it had treated Jones and Wren and many another. So it had treated Enwright. And so it would treat, was already treating, him, George. He did not care. As the steamer approached Greenwich, and the details of the aborted palace grew clearer, and he could distinguish between the genius of Jones and the genius of Wren, he felt grimly and victoriously sure that both Jones and Wren had had the best of the struggle against indifference and philistinism - as he too would have the best of the struggle, though he should die obscure and in penury. He was miserable and resentful, and yet he was triumphant. The steamer stopped at the town-pier.

"Are we there?" said Marguerite. "Already?"

"Yes," said he. "And I think we may as well go back by the same steamer."

She concurred. However, an official insisted on them disembarking, even if they meant to re-embark at once. They, went ashore. The facade of the palace-hospital stretched majestically to the left of them, in sharp perspective, a sensational spectacle.

"It's very large," Marguerite commented. Her voice was nervous.

"Yes, it's rather more than large," he said dryly.

He would not share his thoughts with her. He knew that she had some inklings of taste, but in that moment he preferred to pretend that her artistic perception was on a level with that of William and Mary. They boarded the steamer again, and took their old places; and the menacing problem of their predicament was still between them.

"We can have some tea downstairs if you like," he said, after the steamer had turned round and started upstream.

She answered in tones imperfectly controlled:

"No, thank you. I feel as if I couldn't swallow anything." And she looked up at him very quickly; with the embryo of a smile, and then looked down again very quickly, because she could not bring the smile to maturity.

George thought:

"Am I going to have a scene with her - on the steamer?" It would not matter much if a scene did occur. There was nobody else on deck forward of the bridge. They were alone - they were more solitary than they might have been in the studio, or in any room at No. 8. The steamer was now nearly heading the wind, but she travelled more smoothly, for she had the last of the flood-tide under her.

George said kindly and persuasively:

"Upon my soul, I don't know what the old gentleman's got against me."

She eagerly accepted his advance, which seemed to give her courage.

"But there's nothing to know, dear. We both know that. There's nothing at all. And yet of course I can understand it. So can you. In fact it was you who first explained it to me. If you'd left No. 8 when I did and he'd heard of our engagement afterwards, he wouldn't have thought anything of it. But it was you staying on in the house that did it, and him not knowing of the engagement. He thought you used to come to see me at nights at the studio, me and Agg, and make fun of everything at No. 8 - especially of his wife. He's evidently got some such idea in his head, and there's no getting it out again."

"But it's childish."

"I know. However, we've said all this before, haven't we?"

"But the idea's got to be got out of his head again!" said George vigorously - more dictatorially and less persuasively than before.

Marguerite offered no remark.

"And after all," George continued, "he couldn't have been so desperately keen on - your stepmother. When he married her your mother hadn't been dead so very long, had she?"

"No. But he never cared for mother anything like so much as he cared for Mrs. Lobley - at least not as far back as I can remember. It was a different sort of thing altogether. I think he was perfectly mad about Mrs. Lobley. Oh! He stood mother's death much - much better than hers! You've no idea - "

"Oh yes, I have. We know all about that sort of thing," said George the man of the world impatiently.

Marguerite said tenderly:

"It's broken him."

"Nonsense!"

"It has, George." Her voice was very soft.

But George would not listen to the softness of her voice.

"Well," he objected firmly and strongly, "supposing it has! What then? We're sorry for him. What then? That affair has nothing to do with our affair. Is all that reason why I shouldn't see you in your own home? Or are we to depend on Agg - when she happens to be at her studio? Or are we always to see each other in the street, or in museums and things - or steamers - just as if you were a shop-girl? We may just as well look facts in the face, you know."

She flushed. Her features changed under emotion.

"Oh! George! I don't know what to do."

"Then you think he's determined not to have anything to do with me?"

She was silent.

"You think he's determined not to have anything to do with me, I say?"

"He may change," Marguerite murmured.

"'May change' be dashed! We've got to know where we stand."

He most surprisingly stood up, staring at her. She did not speak, but she lifted her eyes to his with timid courage. They were wet. George abruptly walked away along the deck. The steamer was passing the custom-house again. The tide had now almost slacked. Fresh and heavier clouds had overcast the sky. All the varied thoughts of the afternoon were active in George's head at once: architecture, architects, beauty, professional injustices, girls - his girl. Each affected the others, for they were deeply entangled. It is a fact that he could not put Inigo Jones and Christopher Wren out of his head; he wondered what had been their experiences with women, histories and textbooks of architecture did not treat of this surely important aspect of architecture! He glanced at Marguerite from the distance. He remembered what Agg had said to him about her; but what Agg had said did not appear to help him practically.... Why had he left Marguerite? Why was he standing thirty feet from her and observing her inimically? He walked back to her, sat down, and said calmly:

"Listen to me, darling. Suppose we arrange now, definitely, to get married in two years' time. How will that do for you?"

"But, George, can you be sure that you'll be able to marry in two years?"

He put his chin forward.

"You needn't worry about that," said he. "You needn't think because I've failed in an exam. I don't know what I'm about. You leave all that to me. In two years I shall be able enough to keep a wife - and well! Now, shall we arrange to get married in two years' time?"

"It might be a fearful drag for you," she said. "Because, you know, I don't really earn very much."

"That's not the point. I don't care what you earn. I shan't want you to earn anything - so far as that goes. Any earning that's wanted I shall be prepared to do. I'll put it like this: Supposing I'm in a position to keep you, shall we arrange to get married in two years' time?" He found a fierce pleasure in reiterating the phrase. "So long as that's understood, I don't mind the rest. If we have to depend on Agg, or meet in the streets - never mind. It'll be an infernal nuisance, but I expect I can stand it as well as you can. Moreover, I quite see your difficulty - quite. And let's hope the old gentleman will begin to have a little sense."

"Oh, George! If he only would!"

He did not like her habit of "Oh, George! Oh! George!"

"Well?" He waited, ignoring her pious aspiration.

"I don't know what to say, George."

He restrained himself.

"We're engaged, aren't we?" She gave no answer, and he repeated: "We're engaged, aren't we?"

"Yes."

"That's all right. Well, will you give me your absolute promise to marry me in two years' time - if I'm in a position to keep you? It's quite simple. You say you don't know what to say. But you've got to know what to say." As he looked at her averted face, his calmness began to leave him.

"Oh, George! I can't promise that!" she burst out, showing at length her emotion. The observant skipper on the bridge noted that there were a boy and a girl forward having a bit of a tiff.

George trembled. All that Agg had said recurred to him once more. But what could he do to act on it? Anger was gaining, on him.

"Why not?" he menaced.

"It would have to depend on how father was. Surely you must see that!"

"Indeed I don't see it. I see quite the contrary. We're engaged. You've got the first call on me, and I've got the first call on you - not your father." The skin over his nose was tight, owing to the sudden swelling of two points, one on either side of the bone.

"George, I couldn't leave him - again. I think now I may have been wrong to leave him before. However, that's over. I couldn't leave him again. It would be very wrong. He'd be all alone."

"Well, then, let him be friends with me."

"I do wish he would."

"Yes. Well, wishing won't do much good. If there's any trouble it's entirely your father's fault. And what I want to know is - will you give me your absolute promise to marry me in two years' time?"

"I can't, George. It wouldn't be honest. I can't! I can't! How can you ask me to throw over my duty to father?"

He rose and walked away again. She was profoundly moved, but no sympathy for her mitigated his resentment. He considered that her attitude was utterly monstrous - monstrous! He could not find a word adequate for it. He was furious; his fury increased with each moment. He returned to the prow, but did not sit down.

"Don't you think, then, you ought to choose between your father and me?" he said in a low, hard voice, standing over her.

"What do you mean?" she faltered.

"What do I mean? It's plain enough what I mean, isn't it? Your father may live twenty years yet. Nobody knows. The older he gets the more obstinate he'll be. We may be kept hanging about for years and years and years. Indefinitely. What's the sense of it? You say you've got your duty, but what's the object of being engaged?"

"Do you want to break it off, George?"

"Now don't put it like that. You know I don't want to break it off. You know I want to marry you. Only you won't, and I'm not going to be made a fool of. I'm absolutely innocent."

"Of course you are!" she agreed eagerly.

"Well, I'm not going to be made a fool of by your father. If we're engaged, you know what it means. Marriage. If it doesn't mean that, then I say we've no right to be engaged."

Marguerite seemed to recoil at the last words, but she recovered herself. And then, heedless of being in a public place, she drew off her glove, and drew the engagement ring from her finger, and held it out to George. She could not speak. The gesture was her language. George was extremely staggered. He was stupefied for an instant. Then he took the ring, and under an uncontrollable savage impulse he threw it into the river. He did not move for a considerable time, staring at the river in front. Neither did she move. At length he said in a cold voice, without moving his head:

"Here's Chelsea Pier."

She got up and walked to the rail amidships. He followed. The steamer moored. A section of rail slid aside. The pier-keeper gave a hand to Marguerite, who jumped on to the pier. George hesitated. The pier-keeper challenged him testily:

"Now then, are ye coming ashore or aren't ye?"

George could not move. The pier-keeper banged the rail to close the gap, and cast off the ropes, and the steamer resumed her voyage.

A minute later George saw Marguerite slowly crossing the gangway from the pier to the embankment. There she went! She was about to be swallowed up in the waste of human dwellings, in the measureless and tragic expanse of the indifferent town.... She was gone. Curse her, with her reliability! She was too reliable. He knew that. Her father could rely on her. Curse her, with her outrageous, incredibly cruel, and unjust sense of duty! She had held him once. Once the sight of her had made him turn hot and cold. Once the prospect of life without her had seemed unbearable. He had loved her instinctively and intensely. He now judged and condemned her. Her beauty, her sweetness, her belief in him, her reliability - these qualities were neutralized by her sense of duty, awful, uncompromising, blind to fundamental justice. The affair was over. If he knew her, he knew also himself. The affair was over. He was in despair. His mind went round and round like a life-prisoner exercising in an enclosed yard. No escape! Till then, he had always believed in his luck. Infantile delusion! He was now aware that destiny had struck him a blow once for all. But of course he did not perceive that he was too young, not ripe, for such a blow. The mark of destiny was on his features, and it was out of place there.... He had lost Marguerite. And what had he lost? What was there in her? She was not brilliant; she had no position; she had neither learning nor wit. He could remember nothing remarkable that they had ever said to each other. Indeed, their conversations had generally been rather banal. But he could remember how they had felt, how he had felt, in their hours together.... The sensation communicated to him by her hand when he had drawn off her glove in the tremendous silence of the hansom! Marvellous, exquisite, magical sensation that no words of his could render! And there had been others as rare. These scenes were love; they were Marguerite; they were what he had lost.... Strange, that he should throw the ring into the river! Nevertheless it was a right gesture. She deserved it. She was absolutely wrong; he was absolutely right - she had admitted it. Towards him she had no excuse. Logically her attitude was absurd. Yet no argument would change it. Stupid - that was what she was! Stupid! And ruthless! She would be capable of martyrizing the whole world to her sense of duty, her damnable, insane sense of duty.... She was gone. He was ruined; she had ruined him. But he respected her. He hated to respect her, but he respected her.

A thought leapt up in his mind - and who could have guessed it? It was the thought that the secrecy of the engagement would save him from a great deal of public humiliation. He would have loathed saying: "We've broken it off."

8

INSPIRATION

George, despite his own dispositions, as he went up in the lift, to obviate the danger of such a mishap, was put out of countenance by the overwhelming splendour of Miss Irene Wheeler's flat. And he did not quite recover his aplomb until the dinner was nearly finished. The rooms were very large and lofty; they blazed with electric light, though the day had not yet gone; they gleamed with the polish of furniture, enamel, bookbindings, marble, ivory, and precious metals; they were ennobled by magnificent pictures, and purified by immense quantities of lovely flowers. George had made the mistake of arriving last. He found in the vast drawing-room five people who had the air of being at home and intimate together. There were, in addition to the hostess, Lois and Laurencine Ingram, Everard Lucas, and a Frenchman from the French Embassy whose name he did not catch. Miss Wheeler wore an elaborate Oriental costume, and apologized for its simplicity on the grounds that she was fatigued by a crowded and tiresome reception which she had held that afternoon, and that the dinner was to be without ceremony. This said, her conversation seemed to fail, but she remained by George's side, apart from the others. George saw not the least vestige of the ruinous disorder which, in the society to which he was accustomed, usually accompanied a big afternoon tea, or any sign of a lack of ceremony. He had encountered two male servants in the hall, and had also glimpsed a mulatto woman in a black dress and a white apron, and a Frenchwoman in a black dress and a black apron. Now a third man-servant entered, bearing an enormous silver-gilt tray on which were multitudinous bottles, glasses, decanters, and jugs. George comprehended that aperitifs were being offered. The tray contained enough cocktails and other combinations, some already mingled and some not, to produce a factitious appetite in the stomachs of a whole platoon. The girls declined, Miss Wheeler declined, the Frenchman declined, George declined (from prudence and diffidence); only Lucas took an aperitif, and he took it, as George admitted, in style. The man-servant, superbly indifferent to refusals, marched processionally off with the loaded tray. The great principle of conspicuous ritualistic waste had been illustrated in a manner to satisfy the most exacting standard of the leisured class; and incidentally a subject of talk was provided.

George observed the name of 'Renoir' on the gorgeous frame of a gorgeous portrait in oils of the hostess.

"Is that a Renoir?" he asked the taciturn Miss Wheeler, who seemed to jump at the opening with relief.

"Yes," she said, with her slight lisp. "I'm glad you noticed it. Come and look at it. Do you think it's a good one? Do you like Renoir?"

By good fortune George had seen a Renoir or two in Paris under the guidance of Mr. Enwright. They stared at the portrait together.

"It's awfully distinguished," he decided, employing a useful adjective which he had borrowed from Mr. Enwright.

"Isn't it!" she said, turning her wondrous complexion towards him, and admiring his adjective. "I have a Boldini too."

He followed her across the room to the Boldini portrait of herself, which was dazzling in its malicious flattery.

"And here's a Nicholson," she said.

Those three portraits were the most striking pictures in the salon, but there were others of at least equal value.

"Are you interested in fans?" she demanded, and pulled down a switch which illuminated the interior of a large cabinet full of fans. She pointed out fans painted by Lami, Glaize, Jacquemart. "That one is supposed to be a Lancret," she said. "But I'm not sure about it, and I don't know anybody that is. Here's the latest book on the subject." She indicated Lady Charlotte Schreiber's work in two volumes which, bound in vellum and gold, lay on a table. "But of course it only deals with English fans. However, Conder is going to do me a couple. He was here yesterday to see me about them. Of course you know him. What a wonderful man! The only really cosmopolitan artist in England, I say, now Beardsley's dead. I've got a Siegfried drawing by Beardsley. He was a great friend of mine. I adored him."

"This is a fine thing," said George, touching a bronze of a young girl on the same table as the books.

"You think so?" Miss Wheeler responded uncertainly. "I suppose it is. It's a Gilbert. He gave it me. But do you really think it compares with this Barye? It doesn't, does it?" She directed him to another bronze of a crouching cheetah.

So she moved him about. He was dazed. His modest supply of adjectives proved inadequate. When she paused, he murmured:

"It's a great room you've managed to get here."

"Ah!" she cried thinly. "But you've no idea of the trouble I've had over this room. Do you know it's really two rooms. I had to take two flats in order to fix this room."

She was launched on a supreme topic, and George heard a full history. She would not have a house. She would have a flat. She instructed house-agents to find for her the best flat in London. There was no best flat in London. London landlords did not understand flats, which were comprehended only in Paris. The least imperfect flats in London were two on a floor, and as their drawing-rooms happened to be contiguous on their longer sides, she had the idea of leasing two intolerable flats so as to obtain one flat that was tolerable. She had had terrible difficulties about the central heating. No flats in London were centrally heated except in the corridors and on the staircases. However, she had imposed her will on the landlord, and radiators had appeared in every room. George had a vision of excessive wealth subjugating the greatest artists and riding with implacable egotism over the customs and institutions of a city obstinately conservative. The cost and the complexity of Irene Wheeler's existence amazed and intimidated George - for this double flat was only one of her residences. He wondered what his parents would say if they could see him casually treading the oak parquetry and the heavy rugs of the resplendent abode. And then he thought, the humble and suspicious upstart: "There must be something funny about her, or she wouldn't be asking me here!"

They went in to dinner, without ceremony. George was last, the hostess close to his side.

"Who's the Frenchman?" he inquired casually, with the sudden boldness that often breaks out of timidity. "I didn't catch."

"It's Monsieur Defourcambault," said Miss Wheeler in a low voice of sincere admiration. "He's from the Embassy. A most interesting man. Been everywhere. Seen everything. Read everything. Done everything."

George could not but be struck by the ingenuous earnestness of her tone, so different from the perfunctory accents in which she had catalogued her objects of art.

The dining-room, the dinner, and the service of the dinner were equally superb. The broad table seemed small in the midst of the great mysterious chamber, of which the illumination was confined by shades to the centre. The glance wandering round the obscurity of the walls could rest on nothing that was not obviously in good taste and very costly. The three men-servants, moving soundless as phantoms, brought burdens from a hidden country behind a gigantic screen, and at intervals in the twilight near the screen could be detected the transient gleam of the white apron of the mulatto, whose sex clashed delicately and piquantly with the grave, priest-like performances of the male menials. The table was of mahogany covered with a sheet of plate-glass.

A large gold epergne glittered in the middle. Suitably dispersed about the rim of the board were six rectangular islands of pale lace, and on each island lay a complete set of the innumerable instruments and condiments necessary to the proper consumption of the meal. Thus, every diner dined independently, cut off from his fellows, but able to communicate with them across expanses of plate-glass over mahogany. George was confused by the multiplicity of metal tools and crystal receptacles - he alone had four wine-glasses - but in the handling of the tools he was saved from shame by remembering the maxim - a masterpiece of terse clarity worthy of a class which has given its best brains to the perfecting of the formalities preliminary to deglutition: "Take always from the outside."

The man from the French Embassy sat on the right of the hostess, and George on her left. George had Lois Ingram on his left. Laurencine was opposite her sister. Everard Lucas, by command of the hostess, had taken the foot of the table and was a sort of 'Mr. Vice.' The six people were soon divided into two equal groups, one silent and the other talkative, the talkative three being M. Defourcambault, Laurencine and Lucas. The diplomatist, though he could speak diplomatic English, persisted in speaking French. Laurencine spoke French quite perfectly, with exactly the same idiomatic ease as the Frenchman. Lucas neither spoke nor understood French - he had been to a great public school. Nevertheless these three attained positive loquacity. Lucas guessed at words, or the Frenchman obliged with bits of English, or Laurencine interpreted. Laurencine was far less prim and far more girlish than at the Cafe Royal. She kept all the freshness of her intensely virginal quality, but she was at ease. Her rather large body was at ease, continually restless in awkward and exquisite gestures; she laughed at ease, and made fun at ease. She appeared to have no sex-consciousness, nor even to suspect that she was a most delightful creature. The conversation was disjointed in its gaiety, and had no claim to the attention of the serious. Laurencine said that Lucas ought really to know French. Lucas said he would learn if she would teach him. Laurencine said that she would teach him if he would have his first lesson instantly, during dinner. Lucas said that wasn't fair. Laurencine said that it was. Both of them appealed to M. Defourcambault. M. Defourcambault said that it was fair. Lucas said that there was a plot between them, but that he would consent to learn at once if Laurencine would play the piano for him after dinner. Laurencine said she didn't play. Lucas said she did. M. Defourcambault, invoked once again, said that she played magnificently. Laurencine blushed, and asked M. Defourcambault how he could!... And so on, indefinitely. It was all naught; yet the taciturn three, smiling indulgently and glancing from one to another of the talkers, as taciturn and constrained persons must, envied that peculiar ability to maintain a rush and gush of chatter.

George was greatly disappointed in Lois. In the period before dinner his eyes had avoided her, and now, since they sat side by side, he could not properly see her without deliberately looking at her: which he would not do. She gave no manifestation. She was almost glum. Her French, though free, was markedly inferior to Laurencine's. She denied any interest in music. George decided, with self-condemnation, that he had been deliberately creating in his own mind an illusion about her; on no other hypothesis could either his impatience to meet her tonight, or his disappointment at not meeting her on the night of the Cafe Royal dinner, be explained. She was nothing, after all. And he did not deeply care for Miss Irene Wheeler, whom he could watch at will. She might be concealing something very marvellous, but she was dull, and she ignored the finer responsibilities of a hostess. She collected many beautiful things; she had some knowledge of what they were; she must be interested in them - or why should she trouble to possess them? She must have taste. And yet had she taste? Was she interested in her environment? A tone, a word, will create suspicion that the exhibition of expertise for hours cannot allay. George did not like the Frenchman. The Frenchman was about thirty - small, thin, fair, with the worn face of the man who lives several lives at once. He did not look kind; he did not look reliable; and he offered little evidence in support of Miss Wheeler's ardent assertion that he had been everywhere, seen everything, read everything, done everything. He assuredly had not, for example, read Verlaine, who was mentioned by Miss Wheeler. Now George had read one or two poems of Verlaine, and thought them unique; hence he despised M. Defourcambault. He could read French, in a way, but he was incapable of speaking a single word of it in the presence of compatriots; the least mono-syllable would have died on his lips. He was absurdly envious of those who could speak two languages; he thought sometimes that he would prefer to be able to speak two languages than to do anything else in the world; not to be able to speak two languages humiliated him intensely; he decided to 'take up French seriously' on the morrow; but he had several times arrived at a similar decision.

If Lois was glum, George too was glum. He wished he had not come to the dinner; he wished he could be magically transported to the solitude of his room at the club. He slipped into a reverie about the Marguerite affair. Nobody could have divined that scarcely twenty-four hours earlier he had played a principal part in a tragedy affecting his whole life. He had borne the stroke better than he otherwise would have done for the simple reason that nobody knew of his trouble. He had not to arrange his countenance for the benefit of people who were aware what was behind the countenance. But also he was philosophical. He recognized that the Marguerite affair was over. She would never give way, and he would never give way. She was wrong. He had been victimized. He had behaved with wisdom and with correctness (save for the detail of throwing the ring into the Thames). Agg's warnings and injunctions were ridiculous. What could he have done that he had not done? Run away with Marguerite, carry her off? Silly! No, he was well out of the affair. He perceived the limitations of the world in which Marguerite lived. It was a world too small and too austere for him. He required the spaciousness and the splendour of the new world in which Irene Wheeler and the Ingrams lived. Yea, though it was a world that excited the sardonic in him, he liked it. It flattered authentic, if unsuspected, appetites in him. Still, the image of Marguerite inhabited his memory. He saw her as she stood between himself and old Haim in the basement of No. 8. He heard her.... She was absolutely unlike any other girl; she was so gentle, so acquiescent. Only she put her lover second to her father.... What would Miss Wheeler think of the basement of No. 8?

The chatterers, apropos of songs in musical comedies, were talking about a French popular song concerning Boulanger.

"You knew Boulanger, didn't you, Jules?" Miss Wheeler suggested.

M. Defourcambault looked round, content. He related in English how his father had been in the very centre of the Boulangist movement, and had predicted disaster to the General's cause from the instant that Madame de Bonnemain came on the scene. (Out of consideration for the girls, M. Defourcambault phrased his narrative with neat discretion.) His grandfather also had been of his father's opinion, and his grandfather was in the Senate, and had been Minister at Brussels.... He affirmed that Madame de Bonnemain had telegraphed to Boulanger to leave Paris at the very moment when his presence in Paris was essential, and Boulanger had obediently gone. He said that he always remembered what his mother had said to him: a clever woman irregularly in love with a man may make his fortune, but a stupid woman is certain to ruin it. Finally he related how he, Jules Defourcambault, had driven the General's carriage on a famous occasion through Paris, and how the populace in its frenzy of idolatry had even climbed on to the roof of the carriage.

"And what did you do, then?" George demanded in the hard tone of a cross-examiner.

"I drove straight on," said M. Defourcambault, returning George's cold stare.

This close glimpse into history - into politics and passion - excited George considerably. He was furiously envious of M. Defourcambault, who had been in the middle of things all his life, whose father, mother, and grandfather were all in the middle of things. M. Defourcambault had an immense and unfair advantage over him. To whatever heights he might rise, George would never be in a position to talk as M. Defourcambault talked of his forbears. He would always have to stand alone, and to fight for all he wanted. He could not even refer to his father. He scorned M. Defourcambault because M. Defourcambault was not worthy of his heritage. M. Defourcambault was a little rotter, yet he had driven the carriage of Boulanger in a crisis of the history of France! Miss Wheeler, however, did not scorn M. Defourcambault. On the contrary, she looked at him with admiration, as though he had now proved that he had been everywhere, seen everything, and done everything. George's mood was black. He was a nobody; he would always be a nobody; why should he be wasting his time and looking a fool in this new world?

2

After dinner, in the drawing-room which had cost Irene Wheeler an extra flat, there was, during coffee, a certain amount of general dullness, slackness, and self-consciousness which demonstrated once more Miss Wheeler's defects as a hostess. Miss Wheeler would not or could not act as shepherdess and inspirer to her guests. She reclined, and charmingly left them to manufacture the evening for her. George was still disappointed and disgusted; for he had imagined, very absurdly as he admitted, that artistic luxuriousness always implied social dexterity and the ability to energize and reinvigorate diversion without apparent effort. There were moments during coffee which reminded him of the maladroit hospitalities of the Five Towns.

Then Everard Lucas opened the piano, and the duel between him and Laurencine was resumed. The girl yielded. Electric lights were adjusted. She began to play, while Lucas, smoking, leaned over the piano. George was standing by himself at a little distance behind the piano. He had perhaps been on his way to a chair when suddenly caught and immobilized by one of those hazards which do notoriously occur - the victim never remembers how - in drawing-rooms. Hands in pockets, he looked aimlessly about, smiling perfunctorily, and wondering where he should settle or whether he should remain where he was. In the deep embrasure of the large east bow-window Lois was lounging. She beckoned to him, not with her hand but with a brief, bright smile - she smiled rarely - and with a lifting of the chin. He responded alertly and pleasurably, and went to sit beside her. Such invitations from young women holding themselves apart in obscurity are never received without excitement and never unanswered.

Crimson curtains of brocaded silk would have cut off the embrasure entirely from the room had they been fully drawn, but they were not fully drawn; one was not drawn at all, and the other was only half drawn. Still, the mere fact of the curtains, drawn or undrawn, did morally separate the embrasure from the salon; and the shadows thickened in front of the window. The smile had gone from Lois's face, but it had been there. Sequins glittered on her dark dress, the line of the low neck of which was distinct against the pallor of the flesh. George could follow the outlines of her slanted, plump body from the hair and freckled face down to the elaborate shoes. The eyes were half closed. She did not speak. The figure of Laurencine, whose back was towards the window, received an aura from the electric light immediately over the music-stand of the piano. She played brilliantly. She played with a brilliance that astonished George.... She was exceedingly clever, was this awkward girl who had not long since left school Her body might be awkward, but not her hands. The music radiated from the piano and filled the room with brightness, with the illusion of the joy of life, and with a sense of triumph. To George it was an intoxication.

A man-servant entered with a priceless collection of bon-bons, some of which he deferentially placed on a small table in the embrasure. To do so he had to come into the embrasure, disturbing the solitude, which had already begun to exist, of Lois and George. He ignored the pair. His sublime indifference seemed to say: "I am beyond good and evil." But at the same time it left them more sensitively awake to themselves than before. The hostess indolently muttered an order to the man, and in passing the door on his way out he extinguished several lights. The place and the hour grew romantic. George was impressed by the scene, and he eagerly allowed it to impress him. It was, to him, a marvellous scene; the splendour of the apartment, the richly attired girls, the gay, exciting music, the spots of high light, the glooms, the glimpses everywhere of lovely objects. He said to himself: "I was born for this."

Lois turned her head slowly and looked out of the window.

"Wonderful view from here," she murmured.

George turned his head. The flat was on the sixth story. The slope of central London lay beneath. There was no moon, but there were stars in a clear night. Roofs; lighted windows; lines of lighted traffic; lines of lamps patterning the invisible meadows of a park; hiatuses of blackness; beyond, several towers scarcely discernible against the sky - the towers of Parliament, and the high tower of the Roman Catholic Cathedral: these were London.

"You haven't seen it in daytime, have you?" said Lois.

"No. I'd sooner see it at night."

"So would I."

The reply, the sympathy in it, the soft, thrilled tone of It, startled him. His curiosity about Lois was being justified, after all. And he was startled too at the extraordinary surprises of his own being. Yesterday he had parted from Marguerite; not ten years ago, but yesterday. And now already he was conscious of pleasure, both physical and spiritual, in the voice of another girl heard in the withdrawn obscurity of the embrasure. Yes, and a girl whom he had despised! Yesterday he had seriously believed himself to be a celibate for life; he had dismissed for ever the hope of happiness. He had seen naught but a dogged and eternal infelicity. And now he was, if not finding happiness, expecting it.

He felt disloyal - less precisely to Marguerite than to a vanished ideal. He felt that he ought to be ashamed. For Marguerite still existed; she was existing at that moment less than three miles off - somewhere over there in the dark.

"See the Cathedral tower?" he said.

"Yes," she answered. "What a shame Bentley died, wasn't it?"

He was more than startled, now - he was amazed and enchanted. Something touching and strange in her voice usually hard; something in the elegant fragility of her slipper! Everybody knew that Bentley was the architect of the Cathedral and that he had died of cancer on the tongue. The knowledge was not esoteric; it did not by itself indicate a passion for architecture or a comprehension of architecture. Yet when she said the exclamatory words, leaning far back in the seat, her throat emerging from the sequined frock, her tapping slipper peeping out beneath the skirt, she cast a spell on him. He perceived in her a woman gifted and endowed. This was the girl whom he had bullied in the automobile. She must have bowed in secret to his bullying; though he knew she had been hurt by it, she had given no sign of resentment, and her voice was acquiescent. Above all, she had remembered him.

"You only like doing very large buildings, don't you?" she suggested.

"Who told you?"

"Everard."

"Oh! Did old Lucas tell you? Well, he's quite right."

He had a sudden desire to talk to her about the great municipal building in the north that was soon to be competed for. He yielded to the desire. She listened, motionless. He gave vent to his regret that Mr. Enwright absolutely declined to enter for the competition. He said he had had ideas for it, and would have liked to work for it.

"But why don't you go in for it yourself, George?" she murmured gravely.

"Me!" he exclaimed, almost frightened. "It wouldn't be any good. I'm too young. Besides - "

"How old are you?"

"Twenty-one."

"Good heavens! You look twenty-five at least! I know I should go in for it if I were you - if I were a man."

He understood her. She could not talk well. She could not easily be agreeable; she could easily be rude; she could not play the piano like the delightful Laurencine. But she was passionate. And she knew the force of ambition. He admired ambition perhaps more than anything. Ambition roused him. She was ambitious when she drove the automobile and endangered his life.... She had called him by his Christian name quite naturally. There was absolutely no nonsense about her. Now Marguerite was not in the slightest degree ambitious. The word had no significance for her.

"I couldn't!" he insisted humbly. "I don't know enough. It's a terrific affair."

135

She made no response. But she looked at him, and suddenly he saw the angel that Irene Wheeler and Laurencine had so enthusiastically spoken of at the Cafe Royal!

"I couldn't!" he murmured.

He was insisting too much. He was insisting against himself. She had implanted the idea in his mind. Why had he not thought of it? Certainly he had not thought of it. Had he lacked courage to think of it? He beheld the idea as though it was an utterly original discovery, revolutionary, dismaying, and seductive. His inchoate plans for the building took form afresh in his brain. And the luxury by which he was surrounded whipped his ambition till it writhed.

Curious, she said no more! After a moment she sat up and took a sweet.

George saw, in a far corner, Jules Defourcambault talking very quietly to Irene Wheeler, whose lackadaisical face had become ingenuous and ardent as she listened to him under the shelter of the dazzling music. George felt himself to be within the sphere of unguessed and highly perturbing forces.

3

He left early. Lucas seemed to regard his departure as the act of a traitor, but he insisted on leaving. And in spite of Lucas's great social success he inwardly condescended to Lucas. Lucas was not a serious man and could not comprehend seriousness. George went because he had to go, because the power of an idea drove him forth. He had no intention of sleeping. He walked automatically through dark London, and his eyes, turned within, saw nothing of the city. He did not walk quickly - he was too preoccupied to walk quickly - yet in his brain he was hurrying, he had not a moment to lose. The goal was immensely far off. His haste was as absurd and as fine as that of a man who, starting to cross Europe on foot, must needs run in order to get out of Calais and be fairly on his way.

At Russell Square he wondered whether he would be able to get into the office. However, there was still a light in the basement, and he rang the house-bell. The housekeeper's daughter, a girl who played at being parlourmaid in the afternoons and brought bad tea and thick bread-and-butter to the privileged in the office, opened the front door with bridling exclamations of astonishment. She had her best frock on; her hair was in curling-pins; she smelt delicately of beer; the excitement of the Sunday League excursion and of the evening's dalliance had not quite cooled in this respectable and experienced young creature of central London. She was very feminine and provocative and unparlourmaidish, standing there in the hall, and George passed by her as callously as though she had been a real parlourmaid on duty. She had to fly to her mother for the key of the office. Taking the key from the breathless, ardent

136

little thing, he said that he would see to the front door being properly shut when he went out. That was all. Her legitimate curiosity about his visit had to go to bed hungry.

In the office he switched on the lights in Haim's cubicle, in the pupils' room, and in the principals' room. He enjoyed the illumination and the solitude. He took deep breaths. He walked about. After rummaging for the sketches and the printed site-plan of the town hall projected by the northern city, he discovered them under John Orgreave's desk. He moved them to Mr. Enwright's desk, which was the best one, and he bent over them rapturously. Yes, the idea of entering for the competition himself was a magnificent idea. Strange that it should have occurred not to him, but to Lois! A disconcerting girl, Lois! She had said that he looked twenty-five. He liked that. Why should he not enter for the competition himself? He would enter for it. The decision was made, as usual without consulting anybody; instinct was his sole guide. Failure in the final examination was beside the point. Moreover, though he had sworn never to sit again, he could easily sit again in December; he could pass the exam, on his head. He might win the competition; to be even in the selected first six or ten would rank as a glorious achievement. But why should he not win outright? He was lucky, always had been lucky. It was essential that he should win outright. It was essential that he should create vast and grandiose structures, that he should have both artistic fame and worldly success. He could not wait long for success. He required luxury. He required a position enabling him to meet anybody and everybody on equal terms, and to fulfil all his desires.

He would not admit that he was too young for the enterprise. He was not too young. He refused to be too young. And indeed he felt that he had that very night become adult, and that a new impulse, reducing all previous impulses to unimportance, had inspired his life. He owed the impulse to the baffling Lois. Marguerite would never have given him such an impulse. Marguerite had no ambition either for herself or for him. She was profoundly the wrong girl for him. He admitted his error candidly, with the eagerness of youth. He had no shame about the blunder. And the girl's environment was wrong for him also. What had he to do with Chelsea? Chelsea was a parish; it was not the world. He had been gravely disappointed in Chelsea. Marguerite had no shimmer of romance. She was homely. And she was content with her sphere. And she was not elegant; she had no kind of smartness; who would look twice at her? And she was unjust, she was unfair. She had lacerated his highly sensitive pride. She had dealt his conceit a frightful wound. He would not think of it.

And in fact he could ignore the wound in the exquisite activity of creating town halls for mighty municipalities. He drew plans with passion and with fury; he had scores of alternative schemes; he was a god fashioning worlds.

Having drawn plans, he drew elevations and perspectives; he rushed to the files (rushed - because he was in haste to reach the goal) and studied afresh the schedules of accommodation for other municipal buildings that had been competed for in the past. Much as he hated detail, he stooped rather humbly to detail that night, and contended with it in all honesty. He worked for hours before he thought of lighting a cigarette.

It was something uncanny beyond the large windows that first gently and perceptibly began to draw away his mind from the profusion of town halls on the desk, and so indirectly reminded him of the existence of cigarettes. When he lighted a cigarette he stretched himself and glanced at the dark windows, of which the blinds had not been pulled down. He understood then what was the matter. Dawn was the matter. The windows were no longer quite dark. He looked out. A faint pallor in the sky, and some stars sickening therein, and underneath the silent square with its patient trees and indefatigable lamps! The cigarette tasted bad in his mouth, but he would not give it up. He yawned heavily. The melancholy of the square, awaiting without hope the slow, hard dawn, overcame him suddenly.... Marguerite was a beautiful girl; her nose was marvellous; he could never forget it. He could never forget her gesture as she intervened between him and her father in the basement at Alexandra Grove. They had painted lamp-shades together. She was angelically kind; she could not be ruffled; she would never criticize, never grasp, never exhibit selfishness. She was a unique combination of the serious and the sensuous. He felt the passionate, ecstatic clinging of her arm as they walked under the interminable chain of lamp-posts on Chelsea Embankment. Magical hours!... And how she could absorb herself in her work! And what a damned shame it was that rascally employers should have cut down her prices! It was intolerable; it would not bear thinking about. He dropped the cigarette and stamped on it angrily. Then he returned to the desk, and put his head in his hands and shut his eyes.

He awakened with a start of misgiving. He was alone in the huge house (for the basement was under the house and, somehow, did not count). Something was astir in the house. He could hear it through the doors ajar. His flesh crept. It was exactly like the flap of a washing-cloth on the stone stairs; it stopped; it came nearer. He thought inevitably of the dead Mrs. Haim, once charwoman and step cleaner. In an instant he believed fully in all that he had ever heard about ghosts and spirit manifestations. An icy wave passed down his spine. He felt that if the phantom of Mrs. Haim was approaching him he simply could not bear to meet it. The ordeal would kill him. Then he decided that the sounds were not those of a washing-cloth, but of slippered feet. Odd that he should have been so deluded. Somebody was coming down the long stairs from the upper stories, uninhabited at night. Burglars? He was still very perturbed, but differently perturbed. He could not move a muscle. The suspense as the footsteps hesitated at the cubicle was awful. George stood up straight and called out in a rough voice - louder than he expected it to be:

"Who's there?"

Mr. Enwright appeared. He was wearing beautiful blue pyjamas and a plum-coloured silk dressing-gown and doe-skin slippers. His hair was extremely deranged; he blinked rapidly, and his lined face seemed very old.

"Well, I like this, I like this!" he said in a quiet, sardonic tone. "Sitting at my desk and blazing my electricity away! I happened to get up, and I looked out of the window and noticed the glare below. So I came to see what was afoot. Do you know you frightened me? - and I don't like being frightened."

"I hadn't the slightest notion you ever slept here," George feebly stammered.

"Didn't you know I'd decided to keep a couple of rooms here for myself?"

"I had heard something about it, but I didn't know you'd really moved in. I - I've been away so much."

"I moved in, as you call it, to-day - yesterday, and a nice night you're giving me! And even supposing I hadn't moved in, what's that got to do with your being here? Give me a cigarette."

With hurrying deference George gave the cigarette, and struck a match for it, and as he held the match he had a near view of Mr. Enwright's prosaic unshaved chin. The house was no longer the haunt of lurking phantoms; it was a common worldly house without any mystery or any menace. George's skin was no longer the field of abnormal phenomena. Dawn was conquering Russell Square. On the other hand, George was no longer a giant of energy, initiating out of ample experience a tremendous and superb enterprise. He was suddenly diminished to a boy, or at best a lad. He really felt that it was ridiculous for him to be sketching and scratching away there in the middle of the night in his dress-clothes. Even his overcoat, hat, and fancy muffler cast on a chair seemed ridiculous. He was a child, pretending to be an adult. He glanced like a child at Mr. Enwright; he roughened his hair with his hand like a child. He had the most wistful and apologetic air.

He said:

"I just came along here for a bit instead of going to bed. I didn't know it was so late."

"Do you often just come along here?"

"No. I never did it before. But tonight - "

"What is it you're at?"

"I'd been thinking a bit about that new town hall."

"What new town hall?"

"You know - "

Mr. Enwright did know.

"But haven't I even yet succeeded in making it clear that this firm is not

139

going in for that particular competition?"

Mr. Enwright's sarcastic and discontented tone challenged George, who stiffened.

"Oh! I know the firm isn't going in for it. But what's the matter with me going in for it?"

He forced himself to meet Mr. Enwright's eyes, but he could not help blushing. He was scarcely out of his articles; he had failed in the Final; and he aspired to create the largest English public building of the last half-century.

"Are you quite mad?" Mr. Enwright turned away from the desk to the farther window, hiding his countenance.

"Yes," said George firmly. "Quite!"

Mr. Enwright, after a pause, came back to the desk.

"Well, it's something to admit that," he sneered. "At any rate, we know where we are. Let's have a look at the horrid mess."

He made a number of curt observations as he handled the sheets of sketches.

"I see you've got that Saracenic touch in again."

"What's the scale here?"

"Is this really a town hall, or are you trying to beat the Temple at Karnak?"

"If that's meant for an Ionic capital, no assessor would stand it. It's against all the textbooks to have Ionic capitals where there's a side-view of them. Not that it matters to me."

"Have you made the slightest attempt to cube it up? You'd never get out of this under half a million, you know."

Shaking his head, he retired once more to the window. George began to breathe more freely, as one who has fronted danger and still lives. Mr. Enwright addressed the window:

"It's absolute folly to start on a thing like that before the conditions are out. Absolute folly. Have you done all that tonight?"

"Yes."

"Well, you've shifted the stuff.... But you haven't the slightest notion what accommodation they want. You simply don't know."

"I know what accommodation they ought to want with four hundred thousand inhabitants," George retorted pugnaciously.

"Is it four hundred thousand?" Mr. Enwright asked, with bland innocence. He generally left statistics to his partner.

"Four hundred and twenty-five."

"You've looked it up?"

"I have."

Mr. Enwright was now at the desk yet again.

"There's an idea to it," he said shortly, holding up the principal sheet and blinking.

"I shall go in for it!" The thought swept through George's brain like a fierce flare, lighting it up vividly to its darkest corners, and incidentally producing upon his skin phenomena similar to those produced by uncanny sounds on the staircase. He had caught admiration and benevolence in Mr. Enwright's voice. He was intensely happy, encouraged, and proud. He began to talk eagerly; he babbled, entrusting himself to Mr. Enwright's benevolence.

"Of course there's the Final. If they give six months for the thing I could easily get through the Final before sending-in day. I could take a room somewhere. I shouldn't really want any assistance - clerk, I mean. I could do it all myself...." He ran on until Mr. Enwright stopped him.

"You could have a room here - upstairs."

"Could I?"

"But you would want some help. And you needn't think they'll give six months, because they won't. They might give five."

"That's no good."

"Why isn't it any good?" snapped Mr. Enwright. "You don't suppose they're going to issue the conditions just yet, do you? Not a day before September, not a day. And you can take it from me!"

"Oh! Hurrah!"

"But look here, my boy, let's be clear about one thing."

"Yes?"

"You're quite mad."

They looked at each other.

"The harmless kind, though," said George confidently, well aware that Mr. Enwright doted upon him.

In another minute the principal had gone to bed, without having uttered one word as to his health. George had announced that he should tidy the sacred desk before departing. When he had done that he wrote a letter, in pencil. "It's the least I can do," he said to himself seriously. He began:

"Dear Miss Ingram."

"Dash it! - She calls me 'George,'" he thought, and tore up the sheet. - "Dear Lois, - I think after what you said it's only due to you to tell you that I've decided to go in for that competition on my own. Thanks for the tip. - Yours, George Cannon"

He surveyed the message.

"That's about right," he murmured.

Then he looked at his watch. It showed 3.15, but it had ceased to beat. He added at the foot of the letter: "Monday, 3.30 a.m." He stole one of John Orgreave's ready-stamped envelopes.

In quitting the house he inadvertently banged the heavy front door.

"Do 'em good!" he said, thinking of awakened sleepers.

It was now quite light. He dropped the letter into the pillar-box round the corner, and as soon as he had irretrievably done so, the thought occurred to him: "I wish I hadn't put '3.30 a.m.' There's something rottenly sentimental about it." The chill fresh air was bracing him to a more perfect sanity. He raised the collar of his overcoat.

4

At the club on Tuesday morning Downs brought to his bedside a letter addressed in a large, striking, and untidy hand. Not until he had generally examined the letter did he realize that it was from Lois Ingram. He remembered having mentioned to her that he lived at his club - Pickering's; but he had laid no stress on the detail, nor had she seemed to notice it. Yet she must have noticed it.

"Dear George, - I am so glad. Miss Wheeler is going to her bootmaker's in Conduit Street tomorrow afternoon. She's always such a long time there. Come and have tea with me at the new Prosser's in Regent Street, four sharp. I shall have half an hour. - L.I."

In his heart he pretended to jeer at this letter. He said it was 'like' Lois. She calmly assumed that at a sign from her he, a busy man, would arrange to be free in the middle of the afternoon! Doubtless the letter was the consequence of putting '3.30 a.m.' on his own letter. What could a fellow expect?...

All pretence! In reality the letter flattered and excited him. He thought upon the necktie he would wear.

By the same post arrived a small parcel: it contained a ring, a few other bits of jewellery, and all the letters and notes that he had ever written or scribbled to Marguerite. He did not want the jewellery back; he did not want the letters back. To receive them somehow humiliated him. Surely she might have omitted this nauseous conventionality! She was so exasperatingly conscientious. Her neat, clerk-like calligraphy, on the label of the parcel, exasperated him. She had carefully kept every scrap of a missive from him. He hated to look at the letters. What could he do with them except rip them up? And the miserable trinkets - which she had worn, which had been part of her? As for him, he had not kept all her letters - not by any means. There might be a few, lying about in drawers. He would have to collect and return them. Odious job! And he could not ask anybody else to do it for him.

He was obliged to question Lucas about the Regent Street Prosser's, of which, regrettably, he had never heard. He did not, in so many words, request John Orgreave for the favour of an hour off. He was now out of his articles, though still by the force of inertia at the office, and therefore he informed John Orgreave that unless Mr. John had any objection he proposed to take an hour off. Mr. Enwright was not in. Lucas knew vaguely of the rendezvous, having somewhere met Laurencine.

From the outside Prosser's was not distinguishable from any other part of Regent Street. But George could not mistake it, because Miss Wheeler's car was drawn up in front of the establishment, and Lois was waiting for him therein. Strange procedure! She smiled and then frowned, and got out sternly. She said scarcely anything, and he found that he could make only such silly remarks as: "Hope I'm not late, am I?"

The new Prosser's was a grandiose by-product of chocolate. The firm had taken the leading ideas of the chief tea-shop companies catering for the million in hundreds of establishments arranged according to pattern, and elaborated them with what is called in its advertisements 'cachet.' Its prices were not as cheap as those of the popular houses, but they could not be called dear. George and Lois pushed through a crowded lane of chocolate and confectionery, past a staircase which bore a large notice: "Please keep to the right." This notice was needed. They came at length to the main hall, under a dome, with a gallery between the dome and the ground. The floor was carpeted. The multitudinous small tables had cloths, flowers, silver, and menus knotted with red satin ribbon. The place was full of people, people seated at the tables and people walking about. Above the rail of the gallery could be seen the hats and heads of more people. People were entering all the time and leaving all the time. Scores of waitresses, in pale green and white, moved to and fro like an alien and mercenary population. The heat, the stir, the hum, and the clatter were terrific. And from on high descended thin, strident music in a rapid and monotonous rhythm.

"No room!" said George, feeling that he had at last got into the true arena of the struggle for life.

"Oh yes!" said Lois, with superior confidence.

She bore mercilessly across the floor. Round the edge of the huge room, beneath the gallery, were a number of little alcoves framed in fretted Moorish arches of white-enamelled wood. Three persons were just emerging from one of these. She sprang within, and sank into a wicker arm-chair.

"There is always a table," she breathed, surveying the whole scene with a smile of conquest.

George sat down opposite to her with his back to the hall; he could survey nothing but Lois, and the world of the mirror behind her.

"That's one of father's maxims," she said.

"What is?"

"'There is always a table.' Well, you know, there always is."

"He must be a very wise man."

"He is."

"What's his special line?"

She exclaimed:

"Don't you know father? Hasn't Miss Wheeler told you? Or Mrs.

Orgreave?"

"No."

"But you must know father. Father's 'Parisian' in The Sunday Journal."

Despite the mention of this ancient and very dignified newspaper, George felt a sense of disappointment. He had little esteem for journalists, whom Mr. Enwright was continually scoffing at, and whom he imagined to be all poor. He had conceived Mr. Ingram as perhaps a rich cosmopolitan financier, or a rich idler - but at any rate rich, whatever he might be.

"Of course he does lots of other work besides that. He writes for the Pall Mall Gazette and the St. James's Gazette. In fact it's his proud boast that he writes for all the gazettes, and he's the only man who does. That's because he's so liked. Everybody adores him. I adore him myself. He's a great pal of mine. But he's very strict."

"Strict?"

"Yes," she insisted, rather defensively. "Why not? I should like a strawberry ice, and a lemon-squash, and a millefeuille cake. Don't be alarmed, please. I'm a cave-woman. You've got to get used to it."

"What's a cave-woman?"

"It's something primitive. You must come over to Paris. If father likes you, he'll take you to one of the weekly lunches of the Anglo-American Press Circle. He always does that when he likes anyone. He's the Treasurer.... Haven't you got any millefeuille cakes?" she demanded of the waitress, who had come to renew the table and had deposited a basket of various cakes.

"I'm afraid we haven't, miss," answered the waitress, not comprehending the strange word any better than George did.

"Bit rowdy, isn't it?" George observed, looking round, when the waitress had gone.

Lois said with earnestness:

"I simply love these big, noisy places. They make me feel alive."

He looked at her. She was very well dressed - more stylistic than any girl that he could see in the mirror. He could not be sure whether or not her yellow eyes had a slight cast; if they had, it was so slight as to be almost imperceptible. There was no trace of diffidence in them; they commanded. She was not a girl whom you could masculinely protect. On the contrary, she would protect not only herself but others.

"Haven't you cream?" she curtly challenged the waitress, arriving with ice, lemon-squash, and George's tea.

The alien mercenary met her glance inimically for a second, and then, shutting her lips together, walked off with the milk. At Prosser's the waitresses did not wear caps, and were, in theory, ladies. Lois would have none of the theory; the waitress was ready to die for it and carried it away with her intact. George preferred milk to cream, but he said nothing.

"Yes," Lois went on. "You ought to come to Paris. You have been, haven't you? I remember you told me. We're supposed to go back next week, but if Irene doesn't go, I shan't." She frowned.

George said that positively he would come to Paris.

When they had fairly begun the rich, barbaric meal, Lois asked abruptly:

"Why did you write in the middle of the night?"

Sometimes her voice was veiled.

"Why did I write in the middle of the night? Because I thought I would." He spoke masterfully. He didn't mean to stand any of her cheek.

"Oh!" she laughed nicely. "I didn't mind. I liked it - awfully. It was just the sort of thing I should have done myself. But you might tell me all about it. I think I deserve that much, don't you?"

Thus he told her all about it - how he had arranged everything, got a room, meant to have his name painted on the door, meant to make his parents take their holiday on the north-east coast for a change, so that he could study the site, meant to work like a hundred devils, etc. He saw with satisfaction that the arrogant, wilful creature was impressed.

She said:

"Now listen to me. You'll win that competition."

"I shan't," he said. "But it's worth trying, for the experience - that's what Enwright says."

She said:

"I don't care a fig what Enwright says. You'll win that competition. I'm always right when I sort of feel - you know."

For the moment he believed in the miraculous, inexplicable intuitions of women.

"Oh!" she cried, as the invisible orchestra started a new tune. "Do you know that? It's the first time I've heard it in London. It's the machiche. It's all over Paris. I think it's the most wonderful tune in the world." Her body swayed; her foot tapped.

George listened. Yes, it was a maddening tune.

"It is," he agreed eagerly.

She cried:

"Oh! I do love pleasure! And success! And money! Don't you?"

Her eyes had softened; they were liquid with yearning; but there was something frankly sensual in them. This quality, swiftly revealed, attracted George intensely for an instant.

Immediately afterwards she asked the time, and said she must go.

"I daren't keep Irene waiting," she said. Her eyes now had a hard glitter.

In full Regent Street he put the haughty girl into Irene's automobile, which had turned round; he was proud to be seen in the act; he privately enjoyed the glances of common, unsuccessful persons. As he walked away he smiled to himself, to hide from himself his own nervous excitement. She was a handful, she was. Within her life burned and blazed. He remembered Mr. Prince's remark: "You must have made a considerable impression on her," or words to that effect. The startling thought visited him: "I shall marry that woman." Then another thought: "Not if I know it! I don't like her. I do not like her. I don't like her eyes."

She had, however, tremendously intensified in him the desire for success. He hurried off to work. The days passed too slowly, and yet they were too short for his task. He could not wait for the fullness of time. His life had become a breathless race. "I shall win. I can't possibly win. The thing's idiotic. I might.... Enwright's rather struck." Yes, it was Mr. Enwright's attitude that inspired him. To have impressed Mr. Enwright - by Jove, it was something!

9

COMPETITION

On the face of the door on the third floor of the house in Russell Square the words 'G.E. Cannon' appeared in dirty white paint and the freshly added initials 'A.R.I.B.A.' in clean white paint. The addition of the triumphant initials (indicating that George had kissed the rod of the Royal Institute of British Architects in order to conquer) had put the sign as a whole out of centre, throwing it considerably to the right on the green door-face. Within the small and bare room, on an evening in earliest spring in 1904, sat George at the customary large flat desk of the architect. He had just switched on the electric light over his head. He looked sterner and older; he looked very worried, fretful, exhausted. He was thin and pale; his eyes burned, and there were dark patches under the eyes; the discipline of the hair had been rather gravely neglected. In front of George lay a number of large plans, mounted on thick cardboard, whose upper surface had a slight convex curve. There were plans of the basement of the projected town hall, of the ground floor, of the building at a height of twelve feet from the ground, of the mezzanine floor, of the first, second, third, fourth, and fifth floors; these plans were coloured. Further, in plain black and white, there were a plan of the roof (with tower), a longitudinal section on the central axis, two other sections, three elevations, and a perspective view of the entire edifice. Seventeen sheets in all.

The sum of work seemed tremendous; it made the mind dizzy; it made George smile with terrible satisfaction at his own industry. For he had engaged very little help. He would have been compelled to engage more, had not the Corporation extended by one month the time for sending in. The Corporation had behaved with singular enlightenment. Its schedules of required accommodation (George's copy was scored over everywhere in pencil and ink and seriously torn) were held to be admirably drawn, and its supplementary circular of answers to questions from competitors had displayed a clarity and a breadth of mind unusual in corporations. Still more to the point, the Corporation had appointed a second assessor to act with Sir Hugh Corver. In short, it had shown that it was under no mandarin's thumb, and that what it really and seriously wanted was the best design that the profession could produce. Mr. Enwright, indeed, had nearly admitted regret at having kept out of the immense affair. John Orgreave had expressed regret with vigour and candour. They had in the main left George alone, though occasionally at night Mr. Enwright, in the little room, had suggested valuable solutions of certain problems. In detail he was severely critical of George's design, and he would pour delicate satires upon the idiosyncrasy which caused the wilful boy to 'impurify' (a word from Enwright's private vocabulary) a Renaissance creation with Saracenic tendencies in the treatment of arches and wall-spaces.

Nevertheless Mr. Enwright greatly respected the design in its entirety, and both he and John Orgreave (who had collected by the subterranean channels of the profession a large amount of fact and rumour about the efforts of various competitors) opined that it stood a fair chance of being among the selected six or ten whose authors would be invited to submit final designs for the final award. George tried to be hopeful; but he could not be hopeful by trying. It was impossible to believe that he would succeed; the notion was preposterous; yet at moments, when he was not cultivating optimism, optimism would impregnate all his being, and he would be convinced that it was impossible not to win. How inconceivably grand! His chief rallying thought was that he had undertaken a gigantic task and had accomplished it. Well or ill, he had accomplished it. He said to himself aloud:

"I've done it! I've done it!"

And that he actually had done it was almost incredible. The very sheets of drawings were almost incredible. But they existed there. All was complete. The declaration that the design was G.E. Cannon's personal work, drawn in his own office by his ordinary staff, was there, in the printed envelope officially supplied by the Corporation. The estimate of cost and the cubing was there. The explanatory report on the design, duly typewritten, was there. Nothing lacked.

"I've done it! I've done it!"

And then, tired as he was, the conscience of the creative artist and of the competitor began to annoy him and spur him. The perspective drawing did not quite satisfy - and there was still time. The point of view for the perspective drawing was too high up, and the result was a certain marring of the nobility of the lines, and certainly a diminishment of the effect of the tower. He had previously started another perspective drawing with a lower view-point, but he had mistakenly cast it aside. He ought to finish the first one and substitute it for the second one. 'The perspective drawing had a moral importance; it had a special influence on the assessors and committees. Horrid, tiresome labour! Three, four, five, or six hours of highly concentrated tedium. Was it worth while? It was not. Mr. Enwright liked the finished drawing. He, George, could not face a further strain. And yet he was not content.... Pooh! Who said he could not face a further strain? Of course he could face it. If he did not face it, his conscience would accuse him of cowardice during the rest of his life, and he would never be able to say honestly: "I did my level best with the thing." He snapped his fingers lightly, and in one second had decided to finish the original perspective drawing, and in his very finest style. He would complete it some time during the night. In the morning it could be mounted. The drawings were to go to the north in a case on the morrow by passenger train, and to be met at their destination by a commissionaire common to several competitors; this commissionaire would deliver them to the Town Clerk in accordance with the conditions. In a few minutes George was at work, excited, having forgotten all fatigue. He was saying to himself that he would run out towards eight o'clock for a chop or a steak. As he worked he perceived that he had been quite right to throw over the second drawing; he wondered that he could have felt any hesitation; the new drawing would be immeasurably superior.

Mr. Haim 'stepped up,' discreetly knocking, entering with dignity. The relations between these two had little by little resumed their old, purely formal quality. Both seemed to have forgotten that passionate anger had ever separated them and joined them together. George was young, and capable of oblivion. Mr. Haim had beaten him in the struggle and could afford to forget. They conversed politely, as though the old man had no daughter and the youth had never had a lover. Mr. Haim had even assisted with the lettering of the sheets - not because George needed his help, but because Mr. Haim's calligraphic pride needed to help. To refuse the stately offer would have been to insult. Mr. Haim had aged, but not greatly.

"You're wanted on the telephone, Mr. Cannon."

"Oh! Dash it!... Thanks!"

After all George was no longer on the staff of Lucas & Enwright, and Mr. Haim was conferring a favour.

Down below in the big office everybody had gone except the factotum.

George seized the telephone receiver and called brusquely for attention.

"Is that Mr. Cannon?"

"Yes. Who is it?"

"Oh! It's you, George! How nice to hear your voice again!"

He recognized, but not instantly, the voice of Lois Ingram. He was not surprised. Indeed he had suspected that the disturber of work must be either Lois or Miss Wheeler, or possibly Laurencine. The three had been in London again for several days, and he had known from Lucas that a theatre-party had been arranged for that night to witness the irresistible musical comedy, The Gay Spark, Lucas and M. Defourcambault were to be of the party. George had not yet seen Lois since her latest return to London; he had only seen her twice since the previous summer; he had not visited Paris in the interval. The tone of her voice, even as transformed by the telephone, was caressing. He had to think of some suitable response to her startling amiability, and to utter it with conviction. He tried to hold fast in his mind to the image of the perspective with its countless complexities and the co-ordination of them all; the thing seemed to be retreating from him, and he dared not let it go.

"Do you know," said Lois, "I only came to London to celebrate the sending-in of your design. I hear it's marvellous. Aren't you glad you've finished it?"

"Well, I haven't finished it," said George. "I'm on it now."

What did the girl mean by saying she'd only come to London to celebrate the end of his work? An invention on her part! Still, it flattered him. She was very strange.

"But Everard's told us you'd finished a bit earlier than you'd expected. We counted on seeing your lordship tomorrow. But now we've got to see you tonight."

"Awfully sorry I can't."

"But look here, George. You must really. The party's all broken up. Miss Wheeler's had to go back to Paris tonight, and Jules can't come. Everything's upset. The flat's going to be closed, and Laurencine and, I will have to leave tomorrow. It's most frightfully annoying. We've got the box all right, and Everard's coming, and you must make the fourth. We must have a fourth. Laurencine's here at the phone, and she says the same as me."

"Wish I could!" George answered shortly. "Look here! What train are you going by tomorrow? I'll come and see you off. I shall be free then."

"But, George. We want you to come tonight." There seemed positively to be tears in the faint voice. "Why can't you come? You must come."

"I haven't finished one of the drawings. I tell you I'm on it now. It'll take me half the night, or more. I'm just in the thick of it, you see." He spoke with a slight resentful impatience - less at her over-persuasiveness than at the fact that his mind and the drawing were being more and more separated. Soon he would have lost the right mood, and he would be compelled to re-create it before he could resume the work. The forcible, gradual dragging away of his mind from its passionately gripped objective was torture. He had an impulse to throw down the receiver and run off.

The distant squeaking voice changed to the petulant:

"You are horrid. You could come right enough if you wanted to."

"But don't you understand? It's awfully important for me."

He was astounded, absolutely astounded. She would not understand. She had decided that he must go to the musical comedy and nothing else mattered. His whole future did not matter.

"Oh! Very well, then," Lois said, undisguisedly vexed. "Of course, if you won't, you won't. But really when two girls implore you like that.... And we have to leave tomorrow, and everything's upset!... I do think it's ... However, good night."

"Here! Hold hard a sec. I'll come for an hour or so. What's the number of the box?"

"Fourteen," said the voice brokenly.

Immediately afterwards she rang off. George was hurt and bewildered. The girl was incredibly ruthless. She was mad. Why had he yielded? Only a silly conventional feeling had made him yield. And yet he was a great scorner of convention. He went upstairs again to the perspective drawing. He looked at his watch. He might work for half an hour before leaving to dress. No, he could not. The mood had vanished. The perspective had slipped into another universe. He could not even pick up a pen. He despised himself terribly, despairingly, for yielding.

2

In spite of all this he anticipated with pleasure the theatre-party. He wanted to go; he was glad he was going; the memory of Lois in the tea-palace excited him. And he could refuse a hearing to his conscience, and could prevent himself from thinking uncomfortably of the future, as well as most young men. His secret, unadmitted voluptuous eagerness was alloyed only by an apprehension that after the scene over the telephone Lois might be peevish and ungracious. The fear proved to be baseless.

Owing to the imperfections of the club laundry and the erring humanity of Downs, he arrived late. The Gay Spark had begun. He found a darkened auditorium and a glowing stage. In the dim box Lois and Laurencine were sitting in front on gilt chairs. Lucas sat behind Laurencine, and there was an empty chair behind Lois. Her gesture, her smile, her glance, as she turned to George and looked up, were touching. She was delighted to see him; she had the mien of a child who has got what it wanted and has absolutely forgotten that it ever pouted, shrieked, and stamped its foot. She was determined to charm her uttermost. Her eye in the gloom was soft with mysterious invitations. George looked about the interior of the box; he saw the rich cloaks of the girls hanging up next to glossy masculine hats, the large mirror on the wall, and mother-of-pearl opera-glasses, chocolates, and flowers on the crimson ledge. He was very close to the powerfully built and yet plastic Lois. He could watch her changing curves as she breathed; the faint scent she used rose to his nostrils. He thought, with contained rapture: "Nothing in the world is equal to this." He did not care a fig for the effect of perspective drawings or the result of the competition. Lois, her head half-turned towards him, her gaze lost in the sombre distances of the auditorium, talked in a low tone, ignoring the performance. He gathered that the sudden departure of Irene Wheeler had unusually impressed and disconcerted and, to a certain extent, mortified the sisters, who could not explain it, and who resented the compulsion to go back to Paris at once. And he detected in Lois, not for the first time, a grievance that Irene kept her, Lois, apart from the main current of her apparently gorgeous social career. Obviously an evening at which the sole guests were two girls and a youth all quite unknown to newspapers could not be a major item in the life of a woman such as Irene Wheeler. She had left them unceremoniously to themselves at the last moment, as it were permitting them to do what they liked within the limits of goodness for one night, and commanding them to return sagely home on the morrow. A red-nosed actor, hands in pockets, waddled self-consciously on to the stage, and the packed audience, emitting murmurs of satisfaction, applauded. Conversations were interrupted. George, expectant, gave his attention to the show. He knew little or nothing of musical comedy, having come under influences which had taught him to despise it. His stepfather, for example, could be very sarcastic about musical comedy, and through both Enwright and John Orgreave George had further cultivated the habit of classical music, already acquired in boyhood at home in the Five Towns. In the previous year, despite the calls upon his time of study for examinations, George had attended the Covent Garden performances of the Wagnerian "Ring" as he might have attended High Mass. He knew by name a considerable percentage of the hundred odd themes in "The Ring," and it was his boast that he could identify practically all the forty-seven themes in The Meistersingers. He raved about Ternina in Tristan. He had worshipped the Joachim quartet. He was acquainted with all the popular symphonies of Beethoven, Schubert, Schumann, Mozart, Glazounov, and Tschaikovsky. He even frequented the Philharmonic Concerts, which were then conducted by a composer of sentimental drawing-room ballads, and though he would not class this conductor with Richter or Henry J. Wood, he yet believed that somehow, by the magic of the sacred name of the Philharmonic Society, the balladmonger in the man expired in the act of raising the baton and was replaced by a serious and sensitive artist. He was accustomed to hear the same pieces of music again and again and again, and they were all or nearly all very fine, indisputably great. It never occurred to him that once they had been unfamiliar and had had to fight for the notice of persons who indulged in music exactly as he indulged in music. He had no traffic with the unfamiliar. Unfamiliar items on a programme displeased him. He had heard compositions by Richard Strauss, but he could make nothing of them, and his timid, untravelled taste feared to like them. Mr. Enwright himself was mainly inimical to Strauss, as to most of modern Germany, perhaps because of the new architecture in Berlin. George knew that there existed young English composers with such names as Cyril Scott, Balfour Gardiner, Donald Tovey - for he had seen these names recently on the front page of The Daily Telegraph - but he had never gone to the extent of listening to their works. He was entirely sure that they could not hold a candle to Wagner, and his sub-conscious idea was that it was rather like their cheek to compose at all. He had not noticed that Hugo Wolf had just died, nor indeed had he noticed that Hugo Wolf had ever lived.

Nevertheless this lofty and exclusive adherent of the 'best' music was not prejudiced in advance against The Gay Spark. He was anxious to enjoy it and he expected to enjoy it. The Gay Spark had already an enormous prestige; it bore the agreeable, captivating label of Vienna; and immense sums were being made out of it in all the capitals of the world. George did not hope for immortal strains, but he anticipated a distinguished, lilting gaiety, and in the 'book' a witty and cosmopolitan flavour that would lift the thing high above such English musical comedies as he had seen. It was impossible that a work of so universal and prodigious a vogue should not have unquestionable virtues.

The sight of the red-nosed comedian rather shocked George, who had supposed that red-nosed comedians belonged to the past. However, the man was atoned for by three extremely beautiful and graceful young girls who followed him. Round about the small group was ranged a semicircle of handsome creatures in long skirts, behind whom was another semicircle of young men in white flannels; the scene was a street in Mandalay. The red-nosed comedian began by making a joke concerning his mother-in-law, and another concerning mendacious statements to his wife to explain his nocturnal absences from home, and another concerning his intoxicated condition. The three extremely beautiful and graceful young girls laughed deliriously at the red-nosed comedian; they replied in a similar vein. They clasped his neck and kissed him rapturously, and thereupon he sang a song, of which the message was that all three extremely beautiful and graceful girls practised professionally the most ancient and stable of feminine vocations; the girls, by means of many refrains, confirmed this definition of their status in society. Then the four of them danced, and there was enthusiastic applause from every part of the house except the semicircle of European odalisques lost, for some unexplained reason, in Mandalay. These ladies, the indubitable physical attractions of each of whom were known by the management to fill five or six stalls every night, took no pains whatever to hide that they were acutely bored by the whole proceedings. Self-sufficient in their beauty, deeply aware of the power of their beauty, they deigned to move a lackadaisical arm or leg at intervals in accordance with the respectful suggestions of the conductor.

Soon afterwards the gay spark herself appeared, amid a hysteria of applause.

She played the part of the wife of a military officer, and displayed therein a marvellous, a terrifying vitality of tongue, leg, and arm. The young men in white flannels surrounded her, and she could flirt with all of them; she was on intimate terms with the red-nosed comedian, and also with the trio of delightful wantons, and her ideals in life seemed to be identical with theirs. When, through the arrival of certain dandies twirling canes, and the mysterious transformation of the Burmese street into a Parisian café, these ideals were on the point of realization, there was a great burst of brass in the orchestra, succeeded by a violent chorus, some kicking, and a general wassail, and the curtain fell on the first act. It had to be raised four times before the gratefully appreciative clapping would cease.

The auditorium shone with light; it grew murmurous with ecstatic approval. The virginal face of Laurencine shot its rapture to Lucas as she turned to shake hands with George.

"Jolly well done, isn't it?" said Lucas.

"Yes," said George.

Lucas, too content to notice the perfunctoriness of George's affirmative, went on:

"When you think that they're performing it this very night in St. Petersburg, Berlin, Paris, Brussels, and, I fancy, Rome, but I'm not sure - marvellous, isn't it?"

"It is," said George ambiguously.

Though continuing to like him, he now definitely despised Everard. The fellow had no artistic perceptions; he was a child. By some means he had got through his Final, and was soon to be a junior partner in Enwright & Lucas. George, however, did not envy Everard the soft situation; he only pitied Enwright & Lucas. Everard had often urged George to go to musical comedies more frequently, hinting that they were frightfully better than George could conceive. The Gay Spark gave Lucas away entirely; it gave away his method of existence.

"I don't believe you like it," said sharp Laurencine.

"I adore it," George protested. "Don't you?"

"Oh! I do, of course," said Laurencine. "I knew I should."

Lucas, instinctively on the defence, said:

"The second act's much better than the first."

George's hopes, dashed but not broken, recovered somewhat. After all there had been one or two gleams of real jokes, and a catchiness in certain airs; and the spark possessed temperament in profusion. It was possible that the next act might be diverting.

"You do look tired," said Laurencine.

"Oh no, darling!" Lois objected. "I think he looks splendid."

She was intensely happy in the theatre. The box was very well placed - since

Irene had bought it - with a view equally good of the stage and of the semicircle of boxes. Lois' glance wandered blissfully round the boxes, all occupied by gay parties, and over the vivacious stalls. She gazed, and she enjoyed being gazed at. She bathed herself in the glitter and the gaudiness and the opulence and the humanity, as in tonic fluid. She seemed to float sinuously and voluptuously immersed in it, as in tepid water lit with sunshine.

"Do have a choc.," she invited eagerly.

George took a chocolate. She took one. They all took one. They all had the unconscious pride of youth that does not know itself young. Each was different from the others. George showed the reserve of the artist; Lucas the ease of the connoisseur of mundane spectacles; Laurencine the sturdy, catholic, girlish innocence that nothing can corrupt. And the sovereign was Lois. She straightened her shoulders; she leaned languorously; she looked up, she looked down; she spoke softly and loudly; she laughed and smiled. And in every movement and in every gesture and tone she symbolized the ecstasy of life. She sought pleasure, and she had found it, and she had no afterthought. She was infectious; she was irresistible, and terrible too. For it was dismaying, at any rate to George, to dwell on the fierceness of her instinct and on the fierceness of its satisfaction. To George her burning eyes were wistful, pathetic, in their simplicity. He felt a sort of fearful pity for her. And he admired her - she was something definite; she was something magnificently outright; she did live. Also he liked her; the implications in her glance appealed to him. The peculiar accents in which she referred to the enigma of Irene Wheeler were extraordinarily attractive to that part of his nature which was perverse and sophisticated. "At least she is not a simpleton," he thought. "And she doesn't pretend to be. Some day I shall talk to her."

The orchestra resumed; the lights went out. Lois settled herself to fresh enchantment as the curtain rolled up to disclose the bright halls and staircases of a supper-club. The second act was an amplification and inflammation of the themes of the first. As for the music, George listened in vain for an original tune, even for a tune of which he could not foretell the end from the beginning; the one or two engaging bits of melody which enlivened the first act were employed again in the second. The disdainful, lethargic chorus was the same; the same trio of delicious wantons fondled and kissed the same red-nosed comedian, who was still in the same state of inebriety, and the gay spark flitted roysteringly through the same evolutions, in pursuit of the same simple ideals. The jocularity pivoted unendingly on the same twin centres of alcohol and concupiscence. Gradually the latter grew to more and more importance, and the piece became a high and candid homage to the impulse by force of which alone one generation succeeds another. No beautiful and graceful young girl on the stage blenched before the salacious witticisms of the tireless comedian; on the contrary he remained the darling of the stage. And as he was the darling of the stage, so was he the darling of the audience.

And if no beautiful and graceful young girl blenched on the stage, neither did the beautiful and graceful young girls in the audience blench. You could see them sitting happily with their fathers and mothers and cousins and uncles and aunts, savouring the spectacle from dim stalls and boxes in the most perfect respectability. Laurencine leaning her elbows on the ledge of the box, watched with eager, parted lips, and never showed the slightest sign of uneasiness.

George was uneasy; he was distressed. The extraordinary juxtaposition of respectability and a ribald sexual display startled but did not distress him. If the whole audience was ready to stand it he certainly was. He had no desire to protect people from themselves, nor to blush on behalf of others - whoever they might be. Had anybody accused him of saintliness he would have resented the charge, quite justifiably, and if the wit of The Gay Spark had been witty, he would have enjoyed it without a qualm. What distressed him, what utterly desolated him, was the grossness, the poorness, the cheapness, the dullness, and the uninventive monotony of the interminable entertainment. He yawned, he could not help yawning; he yawned his soul away. Lois must have heard him yawning, but she did not move. He looked at her curiously, pitifully, speculating how much of her luxury was due to Irene Wheeler, and how little to 'Parisian' of The Sunday Journal - for he had been inquiring about the fruits of journalism. The vision of his own office and of the perspective drawing rose seductively and irresistibly in his mind. He could not stay in the theatre; he felt that if he stayed he would be in danger of dropping down dead, suffocated by tedium; and the drawing must be finished; it would not wait; it was the most urgent thing in the world. And not a syllable had any person in the box said to him about his great task. Lois's forearm, braceleted, lay on the front of the box. Unceremoniously he took her hand.

"Bye-bye."

"You aren't going?" Her whisper was incredulous.

"Must."

He gave her no chance to expostulate. With one movement he had seized his hat and coat and slid from the box, just as the finale of the act was imminent and the red-nosed comedian was measuring the gay spark for new lingerie with a giant property-cigar. He had not said good-bye to Laurencine. He had not asked about their departure on the morrow. But he was free.

In the foyer a couple - a woman in a rose plush sortie de bal, and a blade - were mysteriously talking. The blade looked at him, smiled, and left the lady.

"Hallo, old fellow!" It was Buckingham Smith, who had been getting on in the world.

They shook hands.

"You've left Chelsea, haven't you?"

"Yes," said George.

"So've I. Don't see much of the old gang nowadays. Heard anything of old Princey lately?"

George replied that he had not. The colloquy was over in a moment.

"You must come and see my show - next week," Buck Smith called out after the departing George.

"I will," cried George.

He walked quickly up to Russell Square, impatient to steep himself anew in his work. All sense of fatigue had left him. Time seemed to be flying past him, and he rushing towards an unknown fate. On the previous day he had received an enheartening, challenging, sardonic letter from his stepfather, who referred to politics and envisaged a new epoch for the country. Edwin Clayhanger was a Radical of a type found only in the Midlands and the North. For many years Clayhanger's party, to which he was passionately faithful, had had no war-cry and no programme worthy of its traditions. The increasing success of the campaign against Protection, and certain signs that the introduction of Chinese labour into South Africa could be effectively resisted, had excited the middle-aged provincial - now an Alderman - and he had managed to communicate fire to George. But in George, though he sturdily shared his stepfather's views, the resulting righteous energy was diverted to architectural creation.

3

The circumstances in which, about a month later, George lunched with the Ingram family at their flat in the Rue d'Athenes, near the Gare St. Lazare, Paris, had an appearance of the utmost simplicity and ordinariness. He had been down to Staffordshire for a rest, and had returned unrested. And then Mr. Enwright had suggested that it would do him good to go to Paris, even to go alone. He went, with no plan, but having made careful arrangements for the telegraphing to him of the result of the competition, which was daily expected. By this time he was very seriously convinced that there was no hope of him being among the selected six or ten, and he preferred to get the news away from London rather than in it; he felt that he could not face London on the day or the morrow of a defeat which would of course render his youthful audacity ridiculous.

He arrived in Paris on a Wednesday evening, and took a room in a maison meublee of the Rue de Seze. Every inexperienced traveller in Paris has a friend who knows a lodging in Paris which he alleges is better and cheaper than any other lodging - and which is not. The house in the Rue de Seze was the economical paradise of Buckingham Smith, whom George had encountered again at the Buckingham Smith exhibition. Buckingham Smith, with over half his pictures bearing the red seal that indicates 'Sold,' felt justified in posing to the younger George as a cosmopolitan expert - especially as his opinions on modern French art were changing. George spent three solitary and dejected days in Paris, affecting an interest in museums and architecture and French opera, and committing follies. Near the end of the third day, a Saturday, he suddenly sent a threepenny express note to Lois Ingram. He would have telephoned had he dared to use the French telephone. On Sunday morning, an aproned valet having informed him that Monsieur was demanded at the telephone, he had to use the telephone. Lois told him that he must come to lunch, and that afterwards he would be escorted to the races. Dejection was instantly transformed into a gay excitation. Proud of having spoken through a French telephone, he began to conceive romantically the interior of a Paris home - he had seen naught but a studio or so with Mr. Enwright - and to thrill at the prospect of Sunday races. Not merely had he never seen a horse-race on a Sunday - he had never seen a horse-race at all. He perhaps was conscious of a genuine interest in Lois and her environment, but what most satisfied and flattered him, after his loneliness, was the bare fact of possessing social relations in Paris at all.

The Ingram home was up four flights of naked oaken stairs, fairly swept, in a plain, flat-fronted house. The door of the home was opened by a dark, untidy, dishevelled, uncapped, fat girl, with a full apron, dazzling white and rectangularly creased, that had obviously just been taken out of a drawer. Familiarly and amicably smiling, she led him into a small, modest drawing-room where were Lois and her father and mother. Lois was enigmatic and taciturn. Mr. and Mrs. Ingram were ingenuous, loquacious, and at ease. Both of them had twinkling eyes. Mrs. Ingram was rather stout and grey and small, and wore a quiet, inexpensive blue dress, embroidered at the neck in the Morrisian manner, of no kind of fashionableness. She spoke in a low voice, smiled to herself with a benevolence that was not without a touch of the sardonic, and often looked at the floor or at the ceiling. Mr. Ingram, very slim and neat, was quite as small as his wife, and seemed smaller. He talked much and rather amusingly, in a somewhat mincing tone, as it were apologetically, truly anxious to please. He had an extremely fair complexion, and his youthfulness was quite startling. His golden hair and perfect teeth might have belonged to a boy. George leapt immediately into familiarity with these two. But nobody could have less resembled his preconceived image of 'Parisian' than Mr. Ingram. And he could not understand a bit whence or how such a pair had produced their daughter Lois. Laurencine was a far more comprehensible offspring for them.

The dining-room was even less spacious than the drawing-room, and as unpretentious. The furniture everywhere was sparse, but there were one or two rich knick-knacks, and an abundance of signed photographs. The few pictures, too, were signed, and they drew attention. On the table the napkins, save George's, were in rings, and each ring different from the others. George's napkin had the air of a wealthy, stiff, shiny relative of the rest. Evidently in that home the long art of making both ends meet was daily practised. George grew light-hearted and happy, despite the supreme preoccupation which only a telegram could allay. He had keenly the sensation of being abroad. The multiplicity of doors, the panelling of the doors, the narrow planking of the oaken floor, the moulding of the cornices, the shape of the windows, the view of the courtyard from the dining-room and of attics and chimney-cowls from the drawing-room, the closed anthracite stoves in lieu of fires, the crockery, the wine-bottle, the mustard, the grey salt, the unconventional gestures and smiles and exclamations of the unkempt maid - all these strange details enchanted him, and they all set off very vividly the intense, nice, honest, reassuring Englishness of the host and hostess.

It was not until after the others were seated for the meal that Laurencine made her appearance. She was a magnificent and handsome virgin, big-boned, physically a little awkward, candid. How exquisitely and absurdly she flushed in shaking hands with George! With what a delicious mock-furious setting of the teeth and tossing of the head she frowned at her mother's reproaches for being late! This family knew the meaning of intimacy but not of ceremony. Laurencine sat down at her father's left; George was next to her on Mrs. Ingram's right. Lois had the whole of the opposite side of the table.

"Does he know?" Laurencine asked; and turning to George: "Do you know?"

"Know what?"

"You'd better tell him, dad. You like talking, and he ought to know. I shan't be able to eat if he doesn't. It would be so ridiculous sitting here and pretending."

Mrs. Ingram looked upwards across the room at a corner of the ceiling, and smiled faintly.

"You might," she said, "begin by asking Mr. Cannon if he particularly wants to be burdened with the weight of your secrets, my dear child."

"Oh! I particularly do," said George.

"There's no secret about it - at least there won't be soon," said Laurencine.

Lois spoke simultaneously:

"My dear mother, please call George George. If we call him George, you can't possibly call him Mr. Cannon."

"I quite admit," Mrs. Ingram replied to her eldest, "I quite admit that you and Laurencine are entitled to criticise my relations with my husband, because he's your father. But I propose to carry on my affairs with other men just according to my own ideas, and any interference will be resented. I've had a bad night, owing to the garage again, and I don't feel equal to calling George George. I've only known him about twenty minutes. Moreover, I might be misunderstood, mightn't I, Mr. Cannon?"

"You might," said George.

"Now, dad!" Laurencine admonished.

Mr. Ingram, addressing George, began:

"Laurencine suffers from a grave form of self-consciousness - "

"I don't, dad."

"It is a disease akin to conceit. Her sufferings are sometimes so acute that she cannot sit up straight and is obliged to loll and curl her legs round the legs of the chair. We are all very sorry for her. The only treatment is brutal candour, as she herself advocates - "

Laurencine jumped up, towered over her father, and covered his mouth with her hand.

"This simple hand," said Mr. Ingram, seizing it, "will soon bear a ring. Laurencine is engaged to be married."

"I'm not, father." She sat down again.

"Well, you are not. But you will be, I presume, by post-time tonight. A young man of the name of Lucas has written to Laurencine this morning in a certain sense, and he has also written to me. Laurencine has seen my letter, and I've seen hers. But my envelope contained only one letter. Whether her envelope contained more than one, whether the epistle which I saw is written in the style usually practised by the present age, whether it was composed for the special purpose of being shown to me, I do not know, and discretion and nice gentlemanly feeling forbid me to inquire. However - "

At this point, Laurencine snatched her father's napkin off his knees and put it on her own.

"However, my wife and I have met this Mr. Lucas, and as our opinion about him is not wholly unfavourable, the matter was satisfactorily and quickly arranged - even before I had had my bath; Laurencine and I will spend the afternoon in writing suitable communications to Mr. Lucas. I am ready to show her mine for a shilling, but I doubt if five pounds would procure me a sight of hers. Yet she is only an amateur writer and I'm a professional."

There was a little silence, and then George said awkwardly:

"I congratulate old Lucas."

"This news must have astonished you extremely," observed Mr. Ingram. "It must have come as a complete surprise. In fact you are doubtless in the condition known to charwomen as capable of being knocked down with a feather."

"Oh! Quite!" George agreed.

Nevertheless, in spite of his light tone, he regretted the engagement. He did not think Lucas was worthy of the splendid girl. He felt sorry for her. At that moment she faced him bravely, and smiled. Her face had a tremendous deep crimson flush. There was a woman somewhere in the girl! Strange phenomenon!

And another strange phenomenon: if Laurencine had been self-conscious, George also was self-conscious; and he avoided Lois's eyes! Why? He wondered whether the circumstances in which he had come to Paris and entered the Ingram home were as simple and ordinary as they superficially appeared.

"Laurencine," said her mother, "give your father back his serviette!"

"Mine's fallen."

"Never mind, my dear," said Mr. Ingram very benevolently, and he bent down and retrieved Laurencine's napkin, which he kept. "And now," he proceeded, "the serious operation being over and the patient out of danger, shall we talk about something else for a few moments?"

"I should think so indeed!" Laurencine exclaimed, suddenly gay. "George, when shall you know about the competition?"

"Any minute, I might," said he.

They all talked sympathetically to George on the new subject.

After lunch, Lois disappeared. She came back resplendent for the races, when coffee had long been finished in the drawing-room.

"Why aren't you ready, Laure?" she demanded.

"I'm not going, darling."

"Lois," Mr. Ingram exhorted, "don't forget the afternoon is to be spent in literary composition."

"It isn't," Laurencine contradicted. "I may as well tell you I've written all I mean to write in the way of letters for one day. But I don't want to go, really, Lois darling."

"No. She wants to think," Mrs. Ingram explained.

Lois set her lips together, and then glimpsed herself in the large mirror over the anthracite stove. She looked too rich and complicated for that simple drawing-room.

A performance on a horn made itself heard in the street below.

"There he is!" said Laurencine.

She opened a window and ran out on to the balcony and leaned over; then glanced within the room and nodded. George had assumed that Irene Wheeler was the author and hostess of the race-party, and he was not mistaken. Irene's automobile had been sent round to embark him and the girls. Mrs. Ingram urged him to come again the next day, and he said ardently that he would. Mrs. Ingram's 'affair' with him was progressing rapidly.

"But I hope you'll call me George, then," he added.

"I may!" she said. "I may! I may go even further."

Lois and George descended the stairs in silence. He had not seen her, nor written to her, since the night of the comedy when he had so abruptly left the box. Once or twice at the Ingrams' he had fancied that she might be vexed with him for that unceremonious departure. But she was not. The frank sigh of relief which she gave on reaching the foot of the interminable stairs, and her equally frank smile, had no reserve whatever.

The chauffeur's welcoming grin seemed to indicate that he was much attached to Miss Ingram. He touched his hat, bowed, and spoke to her at some length in French. Lois frowned.

"It seems Miss Wheeler doesn't feel equal to going out this afternoon," she translated to George. "But she insists that we shall use the car all the same."

"Is she ill?"

"She's lying down, trying to sleep."

"Well, then, I suppose we'd better use the car, hadn't we?"

Lois said seriously:

"If you don't object, I don't."

4

At Longchamps the sun most candidly and lovingly blessed the elaborate desecration of the English Sabbath. The delicately ornamented grand stands, the flags, the swards, the terraces, the alleys, the booths, the notice-boards, the vast dappled sea of hats and faces in the distant cheaper parts of the Hippodrome, were laved in the descending, caressing floods of voluptuous, warm sunshine. The air itself seemed luminous. The enchantment of the sun was irresistible; it stunned apprehensions and sad memories, obliterating for a moment all that was or might be unhappy in the past or in the future. George yielded to it. He abandoned his preoccupations about the unsatisfactoriness of using somebody else's car in the absence of the owner, about Mr. and Mrs. Ingram's ignorance of the fact that their daughter had gone off alone with him, about Lois's perfect indifference to this fact, about the engagement of Laurencine to a man not her equal in worth, about the strange, uncomfortable effect of Laurencine's engagement upon his attitude towards Lois, and finally and supremely about the competition. He gave himself up to the bright warmth like an animal, and forgot. And he became part of the marvellous and complicated splendour of the scene, took pride in it, took even credit for it (Heaven knew why!), and gradually passed from insular astonishment to a bland, calm acceptance of the miracles of sensuous beatitude which civilization had to offer.

After all, he was born to such experiences; they were his right; and he was equal to them. Nevertheless his conviction of the miraculous fortunately was not impaired. What was impaired was his conviction of his own culture. He was constantly thinking that he knew everything or could imagine everything, and constantly undergoing the shock of undeception; but the shock of the Longchamps Sunday was excessive. He had quite failed to imagine the race-meeting; he had imagined an organism brilliant, perhaps, but barbaric and without form and style; he had imagined grotesque contrasts of squalor,

162

rascality, and fashion; he had imagined an affair predominantly equine and masculine. The reality did not correspond; it transcended his imagination; it painfully demonstrated his jejune crudity. The Hippodrome was as formalized and stylistic as an Italian garden; the only contrasts were those of one elegance with another; horses were not to be seen, except occasionally in the distance when under their riders they shot past some dark background a flitting blur of primary colours with a rumble of muffled thunder; and women, not men, predominated.

On entering the Hippodrome George and Lois had met a group of fashionably attired women, and he had thought: "There's a bunch of jolly well-dressed ones." But as the reserved precincts opened out before him he saw none but fashionably attired women. They were there not in hundreds but in thousands. They sat in rows on the grand stands; they jostled each other on the staircases; they thronged the alleys and swards. The men were negligible beside them. And they were not only fashionably and very fashionably attired - all their frocks and all their hats and all their parasols and all their boots were new, glittering, spick-and-span; were complex and expensive; not one feared the sun. The conception of what those innumerable chromatic toilettes had cost in the toil, stitch by stitch, of malodorous workrooms and in the fatigue of pale, industrious creatures was really formidable. But it could not detract from the scenic triumph. The scenic triumph dazzlingly justified itself, and proved beyond any cavilling that earth was a grand, intoxicating place, and Longchamps under the sun an unequalled paradise of the senses.... Ah! These women were finished - finished to the least detail of coiffure, sunshade-handle, hatpin, jewellery, handbag, bootlace, glove, stocking, lingerie. Each was the product of many arts in co-ordination. Each was of great price. And there were thousands of them. They were as cheap as periwinkles. George thought: "This is Paris."

He said aloud:

"Seems to be a fine lot of new clothes knocking about."

Evidently for Lois his tone was too impressed, not sufficiently casual. She replied in her condescending manner, which he detested:

"My poor George, considering that this is the opening of the spring season, and the place where all the new spring fashions are tried out - what did you expect?"

The dolt had not known that he was assisting at a solemnity recognized as such by experts throughout the clothed world. But Lois knew all those things. She herself was trying out a new toilette, for which doubtless Irene Wheeler was partly sponsor. She could hold her own on the terraces with the rest. She was staggeringly different now from the daughter of the simple home in the Rue d'Athenes.

The eyes of the splendid women aroused George's antipathy, because he seemed to detect antipathy in them - not against himself but against the male in him. These women, though by their glances they largely mistrusted and despised each other, had the air of having combined sexually against a whole sex. The situation was very contradictory. They had beautified and ornamented themselves in order to attract a whole sex, and yet they appeared to resent the necessity and instinct to attract. They submitted with a secret repugnance to the mysterious and supreme bond which kept the sexes inexorably together. And while stooping to fascinate, while deliberately seeking attention, they still had the assured mien of conquerors. Their eyes said that they knew they were indispensable, that they had a transcendent role to play, that no concealed baseness of the inimical sex was hidden from them, and that they meant to exploit their position to the full. These Latin women exhibited a logic, an elegance, and a frankness beyond the reach of the Anglo-Saxon. Their eyes said not that they had been disillusioned, but rather that they had never had illusions. They admitted the facts; they admitted everything - economic dependence, chicane, the intention to seize every advantage, ruthless egotism. They had no shame for a depravity which they shared equally with the inescapable and cherished enemy And it was the youngest who, beneath the languishing and the softness and the invitation deceitful and irresistible, gazed outmost triumphantly to the enemy: "You are the victims. We have tried our strength and your infirmity." They were heroic. There was a feeling in the bright air of melancholy and doom as the two hostile forces, inseparable, inextricably involved together, surveyed the opponent in the everlasting conflict. George felt its influence upon himself, upon Lois, upon the whole scene. The eyes of the most feminine women in the world, denying their smiles and their lure, had discovered to him something which marked a definite change in his estimate of certain ultimate earthly values.

Lois said:

"Perhaps a telegram is waiting for you at the hotel."

"Well, I can wait till I get back," he replied stoutly.

He thought, looking at her by his side:

"She is just like these Frenchwomen!" And for some reason he felt proud.

"You needn't," said Lois, "We can telephone from under the grand stand if you like."

"But I don't know the number."

"We can get that out of the book, of course."

"I don't reckon I can use these French telephones."

"Oh! My poor boy, I'll telephone for you - unless you prefer not to risk knowing the worst."

Yes, her tone was the tone of a strange woman. And it was she who thirsted for the result of the competition.

Controlling himself, submissively he asked her to telephone for him, and she agreed in a delightfully agreeable voice. She seemed to know the entire geography of the Hippodrome. She secured a telephone-cabin in a very business-like manner. As she entered the cabin she said to George:

"I'll ask them if a telegram has come, and if it has I'll ask them to open it and read it to me, or spell it - of course it'll be in English.... Eh?"

Through the half-open door of the cabin he watched her, and listened. She rapidly turned over the foul and torn pages of the telephone-book with her thumb. She spoke into the instrument very clearly, curtly, and authoritatively. George could translate in his mind what she said - his great resolve to learn French had carried him so far.

"On the part of Monsieur Cannon, one of your clients, Monsieur Cannon of London. Has there arrived a telegram for him?"

She waited. The squalor of the public box increased the effect of her young and proud stylishness and of her perfume. George waited, humbled by her superior skill in the arts of life, and saying anxiously to himself: "Perhaps in a moment I shall know the result," almost trembling.

She hung up the instrument, and, with a glance at George, shook her head.

"There isn't anything," she murmured.

He said:

"It's very queer, isn't it? However..."

As they emerged from the arcana of the grand stand, Lois was stopped by a tall, rather handsome Jew, who, saluting her with what George esteemed to be French exaggeration of gesture, nevertheless addressed her in a confidential tone in English. George, having with British restraint acknowledged the salute, stood aside, and gazed discreetly away from the pair. He could not hear what was being said. After several minutes Lois rejoined George, and they went back into the crowds and the sun. She did not speak. She did not utter one word. Only, when the numbers went up for a certain race, she remarked:

"This is the Prix du Cadran. It's the principal race of the afternoon."

And when that was over, amid cheering that ran about the field like fire through dried bush, she added:

"I think I ought to go back now. I told the chauffeur to be here after the Prix du Cadran. What time is it exactly?"

They sat side by side in the long, open car, facing the chauffeur's creaseless back. After passing the Cascade, the car swerved into the Allee de Longchamps which led in an absolutely straight line, two miles long, to the Port Maillot and the city. Spring decorated the magnificent wooded thoroughfare. The side-alleys, aisles of an interminable nave, were sprinkled with revellers and lovers and the most respectable families half hidden amid black branches and gleams of tender green. Automobiles and carriages threaded the main alley at varying speeds. The number of ancient horse-cabs gradually increased until, after the intersection of the Allee de la Reine Marguerite, they thronged the vast road.

All the humble and shabby genteel people in Paris who could possibly afford a cab seemed to have taken a cab. Nearly every cab was overloaded. The sight of this vast pathetic effort of the disinherited towards gaiety and distraction and the mood of spring, intensified the vague sadness in George due to the race-crowd, Lois's silence, and the lack of news about the competition.

At length Lois said, scowling - no doubt involuntarily:

"I think I'd better tell you now. Irene Wheeler's committed suicide. Shot herself." She pressed her lips together and looked at the road.

George gave a startled exclamation. He could not for an instant credit the astounding news.

"But how do you know? Who told you?"

"The man who spoke to me in the grand stand. He's correspondent of The London Courier - friend of father's of course."

George protested:

"Then why on earth didn't you tell me before?... Shot herself! What for?"

"I didn't tell you before because I couldn't."

All the violence of George's nature came to the surface as he said brutally:

"Of course you could!"

"I tell you I couldn't!" she cried. "I knew the car wouldn't be there for us until after the Prix du Cadran. And if I'd told you I couldn't have borne to be walking about that place three-quarters of an hour. We should have had to talk about it. I couldn't have borne that. And so you needn't be cross, please."

But her voice did not break, nor her eyes shine.

"I was wondering whether I should tell the chauffeur at once, or let him find it out."

"I should let him find it out," said George. "He doesn't know that you know. Besides, it might upset his driving."

"Oh! I shouldn't mind about his driving," Lois murmured disdainfully.

5

When the uninformed chauffeur drove the car with a grand sweep under the marquise of the ostentatious pale yellow block in the Avenue Hoche where Irene Wheeler had had her flat, Mr. Ingram and a police-agent were standing on the steps, but nobody else was near. Little Mr. Ingram came forward anxiously, his eyes humid, and his face drawn with pain and distress.

"We know," said Lois. "I met Mr. Cardow at Longchamps. He knew."

Mr. Ingram's pain and distress seemed to increase.

He said, after a moment:

"Alfred will drive you home, dear, at once. Alfred, vous seriez gentil de reconduire Mademoiselle a la rue d'Athenes." He had the air of supplicating the amiable chauffeur. "Mr. Cannon, I particularly want a few words with you."

"But, father, I must come in!" said Lois. "I must - "

"You will go home immediately. Please, please do not add to my difficulties. I shall come home myself as quickly as possible. You can do nothing here. The seals have been affixed."

Lois raised her chin in silence.

Then Mr. Ingram turned to the police-agent, spoke to him in French, and pointed to the car persuasively; and the police-agent permissively nodded. The chauffeur, with an affectation of detachment worthy of the greatest days of valetry, drove off, leaving George behind. Mr. Ingram descended the steps.

"I think, perhaps, we might go to a cafe," said he in a tone which dispersed George's fear of a discussion as to the propriety of the unchaperoned visit to the races.

They sat down on the terrasse of a large cafe near the Place des Ternes, a few hundred yards away from the Avenue Hoche. The cafe was nearly empty, citizens being either in the Bois or on the main boulevards. Mr. Ingram sadly ordered bocks. The waiter, flapping his long apron, called out in a loud voice as he went within: "Deux blonds, deux." George supplied cigarettes.

"Mr. Cannon," began Mr. Ingram, "it is advisable for me to tell you a most marvellous and painful story. I have only just heard it. It has overwhelmed me, but I must do my duty." He paused.

"Certainly," said George self-consciously, not knowing what to say. He nearly blushed as, in an attempt to seem at ease, he gazed negligently round at the rows of chairs and marble tables, and at the sparse traffic of the somnolent Place.

Mr. Ingram proceeded.

"When I first knew Irene Wheeler she was an art student here. So was I. But I was already married, of course, and older than she. Exactly what her age was I should not care to say. I can, however, say quite truthfully that her appearance has scarcely altered in those nineteen years. She always affirmed that her relatives, in Indianapolis, were wealthy - or at least had money, but that they were very mean with her. She lived in the simplest way. As for me, I had to give up art for something less capricious, but capricious enough in all conscience. Miss Wheeler went to America and was away for some time - a year or two. When she came back to Paris she told us that she had made peace with her people, and that her uncle, whom for present purposes I will call Mr. X, a very celebrated railway magnate of Indianapolis, had adopted her. Her new manner of life amply confirmed these statements."

"Deux bocks," cried the waiter, slapping down on the table two saucers and two stout glass mugs filled with frothing golden liquid.

George, unaccustomed to the ritual of cafes, began at once to sip, but Mr. Ingram, aware that the true boulevardier always ignores his bock for several minutes, behaved accordingly.

"She was evidently extremely rich. I have had some experience, and I estimate that she had the handling of at least half a million francs a year. She seemed to be absolutely her own mistress. You have had an opportunity of judging her style of existence. However, her attitude towards ourselves was entirely unchanged. She remained intimate with my wife, who, I may say, is an excellent judge of character, and she was exceedingly kind to our girls, especially Lois - but Laurencine too - and as they grew up she treated them like sisters. Now, Mr. Cannon, I shall be perfectly frank with you. I shall not pretend that I was not rather useful to Miss Wheeler - I mean in the Press. She had social ambitions. And why not? One may condescend towards them, but do they not serve a purpose in the structure of society? Very rich as she was, it was easy for me to be useful to her. And at worst her pleasure in publicity was quite innocent - indeed, it was so innocent as to be charming. Naive, shall we call it?"

Here Mr. Ingram smiled sadly, tasted his bock, and threw away the end of a cigarette.

"Well," he resumed, "I am coming to the point. This is the point, which I have learnt scarcely an hour ago - I was called up on the telephone immediately after you and Lois had gone. This is the point. Mr. X was not poor Irene's uncle, and he had not adopted her. But it was his money that she was spending." Mr. Ingram gazed fixedly at George.

"I see," said George calmly, rising to the role of man of the world. "I see." He had strange mixed sensations of pleasure, pride, and confusion. "And you've just found this out?"

"I have just found it out from Mr. X himself, whom I met for the first time to-day - in poor Irene's flat. I never assisted at such a scene. Never! It positively unnerved me. Mr. X is a man of fifty-five, fabulously wealthy, used to command, autocratic, famous in all the Stock Exchanges of the world. When I tell you that he cried like a child ... Oh! I never had such an experience. His infatuation for Irene - indescribable! Indescribable! She had made her own terms with him. He told me himself. Astounding terms, but for him it was those terms or nothing. He accepted them - had to. She was to be quite free. The most absolute discretion was to be observed. He came to Paris or London every year, and sometimes she went to America. She utterly refused to live in America."

"Why didn't she marry him?"

"He has a wife. I have no doubt in my own mind that one of his reasons for accepting her extraordinary terms was to keep in close touch with her at all costs in case his wife should die. Otherwise he might have lost her altogether. He told me many things about poor Irene's family in Indianapolis which I will not repeat. It was true that they had money, as Irene said; but as for anything else ...! The real name was not Wheeler."

"Has he been over, here long?"

"He landed at Cherbourg last night. Just arrived."

"And she killed herself at once."

"Whether the deed was done immediately before or immediately after his arrival is not yet established. And I need hardly tell you that Mr. X has already fixed up arrangements not to appear in the case at all. But one thing is sure - she had made all the preparations for suicide, made them with the greatest care. The girls saw her yesterday, and both Lois and I spoke to her on the telephone this morning. Not a trace of anything in her voice. I assume she had given a message for Lois to the chauffeur."

"Yes," said George. "We never dreamed - "

"Of course not. Of course not."

"But why did she - "

"Another man, my dear sir! Another man! A young man named Defourcambault, in the French Embassy in London."

"Oh, him!" George burst out. "I know him," he added fiercely.

"You do? Yes, I remember Laurencine saying.... Poor Irene, I fear, was very deeply in love with him. She had written to Mr. X about Defourcambault. He showed me the letter - most touching, really most touching. His answer to it was to come to Europe at once. But poor Irene's death had nothing to do with his coming. She did not know he was coming. She shot herself as she lay in bed, and on the pillow was a letter from this man Defourcambault - well, saying good-bye to her. I saw the letter. Not a letter that I should wish to remember. Perhaps she had told him something of her life. I much fear that Defourcambault will be fetched from London, though I hope not. There would be no object.... No, thank you. I will not smoke again. I only wanted to say this to you. All Paris knows that my daughters were intimate with poor Irene. Now, if anything comes out, if anything should come out, if there's any talk - you see my fear. I wish to assure you, Mr. Cannon, that I had not the slightest suspicion, not the slightest. And yet we journalists cannot exactly be called ingenuous! But I had not the slightest suspicion, nor had my wife. You know the situation between Laurencine and your friend Lucas. You and he are very intimate, I believe. May I count on you to explain everything from my point of view to Mr. Lucas? I could not bear that the least cloud should rest upon my little Laurencine."

"You needn't trouble about Lucas," said George positively. "Lucas 'll be all right. Still, I'll talk to him."

"Thank you very much. Thank you very much. I knew I could rely on you. I've kept you a long time, but I'm sure you understand. I'm thinking only of my girls. Not for anything would I have them know the truth about the affair."

"But aren't they bound to know it?" George asked.

Mr. Ingram was wounded. "I hope not. I hope not," he said gravely. "It is not right that young girls should know such things."

"But surely, sooner or later - "

"Ah! After they are married, conceivably. That would be quite different," he admitted, with cheerfulness. "And now," he smiled, "I'm afraid I've got to go and write the case up for London. I can catch the mail, I think. If not, I must cable. But they hate me to cable when the mail is possible. Can I drop you anywhere?"

Simultaneously he signalled to a taxi and knocked on the window for the attendance of the waiter.

"Thanks. If you're going anywhere near the Place de l'Opera," said George.

6

He was excited, rather than saddened, by the tragic event. He was indeed very excited. And also he had a deep satisfaction, because it seemed to him that he had at last been truly admitted into the great secret fellowship of adult males. The initiation flattered his pride. He left Mr. Ingram at the door of an English newspaper office in the Boulevard des Italiens, and, after vainly asking for telegrams at the hotel, walked away, aimlessly at first, along broad pavements encumbered with the chairs and tables of vast, crowded cafes, and with bright Sunday idlers and sinister street-vendors. But in a moment he had decided that he must and ought to pay a call in the Rue d'Athenes. Mr. Ingram had said nothing about his seeing Lois again, had not referred to Mrs. Ingram's invitation to repeat his visit, might even vaguely object to an immediate interview between him and Lois. Yet he could not, as a man of the world, abandon Lois so unceremoniously. He owed something to Lois and he owed something to himself. And he was a free adult. The call was natural and necessary, and if Mr. Ingram did not like it he must, in the Five Towns phrase, lump it. George set off to find the Rue d'Athenes unguided. It was pleasurable to think that there was a private abode in the city of cafes, hotels, and museums to which he had the social right of entry.

The watching concierge of the house nodded to him politely as he began to mount the stairs. The Ingrams' servant smiled upon him as upon an old and familiarly respected friend.

"Mademoiselle Lois?" he said, with directness.

The slatternly, benevolent girl widened her mouth still further in a smile still more cordial, and led him to the drawing-room. As she did so she picked up a newspaper packet that lay on a table in the tiny hall, and, without putting it on a salver, deposited it in front of Lois, who was alone in the drawing-room. George wondered what Lois would have thought of such an outrage upon

170

established ritual had it happened to her in the home of Irene Wheeler instead of in her own; and then the imagined vision of Irene lying dead in the sumptuous home in the Avenue Hoche seemed to render all established ritual absurd.

"So you've come!" exclaimed Lois harshly. "Mother's quite knocked over, and Laurencine's looking after her. All the usual eau-de-Cologne business. And I should say father's not much better. My poor parents! What did dad want you for?"

The servant had closed the door. Lois had got up from her chair and was walking about the room, pulling aside a curtain and looking out, tapping the mantelpiece with her hand, tapping with her feet the base of the stove, George had the sensation of being locked in a cage with a mysterious, incalculable, and powerful animal. He was fascinated. He thought: "I wanted to see her alone and I am seeing her alone!"

"Well?" she insisted. "What did dad want you for?"

"Oh! He told me a few things about Miss Wheeler."

"I suppose he told you about Jules, and I suppose he told you I wasn't to know on any account! Poor old dad! Instead of feeling he's my father, d'you know what I feel? I feel as if I was his mother. He's so clever; he's frightfully clever; but he was never meant for this world. He's just a beautiful child. How in Heaven's name could he think that a girl like me could be intimate with Irene, and not know about the things that were in her mind? How could he? Why! I've talked for hours with Irene about Jules! She'd much sooner talk with me even than with mother. She's cried in front of me. But I never cried. I always told her she was making a mistake about Jules. I detested the little worm. But she couldn't see it. No, she couldn't. She'd have quarrelled with me if I'd let her quarrel. However, I wouldn't let her. Fancy quarrelling - over a man! She couldn't help being mad over Jules. I told her she couldn't - that was why I bore with her. I always told her he was only playing with her. The one thing that I didn't tell her was that she was too old for him. She really believed she never got any older. When I say too old for him, I mean for her sake, not for his. He didn't think she was too old. He couldn't - with that complexion of hers. I never envied her anything else except her complexion and her money. But he wouldn't marry an American. His people wouldn't let him. He's got to marry into a family like his own, and there're only about ten for him to choose from. I know she wrote to him on Thursday. She must have had the answer this morning. Of course she had a revolver. I've got one myself. She went to bed and did it. She used to say to me that if ever she did it that was how she would do it.... And father tells me not to add to his difficulties! Don't you think it's comic?... But she never told me everything. I knew that. I accused her of it. She admitted it. However..."

Lois spoke in a low, regular murmur, experimentally aware that privacy in

171

a Paris flat is relative. There were four doors in the walls of the drawing-room, and a bedroom on either side. At moments George could scarcely catch her words. He had never heard her say so much at once, for she was taciturn by habit, even awkward in conversation. She glowered at him darkly. The idea flashed through his mind: "There can't be another girl like her. She's unique." He almost trembled at the revelation. He was afraid, and yet courageous, challenging, combative. She had grandeur. It might be moral, or not; but it was grandeur. And - (that touch about the complexion!) - she could remember her freckles! She might, in her hard egotism, in the rushing impulses of her appetites - she might be an enemy, an enemy to close with whom would be terrible rapture, and the war of the sexes was a sublime war, infinitely superior in emotions to tame peace. (And had she not been certified an angel? Had he not himself seen the angel in her?) She dwarfed her father and mother. The conception, especially, of Mr. Ingram at lunch, deliciously playful and dominating, and now with the adroit wit crushed out of him and only a naive sentimentality left, was comic - as she had ruthlessly characterized it. She alone towered formidably over the devastated ruins of Irene's earthly splendour.

He said nothing.

She rang the bell by the mantelpiece. He heard it ring. No answer. She rang again.

"Arrivez donc, jeune fille!" she exclaimed impatiently.

The servant came.

"Apportez du the, Seraphine."

"Oui, mademoiselle."

Then Lois lounged towards the table and tore sharply the wrapper of the newspaper. George was still standing.

"He's probably got something in about her this week - about her soiree last Tuesday. We weren't invited. Of course he went."

George saw the name the Sunday Journal. The paper had come by the afternoon mail, and had been delivered, according to weekly custom, by messenger from Mr. Ingram's office. Lois's tone and attitude tore fatally the whole factitious 'Parisian' tradition, as her hand had torn the wrapper.

"See here," she said quietly, after a few seconds, and gave the newspaper with her thumb indicating a paragraph.

He could hardly read the heading, because it unnerved him; nor the opening lines. But he read this: "The following six architects have been selected by the Assessors and will be immediately requested by the Corporation to submit final designs for the town hall: Mr. Whinburn, Mr.... Mr.... Mr. George E. Cannon ..."

"What did I always tell you?" she said.

And then she said:

"Your telegram must have been addressed wrong, or something."

He sat down. Once again he was afraid. He was afraid of winning in the final competition. A vista of mayors, corporations, town clerks, committees, contractors, clerks-of-works, frightened him. He was afraid of his immaturity, of his inexperience. He could not carry out the enterprise; he would reap only ignominy. His greatest desire had been granted. He had expected, in the event, to be wildly happy. But he was not happy.

"Well, I'm blowed!" he exclaimed.

Lois, who had resumed the paper, read out:

"In accordance with the conditions of the competition, each of the above named will receive a honorarium of one hundred guineas."

She looked at him.

"You'll get that town hall to do," she said positively. "You're bound to get it. You'll see."

Her incomprehensible but convincing faith passed mysteriously into him. A holy dew relieved him. He began to feel happy.

Lois glanced again at the paper, which with arms outstretched she held in front of her like a man, like the men at Pickering's. Suddenly it fell rustling to the floor, and she burst into tears.

She murmured indistinctly: "The last thing she did was for my pleasure - sending the car."

George jumped up, animated by an inexpressible tenderness for her. She had weakened. He moved towards her. He did not consider what he was doing; he had naught to say; but his instinctive arms were about to clasp her. He was unimaginably disturbed. She straightened and stiffened in a second.

"But of course you've not got it yet," she said harshly, with apparent irrelevance.

Seraphine entered bouncingly with the tea. Lois regarded the tray, and remarked the absence of the strainer.

"Et la passoire?" she demanded, with implacable sternness.

Seraphine gave a careless, apologetic gesture.

7

It was late in September, when most people had returned to London after the holidays. John Orgreave mounted to the upper floor of the house in Russell Square where George had his office. Underneath George's name on the door had been newly painted the word 'Inquiries,' and on another door, opposite, the word 'Private.' John Orgreave knocked with exaggerated noise at this second door and went into what was now George's private room.

"I suppose one ought to knock," he said in his hearty voice.

"Hallo, Mr. Orgreave!" George exclaimed, jumping up.

"If the mountain doesn't come to Mahomet, Mahomet must come to the mountain," said John Orgreave.

"Come in," said George.

He noticed, and ignored, the touch of sarcasm in John Orgreave's attitude. He had noticed a similar phenomenon in the attitude of various people within the last four days, since architectural circles and even the world in general had begun to resound with the echoing news that the competition for the northern town hall had been won by a youth not twenty-three years of age. Mr. Enwright had been almost cross, asserting that the victory was perhaps a fluke, as the design of another competitor was in reality superior to George's. Mr. Enwright had also said, in his crabbed way: "You'll soon cut me out"; and, George protesting, had gone on: "Oh! Yes, you will. I've been through this sort of thing before. I know what I'm talking about. You're no different from the rest." Whereupon George, impatient and genuinely annoyed, had retorted upon him quite curtly, and had remembered what many persons had said about Mr. Enwright's wrong-headed jealous sensitiveness - animadversions which he, as a worshipper of Mr. Enwright, had been accustomed to rebut. Further, Lucas himself had not erred by the extravagance of his enthusiasm for George's earth-shaking success. For example, Lucas had said: "Don't go and get above yourself, old chap. They may decide not to build it after all. You never know with these corporations." A remark extremely undeserved, for George considered that the modesty and simplicity of his own demeanour under the stress of an inordinate triumph were rather notable. Still, he had his dignity to maintain against the satiric, and his position was such that he could afford to maintain it.

Anyhow, he preferred the sardonic bearing of his professional intimates to the sycophancy of certain acquaintances and of eager snobs unknown to him. Among sundry telegrams received was one composed regardless of cost and signed 'Turnbull.' He could not discover who Turnbull might be until John Orgreave had reminded him of the wigged, brown, conversational gentleman whom he had met, on one occasion only, at Adela's. In addition to telegrams he had had letters, some of which contained requests for money (demanded even as a right by the unlucky from the lucky), and an assortment of charity circulars, money-lenders' circulars, and bucket-shop lures. His mother's great sprawling letter had pleased him better than any save one. The exception was his stepfather's. Edwin Clayhanger, duly passing on to the next generation the benevolent Midland gibe which he had inherited, wrote:

"Dear George, - It's better than a bat in the eye with a burnt stick. - Yours affectionately, Nunks"

As a boy George had at one period called his stepfather 'Nunks,' but he had not used the appellation for years. He was touched now.

The newspapers had been hot after him, and he knew not how to defend himself. His photograph was implored. He was waylaid by journalists shabby and by journalists spruce, and the resulting interviews made him squirm. He became a man of mark at Pickering's. Photographers entreated him to sit free of charge. What irritated him in the whole vast affair was the continual insistence upon his lack of years. Nobody seemed to be interested in his design for the town hall; everybody had the air of regarding him as a youthful prodigy, a performing animal. Personally he did not consider that he was so very young. (Nevertheless he did consider that he was a youthful prodigy. He could recall no architect in history who had done what he had done at his age.) The town clerk who travelled from the North to see him treated his age in a different manner, the patronizing. He did not care for the town clerk. However, the town clerk was atoned for by the chairman of the new town hall sub-committee, a true human being named Soulter, with a terrific accent and a taste for architecture, pictures, and music. Mr. Soulter, though at least forty-five, treated George, without any appearance of effort, as a coeval. George immediately liked him, and the mere existence of Mr. Soulter had the effect of dissipating nearly all George's horrible qualms and apprehensions about his own competence to face the overwhelming job of erection. Mr. Soulter was most soothing in the matter of specifications and contractors.

"So you've got into your new room," said John Orgreave.

Never before had he mounted to see George either in the new room or in the old room. The simple fact of the presence there of one of the partners in the historic firm below compensated for much teasing sarcasm and half-veiled jealousy. It was a sign. It was a seal authenticating renown.

"Yes."

"I only wanted to give you a message from Adela. The Ingram young woman is staying with us - "

"Lois?" The name shot out of him unbidden.

"Yes. You're humbly supplicated to go to tea to-day. Four o'clock. Thank God I've not forgotten it!"

George arrived fifty-five minutes late at Bedford Park. Throughout the journey thither he kept repeating: "She said I should do it. And I've done it! I've done it! I've done it!" The triumph was still so close behind him that he was constantly realizing it afresh, and saying, wonder-struck: "I've done it." And the miraculous phantasm of the town hall, uplifted in solid stone, formed itself again and again in his enchanted mind, against a background of tremendous new ambitions rising endlessly one behind another like snowy alps.

"Is this what you call four o'clock?" twittered Adela, between cajolery and protest, somewhat older and facially more artificial, but eternally blonde; still holding her fair head on one side and sinuously waving the palm.

"Sorry! Sorry! I was kept at the last moment by a journalist johnny."

"Oh! Of course!" said Adela, pooh-poohing with her lips. "Of course we expect that story nowadays!"

"Well, it was a chap from the Builder, or I wouldn't have seen him. Can't trifle with a trade paper, you know."

He thought:

"She's like the rest of them, as jealous as the devil."

Then Lois came into the room, hatted and gloved, in half-mourning. She was pale, and appreciably thinner; she looked nervous, weak, and weary. As he shook hands with her he felt very self-conscious, as though in winning the competition and fulfilling her prophecy he had done something dubious for which he ought to apologize. This was exceedingly strange, but it was so. She had been ill after the death of Irene Wheeler. Having left Paris for London on the day following the races, he had written to her about nothing in particular, a letter which meant everything but what it said - and had received an answer from Laurencine, who announced that her sister was in bed, and likely to be in bed; and that father and mother wished to be remembered to him. Then he wrote to Laurencine. When the result of the final competition was published he had written again to Lois. It seemed to him that he was bound to do so, for had she not willed and decided his victory? No reply; but there had scarcely been time for a reply.

"Did you get my letter?" he smiled.

"This afternoon," she said gravely. "It followed me here. Now I have to go to Irene's flat. I should have been gone in another minute."

"She will go alone," Adela put in anxiously.

"I shall be back for dinner," said Lois, and to the stupefaction of George she moved towards the door.

But just as she opened the door she turned her head and, looking at George with a frown, murmured:

"You can come with me if you like."

Adela burst out:

"He hasn't had any tea!"

"I'm not urging him to come, my dear. Good-bye."

Adela and George exchanged a glance, each signalling to the other that perhaps this sick, strange girl ought to be humoured. He abandoned the tea.... He was in the street with Lois. He was in the train with her. Her ticket was in his pocket. He had explained to her why he was late, and she had smiled, amiably but enigmatically. He thought: "She's no right to go on like this. But what does it matter?" She said nothing about the competition - not a word of congratulation. Indeed she hardly spoke beyond telling him that she had to choose some object at the flat. He was aware of the principal terms of Irene's will, which indeed had caused the last flutter of excitement before oblivion so quickly descended upon the notoriety of the social star. Irene's renown had survived her complexion by only a few short weeks. The will was of a rather romantic nature. Nobody familiar with the intimate circumstances would have been surprised if Irene had divided her fortune between Lois and Laurencine. The bulk of it, however, went back to Indianapolis. The gross total fell far short of popular estimates. Lois and Laurencine received five thousand pounds apiece, and in addition they were requested to select each an object from Irene's belongings - Lois out of the London flat, Laurencine out of the Paris flat. Lois had come to London to choose, and she was staying with Adela, the sole chaperon available. Since the death of Irene, Mrs. Ingram had been excessively strict in the matter of chaperons.

They took a hansom at Victoria. Across the great square, whose leaves were just yellowing, George saw the huge block of flats, and in one story all the blinds were down. Lois marched first into the lift, masterfully, as though she inhabited the block. She asked no one's permission. Characteristically she had an order from the solicitors, and the keys of the flat. She opened the door without any trouble. They were inside, within the pale-sheeted interior. Scarcely a thing had yet been moved, for, with the formalities of the judicatures of France, England, and the State of Indiana to be complied with, events marched slowly under the sticky manipulation of three different legal firms. Lois and George walked cautiously across the dusty, dulled parquets into the vast drawing-room. George doffed his hat.

"I'd better draw the blinds up," he suggested.

"No, no!" she sharply commanded. "I can see quite well. I don't want any more light."

There was the piano upon which Laurencine had played! The embrasure of the window! The corner in which Irene had sat spellbound by Jules Defourcambault! The portraits of Irene, at least one of which would perpetuate her name! The glazed cases full of her collections!... The chief pieces of furniture and all the chairs were draped in the pale, ghostly sheeting.

Suddenly Lois, rushing to the mantelpiece, cried:

"This is what I shall take."

It was a large photograph of Jules Defourcambault, bearing the words: "A Miss Irene Wheeler. Hommages respectueux de J.D.F."

"You won't!" he exclaimed, incredulous, shocked. He thought: "She is mad!"

"Yes, I shall."

There were hundreds of beautiful objects in the place, and she chose a banal photograph of a despicable creature whom she detested.

"Why don't you take one of her portraits? Or even a fan. What on earth do you want with a thing like that?" His voice was changing.

"I shall take it and keep it for ever. He was the cause of it all. This photograph was everything to her once."

George revolted utterly, and said with cold, harsh displeasure:

"You're simply being morbid. There's no sense in it."

She dropped down into a chair, and the impress of her body dragged the dust-sheet from its gilt arms, exposing them. She put her face in her hands and sobbed.

"You're awfully cruel!" she murmured thickly.

The sobs continued, shaking her body. She was beautifully dressed. Her shoes were adorable, and the semi-transparent hose over her fine ankles. She made a most disturbing, an unbearable, figure of compassion. She needed wisdom, protection, guidance, strength. Every bit of her seemed to appeal for these qualities. But at the same time she dismayed. He moved nearer to her. Yes, she had grandeur. All the costly and valuable objects in the drawing-room she had rejected in favour of the satisfaction of a morbid and terrible whim. Who could have foreseen it? He moved still nearer. He stood over her. He seized her yielding wrists. He lifted her veil. Tears were running down her cheeks from the yellow eyes. She looked at him through her tears.

"You're frightfully cruel," she feebly repeated.

"And what if I am?" he said solemnly. Did she really think him hard, had she always thought him hard - she, the hard one? How strange! Yet no doubt he was hard.

His paramount idea was:

"She had faith in me." It was as if her faith had created the man he was. She was passionately ambitious; so was he.

And when he kissed her wet mouth, and stroked with incredible delicacy those streaming cheeks, he felt himself full of foreboding. But he was proud and confident.

He took her back to Bedford Park. She carried the photograph, unwrapped; but he ventured no comment. She went straight up to her room.

"You must tell Mrs. Orgreave," she said on the stairs.

Adela made a strange remark:

"Oh! But we always intended you to marry Lois!"

PART II

I

THE TRIUMPH

George came into the conjugal bedroom. The hour was about three o'clock in the afternoon. Lois lay on the sofa at the foot of the twin beds. It was perhaps characteristic of her that she sincerely preferred the sofa to her bed. Sometimes in the night, when she could not sleep, she would get up and go sighing to the sofa, and, with nothing but a slippery eiderdown to cover her, sleep perfectly till George arose in the morning. Quite contentedly conventional in most matters of mere social deportment, she often resisted purely physical conventions. A bed was the recognized machine for slumber; hence she would instinctively choose another machine. Also, the sofa was nearer to the ground. She liked to be near the ground. She had welcomed with ardour the first beginnings of the new fashion which now regularly permits ladies to sit on the hearth-rug after a ceremonial dinner and prop their backs with cushions or mantelpieces. Doubtless a trait of the 'cave-woman' that as a girl she had called herself!

She was now stretched on the sofa in a luxurious and expensive ribboned muslin negligee, untidy, pale, haggard, heavy, shapeless, the expectant mother intensely conscious of her own body and determined to maintain all the privileges of the exacting role which nature had for the third time assigned to her. Little Laurencine, aged eight, and little Lois, aged five, in their summer white, were fondling her, tumbling about her, burying themselves in her; she reclined careless, benignant, and acquiescent under their tiny assaults; it was at moments as though the three were one being. When their father appeared in the doorway, she warned them in an apparently awed tone that father was there, and that nursey was waiting for them and that they must run off quietly. And she kissed them with the enormous kiss of a giantess suddenly rendered passionate by a vast uprush of elemental feeling. And they ran off, smiling confidently at their father, giggling, chattering about important affairs in their intolerable, shrieking voices. George could never understand why Lois should attempt, as she constantly did, to instil into them awe of their father; his attitude to the children made it impossible that she should succeed. But she kept on trying. The cave-woman again! George would say to himself: "All women are cave-women."

"Have you come to pack?" she asked, with fatigued fretfulness, showing no sign of surprise at his arrival.

"Oh no!" he answered, and implied that in his over-charged existence packing would have to be done when it could, if at all. "I only came in for one second to see if I could root out that straw hat I wore last year."

"Do open the window," she implored grievously.

"It is open."

"Both sides?"

"Yes."

"Well, open it more."

"It's wide open."

"Both sides?"

"Yes."

"It's so stuffy in this room," she complained, expelling much breath.

It was stuffy in the room. The room was too full of the multitudinous belongings and furniture of wife and husband. It was too small for its uses. The pair, unduly thrown together, needed two rooms. But the house could not yield them two rooms, though from the outside it had an air of spaciousness. The space was employed in complying with custom, in imitating the disposition of larger houses, and in persuading the tenant that he was as good as his betters. There was a basement, because the house belonged to the basement era, and because it is simpler to burrow than to erect. On the ground floor were the hall - narrow, and the dining-room - narrow. To have placed the dining-room elsewhere would have been to double the number of stairs between it and the kitchen; moreover, the situation of the dining-room in all such correct houses is immutably fixed by the code Thus the handiest room in the house was occupied during four hours of the twenty-four, and wasted during the remaining twenty. Behind the dining-room was a very small room appointed by the code to be George's 'den.' It would never have been used at all had not George considered it his duty to use it occasionally, and had not Lois at intervals taken a fancy to it because it was not hers.

The whole of the first floor was occupied by the landing, the well of the staircase, and the drawing-room, which last was inevitably shaped in the resemblance of an L. The small back portion of it over George's den was never utilized save by the grand piano and rare pianists. Still, the code demanded that the drawing-room should have this strange appendage, and that a grand piano should reside in it modestly, apologetically, like a shame that cannot be entirely concealed. Nearly every house in Elm Park Road, and every house in scores of miles of other correct streets in the West End, had a drawing-room shaped in the semblance of an L, and a grand piano in the hinterland thereof. The drawing-room, like the dining-room, was occupied during about four hours of the twenty-four, and wasted during the remaining twenty.

The two main floors of the house being in such manner accounted for, the family and its dependents principally lived aloft on the second and third floors. Eight souls slept up there nightly. A miracle of compression!

George had had the house for ten years; he entered it as a bridegroom. He had stayed in it for seven years because the landlord would only confide it to him on lease, and at the end of the seven years he lacked the initiative to leave it. An ugly house, utterly without architectural merit! A strange house for an architect to inhabit! George, however, had never liked it. Before his marriage he had discovered a magnificent house in Fitzroy Square, a domestic masterpiece of the Adams period, exquisitely designed without and within, huge rooms and many rooms, lovely ceilings, a forged-iron stair-rail out of Paradise; a house appreciably nearer to the centre than the one in Elm Park Road, and with a lower rental. George would have taken the house, had not Lois pointed out to him its fatal disadvantage, which had escaped him, namely, that people simply did not live in Fitzroy Square. Instantly Lois entered Fitzroy Square, George knew himself for a blind fool. Of course the house was impossible. He was positively ashamed to show her the house. She admitted that it was beautiful. So Elm Park Road was finally selected, Elm Park Road being a street where people could, and in fact did, live. It was astounding how Lois, with her small and fragmentary knowledge of London, yet knew, precisely and infallibly, by instinct, by the sound of the names of the thoroughfares, by magic diabolical or celestial, what streets were inhabitable and what were not. And something in George agreed with her.

He now rummaged among hat-boxes beneath the beds, pulled one out, and discovered a straw hat in it.

"Will it do?" he questioned doubtfully.

"Let me look at it."

He approached her and gave her the hat, which she carefully examined, frowning.

"Put it on," she said.

He put it on, and she gazed at him for what seemed to him an unnecessarily long time. His thought was that she liked to hold him under her gaze.

"Well?" he exclaimed impatiently.

"It's quite all right," she said. "What's the matter with it? It makes you look about fourteen." He felt envy in her voice. Then she added: "But surely you won't be able to wear that thing tomorrow?"

"Of course not. I only want it for this afternoon.... This sun."

"Oh!" she cried. "I do think it's a shame I can't go to the Opening! It's just my luck."

He considered that she arraigned her luck much too often; he considered that on the whole her luck was decidedly good. But he knew that she had to be humoured. It was her right to be humoured.

"Yes," he said judicially and rather shortly. "I'm sorry too! But what are you going to do about it? If you can't go, you can't. And you know it's absolutely out of the question." As a fact he was glad that her condition made such an excursion impossible for her. She would certainly have been rather a ticklish handful for him at the Opening.

"But I should so have enjoyed it!" she insisted, with emphasis.

There it was, the thirst for enjoyment, pleasure! The supreme, unslakable thirst! She had always had it, and he had always hardened himself against it - while often, nevertheless, accepting with secret pleasure the satisfactions of her thirst. Thus, for example, in the matter of dancing. She had shared to the full in the extraordinary craze for dancing which had held the West End for several years. Owing to her initiative they had belonged to two dancing clubs whose members met weekly in the saloons of the great hotels. The majority of the members were acutely tedious to George, but Lois was quite uncritical, save on the main point; she divided the members into good dancers and bad dancers. George was a pretty good dancer. He liked dancing. Membership of these clubs involved expense, it interfered with his sleep, it made his early mornings more like defeats than triumphs, it prevented him from duly reading and sketching. But he liked dancing. While resenting the compulsion to outrage his conscience, he enjoyed the sin. What exasperated him was Lois's argument that that kind of thing "did him good" professionally, and was indeed essential to the career of a rising or risen young architect, and that also it was good for his health and his mind. He wished that she would not so unconvincingly pretend that self-indulgence was not what it was. These pretences, however, seemed to be a necessity of her nature. She reasoned similarly about the dinners and theatre-parties which they gave and attended. Next to dancing she adored dinners and theatre-parties. She would sooner eat a bad dinner in company anywhere than a good dinner quietly at home; she would far sooner go to a bad play than to none at all; she was in fact never bored in the theatre or in the music-hall. Never!

Once, by misfortune - as George privately deemed - he had got a small job (erection of a dwelling-house at Hampstead) through a dinner. Lois had never forgotten it, and she would adduce the trifle again and again as evidence of the sanity of her ideas about social life. George really did not care for designing houses; they were not worth the trouble; he habitually thought in public edifices and the palaces of kings, nobles, and plutocrats of taste. Moreover, his commission on the house would not have kept his own household in being for a month - and yet the owner, while obviously proud to be the patron of the celebrated prodigy George Cannon, had the air of doing George Cannon a favour!

And so her ambition, rather than his, had driven them both ruthlessly on. Both were overpressed, but George considerably more than Lois. Lois was never, in ordinary times, really tired. Dinners, teas, even lunches, restaurants, theatres, music-halls, other people's houses, clubs, dancing, changing clothes, getting into autos and taxis and getting out of autos and taxis, looking at watches, writing down engagements, going to bed with a sigh at the lateness of the hour, waking up fatigued to the complexities of the new day - she coped admirably with it all. She regarded it as natural; she regarded it as inevitable and proper. She enjoyed it. She wanted it, and that which she wanted she must have. Yet her attitude to George was almost invariably one of deep solicitude for him. She would look at him with eyes troubled and anxious for his welfare. When they were driving to a dance which he had no desire to attend, she would put her arm in his and squeeze his arm and murmur: "Coco, I don't like you working so hard." (Coco was her pet name for him, a souvenir of Paris.)

He acknowledged that, having chosen her role, she played it well. She made him comfortable. She was a good housekeeper, and a fair organizer generally. She knew how to be well served. He thought that her manner to servants was often inexcusable, but she "kept" her servants, and they would "do anything" for her. Further, except that she could not shine in conversation, she was a good hostess. She never made mistakes, never became muddled, never forgot. Of course she had friends to whom he was indifferent or perhaps slightly hostile, but she was entitled to her friends, as he to his. And she was a good mother. Stranger still, though she understood none of the arts and had no logical taste, she possessed a gift of guessing or of divination which, in all affairs relating to the home, was the practical equivalent of genuine taste. George had first noticed this faculty in her when she put a thousand pounds of her money to a thousand pounds of his stepfather's and they began to buy furniture. The house was beautifully furnished, and she had done her share. And in the alterations, additions, and replacements which for several years she had the habit of springing upon him, she rarely offended him. Still, he knew indubitably that she had not taste, - anyhow in his sense of the term, - and would never, never acquire it. An astonishing creature! He had not finished being astonished at her. In some respects he had not even come to a decision about her. For instance, he suspected that she had "no notion of money," but he could not be sure. She did what she liked with her own income, which was about two hundred a year; that is to say, she clothed herself out of it. Her household accounts were unknown to him; he had once essayed to comprehend them, but had drawn back affrighted.

"Well," she said plaintively. "Now you're here, I think you might sit a bit with me. It's most awfully lonely for me."

"I can't possibly," he said, with calm. "I have to rush off to the club to see Davids about that business."

She ignored his inescapable duties! It was nothing to her that he had a hundred affairs to arrange before his night-journey to the north. She wanted him to sit with her. Therefore she thought that he ought to sit with her, and she would be conscious of a grievance if he did not. 'Lonely!' Because the children were going out for an hour or so! Besides, even if it was lonely, facts were facts, and destiny was destiny and had to be borne.

"What business?"

"You know."

"Oh! That!... Well, can't you go after tea?"

Incurable!

"Here, lass!" he said, with a laugh. "If I stop arguing here I shall miss him."

He bent down, and prepared his lips to kiss her. He smiled superiorly, indulgently. He was the stronger. She defeated him sometimes; she gravely defeated him in the general arrangement and colour of their joint existence; but he was the stronger. She had known it for over ten years. They had had two tremendous, critical, highly dangerous battles. He had won them both. Lois had wanted to be married in Paris. He had been ready to agree until suddenly it occurred to him that French legal formalities might necessitate an undue disclosure as to his parentage and the bigamy of which his mother had been a victim. He refused absolutely to be married in Paris. He said: "You're English and I'm English, and the proper place for us to be married is England." There were good counter-arguments, but he would not have them. Curiously, at this very period, news came from his stepfather of his father's death in America. He kept it to himself. Again, on the night itself of their marriage, he had said to her: "Now give me that revolver you've got." At her protesting refusal he had said: "My wife is not going about with any revolver. Not if I know it!" He was playful but determined. He startled her, for the altercation lasted two hours. On the other hand he had never said a word about the photograph of Jules Defourcambault, and had never seen it. Somewhere, in some mysterious fastness, the mysterious woman kept it.

His lips were close to hers, and his eyes to her eyes. Most persons called her eyes golden, but to him they were just yellow. They had an infinitesimal cast, to which nobody ever referred. They were voluptuous eyes. He examined her face. She was still young; but the fine impressive imprint of existence was upon her features, and the insipid freshness had departed. She blinked, acquiescent. Her eyes changed, melting. He could almost see into her brain, and watch there the impulse of repentance for an unreasonable caprice, and the intense resolve to think in the future only of her husband's welfare. She was like that.... She could be an angel.... He knew that he was hard. He guessed that he might be inordinately hard He would bear people down. Why had he not been touched by her helpless condition? She was indeed touching as she lay. She wanted to keep him near her and she could not. She wanted acutely to go to the north, and she was imprisoned. She would have to pass the night alone, and the next night alone. Danger and great suffering lay in front of her. And she was she; she was herself, with all her terrific instincts. She could not alter herself. Did she not merit compassion? Still, he must go to his club.

He kissed her tenderly. She half lifted her head, and kissed him exactly as she kissed his children, like a giantess, and as though she was the ark of wisdom from everlasting, and he a callow boy whose safety depended upon her sagacious, loving direction.

From the top of the flight of stairs leading from the ground floor, George, waiting till it was over, witnessed the departure of his family for the afternoon promenade. A prodigious affair! The parlourmaid (a delightful creature who was, unfortunately, soon to make an excellent match above her station) amiably helped the nursemaid to get the perambulator down the steps. The parlourmaid wore her immutable uniform, and the nursemaid wore her immutable uniform. Various things had to be packed into the perambulator, and then little Lois had to be packed into it - not because she could not walk, but because it was not desirable for her to arrive at the playground tired. Nursey's sunshade was undiscoverable, and little Laurencine's little sunshade had to be retrieved from underneath little Lois in the depths of the perambulator. Nursey's book had fallen on the steps. Then the tiny but elaborate perambulator of Laurencine's doll had to go down the steps, and the doll had to be therein ensconced under Laurencine's own direction, and Laurencine's sunshade had to be opened, and Laurencine had to prove to the maids that she could hold the sunshade in one hand and push the doll's perambulator with the other. Finally, the procession of human beings and vehicles moved, munitioned, provisioned, like a caravan setting forth into the desert, the parlourmaid amiably waving adieux.

George thought: "I support all that. It all depends on me. I have brought it all into existence." And his reflections embraced Lois upstairs, and the two colleagues of the parlourmaid in the kitchen, and the endless apparatus of the house, and the people at his office and the apparatus there, and the experiences that awaited him on the morrow, and all his responsibilities, and all his apprehensions for the future. And he was amazed and dismayed by the burden which almost unwittingly he bore night and day. But he felt too that it was rather fine. He felt that he was in the midst of life.

As he was cranking his car, which he had left unattended at the kerb, Mrs. Buckingham Smith's magnificent car driven by her magnificent chauffeur, swept in silence up to the door and sweetly stopped. George's car was a very little one, and he was his own chauffeur, and had to walk home from the garage when he had done with it. The contemplation of Buck Smith's career showed George that there are degrees of success. Buck Smith received a thousand pounds for a portrait (in the French manner of painting) - and refused commissions at that. Buck Smith had a kind of palace in Melbury Road. By the side of Buck Smith. George was a struggling semi-failure. Mrs. Buck Smith, the lady whom George had first glimpsed in the foyer of a theatre, was a superb Jewess whom Buck had enticed from the stage. George did not like her because she was apt, in ecstasy, to froth at the mouth, and for other reasons; but she was one of his wife's most intimate friends. Lois, usually taciturn, would chatter with Adah for hours.

"I thought I'd come and see Lois," said Mrs. Buck, effulgently smiling, as George handed her out of the car. "How is the dear thing? You just flying off?"

"You'll do her all the good in the world," George replied. "I can't stop. I have to leave town tonight, and I'm full up."

"Oh yes! The Opening! How perfectly splendid!" Tiny bubbles showed between her glorious lips. "What a shame it is poor Lois isn't able to go!"

"Yes," said George. "But look here! Don't you go and tell her so. That's quite the wrong tack."

"I see! I see!" said Mrs. Buck, gazing at him as one who was capable of subtle comprehensions. "By the way," she added, as she turned to mount the steps, "I ran across Everard Lucas at the Berkeley to-day. Lunching there. I said I was coming here. He told me to tell you, if I saw you, that old Mr. Haim or Home or some such name was dead. He said you'd be interested."

"By Jove!" George ejaculated. "Is he? Haven't seen him for years and years."

2

He got into his car and drove off at speed. Beneath his off-hand words to Mrs. Buckingham Smith he was conscious of a quickly growing, tender sympathy for Marguerite Haim. The hardness in him was dissolved almost instantaneously. He saw Marguerite, who had been adamantine in the difference which separated them, as the image of pliancy, sweetness, altruism, and devotion; and he saw her lips and the rapt glance of her eyes as beautiful as in the past. What a soft, soothing, assuaging contrast with the difficult Lois, so imperious and egoistic! (An unforgettable phrase of Lois's had inhabited his mind for over a decade: "Fancy quarrelling over a man!") He had never met Marguerite since their separation, and for years he had heard nothing whatever about her; he did not under-estimate the ordeal of meeting her again. Yet he at once decided that he must meet her again. He simply could not ignore her in her bereavement and new loneliness. To write to her would be absurd; it would be a cowardly evasion; moreover, he could not frame a letter. He must prove to her and to himself that he had a sense of decent kindliness which would rise above conventional trifles when occasion demanded.

At the top of Elm Park Gardens, instead of turning east towards Piccadilly he turned west in the direction of the Workhouse tower. And thus he exposed the unreality of the grandiose pleas with which professional men impose on their wives and on themselves. A few minutes earlier his appointment at the club (not Pickering's, to which, however, he still belonged, but a much greater institution, the Artists, in Albemarle Street) had been an affair of extreme importance, upon which might depend his future career, for did it not concern negotiations for a London factory, which was to be revolutionary in design, and to cost L150,000, and which, erected, would form a permanent advertisement of the genius of George Cannon? Now he remembered that Sir Isaac Davids, the patron of all the arts and the influencer of commissions, had said that he would probably but not certainly be at the club that afternoon, and he argued that in any event half an hour sooner or later would not make or mar the business. Indeed, he went further, and persuaded himself that between that moment and dinner he had nothing to do except sign a few routine letters at the office. Still, it was just as well that Lois should remain in delusion as to his being seriously pressed for time.

As he curved, slackening and accelerating, with the perfect assurance of long habit, through the swift, intricate, towering motor traffic of Fulham Road, it was inevitable that he should recall the days, eleven years ago, when through a sedate traffic of trotting horses enlivened with a few motors and motor-buses, he used to run down on his motor-cycle to visit Marguerite. It was inevitable that he should think upon what had happened to him in the meantime. His body felt, honestly, no older. The shoulders had broadened, the moustache was fiercer, there were semicircular furrows under the eyes; but he was as slim and agile as ever, and did his morning exercises as regularly as he took his bath. More, he was still, somehow, the youthful prodigy who had won the biggest competition of modern years while almost an infant. He was still known as such, regarded as such, greeted as such, referred to as such at intervals in the Press. His fame in his own world seemed not to have deteriorated. But disappointment had slowly, imperceptibly, eaten into him. He was far off the sublime heights of Sir Hugh Corver, though he met Sir Hugh apparently as an equal on the Council of the Royal Society of British Architects. Work had not surged in upon him. He had not been able to pick and choose among commissions. He had never won another competition. Again and again his hopes had been horribly defeated in these ghastly enterprises, of which two were still pending. He was a man of one job. And a quarter of his professional life had slipped behind him! His dreams were changed. Formerly he had dreamed in architectural forms; now he dreamed in percentages. His one job had been enormous and lucrative, but he had lived on it for a decade, and it was done. And outside it he had earned probably less than twelve hundred pounds.

And if the job had been enormous, his responsibilities were likewise enormous. Home expenses with an increasing family; establishment expenses; a heavy insurance! Slavery to habits! The common story, without the slightest originality in it. The idea recurred continually: it was the fault of Lois, of that embodied, implacable instinct which Lois was! And it was the fault of circumstance, of the structure of society, of existence itself. And it was his fault too. And the whole of the blame would be his if disaster came. Imagine those kids with the perambulator and the doll's perambulator - imagine them in an earthquake! He could see no future beyond, perhaps, eight months ahead. No, he could not! Of course his stepfather was a sure resource. But he could not conceive himself confessing failure to his stepfather or to anybody on earth. Yet, if he did not very soon obtain more work, remunerative and on a large scale ... if he did not ... However, he would obtain more work. It was impossible that he should not obtain it. The matter with Sir Isaac was as good as arranged. And the chances of winning at any rate one of the two competitions were very favourable.... He dismissed every apprehension. His health was too good to tolerate apprehensions permanently. And he had a superstitious faith in his wife's superstitious faith in him, and in his luck. The dark mood quickly faded. It had been induced, not by the spectacle of his wife and family and household seen somehow from a new angle, but by the recollection of the past. Though he often went through dark moods, they were not moods of financial pessimism; they seemed to be causeless, inexplicable, and indescribable - abysses in which cerebration ceased.

3

She was just closing the side gate leading to the studio when he drove up. He recognized her face over the top of the gate. At the first glance it seemed to be absolutely unchanged - the same really beautiful lips, the same nose, the same look in the eyes. Had a decade passed by her and left no trace? He lost his nerve for an instant, and brought the car to a standstill with less than his usual adroitness. She hesitated.

"I was coming to see you," he called out hastily, boyishly, not in the least measuring his effects. He jumped from the car, and said in a lower, more intimate tone: "I've only this minute heard about Mr. Haim. I'm awfully sorry. I thought I'd come along at once."

"How nice of you!" she replied, quite simply and naturally, with a smile. "Do come in."

The tension was eased.

She pulled at the gate, which creaked. He then saw plainly the whole of her figure. She was dressed in black, and wore what the newspaper advertisement called a 'matron's coat.' The decade had not passed by her and left no trace. She had been appointed to a share in the mysterious purpose. Her bust, too, was ampler; only her face, rather pale like the face of Lois, was unaltered in its innocent contours. He felt that he was blushing. He had no instinctive jealousy nor resentment; it did not appear strange to him that this woman in the matron's coat was the girl he had passionately kissed in that very house; and indeed the woman was not the girl - the connexion between the woman and the girl had snapped. Nevertheless, he was extremely self-conscious; but not she. And in his astonishment he wondered at the secretiveness of London. His house and hers were not more than half a mile apart, and yet in eleven years he had never set eyes on her house. Nearly always, on leaving his house, he would go up Elm Park Gardens and turn to the right. If he was not in the car he would never turn to the left. Occasionally he had flown past the end of the Grove in the car; not once, however, had he entered the Grove. He lived in Chelsea and she lived in Chelsea, but not the same Chelsea; his was not the Chelsea of the studios and the King's Road. They had existed close together, side by side, for years and years - and she had been hidden from him.

As they walked towards the studio door she told him that 'they' had buried her father a week ago and that 'they' were living in the studio, and had already arranged to let the lower part of the house. She had the air of assuming that he was aware of the main happenings in her life, only a little belated in the knowledge of her father's death. She was quite cheerful. He pretended to himself to speculate as to the identity of her husband. He would not ask: "And who is your husband?". All the time he knew who her husband was: it could be no other than one man. She opened the studio door with a latchkey. He was right. At a table Mr. Prince was putting sheets of etching-paper to soak in a porcelain bath.

"Well! Well! Well!" exclaimed Mr. Prince warmly, not flustered, not a bit embarrassed, and not too demonstrative. He came forward, delicately drying the tips of his fingers on a rag, and shook hands. His hair was almost white, his thin, benevolent face amazingly lined; his voice had a constant little vibration. Yet George could not believe that he was an old man.

"He only heard to-day about father, and he's called at once," said Marguerite. "Isn't it just like him?"

The last phrase surprised and thrilled George. Did she mean it? Her kind, calm, ingenuous face showed that obviously she meant it.

"It is," said Mr. Prince seriously. "Very good of you, old man."

After some talk about Mr. Haim, and about old times, and about changes, during which Marguerite took off her matron's coat and Mr. Prince gently hung it up for her, they all sat down near to one another and near the unlighted stove. The studio seemed to be precisely as of old, except that it was very clean. Marguerite, in a high-backed wicker-chair, began slowly to remove her hat, which she perched behind her on the chair. Mr. Prince produced a tin of Gold Flake cigarettes.

"And so you're living in the studio?" said George.

"We have the two rooms at the top of the house of course," answered Mr. Prince, glancing at the staircase. "I don't know whether it's quite the wisest thing, with all those stairs; you see how we're fixed" - he glanced at Marguerite - "but we had a fine chance to let the house, and in these days it's as well to be cautious."

Marguerite smiled happily and patted her husband's hand.

"Of course it's the wisest thing," she said.

"Why! What's the matter with these days?" George demanded. "How's the work?"

"Oh!" said Mr. Prince, in a new tone. "I've one or two things that might interest you."

He displayed some prints, and chatted of his labours. He was still etching; he would die etching. This was the etcher of European renown. He referred to the Vienna acquisition as though it was an affair of a few weeks ago. He had disposed of an etching to Stockholm, and mentioned that he had exhibited at the International Show in Rome. He said that his things were attracting attention at a gallery in Bond Street. He displayed catalogues and press-cuttings.

"These are jolly fine," said George enthusiastically, as he examined the prints on his knee.

"I'm glad you like them," said Mr. Prince, pleased. "I think I've improved."

But in spite of his European renown, Mr. Prince had remained practically unknown. His name would not call forth the 'Oh yes!' of recognition from the earnest frequenter of fashionable exhibitions who takes pride in his familiarity with names. The etchings of Prince were not subscribed for in advance. He could not rank with the stars - Cameron, Muirhead Bone, Legros, Brangwyn. Probably he could command not more than two or three guineas for a print. He had never been the subject of a profusely laudatory illustrated article in the Studio. With his white hair he was what in the mart is esteemed a failure. He knew it. Withal he had a notable self-respect and a notable confidence. There was no timidity in him, even if his cautiousness was excessive. He possessed sagacity and he had used it. He knew where he was. He had something substantial up his sleeve. There was no wistful appeal in his eye, as of a man who hopes for the best and fears the worst. He could meet dealers with a firm glance, for throughout life he had subjugated his desires to his resources. His look was modest but independent; and Marguerite had the same look.

"Hallo!" cried George. "I see you've got that here!" He pointed to Celia Agg's portrait of herself as Bonnie Prince Charlie.

"Yes," said Marguerite. "She insisted on me taking it when she gave up painting."

"Gave up painting?"

"Very good, isn't it?" said Mr. Prince gravely. "Pity she ever did give up painting, I think," he added in a peculiar tone.

"Yes, it is," George agreed insincerely, for the painting now seemed to him rather tenth-rate. "But what on earth did she stop painting for?"

Marguerite replied, with reserve:

"Oh! Didn't you know? She's quite gone in for this suffragette business. No one ever sees her now. Not even her people."

"Been in prison," said Mr. Prince, sardonically disapproving, "I always said she'd end in that kind of thing, didn't I, Margy?"

"You did, dear," said Marguerite, with wifely eagerness.

These two respected not only themselves but each other. The ensuing conversation showed that Mr. Prince was somewhat disgusted with the mundane movement, and that Marguerite was his disciple. They were more and more leaving the world alone; their self-sufficiency was increasing with the narrow regularity of their habits. They seldom went out; and when they did, they came home the more deeply convinced that all was not well with the world, and that they belonged to the small remnant of the wise and the sane. George was in two minds about them, or rather about Mr. Prince. He secretly condescended to him, but on the other hand he envied him. The man was benevolent; he spent his life in the creation of beauty; and he was secure. Surely an ideal existence! Yes, George wished that he could say as much for himself. Marguerite, completely deprived of ambition, would never have led any man into insecurity. He had realized already that afternoon that there were different degrees of success; he now realized that there were different kinds of success.

"Well!" he rose suddenly. "I must be off. I'm very busy."

"I suppose you are," said Mr. Prince. Untrue to assert that his glance was never wistful! It was ever so slightly wistful then.

George comprehended that Mr. Prince admired him and looked up to him after all.

"My town hall is being opened tomorrow."

"So I saw," said Mr. Prince. "I congratulate you."

They knew a good deal about him - where he lived, the statistics of his family, and so on. He picked up his hat.

"I can't tell you how I appreciate your coming," said Marguerite, gazing straight into his eyes.

"Rather!" said Mr. Prince.

They were profoundly flattered by the visit of this Bird-of-paradise. But they did not urge him to stay longer.

As he was leaving, the door already open, George noticed a half-finished book-cover design on a table.

"So you're still doing these binding designs!" He stopped to examine.

Husband and wife, always more interested in their own affairs than in other people's, responded willingly to his curiosity. George praised, and his praise was greatly esteemed. Mr. Prince talked about the changes in trade bindings, which were all for the worse. The bright spot was that Marguerite's price for a design had risen to twenty-five shillings. This improvement was evidently a source of genuine satisfaction to them. To George it seemed pathetic that a rise, after vicissitudes, of four shillings in fourteen years should be capable of causing them so much joy. He and they lived in absolutely different worlds.

"This is the last I shall let her do for a long time," observed Mr. Prince. "I shouldn't have let her do this one, but the doctor, who's a friend of ours, said there wouldn't be any harm, and of course it's always advisable to break a connexion as little as possible. You never know...."

George smiled, returning their flattery.

"You aren't going to tell me that that matters to you!"

Mr. Prince fixed George with his eye.

"When the European War starts in earnest I think most of us will need all we've been able to get together."

"What European War?" asked George, with a touch of disdain. "You don't mean to say that this Sarajevo business will lead to a European War!"

"No, I don't," said Mr. Prince very firmly. "Germany's diplomatists are much too clever for that. They're clever enough to find a better excuse. But they will find it, and soon."

George saw that Mr. Prince, having opened up a subject which apparently was dear to him, had to be handled with discretion. He guessed at once, from the certainty and the emotion of Mr. Prince's phrases, that Mr. Prince must have talked a lot about a European War. So he mildly replied:

"Do you really think so?"

"Do I think so? My dear fellow, you have only to look at the facts. Austria undoubtedly annexed Bosnia at Germany's instigation. Look at what led to Algeciras. Look at Agadir. Look at the increase in the German army last July. And look at the special levy. The thing's as clear as day." Mr. Prince now seemed to be a little angry with George, who had moved into the doorway.

"I'll tell you what I think," said George, with the assurance with which as a rule he announced his opinions. "We're Germany's only serious rival. It's us she's up against. She can only fight us on the sea. If she fought us now on the sea she'd be wiped out. That's admitted. In ten years, if she keeps on building, she might have a chance. But not now! Not yet! And she knows it." George did not mention that he had borrowed the whole weighty argument from his stepfather; but he spoke with finality, and was rather startled when Mr. Prince blew the whole weighty argument into the air with one scornful, pitying exhalation.

Mr. Prince said: "Nothing in it! Nothing in it! It's our alliances that will be the ruin of us. We shall be dragged into war. If Germany chooses to fight on land everybody will have to fight on land. When she gets to Paris, what are we going to do about it? We shall be dragged into war. It's the damnable alliances that Sir Edward Grey has let us in for." Mr. Prince fixed George afresh. "That man ought to be shot. What do we want with alliances?... Have you heard Lord Roberts?"

George admitted weakly, and as if ashamed, that he had not.

"Well, you should."

"Oh yes," Marguerite ingenuously put in. "Alfred's been very strong on the European War ever since he heard Lord Roberts speak at Chelsea Town Hall."

George then understood the situation. Mr. Prince, through the hazard of a visit to Chelsea Town Hall, had become obsessed by a single idea, an idea which his natural apprehensions had well nourished. A common phenomenon! George had met before the man obsessed by one idea, with his crude reasoning, his impatience, and his flashing eye. As for himself he did not pretend to be an expert in politics; he had no time for politics; but he was interested in them, and held strong views about them; and among his strongest views was the view that the crudity of the average imperialist was noxious, and a source of real danger. 'That man ought to be shot.' Imagine such a remark! He felt that he must soothe Mr. Prince as he would soothe a child. And he did so, with all the tact acquired at municipal committee meetings in the north.

His last impression, on departure, was that Mr. Prince was an excellent and most lovable fellow, despite his obsession. "Glad to see you at any time," said Mr. Prince, with genuine cordiality, critically and somewhat inimically assessing the car, which he referred to as 'she.' Marguerite had remained in the studio. She was wonderful. She admired her husband too simply, and she was too content, but she had marvellous qualities of naturalness, common sense in demeanour, realism, and placidity. Thanks to her remarkable instinct for taking things for granted, the interview had been totally immune from constraint. It was difficult, and she had made it seem easy. No fuss, no false sentiment! And she looked very nice, very interesting, quite attractive, in her mourning and in her expectancy. A fine couple. Unassuming of course, narrow, opinionated - (he surmised that the last days of the late Mr. Haim had been disciplined) - but no fools either, and fundamentally decent. While condescending to them, he somehow envied them. But he knew what the opinion of Lois about them would be!

<h2 style="text-align:center">4</h2>

After a period of shallow sleep he woke up in the morning factitiously refreshed as the train was rumbling slowly over the high-level bridge. The sun blinked full in his eyes when he looked out through the trellis-work of the bridge. Far below, the river was tinged with the pale blue of the sky. Big ships lay in the river as if they had never moved and never could move; a steamer in process of painting, with her sides lifted above the water, gleamed in irregular patches of brilliant scarlet. A lively tug passed down-stream, proud of her early rising; and, smaller even than the tug, a smack, running close-hauled, bowed to the puffs of the light breeze. Farther away the lofty chimneys sent their scarves of smoke into the air, and the vast skeletons of incipient vessels could be descried through webs of staging. The translucent freshness of the calm scene was miraculous; it divinely intoxicated the soul, and left no squalor and no ugliness anywhere.

Then, as the line curved, came the view of the city beneath its delicate canopy of mist. The city was built on escarpments, on ridges, on hills, and sagged here and there into great hollows. The serrated silhouette of it wrote romance upon the sky, and the contours of the naked earth beyond lost themselves grandly in the mystery of the north. The jutting custom-house was a fine piece of architecture. From the eighteen-forties it challenged grimly the modern architect. On his hasty first visit to the city George had noticed little save that custom-house. He had seen a slatternly provincial town, large and picturesque certainly, but with small sense of form or dignity. He had decided that his town hall would stand quite unique in the town. But soon the city had imposed itself upon him and taught him the rudiments of humility. It contained an immense quantity of interesting architecture of various periods, which could not be appreciated at a glance. It was a hoary place. It went back to the Romans and further. Its fragmentary walls had survived through seven centuries, its cathedral through six, its chief churches through five. It had the most perfect Norman keep within two hundred miles. It had ancient halls, mansions, towers, markets, and jail. And to these the Victorian-Edwardian age had added museums, law courts, theatres; such astonishing modernities as swimming-baths, power-houses, joint-stock banks, lending libraries, and art schools; and whole monumental streets and squares from the designs of a native architect without whose respectable name no history of British architecture could be called complete. George's town hall was the largest building in the city; but it did not dominate the city nor dwarf it; the city easily digested it. Arriving in the city by train the traveller, if he knew where to look, could just distinguish a bit of the town hall tower, amid masses of granite and brick: which glimpse symbolized the relation between the city and the town hall and had its due effect on the Midland conceit of George.

But what impressed George more than the stout, physical aspects of the city was the sense of its huge, adventurous, corporate life, continuous from century to century. It had known terrible battles, obstinate sieges, famines, cholera, a general conflagration, and, in the twentieth century, strikes that possibly were worse than pestilence. It had fiercely survived them all. It was a city passionate and highly vitalized. George had soon begun to be familiar with its organic existence from the inside. The amazing delays in the construction of the town hall were characteristic of the city, originating as they did not from sloth or indecision but from the obduracy of the human will. At the start a sensational municipal election had put the whole project on the shelf for two years, and George had received a compensatory one per cent on the estimated cost according to contract, and had abandoned his hope. But the pertinacity of Mr. Soulter, first Councillor, then Alderman, then Mayor, the true father of the town hall, had been victorious in the end. Next there had been an infinity of trouble with owners of adjacent properties and with the foundations. Next the local contractor, who had got the work through a ruthless and ingenious conspiracy of associates on the Council, had gone bankrupt. Next came the gigantic building strike, in which conflicting volitions fought each other for many months to the devastation of an entire group of trades. Finally was the inflexible resolution of Mr. Soulter that the town hall should not be opened and used until it was finished in every part and every detail of furniture and decoration.

George, by his frequent sojourns in the city, and his official connexion with the authorities, had several opportunities to observe the cabals, the chicane, and the personal animosities and friendships which functioned in secret at the very heart of the city's life. He knew the idiosyncrasies of councillors and aldermen in committee; he had learnt more about mankind in the committee-rooms of the old town hall than he could have learnt in ten thousand London clubs. He could divide the city council infallibly into wire-pullers, axe-grinders, vain nincompoops, honest mediocrities, and the handful who combined honesty with sagacity and sagacity with strength. At beefy luncheon-tables, and in gorgeous, stuffy bars tapestried with Lincrusta-Walton, he had listened to the innumerable tales of the town, in which greed, crookedness, ambition, rectitude, hatred, and sexual love were extraordinarily mixed - the last being by far the smallest ingredient. He liked the town; he revelled in it. It seemed to him splendid in its ineradicable, ever-changing, changeless humanity. And as the train bored its way through the granite bowels of the city, he thought pleasurably upon all these matters. And with them in his mind there gradually mingled the images of Lois and Marguerite. He cared not what their virtues were or what their faults were. He enjoyed reflecting upon them, picturing them with their contrasted attributes, following them into the future as they developed blindly under the unperceived sway of the paramount instincts which had impelled and would always impel them towards their ultimate destiny. He thought upon himself, and about himself he was very sturdily cheerful, because he had had a most satisfactory interview with Sir Isaac on the previous afternoon.

A few minutes later he walked behind a portmanteau-bearing night-porter into the wide-corridored, sleeping hotel, whose dust glittered in the straight shafts of early sunlight. He stopped at the big slate under the staircase and wrote in chalk opposite the number 187: "Not to be called till 12 o'clock, under pain of death." And the porter, a friend of some years' standing, laughed. On the second floor that same porter dropped the baggage on the linoleum and rattled the key in the lock with a high disregard of sleepers. In the bedroom the porter undid the straps of the portmanteau, and then:

"Anything else, sir?"

"That's all, John."

And as he turned to leave, John stopped and remarked in a tone of concern:

"Sorry to say Alderman Soulter's ill in bed, sir. Won't be able to come to the Opening. It's him as'll be madder than anybody, ill or not."

George was shocked, and almost frightened. In his opinion the true intelligence of the city was embodied in Mr. Soulter. Mr. Soulter had been a father to him, had understood his aims and fought for them again and again. Without Mr. Soulter he felt defenceless before the ordeal of the Opening, and he wished that he might fly back to London instantly. Nevertheless the contact of the cool, clean sheets was exquisite, and he went to sleep at once, just as he was realizing the extremity of his fatigue.

He did not have his sleep out. Despite the menace of death, a courageous creature heavily knocked at his door at ten o'clock and entered. It was a page-boy with a telegram. George opened the envelope resentfully.

"No answer."

The telegram read:

"Am told we have got it. - Ponting"

Ponting was George's assistant. The news referred to a competition for an enormous barracks in India - one of the two competitions pending. It had come sooner than expected. Was it true? George was aware that Ponting had useful acquaintanceship with a clerk in the India Office.

He thought, trying not to believe:

"Of course Ponting will swallow anything."

But he made no attempt to sleep again. He was too elated.

5

Through a strange circumstance George arrived late for the Opening lunch in the lower hall, but he was late in grave company. He had been wandering aimlessly and quite alone about the great interiors of the town hall when he caught sight of Mr. Phirrips, the contractor, with the bishop and the most famous sporting peer of the north, a man who for some mystical reason was idolized by the masses of the city. Unfortunately Mr. Phirrips also caught sight of George. "Bishop, here is Mr. Cannon, our architect. He will be able to explain perhaps better - " And in an instant Mr. Phirrips had executed one of those feats of prestidigitation for which he was renowned in contracting circles, left George with the bishop, and gone off with his highly prized quarry, the sporting peer. George, despite much worldliness, had never before had speech with a bishop. However, the bishop played his part in a soothingly conventional way, manipulated his apron and his calves with senile dignity, stood still and gazed ardently at ceilings and vistas, and said at intervals, explosively and hoarsely: "Ha! Very, interesting! Very interesting! Very fine! Very fine! Noble!" He also put intelligent questions to the youthful architect, such as: "How many bricks have been used in this building?" He was very leisurely, as though the whole of eternity was his.

"I'm afraid we may be late for the luncheon," George ventured.

The bishop looked at him blandly, leaning forward, and replied, after holding his mouth open for a moment:

"They will not begin without us. I say grace." His antique eye twinkled.

After this George liked him, and understood that he was really a bishop.

In the immense hubbub of the lower hall the bishop was seized upon by officials, and conducted to a chair a few places to the right of His Worship the Mayor. Though there was considerable disorder and confusion (doubtless owing to the absence of Alderman Soulter, who had held all the strings in his hand) everybody agreed that the luncheon scene in the lower hall was magnificent. The Mayor, in his high chair and in his heavy chain and glittering robe, ruled in the centre of the principal table, from which lesser tables ran at right angles. The Aldermen and Councillors, also chained and robed, well sustained the brilliance of the Mayor, and the ceremonial officials of the city surpassed both Mayor and Council in grandeur. Sundry peers and M.P.'s and illustrious capitalists enhanced the array of renown, and the bishop was rivalled by priestly dignitaries scarcely less grandiose than himself. And then there were the women. The women had been let in. During ten years of familiarity with the city's life George had hardly spoken to a woman, except Mr. Soulter's Scotch half-sister. The men lived a life of their own, which often extended to the evenings, and very many of them when mentioning women employed a peculiar tone. But now the women were disclosed in bulk, and the display startled George. He suddenly saw all the city fathers and their sons in a new light.

The bishop had his appointed chair, with a fine feminine hat on either side of him, but George could not find that any particular chair had been appointed to himself. Eventually he saw an empty chair in the middle of a row of men at the right-hand transverse table, and he took it. He had expected, as the sole artistic creator of the town hall whose completion the gathering celebrated, to be the object of a great deal of curiosity at the luncheon. But in this expectation he was deceived. If any curiosity concerning him existed, it was admirably concealed. The authorities, however, had not entirely forgotten him, for the Town Clerk that morning had told him that he must reply to the toast of his health. He had protested against the shortness of the notice, whereupon the Town Clerk had said casually that a few words would suffice - anything, in fact, and had hastened off. George was now getting nervous. He was afraid of hearing his own voice in that long, low interior which he had made. He had no desire to eat. He felt tired. Still, his case was less acute than it would have been had the august personage originally hoped for attended the luncheon. The august personage had not attended on account of an objection, apropos of an extreme passage in an election campaign speech, to the occupant of the mayoral chair (who had thus failed to be transformed into a Lord Mayor). The whole city had then, though the Mayor was not over-popular, rallied to its representative, and the Council had determined that the inauguration should be a purely municipal affair, a family party, proving to the august and to the world that the city was self-sufficing. The episode was characteristic.

George heard a concert of laughter, which echoed across the room. At the end of the main table Mr. Phirrips had become a centre of gaiety. Mr. Phirrips, whom George and the clerk-of-the-works had had severe and constant difficulty in keeping reasonably near the narrow path of rectitude, was a merry, sharp, smart, middle-aged man with a skin that always looked as if he had just made use of an irritant soap. He was one of the largest contractors in England, and his name on the hoarding of any building in course of erection seemed to give distinction to that building. He was very rich, and popular in municipal circles, and especially with certain councillors, including a labour councillor. George wondered whether Mr. Phirrips would make a speech. No toast-list was visible in George's vicinity.

To George the meal seemed to pass with astounding celerity. The old bishop said grace in six words. The Toast-master bawled for silence. The health of all classes of society who could rely upon good doctors was proposed and heartily drunk - princes, prelates, legislators, warriors, judges - but the catalogue was cut short before any eccentric person could propose the health of the one-roomed poor, of whom the city was excessively prolific. And then the Mayor addressed himself to the great business of the town hall. George listened with throat dry; by way of precaution he had drunk nothing during the meal; and at each toast he had merely raised the glass to his lips and infinitesimally sipped; the coffee was bad and cold and left a taste in his mouth; but everything that he had eaten left a taste in his mouth.

The Mayor began: "My lords, ladies, and gentlemen, - During the building of this - er - er - structure...." All his speech was in that manner and that key. Nevertheless he was an able and strong individual, and as an old trade union leader could be fiercely eloquent with working-men. He mentioned Alderman Soulter, and there was a tremendous cheer. He did not mention Alderman Soulter again; a feud burned between these two. After Alderman Soulter he mentioned finance. He said that that was not the time to refer to finance, and then spoke of nothing else but finance throughout the remainder of his speech, until he came to the peroration - "success and prosperity to our new town hall, the grandest civic monument which any city has erected to itself in this country within living memory, aye, and beyond." The frantic applause atoned for the lack of attention and the semi-audible chattering which had marred the latter part of the interminable and sagacious harangue. George thought: "Pardon me! The city has not erected this civic monument. I have erected it." And he thought upon all the labour he had put into it, and all the beauty and magnificence which he had evolved. Alderman Soulter should have replied on behalf of the town hall committee, and the Alderman who took his place apologized for his inability to fill the role, and said little.

Then the Toast-master bawled incomprehensibly for the twentieth time, and a councillor arose and in timid tones said:

"I rise to propose the toast of the architect and contractor."

George was so astounded that he caught scarcely anything of the speech. It was incredible to him that he, the creative artist, who was solely responsible for the architecture and decoration of the monument, in whose unique mind it had existed long before the second brick had been placed upon the first, should be bracketed in a toast with the tradesman and middleman who had merely supervised the execution of his scheme according to rules of thumb. He flushed. He wanted to walk out. But nobody else appeared to be disturbed. George, who had never before attended an inauguration, was simply not aware that the toast 'architect and contractor' was the classic British toast, invariably drunk on such occasions, and never criticised. He thought: "What a country!" and remembered hundreds of Mr. Enwright's remarks.... Phrases of the orator wandered into his ear. "The competition system.... We went to Sir Hugh Corver, the head of the architectural profession [loud applause] and Sir Hugh Corver assured us that the design of Mr. George Cannon was the best. [Hear, hear! Hear, hear!]... Mr. Phirrip, head of the famous firm of Phirrips Limited [loud applause] ... fortunate, after our misfortune with the original contractor to obtain such a leading light.... Cannot sufficiently thank these two - er officials for the intellect, energy, and patience they have put into their work."

As the speech was concluding, a tactless man sitting next to George, with whom he had progressed very slowly in acquaintance during the lunch, leaned towards him and murmured in a confidential tone:

"Did I tell you both naval yards up here have just had orders to work day and night? Yes. Fact."

George's mind ran back to Mr. Prince, and Mr. Prince's prophecy of war. Was there something in it after all? The thought passed in an instant, but the last vestiges of his equanimity had gone. Hearing his name he jumped up in a mist inhabited by inimical phantoms, and, amid feeble acclamations here and there, said he knew not what in a voice now absurdly loud and now absurdly soft, and sat down, amid more feeble acclamations, feeling an angry fool. It was the most hideous experience. He lit a cigarette, his first that day.

When Mr. Phirrips rose, the warm clapping was expectant of good things.

"When I was a little boy I remember my father telling me that this town hall had been started. I never expected to live to see it finished - "

Delighted guffaws, uproarious laughter, explosions of mirth, interrupted this witty reference to the delays in construction. The speaker smiled at ease. His eyes glinted. He knew his audience, held it consummately, and went on.

In the afternoon there was a conversazione, or reception, for the lunchers and also for the outer fringe of the city's solid respectability. The whole of the town hall from basement to roof was open to view, and citizens of all ages wandered in it everywhere, admiring it, quizzing it, and feeling proudly that it was theirs. George too wandered about, feeling that it was his. He was slowly recovering from the humiliation of the lunch. Much of the building pleased him greatly; at the excellence of some effects and details he marvelled; the entry into the large hall from the grand staircase was dramatic, just as he had had intended it should be; the organ was being played, and word went round that the acoustic (or acoostic) properties of the auditorium were perfect, and unrivalled by any auditorium in the kingdom. On the other hand, the crudity of certain other effects and details irritated the creator, helping him to perceive how much he had learnt in ten years; in ten years, for example, his ideas about mouldings had been quite transformed. What chiefly satisfied him was the demonstration, everywhere, that he had mastered his deep natural impatience of minutiae - that instinct which often so violently resented the exacting irksomeness of trifles in the realization of a splendid idea. At intervals he met an acquaintance and talked, but nobody at all appeared to comprehend that he alone was the creator of the mighty pile, and that all the individuals present might be divided artistically into two classes - himself in one class, the entire remainder in the other. And nobody appeared to be inconvenienced by the sense of the height of his achievement or of the splendour of his triumph that day. It is true that the north hates to seem impressed, and will descend to any duplicity in order not to seem impressed.

The Town Clerk's clerk came importantly up to him and asked:

"How many reserved seats would you like for the concert?"

A grand ballad concert, at which the most sentimental of contraltos, helped by other first-class throats, was to minister wholesale to the insatiable secret sentimentality of the north, had been arranged for the evening.

"One will be enough," said George.

"Are you alone?" asked the Town Clerk's clerk.

George took the ticket. None of the city fathers or their fashionable sons had even invited him to dinner. He went forth and had tea alone, while reading in an evening paper about the Austro-Serbian situation, in the tea-rooms attached to a cinema-palace. The gorgeous rooms, throbbing to two-steps and fox-trots, were crammed with customers; but the waitresses behaved competently. Thence he drove out in a taxi to the residence of Alderman Soulter. He could see neither the Alderman nor Miss Soulter; he learnt that the condition of the patient was reassuring, and that the patient had a very good constitution. Back at the hotel, he had to wait for dinner. In due course he ate the customary desolating table-d'hote dinner which is served simultaneously in the vast, odorous dining-rooms, all furnished alike, of scores and scores of grand hotels throughout the provinces. Having filled his cigar-case, he set out once more into the beautiful summer evening. In broad Side Gate were massed the chief resorts of amusement. The facade of the Empire music-hall glowed with great rubies and emeralds and amethysts and topazes in the fading light. Its lure was more powerful than the lure of the ballad concert. Ignoring his quasi-official duty to the greatest of sentimental contraltos, he pushed into the splendid foyer of the Empire. One solitary stall, half a crown, was left for the second house; he bought it, eager in transgression; he felt that the ballad concert would have sent him mad.

The auditorium of the Empire was far larger than the auditorium of the town hall, and it was covered with gold. The curving rows of plush-covered easy chairs extended backwards until faces became indistinguishable points in the smoke-misted gloom. Every seat was occupied; the ballad concert had made no impression upon the music-hall. The same stars that he could see in London appeared on the gigantic stage in the same songs and monologues; and as in London the indispensable revue was performed, but with a grosser and more direct licentiousness than the West End would have permitted. And all proceeded with inexorable exactitude according to time-table. And in scores and scores of similar Empires, Hippodromes, Alhambras, and Pavilions throughout the provinces, similar entertainments were proceeding with the same exactitude - another example of the huge standardization of life. George laughed with the best at the inventive drollery of the knock-about comedians - Britain's sole genuine contribution to the art of the modern stage. But there were items in the Empire programme that were as awful in their tedium as anything at the ballad concert could be - moments when George could not bear to look over the footlights. And these items were applauded in ecstasy by the enchanted audience. He thought of the stupidity, the insensibility, the sheer ignorance of the exalted lunchers; and he compared them with these qualities in the Empire audience, and asked himself sardonically whether all artists had lived in vain. But the atmosphere of the Empire was comfortable, reassuring, inspiring. The men had their pipes, cigarettes, and women; the women had the men, the luxury, the glitter, the publicity. They had attained, they were happy. The frightful curse of the provinces, ennui, had been conjured away by the beneficent and sublime institution invented, organized, and controlled by three great trusts.

George stayed till the end of the show. The emptying of the theatre was like a battle, like the flight of millions from a conflagration. All humanity seemed to be crowded into the corridors and staircases. Jostled and disordered, he emerged into the broad street, along which huge, lighted trams slowly thundered. He walked a little, starting a fresh cigar. The multitude had resumed its calm. A few noisy men laughed and swore obscene oaths; and girls, either in couples or with men, trudged, demure and unshocked, past the roysterers, as though they had neither ears to hear nor eyes to see. In a few minutes the processions were dissipated, dissolved into the vastness of the city, and the pavements nearly deserted. George strolled on towards the Square. The town hall stood up against the velvet pallor of the starry summer night, massive, lovely, supreme, deserted. He had conceived it in an office in Russell Square when he was a boy. And there it was, the mightiest monument of the city which had endured through centuries of astounding corporate adventure. He was overwhelmed, and he was inexpressibly triumphant. Throughout the day he had had no recognition; and as regards the future, few, while ignorantly admiring the monument, would give a thought to the artist. Books were eternally signed, and pictures, and sculpture. But the architect was forgotten. What did it matter? If the creators of Gothic cathedrals had to accept oblivion, he might. The tower should be his signature. And no artist could imprint his influence so powerfully and so mysteriously upon the unconscious city as he was doing. And the planet was whirling the whole city round like an atom in the icy spaces between the stars. And perhaps Lois was lying expectant, discontented, upon the sofa, thinking rebelliously. He was filled with the realization of universality.

At the hotel another telegram awaited him.

"Good old Ponting!" he exclaimed, after reading it. The message ran:

"We have won it. - Ponting"

He said:

"Why 'we,' Ponting? You didn't win it. I won it."

He said:

"Sir Hugh Corver is not going to be the head of the architectural profession. I am."

He felt the assurance of that in his bones.

2

THE ROLL-CALL

The telephone rang in the principal's room of George's office in Museum Street. He raised his head from the drawing-board with the false gesture of fatigued impatience which, as a business man, he had long since acquired, and took the instrument. As a fact he was not really busy; he was only pretending to be busy; and he rather enjoyed the summons of the telephone, with its eternal promise of some romantic new turn of existence. Nevertheless, though he was quite alone, he had to affect that the telephone was his bane.

"Can Sir Isaac Davids speak to you, sir, from the Artists Club?"

"Put him on."

Immediately came the thick, rich voice of Sir Isaac, with its implications of cynicism and triumphant disdain - attenuated and weakened in the telephone, suggesting an object seen through the wrong end of a telescope.

"Is that you, Cannon?"

"It is," said George shortly. Without yet knowing it, he had already begun to hate Sir Isaac. His criticism of Sir Isaac was that the man was too damnably sure of himself. And not all Sir Isaac's obvious power, and influence, and vast potential usefulness to a young architect, could prevent George from occasionally, as he put it, 'standing up to the fellow.'

"Well, you'd better come along here, if you can. I want to see you," said the unruffled voice of Sir Isaac.

"Now?"

"Yes."

"All right."

As George replaced the instrument, he murmured:

"I know what that means. It's all off." And after a moment: "I knew jolly well it would be."

He glanced round the very orderly room, to which, by judicious furnishing, he had given a severe distinction at no great cost. On the walls were a few interesting things, including a couple of his own perspectives. A neo-impressionist oil-sketch over the mantelpiece, with blue trees and red fields and a girl whose face was a featureless blob, imperiously monopolized the attention of the beholder, warning him, whoever he might be, that the inescapable revolutionary future was now at hand. The room and everything in it, that entity upon which George had spent so much trouble, and of which he had been so proud, seemed futile, pointless, utterly unprofitable.

The winning of the Indian limited competition, coupled with the firm rumour that Sir Isaac Davids had singled him out for patronage, had brilliantly renewed George's reputation and the jealousy which proved its reality. The professional journals had been full of him, and everybody assured everybody that his ultimate, complete permanent success had never been in doubt. The fact that the barracks would be the largest barracks in India indicated to the superstitious, and to George himself, that destiny intended him always to break records. After the largest town hall, the largest barracks; and it was said that Sir Isaac's factory was to be the largest factory! But the outbreak of war had overthrown all reputations, save the military and the political. Every value was changed according to a fresh standard, as in a shipwreck. For a week George had felt an actual physical weight in the stomach. This weight was his own selfish woe, but it was also the woe of the entire friendly world. Every architect knew and said that the profession of architecture would be ruined for years. Then the India Office woke George up. The attitude of the India Office was overbearing. It implied that it had been marvellously original and virtuous in submitting the affair of its barracks to even a limited competition, when it might just as easily have awarded the job to any architect whom it happened to know, or whom its wife, cousin, or aunt happened to know, or whose wife, cousin, or aunt happened to know the India Office - and further, that George ought therefore to be deeply grateful. It said that in view of the war the barracks must be erected with the utmost possible, or rather with quite impossible, dispatch, and that George would probably have to go to India at once. Simultaneously it daily modified George's accepted plans for the structure, exactly as though it was a professional architect and George an amateur, and it involved him in a seemly but intense altercation between itself and the subordinate bureaucracy of a Presidency. It kept George employed. In due course people discovered that business must proceed as usual, and even the architectural profession, despite its traditional pessimism, had hopes of municipalities and other bodies which were to inaugurate public works in order to diminish unemployment.

Nevertheless George had extreme difficulty in applying himself efficiently to urgent tasks. He kept thinking: "It's come! It's come!" He could not get over the fact that it had come - the European War which had obsessed men's minds for so many years past. He saved the face of his own theory as to the immediate impossibility of a great war, by positively asserting that Germany would never have fought had she foreseen that Britain would fight. He prophesied (to himself) Germany's victory, German domination of Europe, and, as the grand central phenomenon, mysterious ruin for George Edwin Cannon. But the next instant he would be convinced that Germany would be smashed, and quickly. Germany, he reckoned superiorly, in 'taking on England' had 'bitten off more than she could chew.'

He knew almost naught of the progress of the fighting. He had obtained an expensive map of Western Europe and some flagged pins, and had hung the map up in his hall and had stuck the pins into it with exactitude. He had moved the pins daily, until little Laurencine one morning, aloft on a chair, decided to change all the positions of the opposing armies. Laurencine established German army corps in Marseilles, the Knockmillydown Mountains, and Torquay, while sending the French to Elsinore and Aberdeen. There was trouble in the house. Laurencine suffered, and was given to understand that war was a serious matter. Still, George soon afterwards had ceased to manipulate the pins; they seemed to be incapable of arousing his imagination; he could not be bothered with them; he could not make the effort necessary to acquire a scientific conception of the western campaign - not to mention the eastern, as to which his ignorance was nearly perfect.

Yet he read much about the war. Some of the recounted episodes deeply and ineffaceably impressed him. For example, an American newspaper correspondent had written a dramatic description of the German army marching, marching steadily along a great Belgian high road - a procession without beginning and without end - and of the procession being halted for his benefit, and of a German officer therein who struck a soldier several times in the face angrily with his cane, while the man stood stiffly at attention. George had an ardent desire to spend a few minutes alone with that officer; he could not get the soldier's bruised cheek out of his memory.

Again, he was moved and even dismayed by the recitals of the entry of the German army into Brussels and of its breaking into the goose-step as it reached the Grande Place, though he regarded the goose-step as too ridiculous and contemptible for words. Then the French defence of Dinant, and the Belgian defence of Liege, failure as it was, and the obstinate resistance at Namur, inspired him; and the engagements between Belgians and Uhlans, in which the clumsy Uhlans were always scattered, destroyed for him the dread significance of the term 'Uhlan.'

He simply did not comprehend that all these events were negligible trifles, that no American correspondent had seen the hundredth part of the enemy forces, that the troops which marched through Brussels were a tiny, theatrical side-show, a circus, that the attack on Liege had been mismanaged, that the great battle at Dinant was a mere skirmish in the new scale of war, and the engagements with Uhlans mere scuffles, and that behind the screen of these infinitesimal phenomena the German army, unimagined in its hugeness, horror, and might, was creeping like a fatal and monstrous caterpillar surely towards France.

A similar screen hid from him the realities of England. He saw bunting and recruits, and the crowds outside consulates. But he had no idea of the ceaseless flight of innumerable crammed trains day and night southwards, of the gathering together of Atlantic liners and excursion steamers from all the coasts into an unprecedented Armada, of the sighting of the vanguard of that Armada by an incredulous Boulogne, of the landing of British regiments and guns and aeroplanes in the midst of a Boulogne wonderstruck and delirious, and of the thrill which thereupon ecstatically shivered through France. He knew only that 'the Expeditionary Force had landed in safety.'

He could not believe that a British Army could face successfully the legendary Prussians with their Great General Staff, and yet he had a mystic and entirely illogical belief in the invincibility of the British Army. He had read somewhere that the German forces amounted in all to the equivalent of over three hundred divisions; he had been reliably told that the British forces in France amounted to three divisions and some cavalry. It was most absurd; but his mysticism survived the absurdity, so richly was it nourished by news from the strange, inartistic colonies, where architecture was not understood. Revelation came to George that the British Empire, which he had always suspected to be an invention of those intolerable persons the Imperialists, was after all something more than a crude pink smear across the map of the world.

Withal he was acutely dejected as he left his office to go to the club.

2

Sir Isaac was sitting quite alone in the large smoking-room of the Artists in Albemarle Street - a beautiful apartment terribly disfigured by its pictures, which had been procured from fashionable members in the fashionable taste of twenty years earlier, and were crying aloud for some one brave enough to put them out of their misery. No interpretation of the word 'artist' could by any ingenuity be stretched to include Sir Isaac. Nevertheless he belonged to the club, and so did a number of other men in like case. The difference between Sir Isaac and the rest was that Sir Isaac did actually buy pictures, though seldom from fashionable painters.

He was a personage of about forty-five years, with a rather prominent belly, but not otherwise stout; a dark man; plenty of stiff black hair (except for one small central bald patch); a rank moustache, and a clean-shaven chin apparently woaded in the manner of the ancient Britons; elegantly and yet severely dressed - braided morning-coat, striped trousers, small, skin-fitting boots, a black flowered-silk necktie. As soon as you drew near him you became aware of his respiratory processes; you were bound to notice continually that without ceasing he carried on the elemental business of existence. Hair sprouted from his nose, and the nose was enormous; it led at a pronounced slope to his high forehead, which went on upwards at exactly the same angle and was lost in his hair. If the chin had weakly receded, as it often does in this type, Sir Isaac would have had a face like a spear-head, like a ram of which the sharp point was the top of his nose; but Sir Isaac's chin was square, and the wall of it perpendicular.

His expression was usually inquisitive, dissatisfied, and disdainful - the effect being produced by a slight lifting of the back of the nostrils and a slight tipping forward of the whole head. His tone, however, often by its bluff good-humour, contradicted the expression. He had in an extreme degree the appearance of a Jew, and he had the names of a Jew; and most people said he was a Jew. But he himself seriously denied it. He asserted that he came of a Welsh Nonconformist family, addicted to christening its infants out of the Bible, and could prove his descent for generations - not that he minded being taken for a Jew (he would add), was indeed rather flattered thereby, but he simply was not a Jew. At any rate he was Welsh. A journalist had described him in a phrase: "All the time he's talking to you in English you feel he's thinking something different in Welsh." He was an exceedingly rich industrial, and had made his money by organization; he seemed always to have leisure.

"Here," he curtly advised George, producing a magnificent Partaga, similar to the one he was himself smoking, "you'd better have this."

He cut the cigar carefully with a club tool, and pushed the match-stand across the table with a brusque gesture. George would not thank him for the cigar.

"You're on that Indian barracks, aren't you?"

"Yes. They're in a Hades of a hurry."

"Well, my factory is in much more of a hurry."

George was startled. He had heard nothing of the factory for a month, and had assumed that the war had scotched the enterprise.

He said:

"Then the war won't stop you?"

Sir Isaac shook his head slowly, with an arrogant smile. It then occurred to George that this man differed strangely from all other men - because the sinister spell of the war had been powerless over him alone. All other men bore the war in their faces and in their gestures, but this man did not.

"I'm going to make munitions now - explosives. I'm going to have the biggest explosives factory in the world. However, the modifications in the general plan won't be serious. I want to talk to you about that."

"Have you got contracts, then, already?"

"No. Both the War Office and the Admiralty have told me they have all the explosives they want," he sneered. "But I've made a few inquiries, and I think that by the time my factory's up they'll be wanting more explosives than they can get. In fact I wish I could build half a dozen factories. Dare say I shall."

"Then you think we're in for a long war?"

"Not specially that. If it's a long war you English will win. If it's a short war the Germans will win, and it will be the end of France as a great power. That's all."

"Won't it be the end of your factory too?"

"Noh!" exclaimed Sir Isaac, with careless compassion in his deep, viscid voice. "If it's a short war, there'll be another war. You English will never leave it alone. So that whatever happens, if I take up explosives, I can't go wrong. It's velvet."

"It seems to me we shall bust up the whole world if we aren't careful, soon."

Sir Isaac smiled more compassion.

"Not at all," he said easily. "Not at all. Things are always arranged in the end - more or less satisfactorily, of course. It's up to the individual to look out for himself."

George said:

"I was thinking of going into the Army."

The statement was not strictly untrue, but he had never formulated it, and he had never thought consecutively of such a project, which did indeed appear too wild and unpractical for serious consideration.

"This recruiting's been upsetting you."

George's vague patriotism seemed to curdle at these half-dozen scornful words.

"Do you think I oughtn't to go into the Army, Sir Isaac?"

"My dear boy, any - can go into the Army. And if you go into the Army you'll lose your special qualities. I see you as the best factory designer we have, architecturally. You've only just started, but you have it in you. And your barracks is pretty good. Of course, if you choose to indulge in sentimentality you can deprive the country of an architect in a million and make it a present of a mediocre soldier - for you haven't got the mind of a soldier. But if you do that, mark my words - you'll only do it to satisfy the egotism that you call your heart, you'll only do it in order to feel comfortable; just as a woman gives a penny to a beggar and thinks it's charity when it's nothing of the sort. There are fellows that go and enlist because they hear a band play."

"Yes," George concurred. He hated to feel himself confronted by a mind more realistic than his own, but he was realistic enough to admit the fact. What Sir Isaac said was unanswerable, and it appealed very strongly to George. He cast away his sentimentality, ashamed of it. And at the same time he felt greatly relieved in other ways.

"You'd better put this Indian barracks on one side as much as you can, or employ some one to help you. I shall want all your energies."

"But I shall probably have to go to India. The thing's very urgent."

Sir Isaac scorned him in a profound gaze. The smoke from their two magnificent cigars mingled in a canopy above them.

"Not it!" said Sir Isaac. "What's more, it's not wanted at all. They think it is, because they're absolutely incapable of thought. They know the word 'war' and they know the word 'barracks.' They put them together and imagine it's logic. They say: 'We were going to build a barracks, and now we're at war. Therefore we must hurry up with the barracks.' That's how they reason, and the official mind will never get beyond it. Why do they want the barracks? If they want the barracks, what's the meaning of what they call 'the response of the Indian Empire'? Are they going to send troops to India or take them away from India? They're going to take them away, of course. Mutiny of India's silent millions? Rubbish! Not because a mutiny would contradict the far-famed 'response of the Indian Empire,' but because India's silent millions haven't got a rifle amongst them. You needn't tell me they've given you forty reasons for getting on with that barracks. I know their reasons. All of 'em put together only mean that in a dull, dim Oxford-and-Cambridge way they see a connexion between the word 'war' and the word 'barracks.'"

George laughed, and then, after a few seconds, Sir Isaac gave a short, rough laugh.

"But if they insist on me going to India - " George began, and paused.

Sir Isaac grew meditative.

"I say, speaking of voyages," he murmured in a tone almost dreamy. "If you have any loose money, put it into ships, and keep it there. You'll double it, you'll treble it.... Any ships. No matter what ships."

"Well, I haven't got any loose money," said George curtly. "And what I want to know is, if they insist on me going to India, what am I to do?"

"Tell them you can't go. Tell 'em your professional engagements won't permit it. They'll lick your boots, and ask humbly if you can suggest any suitable person to represent you. I shall want all your energies, and my factory will be worth more to this country in the war than all the barracks under heaven. Now just bend your eye to these."

He took some papers from his tail-pocket. The discussion grew technical.

3

George sailed down Piccadilly westwards on the top of a motor-bus. The August afternoon was superb. Piccadilly showed more than its usual splendour of traffic, for the class to whom the sacred word 'England' signified personal dominion and a vast apparatus of personal luxury either had not gone away for its holiday or had returned therefrom in a hurry. The newspaper placards spoke of great feats of arms by the Allies. Through the leafage of Hyde Park could be seen uncountable smart troops manoeuvring in bodies. On the top of the motor-bus a student of war was explaining to an ignorant friend that the active adhesion of Japan, just announced, meant the beginning of the end for Germany. From Japan he went to Namur, seeing that Namur was the 'chief bastion' of the defensive line, and that hence the Germans would not be 'allowed' to take it. Almost every motor-bus carried a fine specimen of this type of philosopher, to whom the whole travelling company listened while pretending not to listen. George despised him for his manner, but agreed with some of his reasoning.

George was thinking chiefly about Sir Isaac. Impressive person, Sir Isaac, even if hateful! It was remarkable how the fellow seemed always to have leisure. Organization, of course! Indubitably the fellow's arguments could not be gainsaid. The firing-line was not the only or even the most important part of the national war machine. To suppose otherwise was to share the crude errors of the childlike populace and its Press. Men were useless without guns, guns without shot, shot without explosives; and explosives could not be produced without a factory. The populace would never understand the close interdependence of various activities; it would never see beyond the recruiting station; it was meet only for pity. Sir Isaac had uttered a very wise saying: "Things are always arranged in the end ... It's up to the individual to look out for himself." Sir Isaac was freed from the thrall of mob-sentimentality. He was a super-man. And he was converting George into a super-man. George might have gone back to the office, but he was going home instead, because he could think creatively just as well outside the office as inside - so why should he accept the convention of the ordinary professional man. (Sir Isaac assuredly did not.) He had telephoned to the office. A single consideration appealed to him: How could he now best serve his country? Beyond question he could now serve his country best as an architect. If his duty marched with his advantage, what matter? It was up to the individual to look out for himself. And he, George, with already an immense reputation, would steadily enhance his reputation, which in the end would surpass all others in the profession. The war could not really touch him - no more than it could touch Sir Isaac; by good fortune, and by virtue of the impartiality of his intelligence, he was above the war.... Yes, Sir Isaac, disliked and unwillingly but deeply respected, had cleared his ideas for him.

In Elm Park Gardens he met the white-clad son of a Tory M.P. who lived in that dignified street.

"The very man! Come and make a fourth, will you, Cannon?" asked the youth, dandiacal in flannels, persuasively and flatteringly.

George demanded with firmness:

"Who are the other two?"

"Miss Horton and Gladys What's-her-name."

Why shouldn't he play at tennis? It was necessary to keep fit.

"All right. But not for long, you know."

"That's all right. Hurry up and get into your things."

"Ten minutes."

And in little more than ten minutes he was swinging a racket on the private sward that separates Elm Park Gardens East from Elm Park Gardens West, and is common to the residents of both. He had not encountered Lois at home, and had not thought it necessary to seek her out. He and she were often invited to play tennis in Elm Park Gardens.

The grass was beautifully kept. At a little distance two gardeners were at work, and a revolving sprinkler whirled sprays of glinting water in a wide circle. The back windows of the two streets disclosed not the slightest untidiness nor deshabille; rising irregularly in tier over tier to the high roof-line, they were all open, and all neatly curtained, and many of them had gorgeous sun-blinds. The sound of one or two pianos emerged faintly on the warm, still afternoon. Miss Horton and the slim Gladys were dressed in white, with short skirts, at once elegant and athletic. Miss Horton, very tall and strong, with clear eyes, and a complexion damaged by undue exposure to healthy fresh air, was a fine player of many years' experience, now at the decline of her powers. She played seriously, every stroke conscientious and calculated, and she gave polite, good-humoured hints to the youth, her partner. George and Gladys were together. Gladys, eighteen, was a delightful girl, the raw material of a very sound player; she held herself well, and knew by instinct what style was. A white belt defined her waist in the most enchanting fashion. George appreciated her, as a specimen of the newest generation of English girls. There were thousands of them in London alone, an endless supply, with none of the namby-pambiness and the sloppiness and the blowziness of their forerunners. Walking in Piccadilly or Bond Street or the Park, you might nowadays fancy yourself in Paris ... Why indeed should he not be playing tennis at that hour? The month was August. The apparatus of pleasure was there. Used or unused, it would still be there. It could not be destroyed simply because the times were grave. And there was his health; he would work better after the exercise. What purpose could there be in mournful inactivity? Yet continuously, as he ran about the court, and smiled at Gladys, and called out the score, and exclaimed upon his failures in precision, the strange, physical weight oppressed his stomach. He supposed that nearly everybody carried that physical weight. But did Sir Isaac? Did the delicious Gladys? The youth on the other side of the net was in the highest spirits because in a few days he would be entering Sandhurst.

A butler appeared from the French window of the ground floor of the M.P.'s house, walked down the curving path screened by a pergola, and came near the court with a small white paper in his solemn hand. At a suitable moment he gave the paper to the young master, who glanced at it and stuffed it into his pocket; the butler departed. A few minutes later the players changed courts. While the girls chatted apart, the youth leaped over the net, and, drawing the paper from his pocket, showed it furtively to George. It bore the words:

"Namur has fallen."

The M.P.'s household received special news by telephone from a friend at the War Office.

The youth raised his eyebrows, and with a side-glance seemed to say that there could be no object in telling the women immediately. The next instant the game was resumed with full ardour.

George missed his strokes. Like thousands of other people, untaught by the episode of Liege, he had counted upon Namur. Namur, the bastion, the shoulder of the newly forming line, if not impregnable, was expected to hold out for many days. And it had tumbled like a tin church, and with it the brave edifice of his confidence. He saw the Germans inevitably in Paris, blowing up Paris quarter by quarter, arrondissement by arrondissement, imposing peace, dictating peace, forcing upon Europe unspeakable humiliations. He saw Great Britain compelled to bow; and he saw worse than that. And the German officer, having struck across the face with his cane the soldier standing at attention, would go back to Germany in triumph more arrogant than ever, to ogle adoring virgins and push cowed and fatuous citizens off the pavement into the gutter. The solid houses of Elm Park Gardens, with their rich sun-blinds, the perfect sward, the white-frocked girls, the respectful gardeners, the red motor-buses flitting past behind the screen of bushes in the distance, even the butler in his majestic and invulnerable self-conceit - the whole systematized scene of correctness and tradition trembled as if perceived through the quivering of hot air. Gladys, reliant on the male and feeling that the male could no longer be relied on, went 'off her game,' with apologies; the experience of Miss Horton asserted itself, and the hard-fought set was lost by George and his partner. He reminded the company that he had only come for a short time, and left in a mood of bitter blackness.

215

4

In front of his own house George saw a tradesman's coupe of the superior, discreet sort, with a smart horse (the same being more 'distinctive' than motor-traction), a driver liveried in black, and the initials of the firm in a restrained monogram on the doors. He thought: "She's blueing money again. Of course it's her own, but - " He was extremely sardonic. In the drawing-room he found not only Lois but Laurencine and an attentive, respectful, bright-faced figure rather stylishly dressed in black. This last was fastening a tea-gown on the back of pale Lois, who stood up with a fatigued, brave air. Laurencine sat critically observant on the end of a sofa. The furniture of the room was heaped with tea-gowns, and other garments not very dissimilar, producing a rich and exciting effect. All three women quickened to George's entry.

"Oh! George!" said Lois querulously. "Are you going to play tennis? I wish I could! I'm so glad you came in; we'd no idea you were in the house, had we, Laurencine? Laurencine's giving me a tea-gown. Which of them do you prefer? It's no good me having one you don't like."

He had been unjust to her, then.

"It's really her birthday present," said Laurencine, "only a bit late. Oh! Dear! Darling, do sit down, you're standing too long."

Both Laurencine and the young woman in black regarded Lois with soft compassion, and she sat down. Laurencine too was a mother. But she had retained her girlhood. She was a splendid, powerful, erect creature, handsome, with a frank, benevolent, sane face, at the height of her physical perfection. George had a great fondness for her. Years earlier he had wondered how it was that he had not fallen in love with her instead of with Lois. But he knew the reason now. She lacked force of individuality. She was an adorer by instinct. She adored Lois; Lois could do no wrong. More strange, she adored her husband. Ingenuous simpleton! Yet wise! Another thing was that her mind was too pure. Instead of understanding, it rejected. It was a mind absolutely impregnable to certain phenomena. And this girl still enjoyed musical comedies and their successors in vogue, the revues!

"The Germans have taken Namur," George announced.

The news impressed. Even the young woman in black permitted herself by a facial gesture to show that she was interested in the war as well as in tea-gowns, and apart from its effect on tea-gowns.

"Oh! Dear!" murmured Laurencine.

"Is it serious?" Lois demanded.

"You bet it is!" George replied.

"But what's Sir John French doing, then? I say, Laurencine, I think I shall have that pale blue one, after all, if you don't mind." The black young woman went across to the piano and brought the pale blue one. "George, don't you think so?"

The gown was deferentially held out for his inspection.

"Well, I can't judge if I don't see it on, can I?" he said, yielding superciliously to their mood. Women were incurable. Namur had fallen, but the room was full of finery, and the finery claimed attention. And if Paris had fallen, it would have been the same. So he told himself. Nevertheless the spectacle of the heaped finery and its absorbed priestess was very agreeable. Lois rose. Laurencine and the priestess helped her to remove the white gown she wore, and to put on the blue one. The presence of the male somewhat disturbed the priestess, but the male had signified a wish and the wish was flattering and had to be fulfilled. George, cynically, enjoyed her constraint. He might at least have looked out of the window, but he would not.

"Yes, that's fine," he decided carelessly, when the operation was done. He did not care a pin which tea-gown Lois had.

"I knew you'd like it better," said Lois eagerly. The other two, in words or by demeanour, applauded his august choice.

The affair was over. The priestess began to collect her scattered stock into a light trunk. Behind her back, Lois took hold of Laurencine and kissed her fondly. Laurencine smiled, and persuaded Lois into a chair.

"You will of course keep that on, madam?" the priestess suggested.

"Oh yes, darling, you must rest, really!" said Laurencine earnestly.

"Thank you, madam."

In three minutes the priestess, bearing easily the trunk by a strap, had gone, bowing. Lois's old tea-gown, flung across the head of the sofa, alone remained to brighten the furniture.

The drawing-room door opened again immediately, and a military officer entered. Laurencine sprang up with a little girlish scream and ran to him.

"Oh! Dearest! Have you got them already? You never told me you would have! How lovely you look!"

Blushing with pleasure and pride, she kissed him. It was Everard Lucas. Laurencine had come to Elm Park Road that afternoon with the first news that Everard, through a major known to his late mother, had been offered a commission in a Territorial line regiment. George, who saw Lucas but seldom, had not the slightest idea of this enormous family event, and he was astounded; he had not been so taken back by anything perhaps for years. Lucas was rounder and his face somewhat coarser than in the past; but the uniform had created a new Lucas. It was beautifully made and he wore it well; it suited him; he had the fine military air of a regular; he showed no awkwardness, only a simple vanity.

"Don't you feel as if you must kiss him, Lois darling?" said Laurencine.

"Oh! I certainly must!" Lois cried, forgetting her woes in the new tea-gown and in the sudden ecstasy produced by the advent of an officer into the family.

Lucas bent down and kissed his sister-in-law, while Laurencine beheld the act with delight.

"The children must see you before you go," said Lois.

"Madam, they shall see their uncle," Lucas answered. At any rate his agreeable voice had not coarsened. He turned to George: "What d'you think of it, George?"

"My boy, I'm proud of you," said George. In his tennis-flannels he felt like one who has arrived at an evening party in morning-dress. And indeed he was proud of Lucas. Something profound and ingenuous in him rose into his eyes and caused them to shine.

Lucas related his adventures with the tailor and other purveyors, and explained that he had to 'join his regiment' the next day, but would be able to remain in London for the present. George questioned him about his business affairs.

"No difficulty about that whatever!" said Lucas lightly. "The old firm will carry on as usual; Enwright and Orgreave will have to manage it between them; and of course they wouldn't dream of trying to cut off the spondulicks. Not that I should let that stop me if they did."

"Yes, it's all very well for you to talk like that!" said Lois, with a swift change of tone. "You've got partners to do your work for you, and you've got money.... Have you written to mother, Laurencine?"

George objected to his wife making excuses. His gaze faltered.

"Of course, darling!" Laurencine answered eagerly, agreeing with her sister's differentiation between George and Everard. "No, not yet. But I'm going to tonight. Everard, we ought to be off."

"I've got a taxi outside," said Lucas.

"A taxi?" she repeated in a disappointed tone. And then, as an afterthought: "Well, I have to call at Debenham's."

The fact was that Laurencine wanted to be seen walking with her military officer in some well-frequented thoroughfare. They lived at Hampstead.

Lois rang the bell.

"Ask nurse to bring the children down, please - at once," she told the parlourmaid.

"So this is the new tea-gown, if I mistake not!" observed Lucas in the pause. "Tres chic! I suppose Laurencine's told you all about the chauffeur being run off with against his will by a passionate virgin. I couldn't start the car this morning myself."

"You never could start a car by yourself, my boy," said George. "What's this about the passionate virgin?"

5

George woke up in the middle of the night. Lois slept calmly; he could just hear her soft breathing. He thought of all the occupied bedrooms, of the health of children, the incalculable quality in wives, the touchy stupidity of nurses and servants. The mere human weight of the household oppressed him terribly. And he thought of the adamant of landlords, the shifty rapacity of tradesmen, the incompetence of clerks, the mere pompous foolishness of Government departments, the arrogance of Jew patrons, and the terrifying complexity of problems of architecture on a large scale. He was the Atlas supporting a vast world a thousand times more complex than any problem of architecture. He wondered how he did it. But he did do it, alone; and he kept on doing it. Let him shirk the burden, and not a world but an entire universe would crumble. If he told Lois that he was going to leave her, she would collapse; she would do dreadful things. He was indispensable not only at home but professionally. All was upon his shoulders and upon nobody else's. He was bound, he was a prisoner, he had no choice, he was performing his highest duty, he was fulfilling the widest usefulness of which he was capable ... Besides, supposing he did go insane and shirk the burden, they would all say that he had been influenced by Lucas's uniform - the mere sight of the uniform! - like a girl! He could not stand that, because it would be true. Not that he would ever admit its truth! He recalled Lucas's tact in refraining from any suggestion, even a jocular suggestion, that he, George, ought also to be in uniform. Lucas was always tactful. Be damned to his tact! And the too eager excuses made by Lois in his behalf also grated on his susceptibility. He had no need of excuses. The woman was taciturn by nature, and yet she was constantly saying too much! And did any of the three of them - Lois, Laurencine, and Lucas - really appreciate the war? They did not. They could not envisage it. Lucas was wearing uniform solely in obedience to an instinct.

At this point the cycle of his reflections was completed, and began again. He thought of all the occupied bedrooms.... Thus, in the dark, warm night the contents of his mind revolved endlessly, with extreme tedium and extreme distress, and each moment his mood became more morbid.

An occasional sound of traffic penetrated into the room, - strangely mournful, a reminder of the immense and ineffable melancholy of a city which could not wholly lose itself in sleep. The window lightened. He could descry his wife's portable clock on the night-table. A quarter to four. Turning over savagely in bed, he muttered: "My night's done for. And nearly five hours to breakfast. Good God!" The cycle resumed, and was enlarged.

At intervals he imagined that he dozed; he did doze, if it is possible while you are dozing to know that you doze. His personality separated into two personalities, if not more. He was on a vast plain, and yet he was not there, and the essential point of the scene was that he was not there. Thousands and tens of thousands of men stood on this plain, which had no visible boundaries. A roll-call was proceeding. A resounding and mysterious voice called out names, and at each name a man stepped briskly from the crowds and saluted and walked away. But there was no visible person to receive the salute; the voice was bodiless. George became increasingly apprehensive; he feared a disaster, yet he could not believe that it would occur. It did occur. Before it arrived he knew that it was arriving. The voice cried solemnly:

"George Edwin Cannon."

An awful stillness and silence followed, enveloping the entire infinite plain. George trembled. He was there, but he was not there. Men looked at each other, raising their eyebrows. The voice did not deign to repeat the call. After a suitable pause, the voice cried solemnly:

"Everard Lucas."

And Lucas in his new uniform stepped gravely forward and saluted and walked away.

"Was I asleep or awake?" George asked himself. He could not decide. At any rate the scene impressed him. The bigness of the plain, the summons, the silence, the utter absence of an expression of reproof or regret - of any comment whatever.

At five o'clock he arose, and sat down in his dressing-gown at Lois's very untidy and very small writing-desk, and wrote a letter on her notepaper. The early morning was lovely; it was celestial.

"Dear Davids," the letter began. - That would annoy the fellow, who liked the address respectful. - "Dear Davids, I have decided to join the Army, and therefore cannot proceed further with your commission. However, the general idea is complete. I advise you to get it carried out by Lucas & Enwright. Enwright is the best architect in England. You may take this from me. I'm his disciple. You might ring me up at the office this afternoon. - Yours faithfully, George Cannon"

"P.S. - Assuming you go to Lucas & Enwright, I can either make some arrangement with them as to sharing fees myself, or you can pay me an agreed sum for the work I've done, and start afresh elsewhere. I shall want all the money I can get hold of."

Yes, Sir Isaac would be very angry. George smiled. He was not triumphant, but he was calm. In the full sanity of the morning, every reason against his going into the Army had vanished. The material objection was ridiculous - with Edwin Clayhanger at the back of him! Moreover, some money would be coming in. The professional objection was equally ridiculous. The design for the Indian barracks existed complete; and middle-aged mediocrity could carry it out in a fashion, and Lucas & Enwright could carry it out better than he could carry it out himself. As for Davids, he had written. There was nothing else of importance in his office. The other competition had not been won. If people said that he had been influenced by Lucas's uniform, well, they must say it. They would not say it for more than a few days. After a few days the one interesting fact would be that he had joined. By such simple and curt arguments did he annihilate the once overwhelming reasons against his joining the Army.

But he did not trouble to marshal the reasons in favour of his joining the Army. He had only one reason: he must! He quite ignored the larger aspects of the war - the future of civilization, freedom versus slavery, right versus wrong, even the responsibilities of citizenship and the implications of patriotism. His decision was the product, not of argument, but of feeling. However, he did not feel a bit virtuous. He had to join the Army, and 'that was all there was to it.' A beastly nuisance, this world-war! It was interfering with his private affairs; it might put an end to his private affairs altogether; he hated soldiering; he looked inimically at the military caste. An unspeakable nuisance. But there the war was, and he was going to answer to his name. He simply could not tolerate the dreadful silence and stillness on the plain after his name had been called. "Pooh! Sheer sentimentality!" he said to himself, thinking of the vision - half-dream, half-fancy. "Rotten sentimentality!"

He asked:

"Damn it! Am I an Englishman or am I not?"

Like most Englishmen, he was much more an Englishman than he ever suspected.

"What on earth are you doing, George?"

At the voice of his wife he gave a nervous jump, and then instantly controlled himself and looked round. Her voice was soft, liquid, weak with slumber. But, lying calmly on one side, her head half buried in the pillow, and the bedclothes pushed back from her shoulders, she was wideawake and gazed at him steadily.

"I'm just writing a letter," he answered gruffly.

"Now? What letter?"

"Here! You shall read it." He walked straight across the room in his gay pyjamas only partly hidden by the splendid dressing-gown, and handed her the letter. Moving nothing but her hand, she took the letter and held it in front of her eyes. He sat down between the beds, on the edge of his own bed, facing her.

"Whatever is it?"

"Read it. You've got it," he said, with impatience. He was trembling, aware that the crisis had suddenly leapt at him.

"Oh!"

She had read the opening phrase; she had received the first shock. But the tone of her exclamation gave no clue at all to her attitude. It might mean anything - anything. She shut her eyes; then glanced at him, terror-struck, appealing, wistful, implacable.

"Not at once?"

"Yes, at once."

"But surely you'll at least wait until after October."

He shook his head.

"But why can't you?"

"I can't."

"But there's no object - "

"I've got to do it."

"You're horribly cruel."

"Well, that's me!" He was sullen, and as hard as a diamond.

"George, I shall never be able to stand it. It's too much to expect. It'll kill me."

"Not it! What's the use of talking like that? If I'd been in the Territorials before the war, like lots of chaps, I should have been gone long ago, and you'd have stood it all right. Don't you understand we're at war? Do you imagine the war can wait for things like babies?"

She cried:

"It's no good your going on in that strain. You can't leave me alone with all this house on my shoulders, and so that's flat."

"Who wants to leave you all alone in the house? You can go and stay at Ladderedge, children and nurse and all." This scheme presented itself to him as he spoke.

"Of course I can't! We can't go and plant ourselves on people like that. Besides - "

"Can't you? You'll see!"

He caught her eye. Why was he being so brutal to her? What conceivable purpose was served by this harshness? He perceived that his nerves were overstrung. And in a swift rush of insight he saw the whole situation from her point of view. She was exhausted by gestation; she lived in a world distorted. Could she help her temperament? She was in the gravest need of his support; and he was an ass, a blundering fool. His severity melted within him, and secretly he became tender as only a man can be.

"You silly girl!" he said, slightly modifying his voice, taking care not to disclose all at once the change in his mood.

"You silly girl! Can't you see they'll be so proud to have you they won't be able to contain themselves? They'll turn the whole place upside-down for you. I know them. They'll pretend it's nothing, but mother won't sleep at night for thinking how to arrange things for the best, and as for my cuckoo of an uncle, if you notice something funny about your feet, it'll be the esteemed alderman licking your boots. You'll have the time of your life. In fact they'll ruin your character for you. There'll be no holding you afterwards."

She did not smile, but her eyes smiled. He had got the better of her. He had been cleverer than she was. She was beaten.

"But we shall have no money."

"Read the letter, child. I'm not a fool."

"I know you're not a fool. No one knows that better than me."

He went on:

"And what's uncle's money for, if it comes to that?"

"But we can't spunge on them like that!"

"Spunge be dashed! What's money for? It's no good till it's spent. If he can't spend it on us, who can he spend it on? He always makes out he's fiendishly hard, but he's the most generous idiot ever born."

"Yes, you're awfully like him."

"I'm not."

He was suddenly alive to the marvellous charm of the intimacy of the scene with his wife, in the early summer dawn, in the silent, enchanted house of sleepers, in the disorder of the heaped bedroom. They were alone together, shameless in front of one another, and nobody knew or saw, or could ever know or see. Their relations were unique, the resultant of long custom, of friction, of misunderstanding, of affection, of incomprehensible instincts, of destiny itself. He thought: "I have lived for this sensation, and it is worth living for."

Without the slightest movement, she invited him with her strange eyes, and as she did so she was as mysterious as ever she had been. He bent down responsively. She put her hot, clammy hands on his shoulders, and kept his head at a little distance and looked through his eyes into his soul. The letter had dropped to the floor.

"I knew you would!" she murmured, and then snatched him to her, and kissed him, and kept her mouth on his.

"You didn't," he said, as soon as she loosed him. "I didn't know myself."

But he privately admitted that perhaps she did know. She had every fault, but she was intelligent. Constantly he was faced with that fact. She did not understand the significance of the war; she lacked imagination; but her understanding was sometimes terrible. She was devious; but she had a religion. He was her religion. She would cast the god underfoot - and then in a passion of repentance restore it ardently to the sacred niche.

She said:

"I couldn't have borne it if Everard had gone and you hadn't. But of course you meant to go all the time."

That was how she saved his amour-propre.

"I always knew you were a genius - "

"Oh! Chuck it, kid!"

"But you're more, somehow. This business - "

"You don't mean joining the Army?"

"Yes."

"What rot! There's nothing in it. Fellows are doing it everywhere."

She smiled superiorly, and then inquired:

"How do you join? What are you going to do? Shall you ask Everard?"

"Well - " he hesitated. He had no desire to consult Lucas.

"Why don't you see Colonel Rannion?" she Suggested.

"Jove! That's a scheme. Never thought of him!"

Her satisfaction at the answer was childlike, and he was filled with delight that it should be so. They launched themselves into an interminable discussion about every possible arrangement of everything. But in a pause of it he destroyed its tremendous importance by remarking casually:

"No hurry, of course. I bet you I shall be kept knocking about here for months."

3

IN THE MACHINE

Colonel Rannion was brother of the wife of the man for whom George had built the house at Hampstead. George had met him several times at the dinners and other reunions to which a sympathetic architect is often invited in the dwelling that he has created. Colonel Rannion had greatly liked his sister's house, had accordingly shown much esteem for George, and had even spoken of ordering a house for himself.

Just as breakfast was being served, George had the idea of ringing up the Hampstead people for the Colonel's address, which he obtained at once. The Colonel was staying at the Berkeley Hotel. The next moment he got the Berkeley, and the Colonel in person. The Colonel remembered him instantly. George said he wanted to see him. What about? Well, a commission. The Colonel said he had to leave the hotel in twenty-five minutes. "I can be with you in less than a quarter of an hour," said George - or rather, not George, but some subconscious instinct within him, acting independently of him. The children, with nurse, were in the dining-room, waiting to breakfast with father. They were washed, they were dressed; the dining-room had been cleaned; the pleasant smell of breakfast-cooking wandered through the rooms; since the early talk between George and Lois in the silent, sleeping house the house had gradually come to life; it was now in full being - even to the girl scrubbing the front steps - except that Lois was asleep. Exhausted after the strange and crucial scene, she had dozed off, and had never moved throughout George's dressing.

Now he rushed into the dining-room - "I have to go, nurse. Fardy can't have his breakfast with you!" - and rushed out. A minute previously he had felt a serious need of food after the long, sleepless morning. The need vanished. He scurried up Elm Park Gardens like a boy in the warm, fresh air, and stopped a taxi. He was extremely excited. None but Lois knew the great secret. He had kept it to himself. He might have burst into the kitchen - for he was very apt to be informal - and said: "Well, cook, I'm going into the Army!" What a household sensation the news would cause, and what an office sensation! His action would affect the lives of all manner of people. And the house, at present alive and organic, would soon be dead. He was afraid. What he was doing was tremendous. Was it madness? He had a feeling of unreality.

At the entrance to the Berkeley Hotel lay a large automobile, with a spurred and highly polished military chauffeur. At the door of Colonel Rannion's room was stationed a spurred and highly polished, erect orderly - formidable contrast to the flaccid waiters who slouched palely in the corridors. The orderly went into the room and saluted with a click. George followed, as into a dentist's surgery. It was a small, elegant, private sitting-room resembling a boudoir. In the midst of delicately tinted cushions and flower-vases stood Colonel Rannion, grey-haired, blue-eyed, very straight, very tall, very slim - the slimness accentuated by a close-fitted uniform which began with red tabs and ended in light leggings and gleaming spurs. He conformed absolutely to the traditional physical type of soldier, and the sight of him gave pleasure.

"Good morning. Cannon. Glad to see you." He seemed to put a secret meaning into the last words.

He shook hands as he spoke, firmly, decisively, efficiently.

"I hope I'm not troubling you too much," George began.

"Troubling me! Sit down. You want a commission. The Army wants to give commissions to men like you. I think you would make a good officer."

"Of course I'm absolutely ignorant of the Army. Absolutely."

"Yes. What a pity that is! If you'd only been a pre-war Territorial you might have done three weeks' urgent work for your country by this time." The remark was a polite reproof.

"I might," admitted George, to whom the notion of working for his country had never before occurred.

"Do you think you'd like the Artillery?" Colonel Rannion questioned sharply. His tone was increasing in sharpness.

With an equal sharpness George answered unhesitatingly: "Yes, I should."

"Can you ride?"

"I can ride. In holidays and so on I get on my mother's horses."

"Have you hunted?"

"Never."

"H'm!... Well, I know my friend Colonel Hullocher, who commands the Second Brigade of - er - my Division, is short of an officer. Would you care for that?"

"Certainly."

Without saying anything else Colonel Rannion took up the telephone. In less than half a minute George heard him saying: "Colonel Hullocher.... Ask him to be good enough to come to the telephone at once.... That you, Hullocher?"

George actually trembled. He no longer felt that heavy weight on his stomach, but he felt 'all gone.' He saw himself lying wounded near a huge gun on a battlefield.

Colonel Rannion was continuing into the telephone:

"I can recommend a friend of mine to you for a commission. George Cannon - C-a-n-n-o-n - the architect. I don't know whether you know of him.... Oh! About thirty.... No, but I think he'd suit you.... Who recommends him? I do.... Like to see him, I suppose, first?... No, no necessity to see him. I'll tell him.... Yes, I shall see you in the course of the day." The conversation then apparently deviated to other subjects, and drew to a close.... "Good-bye. Thanks.... Oh! I say. Shall he get his kit?... Cannon.... Yes, he'd better. Yes, that's understood of course. Good-bye."

"That will be quite all right," said Colonel Rannion to George. "Colonel Hullocher thinks you may as well see to your kit at once, provided of course you pass the doctor and you are ready to work for nothing until your commission comes along."

"Oh! Naturally!" George agreed, in a dream. He was saying to himself, frightened, astounded, staggered, and yet uplifted: "Get my kit! Get my kit! But it's scarcely a minute since I decided to go into the Army."

"I may get your commission ante-dated. I haven't all the papers here, but give me an address where I can find you at once, and you shall have them this afternoon. I'll get the Colonel to send them to the Territorial Association to-morrow, and probably in about a month you'll be in the Gazette. I don't know when Colonel Hullocher will want you to report for duty, but I shall see him to-day. You'll get a telegram when you're needed. Now I must go. Which way are you going?"

"I'm going home for my breakfast," said George, writing down his two addresses.

Colonel Rannion said:

"I'm off to Wimbledon. I can drop you in Fulham Road if you like."

In the automobile George received a few useful hints, but owing to the speed of the vehicle the time was far too short for any extensive instruction. The car drew up. For an instant Colonel Rannion became freely cordial. "He must rather have cottoned to me, or he wouldn't have done what he has," thought George, proud to be seen in converse with a staff-officer, waving a hand in adieu. And he thought: "Perhaps next time I see him I shall be saluting him!"

The children and nurse were still at breakfast. Nothing had changed in the house during his absence. But the whole house was changed. It was a house unconvincing, incredible, which might vanish at any moment. He himself was incredible. What had happened was incredible. The screeching voices of the children were not real voices, and the children were apparitions. The newspaper was illegible. Its messages for the most part had no meaning, and such as bore a meaning seemed to be utterly unimportant. The first reality, for George was food. He discovered that he could not eat the food - could not swallow; the nausea was acute. He drank a little coffee, and then went upstairs to see his wife. Outside the bedroom door he stood hesitant. A desolating sadness of disappointment suddenly surged over him. He had destroyed his ambitions, he had transformed all his life, by a single unreflecting and irretrievable impulse. What he had done was terrific, and yet he had done it as though it were naught ... The mood passed as suddenly as it had come, and left him matter-of-fact, grim, as it were swimming strongly on and with the mighty current which had caught him. He went into the bedroom on the current. Lois was awake.

"I've seen Colonel Rannion."

"You haven't, George!"

"Yes, I have. I've just come back."

"Well?"

He replied with his damnable affected casualness: "I'm in the Army. Royal Field Artillery. And so that's that."

"But where's your uniform?"

"I knew you'd say that. I'm in mufti, you see."

2

He promptly received his papers and returned them. His medical examination was quite satisfactory. Then there was no further sign from the Army. The Army might have completely forgotten him; his enrolment in the Army might have been an illusion. Every day and every hour he expected a telegram of command. It was in anticipation of the telegram, curt and inexorable, that he kept harrying his tradesmen. To be caught unprepared by the telegram would be a disaster. But the tradesmen had lessons to teach him, and by the time the kit was approximately completed he had learnt the lessons. Whether the transaction concerned his tunic, breeches, spurs, leggings, cane, sword, socks, shirts, cap, camp field-kit, or any of the numerous other articles without which an officer might not respectably enter the British Army, the chief lesson was the same, namely, that the tradesmen were bearing the brunt of the war. Those who had enrolled and made spectacular sacrifices of homes and careers and limbs and lives were enjoying a glorious game amid the laudations of an ecstatic populace, but the real work was being done in the shops and in the workrooms. The mere aspect of tradesmen was enough to restore the lost modesty of officers. Useless to argue with the tradesmen, to expostulate, to vituperate. The facts were in their favour; the sublime law of supply and demand was in their favour. If the suddenly unloosed military ardour had not been kept down it might have submerged the Island. The tradesmen kept it down, and the Island was saved by them from militarization. Majors and colonels and even generals had to flatter and cajole tradesmen. As for lieutenants, they cringed. And all officers were obliged to be grateful for the opportunity to acquire goods at prices fifty per cent higher than would have been charged to civilians. Within a few days George, who had need of every obtainable sovereign for family purposes, had disbursed some forty pounds out of his own pocket in order to exercise the privilege of defending, at the risk of ruin and death, the ideals of his country.

At the end of the week what, as a civilian, he would have described as his first 'suit' had not been delivered, and he spent Saturday afternoon and Sunday in most uncomfortable apprehension of the telegraph-boy and in studying an artillery manual now known to hundreds of thousands as 'F.A.T.' On the Monday morning he collected such portions of his kit as had to be worn with the 'suit' (leggings, boots, spurs, cap, shirt, collar, etc.), and took them in a taxi to the tailor's, intending to change there and emerge a soldier. The clothes were not ready, but the tailor, intimidated by real violence, promised them for three o'clock. At three o'clock they were still not ready, for buttons had to be altered on the breeches; another hour was needed.

George went to call at Lucas & Enwright's. That office seemed to function as usual, for Everard Lucas alone had left it for the profession of arms. The factotum in the cubicle was a young man of the finest military age, and there were two other good ones in the clerks' room, including a clerk just transferred from George's own office. And George thought of his own office, already shut up, and his glance was sardonic. Mr. Enwright sat alone in the principals' room, John Orgreave being abroad in London in pursuit of George's two landlords - the landlord of his house and the landlord of his office - neither of whom had yet been brought to see that George's caprice for a military career entitled him in the slightest degree to slip out of contracts remunerative to the sacred caste of landlords. Lucas & Enwright had behaved handsomely to George, having taken everything over, assumed all responsibilities, and allotted to George more than a fair share of percentages. And John Orgreave, who in his rough provincial way was an admirable negotiator, had voluntarily busied himself with the affair of the resilition of George's leases.

"Not gone, then?" Mr. Enwright greeted him. "Well, you'd better be going, or I shan't get my chance of being Vice-President."

"What do you mean?"

"Orgreave was at a committee at the Institute this morning. It seems you might have been the next Vice, in spite of your tender years, if you'd stayed. You're becoming the rage, you know."

"Am I?" said George, startled.

He hungered for further details of this great and highly disturbing matter, but Enwright, jealous by nature and excusably jealous by reason of the fact that despite his immense artistic reputation he had never succeeded in being even Vice-President of the Institute, would say no more. Indeed he took a malicious pleasure in saying no more.

The ageing man, more hypochondriacal, thinner, and more wrinkled than ever, was full to the brim of one subject - India. Somebody at the India Office had flattered him by showing a knowledge of his work. The India Office had very graciously agreed to the transfer of the barracks enterprise to Lucas & Enwright, and now Mr. Enwright was for going to India himself. He had never been there. Indian scenery, Indian manners, Indian architecture boiled in his brain. The menace of German raiders would not prevent him from going to India. He had already revisited the photographs of Indian buildings at South Kensington Museum. Moreover, he had persuaded himself that the erection of the barracks formed an urgent and vital part of British war activity.

At the same time he was convinced that the war would soon end, and in favour of Germany. He assumed, as being beyond doubt, that a German army would occupy Paris, and when George, with a wave of the hand, pushed the enemy back and magically rendered Paris impregnable, he nearly lost his temper. This embittered Englishman would not hear a word against the miraculous efficiency of the Germans, whom he admired as much as he hated them. The German military reputation could not have been safer in Potsdam than it was in Russell Square. George, impatient of his master and inspirer, rose to depart, whereupon Mr. Enwright began to talk at large about the terrible derangement of his daily life caused by the sudden disappearance of his favourite barber, deemed now to have been a spy. "But the only barber who ever really understood my chin," said Mr. Enwright. George went, shaking hands perfunctorily. Mr. Enwright was too preoccupied to wish him luck.

The clothes were ready at the tailor's, and they passed the tests. George stood up disguised as a second-lieutenant in the R.F.A., booted, spurred, gloved, nicely managing a cane. He examined himself in the great mirror and was well pleased with his military appearance. In particular, his dark moustache fitted the role excellently.

"Now you'll send the overcoat and all my civilian things down this afternoon, without fail," he said. "I'll let you have an address for the other suit."

And he walked manfully out of the shop. Before he could find himself, a superb serjeant-major strode up, saluted in the highest and strictest perfection, and passed. The encounter was unfortunate. George, taken aback, muddled his share of the rite. Further, the self-consciousness of the potential Vice-President of the Royal Institute of British Architects was so extreme in uniform that it could scarcely have been more extreme had he been thrust by destiny into Oxford Street naked. He returned to the shop and said:

"I think I'll take everything home myself, to make sure. You might get me a taxi."

He crept into his own house furtively with his parcels, like a criminal, though he well knew that the servants would be ready to worship him as a new god. The children were evidently out. Lois was not in the drawing-room. He ran to the bedroom. She lay on the sofa.

"Here I am!" he announced, posing bravely for her inspection.

She did not move for a few seconds. Her eyes were hard-set. Then she gave a tremendous shattering sob, and burst into wild tears. George stooped to pick up a telegram which was lying on the floor. It read:

"You are to report to Adjutant Headquarters Second First West Midland R.F.A. Wimbledon tomorrow Tuesday before noon."

The Army had not forgotten him. Throughout the week his name upon various forms had been under the eye of authority, and at last the order had gone forth.

3

The next morning, after a disturbed night, Lois was taken ill. George telephoned for the doctor, and as soon as he had seen the patient the doctor telephoned for the nurse, and as soon as the doctor had telephoned for the nurse George telephoned for Laurencine. What with George's uniform and approaching departure, and the premature seizure of Lois, the household had, in an exceedingly short time, reached a state of intense excitement and inefficiency. Nurse was with Lois; the children were with cook in the kitchen; the other two servants were noisily and vaguely active on the stairs and the landings. The breakfast had been very badly cooked; the newspapers, with a detailed description of the retreat from Mons, were not glanced at. George was expecting a letter from his mother concerning the arrangements for the visit of Lois and the children to Ladderedge, already decided upon, and no letter had come.

At half-past ten he sent the parlourmaid to get a taxi. Having inspected his luggage in the hall, he went to the telephone again and ascertained that Laurencine had actually started from home. Almost at the same moment a taxi stopped in front of the house. "She's been jolly quick," thought George, meaning the parlourmaid; but going to the window he saw that his stepfather and his mother were in the taxi. He did not rush out to them. He did not move. The comfortable sense of the perfect reliability and benevolence of his 'people' filled and warmed him. They had not written again; they had just come themselves.

He affectionately and critically watched them as they got out of the taxi. Alderman Edwin Clayhanger, undeniably stout, with grey hair and beard, was passing from middle-age into the shadow of the sixties. He dressed well, but the flat crown of his felt hat, and the artificial, exaggerated squareness of the broad shoulders, gave him a provincial appearance. His gesture as he paid the driver was absolutely characteristic - a mixture of the dignified and the boyish, the impressive and the timid. He had descended from the vehicle with precautions, but Mrs. Clayhanger jumped down lightly, though she was about as old and as grey as her husband. Her costume was not successful; she did not understand and never had understood how to dress herself. But she had kept her figure; she was as slim as a girl, and as restless.

George ran to the door, which the feverish parlourmaid had neglected to shut. His mother, mounting the steps, was struck full in the face by the apparition of her son in uniform. The Alderman, behind her, cried mockingly to cover his emotion: "Hallo! Hallo!"

"When did you come up?" asked George quietly, taking his mother's hand and kissing her. She slid past him into the house. Her eyes were moist.

"Last night," the Alderman answered. "Last train. Your mother's idea. All of a sudden. Thought you might be leaving."

"Well, I am," said George. "I have to report at Headquarters at Wimbledon by twelve o'clock. It's rather a good thing you've come. Lois is ill. Oh! Here's my taxi." The parlourmaid had driven up.

"Ill!" exclaimed Mrs. Clayhanger.

"Yes. I've sent for the doctor, and he's sent for the nurse. I'm expecting the nurse every minute."

"You don't mean to say - " Mrs. Clayhanger began.

George nodded.

"She must have had a shock. I knew what it would be for her. It's all very well, but - " Mrs. Clayhanger again left a sentence unfinished.

"I've sent for Laurencine too," said George. "She also may be here any minute."

"Oh!" said the old lady tartly. "I can stay as long as you like, you know. Lois and I get on splendidly."

It was true. They had had one enormous quarrel, which had mysteriously ended by both of them denying superiorly to all males that any quarrel had ever occurred.

"Well, come into the dining-room."

"I think I'll go up and see Lois at once," said Mrs. Clayhanger.

"The doctor's there."

"What if he is?"

The Alderman put in:

"Now look here, missis. Don't startle her."

Mrs. Clayhanger exhaled impatient scorn and went upstairs.

"This your stuff?" the Alderman questioned, pointing with his stick to the kit-bag and strange packages on the hall floor.

"Yes," said George, and to the parlourmaid: "You can put it all in the taxi, May. Come along in, uncle."

"Don't hurry me, boy. Don't hurry me."

"Where are you staying?"

"Russell ... Bit awkward, this about Lois!"

They were now within the dining-room.

"Yes." In the presence and under the influence of his people George at once ceased to be an expansive Londoner, and reverted to the character of the Five Towns.

"I suppose she'll be all right?"

"Doctor seems to think so."

"Yes. They generally are." The Alderman sighed pleasantly and dropped rather heavily into a chair.

"Have a cigarette?"

"No!" The Alderman refused regretfully. "I've got a new rule now. I don't smoke till after dinner."

There was a pause.

"I'm glad we came."

"So'm I."

"You needn't worry about anything. Your mother and I will see to everything. I'll go up and have a talk with Johnnie about the leases."

"Thanks."

"What about money?"

"I'll write you. No hurry."

"What sort of a woman is Laurencine? I've scarcely set eyes on her."

"She's fine."

"She is?"

"Yes."

"Will she hit it off with your mother?"

"Trust her."

"Well, then, I think I'll have one o' them cigarettes."

They smoked in taciturnity, nervous but relieved. They had said what they had to say to each other. After a time George remarked:

"I heard last night there was a chance of me being Vice-President of the Institute this year if I hadn't gone into the Army."

Mr. Clayhanger raised his eyebrows.

"That'll keep all right for later."

"Yes."

Mrs. Clayhanger hurried into the dining-room. She had removed her hat and gloves.

"Lois wants to see you."

"I was just coming up. I've got to go now." He glanced at his watch.

"Go where?" It was like Mrs. Clayhanger to ask a question to which she knew the answer. Her ardent eyes, set a little too close together in the thin, lined, nervous face, burned upon him challengingly.

"I told you! I have to report at Headquarters before noon."

"But you don't mean to say you're going to leave your wife like this! She's very ill."

"I'm bound to leave her."

"But you can't leave her."

The Alderman said:

"The boy's quite right. If he's got to report he's got to report."

"And supposing she was dying?"

"Now, missis, we needn't suppose that. She isn't."

"It would be just the same if she was," Mrs. Clayhanger retorted bitterly. "I don't know what men are coming to. But I know this - all husbands are selfish. They probably don't know it, but they are."

She wept angrily.

"Don't you understand I'm in the machine now, mater?" said George resentfully as he left the room.

In the bedroom Lois lay on her back, pale, perspiring, moaning. He kissed her, glanced at the doctor for instructions, and departed. Lois was not in a condition to talk, and the doctor wished her not to speak. Then George went to the kitchen and took leave of the children, and incidentally of the servants. The nurse was arriving as he re-entered the dining-room; he had seized his cap in the hall and put it on.

"Better give me an address," said the Alderman.

"You might wire during the day," George said, scribbling on a loose leaf from his pocket-book, which he had to search for in unfamiliar pockets.

"The idea had occurred to me," the Alderman smiled.

"Au revoir, mater."

"But you've got plenty of time!" she protested.

"I know," said he. "I'm not going to be late. I haven't the slightest notion where Headquarters are, and supposing the taxi had a break-down!"

He divined from the way in which she kissed him good-bye that she was excessively proud of him.

"Mater," he said, "I see you're still a girl."

As he was leaving, Mr. Clayhanger halted him.

"You said something in your last letter about storing the furniture, didn't you? Have ye made any inquiries?"

"No. But I've told Orgreave. You might look into that, because - well, you'll see."

From the hall he glanced into the dining-room and up the stairs. The furniture that filled the house had been new ten years earlier; it had been anybody's furniture. The passage of ten years, marvellously swift, had given character to the furniture, charged it with associations, scarred it with the history of a family - his family, individualized it, humanized it. It was no longer anybody's furniture. With a pang he pictured it numbered and crowded into a warehouse, forlorn, thick with dust, tragic, exiled from men and women.

He drove off, waving. His stepfather waved from the door, his mother waved from the dining-room; the cook had taken the children into the drawing-room, where they shook their short, chubby arms at him, smiling. On the second floor the back of the large rectangular mirror on the dressing-table presented a flat and wooden negative to his anxious curiosity.

In the neighbourhood of Wimbledon the taxi-driver ascertained his destination at the first inquiry from a strolling soldier. It was the Blue Lion public-house. The taxi skirted the Common, parts of which were covered with horse-lines and tents. Farther on, in vague suburban streets, the taxi stopped at a corner building with a blatant, curved gilt sign and a very big lamp. A sentry did something with his rifle as George got out, and another soldier obligingly took the luggage. A clumsy painted board stuck on a pole at the entrance to a side-passage indicated that George had indeed arrived at his Headquarters. He was directed to a small, frowzy apartment, which apparently had once been the land-lord's sitting-room. Two officers, Colonel Hullocher and his Adjutant, both with ribbons, were seated close together at a littered deal table, behind a telephone whose cord, instead of descending modestly to the floor, went up in sight of all men to the ceiling. In a corner a soldier, the Colonel's confidential clerk, was writing at another table. Everything was dirty and untidy. Neither of the officers looked at George. The Adjutant was excitedly reading to the Colonel and the Colonel was excitedly listening and muttering. The clerk too was in a state of excitement. George advanced towards the table, and saluted and stood at attention. The Adjutant continued to read and the Colonel to murmur, but the Adjutant did manage to give a momentary surreptitious glance at George. After some time the Colonel, who was a short, stout, bald, restless man, interrupted the reading, and, still without having looked at George, growled impatiently to the Adjutant:

"Who's this fellow?"

The Adjutant replied smoothly:

"Mr. Cannon, sir."

The Colonel said:

"He's got a devilish odd way of saluting. I must go now." And jumped up and went cyclonically as far as the door. At the door he paused and looked George full in the face, glaring.

"You came to me with a special recommendation?" he demanded loudly.

"Colonel Rannion kindly recommended me, sir."

"General Rannion, sir. Haven't you seen this morning's Times? You should read your Gazette."

"Yes, sir."

"You're the celebrated architect?"

"I'm an architect, sir."

"I wish you would condescend to answer, yes or no, sir. That's the second time. I say - you're the celebrated architect?"

"Yes, sir."

"Well, remember this. When you come into the Army what you were before you came into the Army has not the slightest importance."

"Yes, sir."

Colonel Hullocher glared in silence for a moment, and was gone. The clerk slipped out after him.

The Adjutant rose: "Now, Cannon, we're all very busy." And shook hands.

4

The same afternoon, indeed within about two hours of his entrance into the Army, George found himself driving back from Wimbledon to London in a motor-bus.

Colonel Hullocher had vanished out of his world, and he had been sent to another and still more frowzy public-house which was the Headquarters of No. 2 Battery of the Second Brigade. He was allotted to No. 2 Battery, subject to the approval of Major Craim, the commanding officer. Major Craim was young and fair and benevolent, and at once approvingly welcomed George, who thereupon became the junior subaltern of the Battery. The other half-dozen officers, to whom he was introduced one by one as they came in, seemed amiable and very well-mannered, if unduly excited. When, immediately before lunch, the Major was called away to lunch with Colonel Hullocher, the excitement of the mess seemed to boil over. The enormous fact was that the whole Division - yeomanry, infantry, and artillery - had been ordered to trek southward the next morning. The Division was not ready to trek; in particular the Second Brigade of its artillery, and quite specially Battery No. 2 of the Second Brigade, was not ready to trek. Nevertheless it would trek. It might even trek to France. Southward was Franceward, and there were those who joyously believed that this First Line Territorial Division was destined to lead the Territorial Army in France.

All the officers had a schoolboyish demeanour; all of them called one another by diminutives ending in 'y'; all of them were pretty young. But George soon divided them into two distinct groups - those who worried about the smooth working of the great trek, and those who did not. Among the former was Captain Resmith, the second in command, a dark man with a positive, strong voice, somewhat similar to George in appearance. Captain Resmith took George very seriously, and promised to initiate him personally into as many technical mysteries as could be compressed into one afternoon. Then a Major Tumulty, middle-aged and pale, came hurriedly into the stuffy room and said without any prologue:

"Now I must have one of you chaps this afternoon. Otherwise I promise you you won't get all the things you want."

Silence fell on the mess.

"The C.O. isn't here, sir," said Captain Resmith.

"I can't help that. I'm not going alone."

"Cannon, you'd better go with Major Tumulty. Major, this is Mr. Cannon, our latest addition."

George only knew about Major Tumulty that he was Major Tumulty and that he did not belong to No. 2 Battery. So far as George was concerned he was a major in the air. After drinking a glass of port with the mess, Major Tumulty suddenly remembered that he was in a hurry, and took George off and put him into a scarlet London-General motor-bus that was throbbing at the door of the public-house, with an ordinary civilian driver at the steering-wheel and a soldier on the step. George felt like a parcel; he had no choice of movement, no responsibility, no knowledge. The mentality of a parcel was not disagreeable to him. But at times, vaguely uneasy, he would start out of it, and ask himself: "What is wrong?" And then the vision of a distant, half-forgotten street called Elm Park Road would rise in his mind and he would remember: "My wife is very ill, and everything is upset at home."

The motor-bus travelled a few yards and stopped; and out of yet another office a soldier carried, staggering, a heavy bag with a brass lock, and dropped it on the floor of the bus between the Major and George; and the bus, after a good imitation by the soldier-conductor of a professional double ting on the bell, went away afresh.

"That's money," said the Major, in his mild, veiled voice, pointing to the bag.

Little by little George learnt that the Major had 'won' the bus 'out of' the War Office, and had been using it daily for several days for the purpose of buying and collecting urgent stores and equipment. The bus had become celebrated within the Division in an astoundingly short time, and on this, the last day preceding the trek, the various units had burdened the good-natured Major with a multitude of commissions.

"I try to keep accounts," said the Major. "But I know I've made a loss every day. I've been in the T.F. ever since there was one, and it has always cost me money. Now, I shall put you in charge of this little book."

The little book was a penny account-book, with pages lettered in pencil A, B, C, D, etc., and items scribbled on each page.

"The letters show the batteries," the Major explained. "I've got a key to the batteries somewhere in my pocket. And here's what I call my grand list." He produced a roll of foolscap. "I like everything orderly. It saves so much trouble, doesn't it? I mean in the end. Now, as I buy things I shall strike them off here, and I want you to strike them off in your book and put down the price from the bill. I always insist on a receipted bill. It saves so much trouble in the end. I meant to bring a file or a clip for the bills, but I forgot. You understand, don't you?"

George answered solemnly and sharply:

"Yes, sir."

The Major weakly cried:

"Hall!"

"Yessir!" The soldier-conductor came to attention.

"Did you tell him to go to Harrods first?"

"Yessir!"

"I think we might go and sit on the top," said the Major. "It's a nice afternoon."

So the two officers went and sat on the top of the motor-bus. The Major gossiped with soothing tranquillity. He said that he was a pianoforte manufacturer; his father, from whom he had inherited, had traded under a German name because people preferred German pianos to English; he now regretted this piece of astuteness on the part of his father; he was trying to sell his business - he had had enough of it.

"Hi! You!" he called, standing up quite unexpectedly and leaning over the front of the bus to hail the driver. "Hi! You!" But the driver did not hear, and the bus drove forward like fate. The Major, who had hitherto seemed to be exempt from the general perturbation of Wimbledon troops, suddenly showed excitement. "We must stop this bus somehow! Why the devil doesn't he stop? I've forgotten the rope-shop."

"I'll stop it, sir," said George, maintaining an admirable presence of mind in the crisis, and he rose and pushed down the knob of the signal-rod at the back of the bus. The bus did actually stop.

"Ah!" murmured the Major, calmed.

The soldier raced upstairs.

"Hall!"

"Yessir."

"Do you know a rope and string shop near the Granville Theatre of Varieties at Walham Green?"

"No, sir."

"Well, there is one. Tell him to stop at the Granville."

"Yessir."

The Major resumed his bland conversation. At Putney they saw the first contents-bill of the afternoon papers.

"How do you think things are going, sir?" George asked.

"It's very difficult to say," answered the Major. "This Mons business is serious."

"Yes, sir."

The discovery of the rope-shop involved a policeman's aid. When the rope had been purchased and new silver brought forth from the bag, and the receipt made out, and the item struck off and the amount entered, and the bus had started again, George perceived that he would soon be passing the end of Elm Park Gardens. Dared he ask the Major to deflect the bus into Elm Park Road so that he might obtain news of Lois? He dared not. The scheme, simple and feasible enough, was nevertheless unthinkable. The bus, with 'Liverpool Street' inscribed on its forehead, rolled its straight inevitable course along Fulham Road, pursued by the disappointed glances of gesturing wayfarers who wanted it to take them to Liverpool Street.

After about two hours of fine confused shopping the Major stopped his bus at a Tube station in the north of London.

"I mustn't forget my pens," said he. "I have to spend three-quarters of my time mewed up in the office, and I don't grumble; but I'm very particular about nibs, and if I don't have my own I cannot work. It's useless to expect it."

Then to the soldier:

"Hall! You go down to Partridge & Cooper's, at the corner of Chancery Lane and Fleet Street, and buy a sixpenny box of their 'No. 6 Velvet' pen-nibs. You understand: 'No. 6 Velvet.'"

"Yessir. With the bus, sir?"

"With the bus. Here's sixpence." He took a coin out of the bag, locked it, and gave the key to George. "And keep an eye on this bag, my boy. You will then come back and wait for us - let me see - outside Piccadilly Tube Station in Jermyn Street."

"Yessir."

The Major and George entered the North London station and proceeded to the lift.

"Tickets!" demanded the lift-man.

The Major halted and gazed at him.

"On service!" said the Major, with resentment and disdain. "A fortnight ago you civilians were raising your hats to us. Now you ask us for tickets! Haven't you grasped yet that there's a war on? Don't you think you'd look better in khaki?" He showed excitement, as at every personal encounter.

The lift-man bowed his head, inarticulately muttering, and the officers passed into the lift, having created a certain amount of interest among the other passengers. The Major was tranquillized in a moment. They came to the surface again at Piccadilly Circus, where at the lift a similar scene occurred.

"Do you know anything about pyjamas?" said the Major.

"Well, sir - "

"I never wear them myself. I'm rather old-fashioned. But I have to buy three pairs - suits for Colonel Hullocher - at Swan & Edgar's. Oh! Bother it! Have you any money? I forgot to take some out of the bag."

The Major purchased the pyjamas with George's money, and his attitude towards the shopman during the transaction was defiant, indicating to the shopman that, though personally he, the Major, never wore pyjamas, he was an expert in pyjamas and not to be gulled. George took the resulting parcel and the receipted bill, and they walked across to Jermyn Street, where surely the bus, with the sixpenny box of pens, was waiting for them. It was perfectly magical. As the vehicle swung with them into the Circus the Major exclaimed:

"We're getting on very well. What do you say to some tea?"

"Certainly, sir."

The bus, having stopped by order at the second tea-house on the left in Piccadilly, was immediately assaulted, without success, by several would-be passengers. A policeman, outraged by the spectacle of a bus stationary at a spot where buses are absolutely forbidden to be stationary, hurried forward in fury. But the Major, instantly excited, was ready for him.

"This motor-bus is a military vehicle on service, and I'll thank you to mind your own business. If you've any complaints to make, you'd better make them to Lord Kitchener."

The policeman touched his hat.

"They have music here," said the Major mildly, entering the tea-house. "I always like music. Makes things so much jollier, doesn't it?"

During tea the Major inquired about George's individual circumstances, and George said that he was an architect.

"Student of bricks and mortar, eh?" said the Major benevolently. "How long have you been in the Army?"

"Rather less than half a day, sir."

The Major, raising his eyebrows, was very interested and kind. Perceiving that he had virgin material under his hands, he began to shape the material, and talked much about the niceties of the etiquette of saluting. George listened, yet at intervals his attention would wander, and he would be in Elm Park Road. But the illusion of home was very faint. His wife and family seemed to be slipping away from him. "How is it," he thought, "that I am not more upset about Lois than I am?" The various professional and family matters which in his haste he had left unsettled were diminishing hourly in their apparent importance. He came back to the tea-house with a start, hearing the Major praise his business capacity as displayed during the afternoon. The friendly aspect of the thin, pallid face inspired him with a sort of emotional audacity, and in ten words he suddenly informed the Major of his domestic situation.

"H'm!" said the Major. "I'm a bachelor myself."

There was a pause.

"I'll give you a tip," said the Major, resuming the interrupted topic. "War is a business. The more business capacity you have, the more likely you are to succeed. I'm a business man myself."

On leaving the tea-house they discovered the military vehicle surrounded by an enchanted multitude who were staring through its windows at the merchandise - blankets, pans, kettles, saddles, ropes, parcels, stoves, baskets, and box of nibs - within, while the policeman strove in vain to keep both the road and the pavement clear. George preceded the Major, pushing aside with haughty military impatience the civilians so reluctant to move. He felt as though he had been in the Army for years. No longer did his uniform cause him the slightest self-consciousness.

At Wimbledon in the dusk the bus was met by several military wagons each from a different unit, and each anxious to obtain goods. This piece of organization rather impressed George.

"Well, my boy," said the Major, "you'd better go and report yourself. You've been a great help to me."

George saluted according to the Major's own doctrine, and departed. At Battery Headquarters he met Captain Resmith.

"How did you get on with Auntie?" asked Resmith in his loud, firm voice.

George winked.

Resmith gave a scarcely perceptible smile.

"Look here," he said. "I'm just going round the horse-lines. If you'll come with me I'll show you a thing or two, and we can choose a mount for you. Then after dinner if you like I'll take you through the orders for tomorrow. By the way, there's a telegram for you."

The telegram read:

"Girl. Everything fairly satisfactory. Don't worry too much. Laurencine sleeps here. - NUNKS"

The telegram was entirely characteristic of his stepfather - curt, exact, realistic, kind.

He thought:

"Three girls, by Jove!"

5

The early sun, carrying into autumn the tradition of a magnificent summer, shone on the artillery camps. The four guns of the No. 2 Battery of the Second Brigade were ranged side by side in the vast vague space in front of the officers' hutments. Each gun had six horses in three pairs, and a rider for each pair. On the guns and the gun-teams everything glittered that could glitter - leather, metal, coats of horses, faces of men. Captain Resmith rode round, examining harness and equipment with a microscope that he called his eye. George rode round after him. Sometimes Captain Resmith spoke to a N.C.O., sometimes even to a man, but for the most part the men stared straight in front of them into eternity. Major Craim trotted up. Captain Resmith approached the Major and saluted, saying in his best military voice:

"The Battery is all correct and ready to move off, sir."

The Major in his drawing-room voice replied:

"Thank you, Captain Resmith."

Silence reigned in No. 2 Battery, except for the faint jingling restlessness of the horses.

Then Colonel Hullocher and his Adjutant pranced into sight. The Adjutant saluted the Major and made an inquiry. The Major saluted, and all three chatted a little.

George, who had accompanied Captain Resmith into the background, murmured to him, as cautiously as a convict talking at exercise:

"He's got his knife into me."

"Who?"

"The Colonel."

"Don't you know why?"

"No. I was specially recommended to him."

"Well, that's one reason, isn't it? But there was a difficulty between him and the Major as to when you should come. The old man got the better of him - always does. But he's a good officer."

"Who?"

"Hullocher. Shut up."

These two had reached familiarity with the swiftness characteristic of martial life.

During the brief colloquy Resmith had sat very upright on his horse, the chin slightly lifted, the head quite still, even the lips scarcely moving to articulate. Colonel Hullocher seemed now to be approaching. It was a false alarm. The Colonel and his Adjutant pranced off. After a long time, and at a considerable distance, could just be heard the voice of the Colonel ordering the Brigade to move. But No. 2 Battery did not stir for another long period. Suddenly, amid a devolution of orders, No. 2 Battery moved. The Major, attended by his trumpeter, and followed by the Battery staff of range-takers, director-men, telephonists, and the serjeant-major, inaugurated a sinuous procession into the uneven, rutted track leading to the side-road. Then the guns one by one wheeled to the right, the horses' hoofs stamping into the damp ground as they turned, and became part of the procession. Then the quartermaster and other N.C.O.'s and men joined; and last were Captain Resmith, attended by his trumpeter, and George. Resmith looked over his shoulder at the Third Battery which surged behind. There were nearly two hundred men and over a hundred and fifty horses and many vehicles in the Battery. The Major was far out of sight, and the tail of the column was equally out of sight in the rear, for the total length of Major Craim's cavalcade exceeded a mile; and of the Brigade three miles, and two other similar Brigades somewhere in the region of Wimbledon were participating in the grand Divisional trek.

Captain Resmith cantered ahead to a bend in the track, and anxiously watched a gun-team take the sharp curve, which was also a sharp slope. The impression of superb, dangerous physical power was tremendous. The distended nostrils of horses, the gliding of their muscles under the glossy skin, the muffled thud of their hoofs in the loose soil, the grimacing of the men as they used spur and thong, the fierce straining of straps and chains, the creaking, the grinding, and finally the swaying of the 90-millimetre gun, coddled and polished, as it swung helplessly forward, stern first, and its long nose describing an arc in the air behind - these things marvellously quickened the blood.

"Good men!" said Captain Resmith, enthusiastic. "It's great, isn't it? You know, there's nothing so fine as a battery - nothing in the whole world."

George heartily agreed with him.

"This is the best Battery in the Division," said Resmith religiously.

And George was religiously convinced that it was.

He was astoundingly happy. He thought, amazed, that he had never been so happy, or at any rate so uplifted, in all his life. He simply could not comprehend his state of bliss, which had begun that morning at 6.30 when the grey-headed, simple-minded servant allotted to him had wakened him, according to instructions, with a mug of tea. Perhaps it was the far, thin sound of bugles that produced the rapturous effect, or the fresh air blowing in through the broken pane of the hut, or the slanting sunlight, or the feeling that he had no responsibility and nothing to do but blindly obey orders.

He had gone to sleep as depressed as he was tired. A sense of futility had got the better of him. The excursion of the afternoon had certainly been ridiculous in a high degree. He had hoped for a more useful evening. Captain Resmith had indeed taken him to the horse-lines, and he had tried a mount which was very suitable, and Captain Resmith had said that he possessed a naturally good seat and hands, and had given him a few sagacious tips. It was plain to him that Resmith had the Major's orders to take him in tutelage and make an officer of him. But the satisfactoriness of the evening had suddenly ceased. Scarcely had Resmith begun to expound the orders, and George to read the thrilling words, 'Second Lieutenant G.E. Cannon to ride with Captain Resmith,' when the mess had impulsively decided to celebrate the last night in camp by a dinner at the hotel near the station, and George, fit for nothing more important, had been detailed to run off and arrange for the rich repast. The bulk of the mess was late to arrive, and George spent the time in writing a descriptive and falsely gay letter on slips of yellow Army paper to Lois. The dinner, with its facile laughter and equally facile cynicism, had bored him; for he had joined the Army in order to save an Empire and a world from being enslaved. He had lain down in his truckle-bed and listened to the last echoing sounds in the too-resonant corridor of the hutments, and thought of the wisdom of Sir Isaac Davids, and of the peril to his wife, and of the peril to the earth, and of his own irremediable bondage to the military machine. He, with all his consciousness of power, had been put to school again; deprived of the right to answer back, to argue, even to think. If one set in authority said that black was white, his most sacred duty was to concur and believe. And there was no escape....

And then, no sooner had he gone to sleep than it was bright day, and the faint, clear call of bugles had pierced the clouds of his depression and they had vanished! Every moment of the early morning had been exquisite. Although he had not been across a horse for months, he rode comfortably, and the animal was reliable. Resmith in fact had had to warn him against fatiguing himself. But he knew that he was incapable of fatigue. The day's trek was naught - fifteen miles or less - to Epsom Downs, at a walk!... Lois? He had expected a letter from 'Nunks' or his mother, but there was no letter, and no news was good news, at any rate with 'Nunks' in charge of communications. Lois could not fail to be all right. He recalled the wise generalization of 'Nunks' on that point ... Breakfast was a paradisiacal meal. He had never 'fancied' a meal so much. And Resmith had greatly enheartened him by saying sternly: "You've got exactly the right tone with the men. Don't you go trying to alter it." The general excitement was intense, and the solemn synchronizing of watches increased it further. An orderly brought a newspaper, and nobody would do more than disdainfully glance at it. The usual daily stuff about the war!... Whereas Epsom Downs glittered in the imagination like a Canaan. And it lay southward. Probably they were not going to France, but probably they would have the honour of defending the coast against invasion. George desired to master gunnery instantly, and Resmith soothed him with the assurance that he would soon be sent away on a gunnery course, which would give him beans. And in the meantime George might whet his teeth on the detailed arrangements for feeding and camping the Battery on Epsom Downs.

This organization gave George pause, especially when he remembered that the Battery was a very trifling item in the Division, and when Resmith casually informed him that a Division on the trek occupied fifteen miles of road. He began to perceive the difference between the Army and a circus, and to figure the Staff as something other than a club of haughty, aristocratic idlers in red hats. And when the Battery was fairly under way in the side-road, with another Battery in front and another Battery behind, and more Artillery Brigades and uncounted Infantry Brigades and a screen of Yeomanry all invisibly marching over the map in the direction of Epsom, and bound to reach a certain lettered square on the map at a certain minute - when this dynamic situation presented itself to the tentacles of his grasping mind, he really did feel that there could be no game equal to war.

The Battery 'rode easy,' the men were smoking, talking, and singing in snatches, when suddenly all sounds were silenced. Captain Resmith, who had been summoned to the Major, reined in his horse, and George did likewise, and the Battery passed by them on the left. The Major's voice was heard:

"No. 2 Battery. Eyes - right!"

George asked:

"What's this?"

"C.R.A.'s ahead," murmured Resmith.

Then another officer cried:

"Right section. Eyes - right."

And then an N.C.O. bawled:

"A sub-section. Eyes - right."

Then only did George, from the rear, see the drivers, with a simultaneous gesture, twist their heads very sharply to the right, raise their whips, and fling the thongs over the withers of the hand-horses, while the section-officer saluted.

Another N.C.O. bawled:

"B sub-section. Eyes - right."

And the same action followed.

Then another officer cried:

"Left section. Eyes - right."

So the rite proceeded.

Resmith and George had now gone back to their proper places. George could see the drivers of the last gun gathering up the whip thongs into their hands preparatory to the salute. C sub-section received the command.

And then, not many yards ahead, the voice of an N.C.O.:

"D sub-section. Eyes - right."

Heads turned; whips were raised and flung outwards; horses swerved slightly.

"Get ready," muttered Resmith to George.

The figure of the C.R.A., Brigadier-General Rannion, motionless on a charger, came into view. George's heart was beating high. Resmith and he saluted. The General gazed hard at him and never moved. They passed ahead.

The officer commanding the Third Battery had already called:

"Battery. Eyes - right."

The marvellous ceremonial slipped rearwards. George was aware of tears in his eyes. He was aware of the sentiment of worship. He felt that he would have done anything, accomplished any deed, died, at the bidding of the motionless figure on the charger. It was most curious.

There was a terrific crash of wood far behind. Resmith chuckled.

"One of those G.S. wagons has knocked down the Automobile Club 'Cross-Roads' sign," he said. "Good thing it wasn't a lamp-post! You see, with their eyes right, they can't look where they're going, and the whip touches up the horses, and before you can say knife they're into something. Jolly glad it's only the Am. Col. Jones will hear of this." He chuckled again. Jones was the Captain commanding the Ammunition Column.

The order ran down the line:

"Eyes - front."

Soon afterwards they came to some policemen, and two girls in very gay frocks with bicycles, and the cross-roads. The Battery swung into the great high road whose sign-post said, 'To Ewell and Epsom.' Another unit had been halted to let the Artillery pass into its definitive place in the vast trek. It was about this time that George began to notice the dust. Rain had fallen before dawn and made the roads perfect; but now either all the moisture had evaporated in the blazing sun, or the Battery had reached a zone where rain had not fallen. At first the dust rose only in a shallow sea to the height of fetlocks; but gradually it ascended and made clouds, and deposited a layer on the face and on the tongue and in the throat. And the surface itself of the road, exasperated by innumerable hoofs and wheels, seemed to be in a kind of crawling fermentation. The smell of humanity and horses was strong. The men were less inclined to sing.

"Left!" yelled a voice.

And another:

"Left!"

And still another, very close on the second one:

"LEFT!"

"Keep your distances there!" Resmith shouted violently.

A horn sounded, and the next moment a motor-car, apparently full of red-hats, rushed past the Battery, overtaking it, in a blinding storm of dust. It was gone, like a ghost.

"That's the Almighty himself," Resmith explained, with unconscious awe and devotion in his powerful voice. "Gramstone, Major-General."

George, profoundly impressed (he knew not why), noticed in his brain a tiny embryo of a thought that it might be agreeable to ride in a car.

A hand went up, and the Battery stopped. It was the first halt.

"Look at your watch," said Resmith, smiling.

"Ten to, exactly."

"That's right. We have ten minutes in each hour."

All dismounted, examined horses for galls, and looked at their shoes, took pulls at water-bottles, lit cigarettes, expectorated, coughed, flicked at flies with handkerchiefs. The party also went past, and shortly afterwards returned with the stretcher laden.

6

It was after the long halt at midday that the weather changed. The horses, martyrized by insects, had been elaborately watered and fed with immense labour; officers and men had eaten rations and dust from their haversacks, and for the most part emptied their water-bottles; and the march had been resumed in a temper captious and somewhat exacerbated.

"Get your horse away; he's kicking mine!" said Captain Resmith impatiently to George, reflecting the general mood. And George, who was beginning to experience fatigue in the region of the knees, visited on his horse the resentment he felt at Resmith's tone.

At precisely that moment some drops of rain fell. Nobody could believe at first that the drops were raindrops for the whole landscape was quivering in hot sunshine. However, an examination of the firmament showed a cloud perpendicularly overhead; the drops multiplied; the cloud slowly obscured the sun. An almost audible sigh of relief passed down the line. Everybody was freshened and elated. Some men with an instinct for the apposite started to sing:

"Shall we gather at the river?"

And nearly the whole Battery joined in the tune. The rain persevered, thickening. The sun accepted defeat. The sky lost all its blue. Orders were given as to clothing. George had the sensation that something was lacking to him, and found that it was an umbrella. On the outskirts of Ewell the Battery was splashing through puddles of water; the coats of horses and of men had darkened; guns, poles, and caps carried chaplets of raindrops; and all those stern riders, so proud and scornful, with chins hidden in high, upturned collars, and long garments disposed majestically over their legs and the flanks of the horses, nevertheless knew in secret that the conquering rain had got down the backs of their necks, and into their boots and into their very knees but they were still nobly maintaining the illusion of impermeability against it.

247

The Battery, riding now stiffly 'eyes front,' was halted unexpectedly in Ewell, filling the whole of the village, to the village's extreme content. Many minutes elapsed. Rumour floated down that something, was wrong in front. Captain Resmith had much inspectorial cantering to do, and George faithfully followed him for some time. At one end of the village a woman was selling fruit and ginger-beer to the soldiers at siege prices; at the other, men and women out of the little gardened houses were eagerly distributing hot tea and hot coffee free of charge. The two girls from the crossroads entered the village, pushing their bicycles, one of which had apparently lost a pedal. They wore mackintoshes, and were still laughing.

At length George said:

"If you don't mind I'll stick where I am for a bit."

"Tired, eh?" Resmith asked callously.

"Well! I shall be if I keep on."

"Dismount, my canny boy. Didn't I tell you what would happen to you? At your age - "

"Why! How old d'you think I am?"

"Well, my canny boy, you'll never see thirty again, I suppose."

"No, I shan't. Nor you either."

Captain Resmith said:

"I'm twenty-four."

George was thunder-struck. The fellow was a boy, and George had been treating him as an equal! But then the fellow was also George's superior officer, and immeasurably his superior in physique. Do what he would, harden himself as he might, George at thirty-three could never hope to rival the sinews of the boy of twenty-four, who incidentally could instruct him on every conceivable military subject. George, standing by his sodden horse, felt humiliated and annoyed as Resmith cantered off to speak to the officer commanding the Ammunition Column. But on the trek there was no outlet for such a sentiment as annoyance. He was Resmith's junior and Resmith's inferior, and must behave, and expect to be behaved to, as such.

"Never mind!" he said to himself. His determination to learn the art and craft of war was almost savage in ferocity.

When the Battery at length departed from Ewell the rain had completed its victory but at the same time had lost much of its prestige. The riders, abandoning illusion, admitting frankly that they were wet to the skin, knowing that all their clothing was soaked, and satisfied that they could not be wetter than they were if the bottom fell out of the sky, simply derided the rain and plodded forward. Groups of them even disdained the weather in lusty song. But not George. George was exhausted. He was ready to fall off his horse. The sensation of fatigue about the knees and in the small of his back was absolute torture. Resmith told him to ride without stirrups and dangle his legs. The relief was real, but only temporary. And the Battery moved on at the horribly monotonous, tiring walk. Epsom was incredibly distant. George gave up hope of Epsom; and he was right to do so, for Epsom never came. The Battery had taken a secondary road to the left which climbed slowly to the Downs. At the top of this road, under the railway bridge, just before fields ceased to be enclosed, stood the two girls. Their bicycles leaned against the brick wall. They had taken off their mackintoshes, and it was plain from their clinging coloured garments that they too were utterly drenched. They laughed no more. Over the open Downs the wind was sweeping the rain in front of it; and the wind was the night wind, for the sky had begun to darken into dusk. The Battery debouched into a main road which seemed full of promise, but left it again within a couple of hundred yards, and was once more on the menacing, high, naked Downs, with a wide and desolate view of unfeatured plains to the north. The bugles sounded sharply in the wet air, and the Battery, now apparently alone in the world, came to a halt. George dropped off his horse. A multiplicity of orders followed. Amorphous confusion was produced out of a straight line. This was the bivouacking ground. And there was nothing - nothing but the track by which they had arrived, and the Downs, and a distant blur to the west in the shape of the Epsom Grand Stand, and the heavy, ceaseless rain, and the threat of the fast-descending night. According to the theory of the Divisional Staff a dump furnished by the Army Service Corps ought to have existed at a spot corresponding to the final letter in the words 'Burgh Heath' on the map, but the information quickly became general that no such dump did in practice exist. To George the situation was merely incredible. He knew that for himself there was only one reasonable course of conduct. He ought to have a boiling bath, go to bed with his dressing-gown over his pyjamas, and take a full basin of hot bread-and-milk adulterated by the addition of brandy - and sleep. Horses and men surged perilously around him. The anarchical disorder, however, must have been less acute than he imagined, for a soldier appeared and took away his horse; he let the reins slip from his dazed hand. The track had been transformed into a morass of viscous mud.

7

It was night. The heavy rain drove out of the dark void from every direction at once, and baptized the chilled faces of men as though it had been discharged from the hundred-holed rose of a full watering-can. The right and the left sections of the Battery were disposed on either side of the track. Fires were burning. Horse-lines had been laid down, and by the light of flickering flames the dim forms of tethered animals could be seen with their noses to the ground pessimistically pretending to munch what green turf had survived in the mud. Lanterns moved mysteriously to and fro. In the distance to the west more illuminations showed that another unit had camped along the track. The quartermaster of No. 2, had produced meagre tinned meats and biscuits from his emergency stores, and had made a certain quantity of tea in dixies; he had even found a half-feed of oats for the horses; so that both horses and men were somewhat appeased. But the officers had had nothing, and the Army Service Corps detachment was still undiscoverable.

George sat on an empty box at the edge of the track, submissive to the rain. Resmith had sent him to overlook men cutting straight branches in a wood on Park Downs, and then he had overlooked them as, with the said branches and with waterproofs laced together in pairs, they had erected sleeping shelters for the officers under the imperfect shelter of the sole tree within the precincts of the camp. From these purely ornamental occupations he had returned in a condition approximating to collapse, without desire and without hope. The invincible cheerfulness of unseen men chanting music-hall songs in the drenched night made no impression on him, nor the terrible staccato curtness of a N.C.O. mounting guard. Volition had gone out of him; his heart was as empty as his stomach.

Then a group of officers approached, with a mounted officer in the middle of them, and a lantern swinging. The group was not proceeding in any particular direction, but following the restless motions of the uneasy horse. George, suddenly startled, recognized the voice of the rider; it was Colonel Hullocher's voice. The Brigade-Commander had come in person to investigate the melancholy inexcusable case of No. 2 Battery, and he was cursing all men and all things, and especially the Divisional Staff. It appeared that the Staff was responsible for the hitch of organization. During the day the Staff had altered its arrangements for No. 2 Battery of the Second Brigade, and had sent an incomplete message to the Army Service Corps Headquarters. The A.S.C. had waited in vain for the completion of the message, and had then, at dark, dispatched a convoy with provender for No. 2 with instructions to find No. 2. This convoy had not merely not found No. 2 - it had lost itself, vanished in the dark universe of rain. But let not No. 2 imagine that No. 2 was blameless! No. 2 ought to have found the convoy. By some means, human or divine, by the exercise of second sight or the vision of cats or the scent of hounds, it ought to have found the convoy, and there was no excuse for it not having done so. Such was the expressed opinion of Colonel Hullocher, and a recital by Major Craim of the measures taken by him did nothing to shake that opinion.

"How exactly do you stand now?" the Colonel fiercely demanded.

"The men and the horses will manage fairly well with what they've had, sir," said the Major; and he incautiously added: "But my officers haven't had anything at all."

The Colonel seized the opening with fury.

"What the devil do I care for your officers? It's your horses and your men that I'm thinking about. It's tomorrow morning that I'm thinking about. I - "

The horse, revolving, cut short his harangue.

"Keep that d - d lantern out of his eyes!" cried the Colonel.

George jumped up, and as he did so the water swished in his boots, and a stream poured off his cap. The horse was being fatally attracted towards him. The beam of the lantern fell on him, illuminating before his face the long slants of rain.

"Ha! Who's this?" the Colonel demanded, steadying the horse.

George smartly saluted, forgetting his fatigue.

"You, is it? And what are you supposed to be doing? Look here - " Colonel Hullocher stopped in full career of invective, remembering military etiquette. "Major, I suggest you send Mr. Cannon with some men to find the convoy." The Major having eagerly concurred, the Colonel went on: "Take a few men and search every road and track between here and Kingswood Station - systematically. Kingswood's the rail-head, and somewhere between here and there that convoy is bound to be. Systematically, mind! It's not a technical job. All that's wanted is common sense and thoroughness."

The Colonel's gaze was ruthlessly challenging. George met it stiffly. He knew that the roads, if not the tracks, had already been searched. He knew that he was being victimized by a chance impulse of the Colonel's. But he ignored all that. He was coldly angry and resentful. Utterly forgetting his fatigue, he inimically surveyed the Colonel's squat, shining figure in the cavalry coat, a pyramid of which the apex was a round head surmounted by a dripping cap.

"Yes, sir," he snapped.

By rights the tyrant ought to have rolled off his horse dead. But Colonel Hullocher was not thus vulnerable. He could give glance for glance with perhaps any human being on earth, and indeed thought little more of subalterns than of rabbits.

He finished, after a pause:

"You will be good enough, Major, to let this officer report to me personally when he has found the convoy."

"Certainly, sir."

The horse bounded away, scattering the group.

Rather less than half an hour later George had five men (including his own servant and Resmith's) and six lanterns round a cask, on the top of which was his map. There were six possible variations of route to Kingswood Station, and he explained them all, allotting one to each man and keeping one for himself. He could detect the men exchanging looks, but what the looks signified he could not tell. He gave instructions that everybody should go forward until either discovering the convoy or reaching Kingswood. He said with a positive air of conviction that by this means the convoy could not fail to be discovered. The men received the statement with strict agnosticism; they could not see things with the eye of faith, fortified though they were with tea and tinned meats. An offered reward of ten shillings to the man who should hit on the convoy did not appreciably inspirit them. George himself was of course not a bit convinced by his own argument, and had not the slightest expectation that the convoy would be found. The map, which the breeze lifted and upon which the rain drummed, seemed to be entirely unconnected with the actual facts of the earth's surface. The party mounted tired, unwilling horses and filed off. Some soldiers in the darkness, watching the string of lanterns, gave a half-ironical 'Hurrah.' One by one, as the tracks bifurcated, George dispatched his men, with renewed insistent advice, and at last he and his horse were alone on the Downs.

His clothes were exceedingly heavy with all the moisture they had imbibed. Repose had mitigated his fatigue, but every slow, slouching step of the horse intensified it again - and at a tremendous rate. Still, he did not care, having mastered the great truth that he would either tall off the horse in exhaustion or arrive at Kingswood - and which of the alternatives happened did not appear to him to matter seriously. The whole affair was fantastic; it was unreal, in addition to being silly. But, real or unreal, he would finish it. If he was a phantom and Kingswood a mirage, the phantom would reach the mirage or sink senseless into astral mud. He had Colonel Hullocher in mind, and, quite illogically, he envisaged the Colonel as a reality. Often he had heard of the ways of the Army, and had scarcely credited the tales told and printed. Well, he now credited them. Was it conceivable that that madman of a Colonel had packed him, George, off on such a wild and idiotic errand in the middle of the night, merely out of caprice? Were such doings -

He faintly heard voices through the rain, and the horse started at this sign of life from the black, unknown world beyond the circle of lantern-light. George was both frightened and puzzled. He thought of ghosts and haunted moors. Then he noticed a penumbra round about the form of what might be a small hillock to the left of the track. He quitted the track, and cautiously edged his horse forward, having commendably obscured the lantern beneath his overcoat. The farther side of the hillock had been tunnelled to a depth of perhaps three feet; a lantern suspended somehow in the roof showed the spade which had done the work; it also showed, within the cavity, the two girls who had accompanied the Brigade from Wimbledon, together with two soldiers. The soldiers were rankers, but one of the girls talked with perfect correctness in a very refined voice; the other was silently eating. Both were obviously tired to the limit of endurance, and very dirty and draggled. The gay colours of their smart frocks had, however, survived the hardships of the day. George was absolutely amazed by the spectacle. The vagaries of autocratic

Colonels were nothing when compared to this extravagance of human nature, this glimpse of the subterranean life of regiments, this triumphant and forlorn love-folly in the midst of the inclement, pitiless night. And he was touched, too. The glimmer of the lantern on the green and yellow of the short skirts half disclosed under the mackintoshes was at once pathetic and exciting. The girl who had been eating gave a terrible scream; she had caught sight of the figure on horseback. The horse shied violently and stood still. George persuaded him back into the track and rode on, guessing that already he had become a genuine phantom for the self-absorbed group awakened out of its ecstasy by the mysterious vision of a nightrider.

Half a mile farther on he saw the red end of a cigarette swimming on the sea of darkness; his lantern had expired, and he had not yet tried to relight it.

"Hi there!" he cried. "Who are you?"

The cigarette approached him, in a wavy movement, and a man's figure was vaguely discerned.

"A.S.C. convoy, sir."

"Where are you supposed to be going to?"

"No. 2 Battery, Second Brigade, sir. Can't find it, sir. And we've got off the road. The G.S. wagon fell into a hole and broke an axle, sir."

"And what do you think you're doing?"

"Waiting for daylight, sir."

The man's youthful voice was quite cheerful.

"D'you know what time it is?"

"No, sir."

"How many other vehicles have you got?"

"Three altogether, sir. Six horses."

"Well, I'm from No. 2 Battery, and I'm looking for you. You've unharnessed, I suppose."

"Oh yes, sir, and fed."

"Well, you'd better harness up your other two carts like lightning and come along with me. Show me the way. We'll see about the G.S. wagon later on."

"It's about a hundred yards from here, sir."

For the second time that evening George forgot fatigue. Exultation, though carefully hidden, warmed and thrilled every part of his body. Tying his horse behind one of the vehicles, he rode comfortably on hard packages till within sight of the Battery camp, when he took saddle again and went off alone to find a celebrated inn near the Epsom Grand Stand, where Colonel Hullocher and other grandees had billeted themselves. The Colonel was busy with his Adjutant, but apparently quite ready to eat George.

"Ah! You, is it? Found that convoy?"

George answered in a tone to imply that only one answer was

conceivable:

"Yes, sir."

"Brought it back?"

"Part of it, sir."

He explained the circumstances.

The Colonel coughed, and said:

"Have a whisky-and-soda before you go?"

George reflected for an instant. The Colonel seemingly had a core of decency, but George said in his heart: "I've not done with you yet, my fat friend." And aloud, grimly.

"Thank you very much, sir. But I shall ask you to excuse me."

Both the Colonel and the Adjutant were pardonably shaken by this unparalleled response.

The Colonel barked:

"Why? Teetotaller?"

"No, sir. But I've eaten nothing since lunch, and a glass of whisky might make me drunk."

Colonel Hullocher might have offered George some food to accompany the whisky, but he did not. He had already done a marvel; a miracle was not to be expected. He looked at George and George looked at him.

"No doubt you're right. Good night."

"Good night, sir." George saluted and marched off.

8

He prepared to turn in. The process was the simplest in the world. He had only to wrap a pair of blankets round his soaked clothes, and, holding them in place with one hand, creep under the shelter. There were four shelters. The Major had a small one, nearest the trunk of the tree, and the others were double shelters, to hold two officers apiece. He glanced about. The invisible camp was silent and still, save for a couple of lieutenants who were walking to and fro like young ducks in the heavy rain. Faint fires here and there in the distance showed how the troops were spread over the Downs. Heaven and earth were equally mysterious and inscrutable. He inserted himself cautiously into the aperture of the shelter, where Resmith already lay asleep, and, having pushed back his cap, arranged his right arm for a pillow. The clammy ground had been covered with dry horse-litter. As soon as he was settled the noise of the rain ceaselessly pattering on the waterproof became important. He could feel the chill of the wind on his feet, which, with Resmith's, projected beyond the shelter. The conditions were certainly astounding. Yet, despite extreme fatigue, he was not depressed. On the contrary he was well satisfied. He had accomplished something. He had been challenged, and had accepted the challenge, and had won. The demeanour of the mess when he got back to the camp clearly indicated that he had acquired prestige. He was the man who had organized an exhaustive search for the convoy and had found the convoy in the pitchy blackness. He was the man who had saved the unit from an undeserved shame. The mess had greeted him with warm food. Perhaps he had been lucky - the hazard of a lighted cigarette in the darkness! Yes, but luck was in everything. The credit was his, and men duly gave it to him, and he took it. He thought almost kindly of Colonel Hullocher, against whom he had measured himself. The result of the match was a draw, but he had provided the efficient bully with matter for reflection. After all, Hullocher was right. When you were moving a Division, jobs had to be done, possible or impossible; human beings had to be driven; the supernatural had to be achieved. And it had been! That which in the morning existed at Wimbledon now existed on the Downs. There it lay, safe and chiefly asleep, in defiance of the weather and of accidents and miscarriage! And the next day it would go on.

The vast ambitions of the civilian had sunk away. He thought, exalted as though by a wonderful discovery:

"There is something in this Army business!"

He ardently desired to pursue it further. He ardently desired sleep and renewal so that he might rise afresh and pursue it further. What he had done and been through was naught, less than naught. To worry about physical discomforts was babyish. Inviting vistas of knowledge, technical attainment, experience, and endurance stretched before him, illuminating the night. His mind dwelt on France, on Mons, on the idea of terror and cataclysm. And it had room too for his wife and children. He had had no news of them for over twenty-four hours; and he had broken his resolve to write to Lois every day; he had been compelled to break it. But in the morning, somehow, he would send a telegram and he would get one.

"If it's true the French Government has left Paris - "

The nocturnal young ducks were passing the shelter.

"And who says it's true? Who told you, I should like to know?"

"The Major has heard it."

"Rats! I lay you a fiver the Allies are in Berlin before Christmas."

Arnold Bennett

Clayhanger

In this, the first volume of an ambitious trilogy intending to trace the parallel lives of a man and woman from youth to marriage and from marriage to old age, Bennett introduces the character of Edwin Clayhanger. A sober portrait of a boy growing up under a tyrannical father contrasts with young Edwin's glimpses of the mysterious and tantalizing Hilda Lessways. As the lives of these two characters unfold before us, Bennett uses autobiographical detail to beautifully depict the constraints and spiritual adventures of young life in the Potteries.

Hilda Lessways

In the second volume of the Clayhanger trilogy, events in *Clayhanger* are retold from the perspective of Hilda Lessways, who is embarking on a relationship with Cannon, a charismatic entrepreneur, whose success has taken him from the Five Towns to Brighton. As Hilda's fascination with the young Clayhanger grows, one of Bennett's most living heroines must face up to her conflicting emotions, and the reality of her hopes and tragedies.

These Twain

In *Clayhanger* and *Hilda Lessways*, Bennett followed the development of a relationship from two very different perspectives. He now draws these perspectives together in a finale that sees the two young protagonists embarking upon married life. One might expect a fairy tale romance, but both Edwin and Hilda are extremely strong-willed, and this clash of personalities makes for a marriage that often hovers on the brink of failure.

This concluding volume of the Clayhanger trilogy contains some of Bennett's very finest work, depicting superb scenes from provincial life and painting a powerful picture of the conflict of wills in an inharmonious marriage.

Arnold Bennett

A Man from the North

Fleeing a drab and dead-end existence, Richard Larch moves south from Bursley to London, intent on pursuing a career as a writer. He is also looking for companionship and love, but finds his high hopes dashed when life in the capital is fraught with difficulties, and the glittering career proves to be more elusive than anticipated.

Melancholic and starkly realistic, *A Man from the North* is Arnold Bennett's first novel.

The Old Wives' Tale

Arnold Bennett's masterpiece, *The Old Wives' Tale*, chronicles the lives of sisters Constance and Sophia Baines, daughters of a Bursley draper. Constance, a conventional and sombre young woman, marries the shop's chief assistant, while the spirited and adventurous Sophia elopes to Paris with Gerald Scales, an irresistible but unprincipled cad. This is the utterly compelling story of their lives and loves, their triumphs and despair from early teens to old age, told with Arnold Bennett's characteristic insight and truthfulness.

How to Live on 24 Hours a Day

'You have to live on…twenty-four hours of daily time. Out of it you have to spin health, pleasure, money, content, respect, and the evolution of your immortal soul'.

This timeless classic is one of the first 'self-help' books ever written and was a best-seller in both England and America. It remains as useful today as when it was written, and offers fresh and practical advice on how to make the most of 'the daily miracle' of life.

'Mr Bennett writes with his usual crispness, point
and humour' – *Times of London*